D0240099

LANCASHIRE COUNTY LIBRARY

3011813919865 4

THE
ANARCHISTS'
CLUB

ALSO BY ALEX REEVE

The House on Half Moon Street

ALEX REEVE

THE
ANARCHISTS'
CLUB

R A V E N BOOKS
LONDON · OXFORD · NEW YORK · NEW DELHI · SYDNEY

LANCASHIRE COUNTY LIBRARY	
3011813819865 4	
Askews & Holts	30-Apr-2019
AF AFC	£12.99
CPP	

RAVEN BOOKS
Bloomsbury Publishing Plc
50 Bedford Square, London, WC1B 3DP, UK

BLOOMSBURY, RAVEN BOOKS and the Raven Books logo are trademarks of Bloomsbury
Publishing Plc

First published in Great Britain 2019

Copyright © Alex Reeve, 2019
Illustrations © Martin Lubikowski, ML Design, 2019

Alex Reeve has asserted his right under the Copyright, Designs and Patents Act, 1988, to be
identified as Author of this work

All rights reserved. No part of this publication may be reproduced or transmitted in any form or
by any means, electronic or mechanical, including photocopying, recording, or any information
storage or retrieval system, without prior permission in writing from the publishers

A catalogue record for this book is available from the British Library

ISBN: HB: 978-1-5266-0416-3; TPB: 978-1-5266-0417-0; EBOOK: 978-1-5266-0418-7

2 4 6 8 10 9 7 5 3 1

Typeset by Integra Software Services Pvt. Ltd.
Printed and bound in Great Britain by CPI Group (UK) Ltd, Croydon CR0 4YY

To find out more about our authors and books visit www.bloomsbury.com
and sign up for our newsletters

For Seth and Caleb

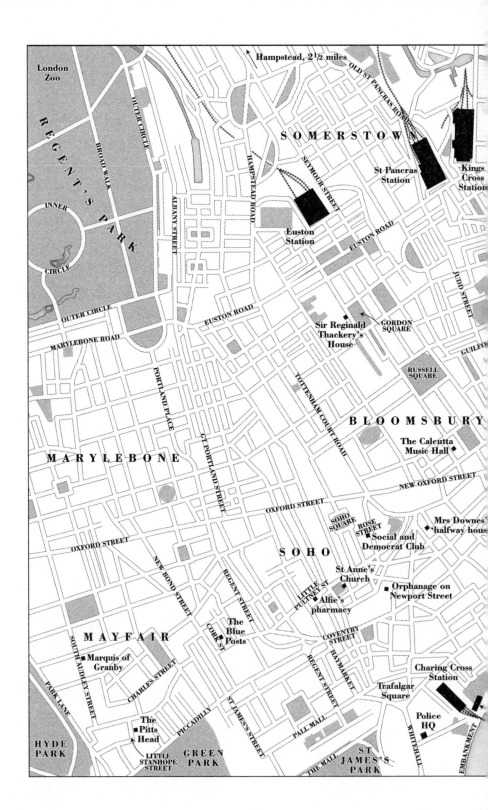

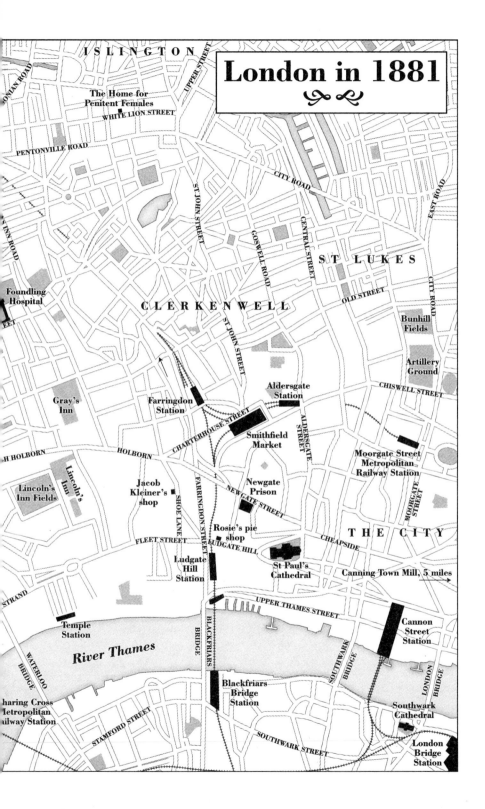

London in 1881

I MET DORA HANNIGAN just once, on a Saturday afternoon in March, when the rain was coming down so hard outside I could barely see across the street. She pushed open the door of the pharmacy and came in, ushering two soaked and shivering children in front of her, their clothes clinging to their skin. The boy knelt by the hearth, his jacket sleeves rucked up on his wrists like an accordion, and his younger sister copied him, her fingers wriggling in the warmth.

I went back to my book, not paying them much attention, assuming they were simply sheltering from the weather. But after a while, I noticed the mother throwing glances in my direction. She produced a hand mirror from her bag, turning from side to side and straightening her hat, but I could see her face reflected and that meant she could see mine too.

'Let me know if you need any help,' I said.

'I will,' she replied, with a hint of an accent I couldn't place.

The little girl grew bored and clambered on to the dentistry chair, picking at the leather with her fingernails and surveying the room like a queen who'd inherited the throne too young.

'What's this for?' she asked.

She couldn't have been more than seven years old, but she was unusually confident, demanding answers from an adult man she didn't know.

I put down my book and came out from behind the counter. Her mother's gaze followed me.

'You see this?' I crouched down and indicated the pump mechanism. 'It makes the drill go round and round, so you can mend people's teeth.'

The little girl grinned, showing me her own, milky white and missing a couple at the front. She slid off the chair and started pushing on the pump with her foot, giggling as the drill danced and rattled in its holder.

I could understand her curiosity – I would have been the same at her age – but Alfie wouldn't thank me if he came home to find his precious chair damaged, so I steered her back next to her brother.

'Don't be difficult,' he hissed at her, his mouth fixed in a hard line.

He shared his sister's shock of black, curly hair and dark eyes, but not her pleasant disposition. The little girl made a face at him and squirmed closer to the fire, blowing on the cinders to make them glow and crackle.

Their mother watched them with a thoughtful stillness. A drop of rainwater fell from the hem of her sleeve on to the floor. She shook herself – a rapid, impatient movement – and turned to me.

'I'd like some bromide, if you have it,' she said. 'But I can only afford sixpence. How much will that buy?'

I searched along the shelf until I found a half-full jar of the stuff: bromide of potash. I was no expert. It looked exactly like salt to me.

'One ounce.'

I was weighing it out when she spoke again. 'If I might have four ounces, or five, I'll return tomorrow with more money.'

'Do you have credit here?'

She shook her head. 'Not at present.'

'Then I'm afraid I can't make that arrangement. You'll have to come back later and speak to the owner.'

I was only filling in as a favour to Alfie, my landlord and the proprietor of the establishment, who was out with his *friend*, as he described Mrs Gower. He'd said he would be back shortly after lunch, but the clock had already struck three and there was no sign of him. I didn't mind. I had nothing better to do, and his twelve-year-old daughter Constance always remembered a pressing engagement whenever he wanted to spend time with Mrs Gower.

'If you would be prepared to extend me credit on your own authority, I'll pay you double tomorrow. That's a profit of two and six. You'd have the option of keeping it for yourself, of course.'

I must admit I was surprised, and considerably insulted. Did she really think I would betray Alfie's trust so easily?

'No, I can't do that. Would you still like the one ounce?'

She narrowed her eyes. 'Yes please.'

I put her sixpence into the money drawer and thrust the bromide into her hand. She took it with a nod, which I didn't return.

As they were leaving, she looked back, meeting me straight in the eyes. 'You're an honest person,' she said.

I wasn't sure whether she meant it as a compliment or not.

I gave them no more thought for the next few days. Every morning, I went to work as a porter at St Thomas's Hospital and every evening I came home. Once a week I played chess. Some might call it predictable, or even monotonous, but I was content. I had experienced excitement before and wanted nothing more of it.

I was therefore quite perturbed when, arriving back from work on the following Thursday, I was met at the pharmacy door by Constable Pallett. He was younger than me, but larger in every dimension, with a soft, gentle face and fists like the great, iron cleats on the docks.

'Mr Stanhope,' he greeted me, with his usual unbending courtesy, like a bank manager about to foreclose.

'What can I do for you, Constable?'

I was keeping my voice steady, but it was always in my head, that thought: am I discovered? Is this the moment?

I unlocked the door and he followed me inside, removing his helmet, which would otherwise have scraped the ceiling.

'It's a delicate matter, sir. We'd like your help, if you don't mind.'

'With what?'

I was watching him carefully. His boots were caked with mud and his jacket was streaked as if he'd wiped his grubby hands down it. But he was perfectly at ease, idly rocking Alfie's new scales with one finger.

'It's a curiosity and no mistake.' I had the feeling he was quoting someone else. 'Detective Inspector Hooper's in charge.'

'I don't know him. Is he a good man?'

'He was hoping you might be able to shed some light on an occurrence.'

I noted that he hadn't answered my question. And an 'occurrence' could mean almost anything: a ship sunk, a loved one murdered, a brawl in a bar, a pair of gloves borrowed and not returned.

'What's happened?'

'He asked me not to divulge any details, sir. He said he wants to see your natural reaction without the benefit of prior notice, as it were. He was very insistent on the point.'

'And if I refuse?'

He looked surprised. 'A crime has been committed. It's best you come with me.'

We headed north through Soho, Pallett striding resolutely along the pavement and tipping his helmet to the people we passed. I noticed them eyeing me, probably wondering why I was scurrying along behind a policeman. Was I a victim or a suspect? I couldn't have told them. I had the urge to slow down, take a side street and run. I had done it before.

'Where are we going?'

'Rose Street, sir.'

I knew it a little from the pub at the entrance, which had been built around the street and over it, creating a passageway through the building itself. Alfie drank there often and had once persuaded me to join him and his old army comrades. They welcomed me warmly and wouldn't permit me to buy a round, gathering together so tightly our shoulders were touching. They took turns telling stories, which they clearly all knew by heart, of their time overseas, and then laughed and threw back their ales.

I left early. I didn't want any new friends.

Pallett and I reached Rose Street and instinctively ducked as we entered the passageway, stepping between the drunks and vagrants crammed in like baby mice. On the other side, the sunken road was flooded by a brown, muddy lake that seeped into my socks through the holes in my shoes. High on one wall, an artisan's symbol had been sculpted in metal, a man's arm holding a hammer, threatening to crush anyone who dared pass.

I couldn't imagine why I had been brought here. With a cramp in my stomach, I wondered if I was being called upon to identify the body of someone I knew, and immediately thought of Alfie and Jacob and then, because my mind always turned towards the blackest of outcomes, Constance.

It couldn't be so. Why would any of them be here, in this street? And if they were, why would I be called upon first? They had families of their own.

Pallett stopped at number 6, an unremarkable door, slightly ajar, next to a shuttered window. I could hear noises within; the hushed, insistent tones of people who were frightened and trying to decide what to do about it.

He pushed open the door and went inside, but I hesitated on the step, my palms itching.

'Mr Stanhope?' he called over his shoulder. 'This way, sir.'

The narrow hallway was dark and crowded with people, mostly tradesmen and a few women, dressed simply and respectably. The wall was hung with advertisements for events and speakers, but I couldn't read their names in the half-dark. We passed rooms on the left and right, one filled with beds and another laid out for a meeting, the table piled with papers and pamphlets.

At the end, a back door opened into a sheltered courtyard where oil lamps had been hung from wooden stairs, hissing and flickering. It wasn't raining, but everything was wet, as if the sun never found its way down between the buildings.

A group of five or six men were standing in a circle, and one of them, with his right hand in his baggy suit pocket and the other scratching his unkempt beard, squinted in my direction. His face was ashen. Another fellow touched his elbow, an attempt to comfort him, but he barely seemed to notice. I realised with a prickle of blood in my cheeks that I knew him. Or I had known him, a long time ago. I had no desire to meet him again.

Of course, he couldn't possibly remember me; I was so changed.

'Over here, Mr Stanhope,' said Pallett, and led me towards the centre of the courtyard.

A tall fellow with a long nose came towards us, picking his way through the shallows like a fastidious heron.

'I'm Detective Inspector Hooper,' he said, in an accent that one born in the slums might consider upper class, but, to one familiar with the upper class – my father's small-town ministry reached all kinds – sounded merely affected.

I glanced at Pallett, whose expression was blank.

'Why am I here?'

'A tragedy, a crime and, may I say, a curiosity.' Hooper rubbed his hands together and grinned, showing me an expensively assembled row of teeth. 'Come and see for yourself.'

I followed him towards the gaggle of men, who dispersed as we approached. One of them, with heavy whiskers and a blunt, bullish face, was writing in a notebook. He nodded to me, but I took no notice. I was more concerned with what they had been looking at.

It was a grave, of a sort, but no more than two feet deep, dug roughly out of the earth and sodden. A woman was lying within, eyes closed, her hair fanning out on the surface of the water. Her lips were dark, and her skin was grey and bloated. At her chest, an inch below her breast-bone, a fierce rip in her blouse was marked by a bloodstain blossoming like a red water lily. I recognised her at once as the woman who had come into the pharmacy, who had purchased bromide but had seemed more interested in me.

Having spent two years as the secretary to a surgeon, I had seen hundreds of corpses – crushed, knifed, poisoned, beaten and drowned – but it was still shocking to see some-one in death whom I had met in life.

'Stabbed in the gut,' stated Hooper in a matter-of-fact tone. 'Her name's Dora Hannigan. Did you know her?'

'No. Why have you asked me to come here?'

Of course, I didn't know her. Not really. Meeting some-one once isn't *knowing* them, and I didn't want anything to do with this. I wanted to go home and eat Constance's attempt at stew and sip a glass of Alfie's whisky and read my book by my bedroom window. Even so, something chafed inside me. My denial somehow made her seem more dead.

'Interesting.' He pulled a piece of paper from his pocket. 'This was in her purse.'

He turned it round to show me, and I was amazed to read my name and address, written in a neat, flowing hand. Apparently, this woman, Dora Hannigan, hadn't come in simply to buy an ounce of bromide or escape the storm; she had sought me out *by name*. And yet she hadn't given me any indication of it at the time; she hadn't introduced herself or asked who I was.

Why had she walked through my door that day, so shortly before her death? No, before her *murder*.

'I told you, I don't know her.'

Hooper nodded. I had the impression he wanted me to think he believed me, though I was certain he didn't.

'Have you been here before?'

'No, never.'

He sniffed and surveyed the courtyard, which was narrower than the buildings were tall, lending it an ecclesiastical air.

'These people call it a *club*,' he said with a sneer. 'They're radicals and anarchists, planning an end to all that's proper and industrious. Scoundrels, the lot of 'em.'

He didn't seem to care that the men sitting on the steps were well within earshot, hats in their hands and heads lowered, or that the woman leaning on the balustrade above us was humming 'Nearer, My God, to Thee', her expression peaceful even as her tears fell.

There was no sign of Mrs Hannigan's children. I wondered where they were. But I couldn't ask Hooper about them now, not after saying I didn't know their mother.

I felt another pinch of guilt.

'It doesn't look as though anything was stolen,' I said. 'She still has her necklace and shoes.'

'Nothing was stolen *as far as we know*,' Hooper admitted. 'If you don't mind me making the observation, Mr …' He waved a hand trying to remember my name. I didn't help him. 'You don't sound very shocked. Most people would be highly disturbed to see something like this.'

I realised why he'd brought me here with such secrecy. He thought Dora Hannigan and I had known each other, that I had killed her and, on seeing my handiwork so exposed, would break down in tears and admit my guilt. He was disappointed by my sanguinity.

'I work in a hospital. Not much disturbs me any more. Can I go now?'

I was regretting coming to this place with Pallett. I risked a glance towards the man I had recognised from before, but he had his back to me, fidgeting and moving his weight from foot to foot as if unable to keep still. I was still staring at him as he turned, and I only just averted my eyes in time. Had I learned nothing?

'She was unmarried,' Hooper continued, not answering my question. 'But she wasn't a prostitute as far as we can tell.'

'Why would you think she was?'

'She's dead, isn't she?' He scowled at the men on the steps, and one of them, with a bald head and hard eyes, scowled right back, unblinking. 'If it's not robbery, it's usually the other thing. Maybe she's someone's mistress. Crime of passion. Are you married?'

'No. And crimes of passion are generally more …' I struggled for the word, staring down at her. In the meagre lamplight she looked as if she'd been set in amber. 'They're more *savage*. They're messy and it shows on the deceased. This is too clean. Will you be sending the body to a surgeon?'

Hooper smoothed his moustache. 'What's the point? The cause of death is obvious.'

'Perhaps. Is there blood on her back as well?'

The detective nodded at Pallett, who sighed deeply and crouched down beside the hole, collapsing its edges and submerging his boots in mud. He took her arm and pulled her on to her side, so her face lolled under the water. I had the urge to beg him to let her fall back, so she could breathe, but of course that was foolishness.

Her dress was torn to the right of her spine. Whatever had been used to stab her was long and sharp, going all the way through.

'A sword perhaps,' said Hooper. He made a thrusting motion with an imaginary weapon. 'Do you own a sword?'

'No, of course not. Is there another way into the court-yard, other than the way we came?'

Pallett pointed towards the darkest corner. 'There's a back gate.'

'Why do you want to know?' asked Hooper, with a note of irritation.

'She may have been killed somewhere else and brought here.'

He rolled his eyes. 'I doubt that. Someone in this midden is the killer. Stands to reason.'

I fetched one of the lamps and squatted beside her, study-ing the tiny lines around her eyes, the long-healed scar on her jawline. I couldn't understand how anyone could take another person's life this way. Still, I told myself, I had examined hundreds of corpses before, and always with the same aim: to find out how they had died. It was all I could do for her now.

Her clothes were all in place, so she was spared that, at least. I took a deep breath and closed my eyes, memories pulling at me. The courtyard spun and slowly settled.

'There are no signs of a struggle,' I said.

Hooper pursed his lips, embarrassed to be hanging on the words of a man he'd brought here as a suspect. 'She couldn't fend him off, could she? Just a woman.'

'It's unusual, though, in my experience.' I took her hand, pulling up her sleeve and turning her palm upwards. Accustomed to cadavers as I was, it still felt strangely intimate. 'No cuts, wounds or bruises from a fight. If someone attacked me with a sword, I'd try to deflect the blade. Wouldn't you?'

'Maybe she was taken by surprise.' He clapped his hands together. 'Or maybe she was stabbed in the back! That would explain it.'

'By surprise perhaps, but not in the back. Look here. The wound on her front is wider than the one in her back, so the blade was tapered. A dagger or a shortsword.'

Beneath her hair, her neck was purple and mottled. I pressed my finger against her skin, and the mottling didn't change. 'Livor mortis has set in and her blood has already congealed. She's been dead for twelve hours at least, I would say.'

Hooper shook his head with a condescending smirk. 'You're wrong. She's not stiff yet, so it happened some time today. Like I said, must've been someone local.'

I was growing impatient. In my experience the police could see about as far as their fists could reach, and no further. 'She's lying in cold, wet ground, and that can delay rigor mortis significantly. This happened more than twelve hours ago, but probably less than thirty-six.'

Pallett wiped his hands down his jacket. 'And where were you during those hours, Mr Stanhope?'

'Aside from being asleep, I was working at St Thomas's Hospital and drinking whisky with my landlord until late. He can vouch for me.'

Hooper pulled a tortoiseshell pen from his pocket and wrote that down, slowly and carefully. A drizzle had started, and he had to hunch over his notebook to keep the paper from being soaked.

'Right then. You can go now, Mr Stanhope. We'll let you know if we have more questions for you.' He turned abruptly towards Pallett, thumbing in the direction of the group of men. 'We should have a chat with this lot, especially that shifty fellow. What was his name?'

'Duport, sir,' said Pallett. 'John Duport.'

'Yes, him. Let's see if he has a sword or something similar.'

I was covered in mud and starting to shiver. I bent down to push Dora Hannigan's hair from her forehead and noticed something glinting at her neck: a silver locket. I opened it up.

The pictures inside had survived the water. They weren't well drawn, and I wouldn't have known who they depicted if I hadn't seen the living subjects a few days before: the dour boy and inquisitive girl, one either side, facing each other across the hinge.

'Detective!' I called after Hooper.

He looked back at me, frowning, appearing surprised I was still there. 'It's Detective *Inspector*.'

I held up the locket. 'She had a son and daughter. Where are they now?'

'She was unmarried, like I said.'

I ignored his idiocy. 'You should ask the people here if anyone has them.'

He raised his eyebrows and cast around as if they might be hiding behind a water barrel. 'I suppose so. See to it, Pallett.'

He stood under one of the lamps, reading his notes. He hadn't thanked me.

A man approached and put out his hand to pull me upright, which I ignored. He was the large, whiskered fellow I'd seen earlier.

'J. T. Whitford,' he announced. 'The *Daily Chronicle*. And you are?'

'Cold,' I replied. 'And wet. And keen to get home.'

I rarely read a newspaper, but even if I did, it wouldn't be the *Daily Chronicle*, a salacious rag filled with gossip about actors' latest dalliances and hysterical warnings about rabies epidemics. I had no idea why anyone would read such claptrap.

Whitford pulled out a notebook and pencil. Today, everyone seemed to want to write down what I had to say. 'When did you first meet Mrs Hannigan?'

He had a blunt accent that I thought might come from Yorkshire. My sister, who could place a voice to any county south of Hadrian's Wall, could have told me for sure, down to the nearest town probably.

'Never.'

'Are you a member here or just a radical sympathiser?'

'What?'

He rolled his eyes. 'Look, these coppers'll spill the whole story for fourpence. A cigarette, most of 'em. You might as well tell me what you're doing here.'

'I'm sorry, I can't help you.'

I pushed past him, intending to leave, but then stopped. The man I had recognised, with the ragged beard and unlaundered suit, was staring at me. He glanced quickly at Hooper, who was still flicking through his papers, and beckoned me to follow him away from the others, beneath the gallery, where ice left over from January's blizzards was still clinging to the ground. I ignored him, but he waved more insistently, and I feared he would call out my name if I didn't respond. It was a risk I couldn't take.

He was huddled against the wall, so deep in the shadows I could hardly see him. He grabbed my sleeve and pulled me closer, almost hissing into my ear.

'Why are you here? Tell me. Be quick.'

Despite his urgency, his voice was well-mannered and clipped, every consonant pronounced perfectly.

'I will not,' I said, trying to pull away from him without anyone noticing.

'Dora must've kept your name and address. That's it, isn't it?' He stepped into the lamplight, his eyes shining orange. 'But this could be good news. You can help us. You'll do it, won't you?'

'I don't even know who you are.'

'Of course you do. We met in Enfield – goodness, it must be ten years ago. More, even. Our mothers tried to … well, it seems pretty foolish now, wouldn't you say? My word, and to think of what might've happened.'

'I don't know you.'

'Yes, you do. I'm …' He dropped his voice to a whisper. 'I'm John Thackery. And you're Lottie Pritchard. Or you used to be. And I'm certain you remember me full well.'

I could feel myself shaking and clasped my hands together, pinching the skin fiercely between my thumb and forefinger. I wished I had refused to come to this place, and I wished I had acknowledged having met Dora Hannigan, and I wished most of all that I had not come face to face with this man.

'What are you talking about?'

'I need an alibi for yesterday,' he said. 'And unless you want your secret exposed right now to these policemen, you're going to provide one.'

2

WHEN I WAS FIFTEEN and living with my family in Enfield, a businessman and his family moved into the area. They took up residence in the grandest house, hired a dozen servants and starting riding around the town in a regal carriage pulled by two black horses who picked up their hooves like dancers. He was in the jute business, making cheap cloth for sacks and cart covers, and had taken a share in a mill at Ponder's End, employing dozens of local men. My father was deeply impressed. He talked about it every time we sat down to dinner:

'Mr Thackery said the jute crop looks very promising this year.'

'Have you seen the walled garden Mr Thackery has built? It might be the best in Middlesex.'

'Mr Thackery thinks the Liberal government will fall soon.'

And so on, until we were all sick of hearing about him.

My father started angling his sermons towards Mr Thackery's interests too, beseeching his flock to work hard and show due respect for their betters. At the time I took no interest, but afterwards I concluded he must have been hoping for a substantial donation to the church or to achieve the kind of influence that might one day lead to a bishopric.

My mother had a different objective. The Thackery family had two sons, one very small, but the other, John, was a year or so older than me. She invited the Thackerys to tea and placed John and me on the velvet settee together, casting sidelong glances at us while Mrs Thackery instructed her on crochet hooks and the men talked about the disestablishment of the Irish Church, which they naturally opposed, and the exorbitant cost of labour.

John was a pleasant lad, I thought, and quite amusing. Not for one second did he honour his father, instead rolling his eyes quite blatantly at Mr Thackery's more grandiose outpourings. He even made a sly motion of slitting his own throat when he heard he was expected to go into the army, making me snort audibly, garnering a frown from my mother and a smirk from my older sister, Jane, who was newly engaged to be married and plainly found my discomfort amusing.

I rarely saw John over the summer, and it was not until mid-October that we spoke properly. The congregation was milling around after a morning service, and we found ourselves on the same bench, swishing the autumn leaves with our feet. Outside of his parents' orbit he was surprisingly shy, and sat fiddling with his fingers, gazing mutely at the tombstones, until he hit upon the idea of making up biographies for the deceased.

'Edith Charm, beloved wife and mother, seventeen ninety-two to eighteen fifty-five. She was a local witch, you know. She cursed the village men and turned them into dogs.'

I laughed, imagining what my father would say to that. 'What a horrible story.'

'Yes, it was. They attacked each other with tooth and fang, until every last one of them was dead.'

'How unkind.'

'Not at all.' He attempted to centre his necktie, without success. 'They deserved it. They'd tried to trap her, you see, and imprison her in a cage.'

'But still.'

'And it was for the best in the end.' He pointed towards the fields stretching out in the distance, beyond the houses. 'Afterwards, she turned herself and her friends into sheep, so they could live together freely and without violence. No dogs left to bite them or humans to confine them.'

When it was time to go, he was awkward again. He probably knew what my mother had in mind, and was embarrassed, believing I wanted it too. Nothing could have been further from the truth. I was already saving for my escape, earning threepences for teaching arithmetic to local children. But I was fascinated by how he talked, how he held himself, how he took up space on the bench, his legs splayed out or one foot propped up on the opposite knee. He was my model, my exemplar, far more so than Oliver, my older brother, who was away training for the army and already a man. Oliver was born a man, somehow. He had reached my father's height, over six feet, by the age of sixteen, and at nineteen he was broad and strong enough to pick up a pew on his own. I could never be like Oliver. But John was boyish and slight, with a diffident manner and a sharp wit. I could imagine myself like him.

On the day I left home, tearing myself from my mother's arms and dashing down the hill towards the station, actually passing my father coming the other way without him so much as glancing at this slim young man with reddened eyes and badly cut hair, I never considered I might see John Thackery again.

And now here he was, eleven years later, turning up like a ghost, dragging the chains of my previous existence behind him.

He was as crumpled as I remembered, wearing loose trousers and a bowler hat with a boot-shaped dent in the brim. But there was something curious about his clothes: despite his dishevelment, I would have expected them to be expensive, made of good-quality cloth and lined, as befits the elder son of a wealthy mill owner. But these were the garments of a man who worked for a living. He resembled a university professor fallen on hard times.

'We need to talk properly,' he said, his tone pleasant but firm. 'I have an office here we can use.'

'I'm very busy,' I replied, trying to sound efficient and slightly harried, the kind of person who hasn't the time to stop for a chat. 'You've mistaken me for someone else.'

'We'll see.' He cleared his throat loudly and made as if to wave to Hooper.

'All right,' I said quickly, hating the words as soon as they were out of my mouth. 'I'll listen to what you have to say.'

'Good.' He raised his hand as if about to clap me on the shoulder, but then lowered it again. 'Come with me.'

It was late March, and seagulls were crying over the rooftops, gathering in flocks ready to head back to the coast. I looked longingly at the back gate. If I simply marched out, what could he do? I answered my own question: he could tell the police about me. And even if he didn't, I would always fear that he might.

I followed him through one of the doors into a small kitchen, where two women were rocking babies, onwards along a corridor piled with open sacks of old clothes and rags, and into an empty hall where dozens of chairs had been arranged in rows. The sound of our shoes echoed off the walls.

It was clear that this building was much larger than I had supposed. I was acutely aware that I was accompanying a man I hadn't seen in many years, and that he might be involved in a murder. I looked back the way we'd come, our damp footprints chasing us across the woodblock floor, and tried to remember the route we'd taken.

He led me up a flight of stairs to a narrow landing, ducking under a low lintel, his hands behind his back as if he was strolling through a museum. Finally, he stopped next to a door cut down diagonally to fit beneath the gable.

'Mind your head.'

I followed him inside and went to close the door, but he put his hand on it.

'No, please,' he said, his face flushing. 'I prefer it open.'

The room had a writing desk under the window, a tray of unwashed teacups, two club chairs and walls lined with bookshelves. I suffered a pang of jealousy, picturing myself having a study like this one, spending my days reading and practising chess openings. More books were piled on the floor and desk, with titles like *Progress and Poverty* and *Principles of Political Economy*. Not what I would have chosen.

Thackery perched on the edge of his desk while I stood. I didn't want him to think I was staying.

'It's Leo now, isn't it?' he said.

'Mr Stanhope,' I replied, sounding pompous even to myself.

He studied my face, cocking his head to one side, his eyes straying downwards. I pulled my jacket tighter, but his expression was one of wonder rather than revulsion.

'I wouldn't have believed it,' he said. 'It's quite remarkable.'

'What is?'

I was keeping my voice calm and friendly even though I knew what he was thinking: that I could mimic masculinity quite well considering my limitations, rather as one might applaud a dog wearing a waistcoat. *Bravo! It's almost like the real thing.*

He ignored my question. 'You left so suddenly. Everyone was talking about it. I mean, it's not something that can easily be explained away.' I said nothing, and he sighed, still examining me, seeming most interested in the length of my shoes. He couldn't know they were stuffed with newspaper. 'We have many things to discuss, but first you must acknowledge that we know each other. I won't speak further unless you do.'

I took a deep breath and closed my eyes. We were alone, and there was no point in denying the truth. And I needed to know what he intended.

'Very well. We know each other. Now what of it?'

'After you left, most people thought the obvious, I'm afraid.'

'Which was?'

'That you'd been sent away for reasons of impropriety … a young lady, you know, you wouldn't be the first. My father even asked if we had … well, he thought perhaps you'd tempted me astray. I think he rather hoped you had, though he's always convinced everyone is after his money.' His face took on a sour expression. 'Your father told everyone you'd gone away to France, but no one believed it. The reverend's daughter, you know, it's like a joke, isn't it? And, if it was true, why did your mother stay in bed for a month afterwards? It didn't hold water.'

I felt a lump rise in my throat. Before I had left home, I promised my mother I would write to her and had meant it at the time. But I never did. Much later, I discovered that she had pined for her youngest child, her jewel, every day for the rest of her life. The most difficult is always the favourite.

'A few people thought you were dead,' he continued. 'There was a suggestion we should dig up the churchyard and open all the coffins.'

'I don't have time for your reminiscences.'

I turned towards the door and he put up his hands in surrender.

'Please, sit down, Lott— Leo.' I remained standing, holding my bowler in my hands. It was new and shiny, and droplets of water had beaded on the brim like gemstones. 'There are things you need to know. We don't have time for all of it, under the present circumstances.' His voice caught, just a fraction. 'But we should meet properly, and soon. There's this thing called the greater good. Do you know what that means?' He paused as if expecting me to answer, but I didn't. He smiled thinly, acknowledging my silence as deliberate. 'It means that sometimes we do things that seem wrong, but they lead to a better thing in the future.'

'What are you talking about?'

'I'm saying that you really do need to help me with this. If you refuse, it will be the worse for you. I'll tell everyone who and what you are. If I must be exposed, so will you be.'

He seemed entirely serious, and yet I still found it hard to accept that he was blatantly threatening me. What had I done to make him hate me so? All the care I took, day after day: the trials of finding the right clothes, the endless washing and drying of sanitary cloths, the salving of my bleeding sores where my binding chafed my skin, and most of all, the constant alertness to my voice, my stance, the way I used my hands and the exact blitheness of my laugh, much of which had been modelled on him; after all that, he would betray me? If it wasn't so tragic it would be funny.

I took a deep breath. 'What exactly do you want?'

'You must tell the police we were together all of yesterday, including the evening.'

'But we weren't.'

'I know, but I want you to say that we were. Not here, somewhere else.' He scratched his head, thinking. 'Say we went to Alexandra Park. There's a horse show on, and the two of us spent the day there and had a friendly drink afterwards.'

'I've already told the police the truth.'

He gave me a condescending smile. 'Yes, but the memory plays tricks, doesn't it, especially when you're under stress. Seeing a dead body like that, it's easy to get confused about dates and times and so forth. Tell them we were together, and I'll do likewise, so our story is the same.'

He was behaving as if we were close friends concocting an excuse for a drunken night out, but we were virtually strangers, and Dora Hannigan had been buried just a few yards from this little room.

'I won't lie for you to cover up a murder.'

'What?' He looked genuinely shocked. 'No, of course not. Good Lord, I had thought … I mean, you can't possibly think I would do a thing like that, let alone …' Again, his voice caught, and he had to pause, swallowing hard '… let alone to Dora.'

I frowned, not understanding. 'Then why do you want me to lie?'

Despite having insisted we needed to hurry, he seemed content to take his time, sliding his finger around the top of a teacup as if he were trying to make it sing. I wondered if he washed up his own dirty crockery, or if he was waiting for a maid to come and do it for him.

'The things my father cares about, they don't interest me. Did you know he was knighted last year? He's *Sir* Reginald Thackery now, never mind that he made every penny of his fortune exploiting the men who work for him in conditions you wouldn't credit, while he's never so much as pulled a jute stalk in his life. The new mill's not like the one you remember. That was almost pleasant by comparison. This one's in Whitechapel, and it's vast and black, groaning all day and night. It's like being in hell.' He was staring straight ahead, and I had the feeling he wasn't properly with me at all, but was reliving the memory of standing in that factory, consumed by the ghastliness of it. 'With the fumes and dust, you can hardly see a thing. And the noise! An hour in that place and you can't hear your own voice afterwards. And yet men spend their whole lives there.'

'What does any of this have to do with me?'

He looked at me with something close to amazement. 'It has to do with everyone! That's what we're trying to do, transform our economy. Our *society*. Henry Hyndman has spoken here, and Johann Most.' He produced a pamphlet from the shelf, presumably by this Johann Most fellow, and started waving it at me. 'They are remarkable men. They say that all property is truly theft because it's been taken from the people by the rich, and the workers will rise up to reclaim what's theirs.'

'I doubt it would appeal to me.'

I had no interest in who was in government. Both sides would despise me equally.

He closed his eyes and seemed to be mumbling to himself, like a child trying to memorise a poem. 'I'm sorry, I've strayed from my point, but I feel so strongly that justice needs to be served. It was my father who killed Dora. He murdered her as certainly as if he'd come here himself, although of course he wouldn't. Even the task of killing can be loaded on to the backs of other men.'

Despite myself, I was curious. 'What makes you think it was him?'

Thackery wiped his eyes and took a moment to control his breathing. 'Dora used to work for the family, years ago, before we moved to Enfield. She had good cause to hate him, believe me.'

Sir Reginald wouldn't be the first gentleman to force himself on a servant, I thought. But that would have to be at least twelve years ago. It didn't seem a likely motive for murder now.

On the other hand, it wasn't completely implausible either. Taken in the purely physical, Sir Reginald had been ordinary, of average height and build, losing his hair, not particularly striking in any way. And yet he exuded a sort of confidence, such as I'd never encountered before or since, as though everything he did or said was somehow *correct*, and even when he expressed an opinion as a mere passing remark, it was something you should listen to and act upon. His certitude was almost tangible. I could still picture him standing in the church after one of my father's services, greeting his fellow parishioners as if he was a visiting dignitary doing them the honour of a handshake.

Yes, I thought. He might be capable of ordering a murder.

'The police think some fellow named Duport is involved,' I said. 'That's who they said they wanted to speak to next.'

'Ah, is that so? They mentioned Duport specifically, did they?'

'Yes. Could he have been acting on your father's orders?'

Thackery went red and picked another volume off the shelf, flipping through the pages. 'I say, do you remember that bookshop in Enfield, on the London Road? Did you ever go in there?'

'I suppose so.'

I was shivering and annoyed. Of course I'd been in there; it was the only bookshop in the town, and I'd known every nook and cranny of it. Mr Heffernan had treated me like his own granddaughter. He used to save me slices of cake.

'I went in a few times. The old man had a fancy for Chartism. Do you know what that is?'

'Politics.'

A look of impatience crossed his face. 'It was a *movement*. It meant treating all men fairly, paying decent wages and providing humane working conditions. The old man had dozens of books about it.' He sighed at the memory. 'I don't suppose he sold many of them in Enfield, all things considered, except to me. I started with Carlyle's *The French Revolution*.' He held up the book to show me the title on the spine. 'Not this actual copy. It was the first volume, and this is the second.'

'Is there a point to this story?'

He gave me another impatient look. He really didn't understand why everyone wasn't fascinated by the same things as him. 'I took it straight to the park and sat reading for hours. Such ideas Carlyle had! Such acuity! I'd never read anything like it. I was transfixed.'

'Good for you, but I haven't got time for this.'

I put on my hat and stood up. Thackery stood also, placing the volume on his desk and resting his hand on it, as if swearing on a Bible.

'You should stay. There are things you need to know.'

'I've heard enough.'

As I was leaving, he called after me: 'Remember, you were with me all of yesterday at the horse show. If you don't say that, I will tell the police about you. I have proof, if I need it, of who you truly are.'

I stormed down the corridor, intending to put as much distance between myself and John Thackery as I could.

If he did as he was threatening, every friend and acquaintance I had would shun me. Even Jacob, who knew exactly what I was, would have to deny it to avoid incriminating himself.

I would be convicted, perhaps for sexual offences and certainly for fraud. I held a position at the hospital as a man, not to mention my lodging with Alfie. The police would say I had claimed to be someone I was not. I would be imprisoned as Lottie Pritchard in a women's prison and they would try to cure me. They would administer chemicals to douse my senses and, if those failed, run electricity through my head. But even that wasn't the worst. On those nights when I awoke sweating and gripping the blankets, my throat hoarse, it was another dread that crawled through my guts and reached its fingers into my throat: cauterisation.

I had heard of doctors burning away the location, the very nub, of sexual pleasure, such that nothing was left, and a woman lusting after other women, as the doctors would believe me to be, would have that urge removed for ever. It was supposed to relieve wicked thoughts and allow the insanity to fade, but how was that possible? How could the doctor know, as he sets fire to another person's skin, that it is the insanity which dissipates and not something else, something more precious? What if what's lost is the *self*, that indefinable thing that makes us who we are?

What would be left behind if my *self* was burned away?

The thought of it almost made me sick.

I stopped. I had lost my bearings and was in an unfamiliar room containing what looked like a small printing press. I turned and went out through a different door, this time into a hallway leading to a dormitory filled with empty beds. An old woman was standing at the window and she started, crossing her arms over her chest.

'It's all right,' I assured her. 'How do I get out of here?'

She shook her head and started babbling in a language I didn't understand, and then threw up her hands and said what appeared to be the only English word she knew: 'Italian.'

'Oh, I see. Excuse me.'

I went to the window, trying to orientate myself. I was looking down on the courtyard, where Dora Hannigan's body was being carried away on a stretcher by two policemen. Hooper was holding a wad of paper under a lamp and flicking through it, appearing to get more and more furious as he turned the pages. When he'd finished, he shouted, 'Search every room. The whole place.'

He looked up at the window, and I thought perhaps he'd caught sight of me. I stepped back into the shadows, and hurried out, finding my way through a succession of corridors to the stairs, where I almost careered into Pallett.

'Good grief,' I said to him. 'This place is impossible!'

He nodded solemnly. 'It's a rabbit warren and no mistake.'

'I thought this was a club of some kind. Why are all these people living in it?'

'They're radicals, sir.'

He seemed to think that was explanation enough.

In the courtyard, bats were making patterns in the lamplight above us, snatching insects out of the air. To my horror John Thackery was talking to Hooper. He pointed in my direction. 'Of course, Detective Inspector,' I heard him say. 'I was with Mr Stanhope all day, at the horse show in Alexandra Park, and then we went to the pub. We were there until late, weren't we, *Leo*?'

'Is that right, Mr Stanhope?' asked Hooper.

I stood with my mouth open for what felt like an eternity. 'I … which day?'

'*Yesterday.* Were you at the horse show or not?'

I nodded, not properly aware I was doing it.

Hooper pulled out his pen and notebook. 'Didn't you say before you were with your landlord drinking whisky?'

'Um … yes, no, I misspoke. That was the day before. I'm sorry.'

He made a note, glancing at Thackery and me in turn.

'If you're not telling the truth, I'll find out,' he said. 'I'm going to check every detail. I've sent for more men already. This case has become our highest priority.'

'Why? Was Miss Hannigan someone important?'

Murders were commonplace in the city. I didn't understand why the police would give this one special attention.

Hooper stepped towards me, seeming even taller. I could see up his nose. 'You mind your own business. I'll be seeing you both again.' He tipped his hat to me and Thackery in turn. 'Mr Stanhope. Mr Duport.'

Mr Duport?

Once Hooper had gone, I wheeled round and glared at Thackery. '*You're* Mr Duport? You're the man the police suspect is the murderer?'

'Well, yes, that's true. But I didn't do it.'

I thumped the wall with my fist. 'Why didn't you tell me? And why are you using a false name?'

'I tried to explain before, but you rushed out. That book I bought in Enfield, by Thomas Carlyle. When I got home, my father threw it away. He told me I must never look at such seditious nonsense again and wrote a letter to the mayor suggesting that the bookshop should be closed down. He thought the owner had known who I was and had pushed the book upon me as a way of making a point. But he was wrong; the old fellow had no idea. The next time I went in I called myself by a different name: John Duport. When I came here a couple of years ago, I didn't want everyone knowing who I was related to, and I remembered the name. So, you see, we're not so different, you and me. We both chose to be someone new.'

I stared at him, not believing what I was hearing. I had mentioned the name Duport to him and he hadn't admitted it was his own alias. He had deceived me, straight to my face.

He produced a pocket watch from his waistcoat. 'Stick to our story and we'll both be fine. Look, it's getting late and I have to go, but we must talk properly, and soon.'

'I want nothing more to do with you,' I said. 'Nothing at all. *Ever.*'

I emphasised the last word by slicing the air between us with my hand. He didn't notice or, if he did, he didn't care.

'There are things I need to tell you. Very important things. We need to talk like civilised … well, men. Come to the Marquis of Granby pub on South Audley Street. Do you know it? Good, I can see that you do. Tomorrow at seven-thirty.'

And with that, he scurried away towards the house, leaving me alone but for the bats and one young constable, who was walking around the courtyard unhooking the lamps.

When he reached the last one, he paused. 'Are you all right, sir?'

I nodded, and he snuffed it out, leaving me in near darkness.

I had lied to the police about a murder. And I had given an alibi to their top suspect.

3

SOMEWHERE IN THE DISTANCE, a clock was striking the hour. Was it nine o'clock, or ten? I had completely lost track.

Outside, on Rose Street, a man was standing under the eaves to avoid the drips. I recognised him as the journalist who had spoken to me earlier: Mr Whitford. I lowered my face and hurried onwards, avoiding eye contact.

'Mr Stanhope!' he called after me, proving that he'd discovered my name. 'Any comment for the *Daily Chronicle*? Are you an anarchist? How well did you know Miss Hannigan? When did you first meet her? Do you know why she was killed?'

I just wanted to get home. I was determined not to tell him anything.

'I have no idea. I gave the police some help, that's all.'

I set off down the passageway, picking a path between the curled figures sleeping under blankets. Behind me, I could hear Whitford in pursuit. He caught up with me at the corner of Greek Street, which was as hectic as ever.

'They sent Hooper, their senior man. He doesn't generally soil himself with this sort of thing.'

'What sort of thing?' I hated that I was intrigued.

He took off his hat and beat it against his leg, sending a sparkling spray of water over his shoes. 'Hooper prefers taking his carriage to Mayfair and dealing with a better class of criminal as a rule, especially when the top brass want things kept quiet. He has a reputation for being ... how shall I put this? A prudent man, you might say. Or a lackey of the wealthy and powerful perhaps, depending on your point of view.'

'I wish you luck, Mr Whitford. Good evening.'

He kept pace with me as I lengthened my stride. For a fellow of such ample girth he was surprisingly energetic.

'See, that's what's got me inquisitive, Mr Stanhope. They sent Hooper to make sure the right story gets told. Right for *them*, of course. It's a matter of note, you see, a murder in the house of socialists and anarchists. Either the victim's one of 'em, which is a warning to all, or the murderer is, which is better still. Or both, of course, which is best of all.'

'I have nothing to do with any of this. Please leave me alone.'

He grabbed my sleeve, not aggressively, more earnestly, trying to convince me. 'I want to find out the truth, Mr Stanhope. The police found some papers. I was told they were plans to commit an act of vandalism on a large scale. A very large scale indeed. Was Mrs Hannigan part of it, do you suppose?'

'Goodbye, Mr Whitford.'

I pulled my hat low over my brow and crossed the road between two carts queuing behind a donkey that was tail up, depositing its load while a boy caned it mercilessly.

'You're an interesting chap, Mr Stanhope,' Whitford shouted. When I didn't reply, he shouted louder: 'I'll find out the truth in the end, you know.'

The truth is not so simple, I thought. The truth is that I am a man, from the soles of my feet to the top of my head. I have a man's thoughts and a man's desires. And yet, if you were to look at my skin, Mr Whitford, heaven forbid, you would think I was female. That would be your truth. Whose truth is more important, do you think: yours or mine?

Such self-obsession I had. I hardly warranted it. He wanted a story about murder and scandal for his ghastly newspaper. None of us mattered to him; not me, not Dora Hannigan. Not even her children.

I had forgotten about her children.

I hurried back to where Whitford was still standing, writing in his notebook.

'There's one thing,' I said, cursing myself for almost escaping, but not quite.

'Changed your mind?' he said, looking up. 'Good for you.'

'Dora Hannigan had two children. A boy and a girl. She had their pictures in a locket. Do you know where they are now?'

'A boy and a girl,' he repeated. 'How old and what are their names?'

'I don't know. The brother's the elder, perhaps nine or ten.'

'Just nippers.' He paused, sucking his pencil, and then wrote some more. 'Could've been taken, I s'pose. Or worse.'

A fearful image formed in my mind of another shallow hole in that courtyard.

'How did the police find their mother's body?'

'A dog dug 'er up.'

I nodded. 'All right. Good.'

He looked at me quizzically. 'Why is that good?'

'If the children were buried there, the dog would've found them too. There's a reason why cemeteries have deep graves.' I was thinking professionally again. It was a comfort, like streetlamps on a dark night. I could see my way. 'Ask around, will you? If they're lost, the police need to start looking for them.'

'I will.' He blew out his cheeks and we were both silent, contemplating two small children lost in the city.

We shook hands, and this time I really did walk away, crossing over quickly and causing a cab driver to pull on his reins and bark abuse at me. I strode swiftly onwards, a man among all the other men, rushing home or spilling out from the pubs on to the pavement, talking, laughing and whistling. I was exactly like them, as far as anyone could tell.

When I came in through the back door, Constance was setting out some laundry on the rack in front of the stove. It was much earlier than I had thought, only a little after eight o'clock.

'Have you been with Mr Kleiner?' she asked.

'No, someone else. Someone I used to know.'

She raised her eyebrows, and I could see her brain working. She liked to treat me as the unwilling hero of a romantic novella, with her as the author, chivvying me towards matrimony. Two weeks previously, I had asked her why she was so determined that I should be married and her father not, and she replied that my not knowing the answer to that question was exactly why I needed a good woman to take me in hand.

'Was it a lady?'

'No.'

'A friend? You need to meet some new people.' She didn't approve of Jacob. 'It's no use being lonely, Mr Stanhope.'

'I'm not lonely, thank you.' I folded my arms, slightly piqued by her nosiness. It didn't dissuade her.

'What happened to that lady who came here before?'

I cursed myself for blushing. 'As far as I know she's still running her pie shop.'

'You liked her, I could tell. What was her name again?'

'Flowers. Rosie Flowers.'

It was a silly name, bequeathed to her by her late husband.

'You should go and see Mrs Flowers. I'm sure she could cure your loneliness for you.'

She nodded firmly, certain she was right. Certainty is easy when you're twelve.

I trudged upstairs to my room and lay on the bed with my face buried in a blanket. I remembered how it had been, a year before, the last time I was caught up in something. My side still felt stiff every night, and there was worse, much worse; things I wouldn't name or think about. Since then, my life had become uneventful. It was numbness, rather than happiness, but it was all I wanted. I couldn't bear the thought that John Thackery might take it away from me.

I was supposed to play chess that evening but couldn't face it, so I dozed, and for a while was beset by the darkest of thoughts, my fears and memories mixing: light against a slanting ceiling, the taste of salt water in my mouth and the acrid stink of scorched meat. But I surfaced, blinking, when I remembered poor Dora Hannigan and her two children. How selfish I was; how crass. She was dead, and they were lost, and all I could think about was my own troubles.

Better if I went out to play chess with Jacob, especially as he had been known, on extremely rare occasions, to offer useful advice.

———

When I got to the Blue Posts pub it was packed, and I couldn't see Jacob. Then I heard the unmistakeable growl of his voice at the bar.

'Wait your turn!'

I squeezed through, explaining that my friend was aged and needed help carrying the drinks. When I reached him, he was confronting a large fellow with oil on his hands.

I was surprised when the fellow laughed. 'Sorry, old man. Didn't see you there.'

Jacob curled his lip. 'I'm not bloody invisible.'

His fingers were turning white on the hook of his cane. He started to raise it, and I feared there would be violence, albeit of a brief and one-sided variety.

I put my hand on his arm. 'Shall I take over? You go and find us a table.'

All the other members of the chess club played in the calm of the upstairs room, but Jacob had injured his leg a few months previously, tripping over a kerb near Southwark Park despite, he claimed, being as sober as a Nazirite. The stairs were steep, so we had taken to playing downstairs amidst the throng.

He waved a hand, apparently dismissing me, the bar, London and the whole of England in a single gesture. 'You're late. Five times I've asked the barman to serve me, but always someone else comes first. I ask for an ale, a porter, two whiskies and a chess set. Five times. Always another customer, as if my money isn't good enough for this *distinguished* place.' He waved his hand again, this time aiming at the peeling walls and collapsing furniture. 'We should go somewhere else. The beer here tastes like piss and they water down the whisky.'

I steered him outside, where the air was less dense – the best that could ever be said for London's noxious atmosphere.

He took off his hat and wiped his brow, and I could see the pink skin of his scalp beneath his grey hair. 'That oaf is lucky I'm not still young.' He tapped his cane on the ground as if considering rushing back to strike the fellow after all. 'I was strong once, you know. I used to pull ships along the docks in Nikolaev; just me, on my own, hauling ships weighing tens of tons to be unloaded. They used to call me *medved*. The bear. No one argued with me in those days. They were afraid of me. I could have pulled their arms from their sockets, just like that.' He mimed the motion and made a sucking sound with his mouth, and then a pop. 'Now I am an old man, and no one is afraid of me. Not even you.'

Lilya, his wife, had once confided that she didn't believe he had ever truly hauled boats along the docks in Nikolaev, despite the stories he liked to tell. She said he'd been a jeweller's assistant before she met him, and then a jeweller, until they'd been evicted from their home and forced to flee across

Europe. He was a jeweller still, spending his days peering through an eyeglass at the fine details of brooches and bracelets. I didn't mind the pretence. If he wanted to convince himself that he'd once been a feared man with thighs like tree roots, who was I to deny him? Me, of all people?

'Is your leg getting worse?'

'Everything's getting worse. All of me. Never grow old, Leo, my friend. When you're young, your body and mind are one and the same. You think to speak, and you speak. Your voice does not creak and whine like an old door. You think to pick up a glass, and you pick it up. You think to stand, and you stand. Not so when you're old. You think to stand, and you ache and shake and groan, and forget why you wanted to stand, and eventually it's easier to stay seated.'

'That's not an answer. Is it still hurting you?'

He shrugged, leaning on his stick. 'That's a young man's question. My back hurts, my neck, my feet. They punish me! They hate me! How can I tell which pain is greater or lesser? At least it means I'm still alive.' He pointed his cane west, towards Hyde Park. 'Let's go to that place on your street. You know the one. What's it called again?'

'Very funny.'

'Little Stanhope Street!' He grinned impishly, waggling his beard. 'Your very own. How I envy you! There is no Kleiner Street.'

The pub was called the Pitt's Head, which I thought made it sound like a coal mine, and in truth the place was hardly better than that; dismal and dark with walls browned by years of smoke, and a boneyard of armchairs, padding spiked by their own skeletons, cushions bursting through their seams. But at least it was quiet and there was less likelihood Jacob would get us into a fight. We found a quiet corner near the fireplace and laid out the pub's hoary chess set.

'So?' he said, his way of inviting me to speak.

I told him about the murder, and John Thackery, who called himself John Duport. I even told him about Dora Hannigan's visit to the pharmacy, though not that I'd lied to the police about it. I was too ashamed. She had been a living, breathing person, and I had erased our encounter like a clerk rubbing out his mistakes. And that was *before* John Thackery had threatened to expose me. It was my own action, unforced.

I took a deep gulp of my porter.

'You say this Thackery is wealthy?' Jacob said, pulling a cigar box from his pocket and opening it up. 'Maybe there's something in it for you, if you help him.'

'His father, not him.'

'If his father's wealthy, he is too. That's how wealth works.'

I advanced my queen's pawn two squares and sipped my drink. Jacob was three-quarters down his ale already, and he eyed me over the glass.

'That woman's death, do you think it was him? Is he the killer?'

Despite everything that had happened, I couldn't deny that some part of me retained a liking for John Thackery – not perhaps the man he was now, but the boy he had been back in Enfield, with his restless hands and the thin fuzz of hair on his chin, like the fur on a caterpillar cocoon.

'I don't know. When we were younger, John was always quite gentle. But he's more … fervent now. He asked to meet me again tomorrow.'

Jacob swapped his empty glass for my half-full one, and sat back, sucking on his cigar, exhaling slowly, almost chewing on the smoke as it left his mouth. 'And you're planning to do it, are you? Spend time with your old pal *John.*'

I sensed he was anxious, concerned for my well-being, but perhaps something else as well. He was my only friend other than Alfie, who was also my landlord. I rarely considered that I was Jacob's only friend too, and he might be jealous of any other I might make.

'He's not my *pal*. I was hardly the same person last time I met him, was I? And he said he had information for me. Something important. There are things I don't understand about all this. The dead woman had my name and address. She came to the pharmacy. It can't be a coincidence.' I indicated his rank of untouched pieces. 'Are you playing or not?'

He grimaced and matched my pawn, seasoning his jacket with ash.

'She's dead now. What difference does any of it make? She won't come back to life.'

'I know, but … she had two children as well. They're missing.'

He took a deep breath. 'How long?'

'I don't know exactly. A day, maybe two.'

He nodded, his lips pressed together. He had seven children of his own and loved them devotedly, though he tried his best to hide it.

'That's very sad,' he said. 'But not your problem.' He blew out another thick coil of smoke. 'You of all people have cause to be careful.'

Most of the time, Jacob ignored what I was under these clothes, treating me as a young man in need of his guidance and wisdom. Whenever reminded, he shrugged and offered nothing. I think he imagined my previous life was a part I'd once performed in a play or a character I'd made up, which wasn't all that far from the truth. I had been constructed from little more than petticoats and bonnets, and hadn't been sure there was anyone real inside.

'Are you listening to me, Leo? I said you must be careful. You have a history of foolishness.' He put his hand on my arm and squeezed it. 'Remember what you said you wanted? A quiet life. No problems and no excitements.' He drained my glass. 'And a dog. Did you get a dog?'

'No.'

'Why not? Every man should have a dog.'

'You don't have a dog.'

'Lilya has a dog. It's our dog.'

'He's her dog.'

'You're avoiding the point.' He produced another half a cigar from the box and lit it, surveying me through the smoke. 'You never do what's best for you.'

I moved my queen's knight to aggress his pawn.

'I want to know what he has to say, that's all.'

I'd spoken more sharply than I intended, and he sat back, his moustache twitching. 'You're like another son to me, Leo, you know that, don't you?'

'Of course I do.'

I looked away towards the bar while he wiped his eyes.

When I looked back, he was moving a pawn to defend the one my knight was threatening. His hand was shaking, and he had to take care to place his piece without knocking over another, and then it was my turn to wipe my eyes.

4

THE MARQUIS OF GRANBY was a decrepit pile of bricks and wooden pillars that had somehow survived while the rest of Mayfair grew higher and wealthier around it. As ever, it stank. I couldn't determine the exact combination of substances that permeated the walls and furniture to create such an odour, but they seemed to include stale beer, cigar smoke, lamp oil, blood, bile, flatulence and the vague odour of poultry, making me wonder whether a pigeon had become stuck in the chimney.

Unsurprisingly, the place was almost empty, and what patrons it had were old men at rickety tables, nursing ales and reading brown, curling newspapers. They looked as if they'd been coming here for decades, crumbling along with the plasterwork.

John Thackery was sitting in the most visible spot at the bar, his dented hat in front of him. Seeing him there, I felt strangely fearful. He was like a door into a room I didn't want to enter. But if I left, I would never find out what he wanted to tell me, and it might relate to Dora Hannigan's children. I could still picture the little girl's grin as she pushed the pedal on Alfie's dentistry chair.

'What do you have to say to me, Mr Thackery? Or should I call you Mr Duport?'

He peered at me, at my face, my hair, my chin. 'Call me John, please. We've known each other a long time.'

'We knew each other briefly, a long time ago. It's not the same thing.'

I wouldn't pretend we were old friends after he'd so recently blackmailed me into lying for him.

He nodded, accepting my correction. 'I didn't want all this to happen. I'm trying very hard to do the right thing, but it's become rather *complicated*. Sit down. Please. I'll get you a drink.' He summoned the barman and ordered a half-pint of Indian Pale Ale without further consulting me.

I generally avoided stools, but had no choice on this occasion, so I arranged my coat to hang down at the back and obscure my hips.

'How did you find me? And what do you need an alibi for, if it's not murder?'

He attempted, unsuccessfully, to straighten his necktie, looking exactly like the young man I had once known. 'That doesn't concern you.'

'None of it concerns me.' I had spoken too loudly, and two old fellows looked round, unused to having their quietude interrupted. I lowered my voice. 'Her children are missing. Do you have any idea where they are?'

He took a sip of his drink and gazed at me blankly, apparently having given them no thought at all. 'I'm sure they'll turn up. You need to know that I would never do anything to hurt Dora.' His voice cracked, and he had to swallow to keep it under control. 'She was very precious to me.'

'I see.'

'It's not what you're thinking, but believe me, I would give anything to have her here again, alive and well. Anything.'

There were tears in his eyes, and one of them ran down his face and into his beard. 'Dora was my governess when I was a boy. She wasn't afraid of anything or anyone. She had such belief, such commitment. I didn't realise until later how much influence she'd had on me.'

I thought back. 'Your governess? I don't remember her.'

He shook his head, watching his own reflection in the glass behind the bar. 'It was before we came to Enfield, when we still lived in London. She came when I was ten, and two years later they packed me off to boarding school. When I got home at Christmas they'd already sent her away.' He drew in a deep breath. 'I was inconsolable. Afterwards, I discovered what he'd done to her. My father, I mean.'

I felt a clutch in my stomach, and realised I was twisting the bar towel between my fists.

'What had he done?'

Thackery took a long time to reply, several times opening his mouth as if to speak before closing it again. I sensed he still thought of me as a girl and wanted to protect my gentle nature, which actually brought a smile to my face, albeit of the bitterest type.

Finally, he almost whispered, 'The worst thing.' He looked at me squarely for the first time. 'Worse than you can imagine. That's how I know it was him who killed her.'

I couldn't help but feel compassion for him, sitting here in this stinking pub and telling me about a woman he had clearly loved like an aunt.

'I'm sorry, John, I really am.'

'She was the kindest person I've ever known. She said we shouldn't force you to cooperate and insisted that I give her your address at that pharmacy. She visited several times before she finally met you.'

'Why?'

'She wanted to see if you could be bribed to help us instead. But she decided you couldn't and demanded that we leave you alone.' He rubbed his eyes and drew his fingers down his face. 'Too late for that now, I'm afraid.'

I thought back to our encounter in the shop. She had asked if I would extend her a line of credit in return for a personal profit. Had that been a test?

'She was right. I'm an honest man.' I said.

He took a sip of his beer and wiped his mouth with the back of his hand, accidentally angling his elbow towards my face, forcing me to lean away from him.

'Was she? Seems to me you lied quite well to that policeman. I suppose you've had a lot of practice.'

'I only lied because you gave me no choice.' I picked up my hat. 'This is pointless.'

'Wait,' he insisted. 'There's something else I have to tell you.'

'What is it?'

He looked down at his glass, swirling his beer so it nearly over-brimmed. 'I envied you terribly back then, you know. You and your brother and sister. I would've given *anything* to have had the reverend as a father instead of my own. The reverend and I used to talk in his study, and sometimes he lent me books from his collection.' He smiled at the memory. 'John Stuart Mill and Jonathan Swift. I devoured them in days and couldn't wait to discuss them with him. When we moved back to London, I didn't miss much about Enfield. Dull little town. But I missed the reverend.'

'You don't know anything about him,' I said, in a voice so low it was almost a whisper. My hatred for my father was far beyond shouting and stamping my feet, childish displays aimed at winning sympathy or apology. I cared not a jot for either of those. My anger was a cold, sharp blade, in and out with barely a murmur. 'When my mother was sick, in her last weeks, Jane told me that he wouldn't stay with her or speak to her. He wouldn't even tend to his dying wife.'

'I'm sure that's not correct. He's a decent man.' He shook his head sadly, rubbing his thumb across his knuckles. 'Look, this should really come from your brother or sister. But you need to know. Your father's very sick. I'm afraid he's dying.'

I had only seen my father once since I left home, though he hadn't noticed me. It was shortly after I started as a porter in Westminster, and I was on my way to the late shift, strolling down Whitehall on a fine summer day. Ahead of me on the pavement was a man with a small dog, a terrier such as my father favoured. The dog stopped to sniff something, and the man turned, and there he was. I almost bumped into him. It was as if a memory had come to life.

He mumbled something to the dog and carried on, so I followed him, studying the thin strands of hair on the back of his neck and his bony hand as it held the leash. He was still tall, over six feet, and broad-bellied, but more stooped than I remembered. When I was young he used to walk at high speed, in great strides that I had to scamper to keep up with. No longer. Now, he was stiff-legged, waving his thanks to an omnibus driver who had stopped to let him cross the road. I continued onwards to the hospital, none the wiser about why he was there or where he was going.

And now he was dying, apparently. I searched inside myself, but this new information seemed illusory, a story about another man. I didn't believe my father could ever die. He was like an old stone wall that might weather and crack but would never crumble away completely.

'I stayed in touch with him,' John said. 'Especially after your mother … well, after she died. I heard he was very sick, so I went to visit him. He seemed extremely weak, I'm afraid. You must visit him soon, before it's too late.'

'I won't do that.'

He wasn't facing me, but I could see his angry expression in the mirrored glass behind the bar. He took a rapid gulp of his beer, almost slamming the tankard back down on the counter.

'Why on earth not?'

'Goodbye, John,' I said, and marched out into the evening.

The following Monday, Alfie returned late, having been out for dinner with Mrs Gower. They had seen a lot of each other over the previous six months; twice weekly or more, having a common interest in walking around parks and admiring the flora, though it was recently acquired in his case.

He shook his umbrella and brushed the rainwater from his new coat, which had velvet lapels and a purple silk lining. He was sporting his new top hat as well, which he had become extremely fond of, often leaving it on the counter where everyone could see it.

49

'Shall we have a whisky, Leo?'

He seemed excited to share his news.

A whisky was what I needed. It was one of my great delights, sitting side by side with Alfie, elbows on the counter, talking or remaining pleasantly silent while the light dimmed and the liquid in our glasses grew black. It occurred to me that if John Thackery chose to betray me, I might not be able to enjoy many more.

'We walked back through the Botanic Gardens,' Alfie said, as he poured. 'She mentioned she'd like to be married again, some day.' He must have noticed my disquiet because he patted my shoulder. 'You'll always have a home here, Leo. Nothing will change that.'

'I know.'

He still thought he owed me a debt of gratitude, crediting me as the author of his financial recovery, following a long period of decline. I had asked a local businesswoman to send all her staff, and those of her friends in the industry, to Alfie to get their teeth fixed. That was more than a year ago, and word of his talents had travelled widely since. Of course, what remained unspoken was the exact nature of the businesswoman's trade. No one wants to be known as the whores' dentist. But still, these days he could afford to buy expensive new coats and top hats, not to mention court a widow who owned a house in Pimlico with servants and a horse and carriage.

All the changes happening; I felt as if everyone was on a road to somewhere, crissing and crossing, all except me. I wished everything would stay still.

'Do you want to be married again?'

'Yes, I think it's time.'

'So, you're going to ask her, are you?'

His face darkened, and he bit his lip. 'Not yet. I haven't mentioned it to Constance. But she'll be delighted, I'm sure. She needs a mother at her age, and Mrs Gower is a fine woman.'

I almost felt sorry for Alfie's new belle. Constance's silences could be wintry, and she was capable of the most formidable politeness, which had been known to reduce seasoned adults almost to tears.

'You'll have to tell her soon,' I said.

He nodded, his mood sagging at the thought of it.

We didn't talk for a while, each musing on our respective futures, until Alfie raised his eyebrows at me. 'Constance told me you'd had a lady-friend yourself, a few months back.'

'Mrs Flowers and I were amicable for a short while, that's all.'

He chuckled, unable to help himself. 'I'm sorry, Leo, but it's made such a difference to me to have someone. It could make a difference to you too. You can't just sit around all the time. You have to go out and see people.'

'I do see people. I go to work and I play chess with Jacob every Thursday.'

He laughed again. 'Chess with Jacob will certainly keep you cosy on those long, cold nights.'

I didn't laugh with him. At one time, I used to imagine myself coming home to a bustling wife, kissing her and pulling her on to my lap as she told me about her day and I told her about mine. I could almost feel her head on my shoulder and her hair tickling my cheek. But the woman I had loved was dead, and in the unlikely event I ever found another who would overlook my obvious affliction, I would be importuning her to commit fraud, and that would be a poor exchange indeed.

'I do wish people would stop telling me what's good for me,' I said, aware that I was sounding sour. I understood that he wished me to be happy, but his insistence upon the method of it was wearying.

'All right.' He was staring at the rows of bottles and packets displayed in the window, but then leapt up from his chair. 'Bloody hell,' he exclaimed, pointing. 'Those urchins again!'

In the doorway, two figures were huddled together, sheltering from the rain.

'What difference does it make?' I asked, curious why Alfie was so bothered. He wasn't normally one to make a fuss about such things.

'They were there this morning when I opened.' He fished his keys out of his pocket. 'That exact spot. A customer had to move them to get into the shop. It's a bit much.'

He unlocked the door and threw it open. One of the urchins squeezed closer to the other, and I had a brief view of scared eyes and dark, curly hair. The city was riddled with children like these, sleeping on benches, under trees, in doorways, begging on pavements, rifling through bins for scraps and knocking on doors selling posies of flowers stolen from parks and cemeteries.

'Please go somewhere else,' Alfie said, handing each of them a farthing. He wasn't an unkind man.

They took the money and started to move away, clutching on to each other, shivering in the cold. The smaller one looked back, and I realised who she was. Who they both must be.

They were the children of Dora Hannigan.

5

'WAIT!' I CALLED AFTER them.

They stumbled on, into the brief light from next door's window and then the shadow beyond. I might have lost them altogether if a young gentleman hadn't been pushing a bicycle along the pavement in the opposite direction, forcing them to stop.

'I just want to talk to you,' I said.

They shuffled back towards the doorway, the boy leading his sister by the hand. She looked exhausted, almost falling down where she stood, pressing against his arm for comfort.

'What are you doing here?' I asked.

Neither of them answered. The boy was as grim-faced as when I'd last seen him, except now he kept his eyes fixed on Alfie, being sure to stay out of his reach.

Alfie stared at me in astonishment. 'Do you *know* them?'

'Not exactly.' And then more quietly so the children wouldn't hear. 'Their mother was killed. I'll take care of it. You go to bed.'

He seemed doubtful. 'All right, but don't get caught up in this, Leo. Remember what happened last time.'

'I'll lock up.'

I opened the door wide, but the children didn't move.

'Come on,' I said to them. 'It's warmer indoors.'

The boy looked at his sister, and in they came, hand in hand.

I wasn't sure what to do next. The police should certainly speak to them, but it was late in the evening and Hooper would most likely be at home. He didn't seem the type to work long shifts.

'Do you know what happened to your mother?' I asked. 'Were you at the club on Rose Street when it happened? What did you see?' The little girl edged behind her brother, peeping at me from around his shoulder.

Perhaps I had been taking too direct an approach. I changed tack.

'Do you have a father?'

The boy took a step sideways and glanced at the door out of the corner of his eye. His grip on his sister's hand tightened.

I really had no idea how to speak to children. I supposed Constance had been about this boy's age when I had first met her, but I probably didn't say more than two words to her in those first few months. And anyway – and there was truly no other way to express this – she was Constance. It was not the same.

I tried to remember how it felt to be this young, and how people used to speak to me. The one adult I had known well, aside from my parents, was Bridget, our maid. I used to spend hours with her in the kitchen, dipping a thumb into the molasses and stealing pinches of sugar while she prattled about whatever came into her head: an acquaintance she'd met, a new shop she'd been to, a joke she'd heard. She was so garrulous that if I hadn't been there

I swear she would've chattered to the stove, or the pastry, or her fingers.

I couldn't be like Bridget; I couldn't say that many words in a whole month. But there was *something* I could take from my time in that kitchen.

'Would you like some porridge?' I asked, and they nodded in unison.

They ate fast and skilfully, skimming their spoons across the top for the coolest part before digging in properly, and finally, when all but the dregs had been consumed, running their fingers around the bowl and sucking them clean.

I watched, envious of their voraciousness. I could never eat like that. Jacob sometimes said I resembled a scarecrow, which was fine coming from him, a man with holes in the elbows of his jacket and buttons missing from his shirts. But he never wondered *why* I starved myself. I relished those soft curves on a woman, but not on me. Never on me.

When the children had finished their porridge and munched their way through an apple each from Alfie's store, cores and all, and downed two cups of boiled water, and eaten two pieces of bread with honey, and asked for more and been declined for the sake of their stomachs, I sat down at the table with them.

'Do you want to see a trick?' I asked.

I fished ten coins from my pocket and balanced them on the back of my forefinger. In one movement, I snatched them out of the air ... or I intended to anyway. Actually, I was a fraction too slow, being out of practice, and sprayed them across the room.

'Damn it! Wait.'

I scrabbled around the floor picking up the coins while the children watched, unsure whether this was part of the trick or I was some kind of idiot.

Once again, I balanced the pennies and farthings on the back of my finger, and this time caught them perfectly. It was as if they'd disappeared from out of the air. The girl yawned and laid her head on her arms on the table, but the boy's eyes widened and he put out his hand for the coins.

I made myself a pot of tea while he tried the trick for himself. He had already worked up to five coins by the time the kettle boiled, somewhat dampening my sense of achievement.

'What's your name?' I asked him.

His mouth was set hard, as though he was wondering whether to tell me. Eventually he muttered, 'Aiden.'

'And your sister?'

He put his hand on her forearm. She opened a bleary eye and closed it again, falling instantly back to sleep.

'She's Ciara.'

He used words frugally, as if he was feeding treats to a dog to keep it docile.

'How old are you?' He said nothing, and I took a sip of my tea. Upstairs, I could hear snoring from Alfie's room. 'Eight, maybe?'

'Ten,' he answered quickly. No child wants to be thought of as younger than they actually are.

'And Ciara?'

He frowned, looking up at the ceiling. He seemed to be genuinely trying to remember. 'Six.'

Constance's cat, Colly, sprang up on to the table and nosed towards Ciara's bowl, and Aiden stretched forwards to stroke her tabby fur, his head cocked on one side.

'Do you have a cat?' I asked.

He shook his head. 'We had a dog, once. We called him Patch because he had a patch over one eye.'

Not much imagination there, I thought, but at least it was a conversation. He had the resilience of all children. His mother was dead, and yet here he was, talking and drinking a cup of water as if the world had not changed. Then it occurred to me that he might not know. If that was the case, I would have to tell two children that their mother had been murdered. How did one do that?

He was restless, drumming his fingers on the table and squirming in his seat as though an agitation was building up within him, and he might leap up at any moment and run from the room.

'Were you living at the club on Rose Street?' I asked him, keeping my voice low and calm.

He shrugged, which I took to mean yes. His eyes remained harsh, watching me from under a fierce brow.

'Do you have anywhere to stay now?'

He shook his head and yawned a childish yawn, mouth wide and uncovered, no hint of self-consciousness.

Again, I wondered what I should do. I couldn't turn them out. Two innocents like these, in well-patched clothes and with all their limbs and eyes intact, they would be taken for certain. They would be put to work, and in another few years, perhaps very few, this little girl would be being sold on the street. Virgins were highly prized and could be freshly deflowered three or four times a night.

I shook myself. That would not happen to these children. I wouldn't allow it.

'You can stay here tonight,' I said. 'Tomorrow, I'll work out what to do with you. Do you understand?'

Ciara didn't wake when I picked her up. She rested her head on my shoulder, her feet dangling limply. Aiden followed us upstairs and removed his boots before entering my room. His hair, freed from his cap, was tightly curled around his head like a jet-black helmet. He took off his jacket and trousers and stood in his small-clothes, narrow and pale, his shoulders like hazelnuts and his legs like wheat-stalks. I laid his sister on my bed, intending shortly to move her on to the floor, but she curled up beneath the blanket and her brother crawled in beside her. He was asleep in seconds.

I sat on my chair for a while, listening to their slow breathing, and then lay resentfully on the rug.

I hadn't been able to change, and, worse, the cotton bandage I wore to flatten my breasts beneath my shirt was damp and abrading my skin. I called it my cilice after the sackcloth vests worn by Christian monks, though I bore it not to repent my sins but to hide them. I sought no forgiveness from God.

I could take it off easily enough, but how would I tie a new one in the morning without the children noticing? I had no choice but to suffer.

Tomorrow, I would take them to Detective Hooper on my way to work. And after that? They would likely go to relatives, I supposed, who probably wouldn't be thrilled by the extra mouths to feed. And if no relatives existed, where would they go, the children of an unwed mother? My eyes strayed towards the bookshelf, to *Oliver Twist*; I had first read it at age twelve, and the terror of the workhouse had never left me.

Sleep would not come. It wasn't yet close to dawn; no clatter of carts along the cobbles of Soho and no chorus of birds in the nearby churchyard. Even the stray dogs, normally disposed to bark and howl all night to one another across the city like a canine telegraph, were hushed. Everyone was asleep but me.

The scene of their mother's murder was plaguing me. To start with, there was no way to tell whether she had been killed where she was buried or if her body had been transported to that dank courtyard from somewhere else.

If she'd been killed in the courtyard, why hadn't anyone been alerted by the commotion? Surely, if someone was attacked in that small space, surrounded by lodgings, they would scream for help.

But if she'd been transported, then why to that spot? Awful as it was to contemplate, wouldn't it be easier to tip her into a canal or leave her in some alley?

Neither option appeared to make any sense.

I wondered if the children knew the answer. Part of me hoped they did, so the criminal would be caught, but another part hoped not, in case that criminal was John Thackery. I went cold at the thought and pinched myself hard under my armpit with the nails of my thumb and forefinger, gritting my teeth at the pain. What a self-regarding oaf I was, wishing the children had not witnessed their mother's murder for my own sake, rather than theirs.

I was halfway between sleeping and waking when I heard a noise, a thin shriek. I jumped up, fumbling for a match. Aiden was awake too, kneeling on my bed.

I heard him grunt with effort, and then mutter, 'Not now.'

He was crouching over Ciara, holding her shoulders while she thrashed to and fro. She was shaking and kicking as though overtaken by hysteria. It was she who had cried out, but now she was silent, aside from her teeth grinding together in her mouth.

I lit the candle and held it up. 'What's wrong with her?'

Aiden continued restraining his sister, accepting the blows and scratches from her flailing hands. She was completely unaware of us. Her eyes were rolled back in her head.

'It happens sometimes,' he said.

I took her hand, feeling the spasms and convulsions gradually diminishing, until finally they ceased altogether and she closed her eyes.

I was left gasping, my heart dancing in my chest, but she curled up and immediately went back to sleep. Aiden lay down next to her and closed his eyes too, apparently content to resume his dreams as if nothing of note had occurred.

I, on the other hand, lay awake for two further hours at least, gazing up at the blackness, startling every time one of them moved.

———

I wasn't sure how pleased Alfie would be that I had chosen to accommodate the children overnight, so in the morning I told them to wait in my room.

My clothes were still damp. I had another pair of trousers, fortunately, but only one jacket, so I took it downstairs and arranged it in front of the stove. Constance was pottering about boiling porridge, and the homely aroma of drying wool and mulling oats almost made me forget the events of the previous day.

'A letter came for you,' she said, and handed me a crisp white envelope with LEO STANHOPE and my address written on the front.

I knew Jane's handwriting as well as my own. Indeed, it was she who had taught me to write, even before I went to school, sitting patiently at our kitchen table while I inscribed each shape on the paper. She delighted in my progression from single letters to whole words and then sentences, and had kissed my cheek and clapped her hands when I completed the entirety of the Lord's Prayer without a single mistake. And yet, I had never before seen my proper name written in her hand.

The last time I had met her, more than a year before, she'd told me she missed her sister, Lottie, every day, but never wanted to see me at her door again. I was certain the only reason she was writing now was to tell me about our father. He must either have died or be close to it.

'Thank you, Constance,' I said, and tossed the letter unopened on to the fire.

I either had a family or I didn't. There could be no half-way point.

An hour later, I set out with the orphans, leading the way south towards the Metropolitan Police Station. People were wrapped up in their coats and scarves, hurrying to get to work, exactly as I would normally be doing. On Archer Street, where the houses had front yards, a barefoot lad of about Aiden's age emerged from under a tarp sheet tied between a metal fence and the window frames. The two boys eyed each other as we passed.

We had reached the edge of Trafalgar Square when Aiden stopped. Ciara stopped too, half hiding behind her brother. A man pushing a handcart full of plucked chickens swore as he manoeuvred around us.

Aiden turned his dark eyes on me. 'Where are we going?' he asked.

'I'm taking you to the police.'

'Why?'

'They'll want to know what happened. And they'll decide what to do with you.'

He took Ciara's hand. 'Thank you for the food, Mr Stanhope.'

I stepped towards him, realising too late what he was about to do.

He spun and darted away, pulling his sister after him. One moment they were there, and the next they were gone.

6

I TOOK A COUPLE of seconds to respond, too shocked to move, and perhaps, just briefly, feeling I should let them go. But still, I set off after them. They weren't my responsibility, but they were my *something*; something I didn't yet know the name of.

Aiden sprinted across the street, dragging Ciara behind him, and I galloped in pursuit, overtaking pedestrians on their way to work and costermongers setting up for the day, vaulting over a tray of chestnuts. Aiden didn't seem to know where he was going, and dashed along Orange Street, which was almost deserted, glancing back over his shoulder. Seeing me, he accelerated, and would have escaped completely, but for Ciara. In his haste, he pulled her too hard and she tripped on a kerb, sprawling on to her hands and knees. He hoisted her to her feet, but she had grazed her palms and was too shocked to move.

I caught up with them, gasping for breath, my lungs burning. I wasn't used to physical exertion and wanted nothing more of it.

'Are you hurt, Ciara?'

Her teeth were gritted and her face was pale, but she wasn't crying. She opened her hands, and they were speckled red and brown with blood and dirt. They looked sore, but not seriously harmed.

I turned to Aiden. 'Why did you run?'

He glared at me with such ferocity I had to take a step backwards. His fists were clenched, and he was shaking as though he might rush at me.

Just as quickly, it passed. He licked his lips and stood up straight.

'You were taking us to the *police*.'

He made it sound as though I had threatened to feed them to wild dogs.

'You have to trust me,' I assured him. 'I'll make sure you're treated properly. I promise.'

I felt uncomfortable making such a guarantee, but it was the only way I could persuade them to come with me. I couldn't pick them up and carry them.

He looked up and down the road, fixing his gaze on two soldiers walking side by side towards the barracks.

'Mummy said you were an honest man.'

'I am.'

On impulse, I stuck out my hand for him to shake, which was something I normally avoided, conscious of the short-ness of my fingers, and my knuckles like knots in pieces of string. After a pause that seemed like minutes, he took my hand and looked me in the eye, and I had a glimpse of him as the man he might become: stubborn, staunch and perhaps a little severe.

'What will the police ask us?'

I closed my eyes, wishing I had not delayed telling them about their mother. If they didn't already know she was dead, I would be giving them that news here, now, on this pavement. I should've dealt with it back at the pharmacy, but there hadn't been enough time.

Was that true? I pinched the skin between my thumb and forefinger, angry at myself for not being honest: there had been enough time, but I had been too scared. I didn't want to see their grief, answer their questions and give them comfort. I didn't want to *feel* anything.

Now they would suffer for my cowardice.

'Do you know about your mother?' I asked them, as gently as I could.

Ciara pulled away, her body tensing, her eyes fixed on Aiden. He straightened his shoulders, trying to be brave.

'She's dead,' he said.

I wondered what reserves of spirit a person must possess to put it so simply. If he and his mother's positions were reversed, and she had lost him, she would never recover. I had seen a woman bloody her hands from beating them on the floor of the children's ward in her woe. How hard it must be to love someone so utterly, knowing they will never love you as much in return.

'The police will ask you about her,' I said, speaking slowly. 'You must tell them the truth.'

He shivered and picked at his fingers. 'I didn't see what happened.'

I was relieved. At least he would be spared that ordeal. 'Then you should tell them so.'

'Ciara did, though.'

I looked down at her, seeing only her black, curly hair, tied with one of Constance's ribbons. This child had watched her mother being murdered. No wonder she was behaving so differently. The Ciara I'd first met, the bumptious little girl who had climbed on to the dentist's chair and fiddled with the mechanism, was buried far away inside her, perhaps for ever.

'Did she see who it was?' I asked quietly.

Aiden bit his lip. I was sure he was going to say 'John Duport', but he didn't. In fact, he didn't say anything at all for a while, but then gathered himself and leaned towards me.

'She's a silly girl.' He shoved his hands into his pockets. 'She makes things up. She always has.'

'What did she see?'

'Remember, you promised.'

'I know. Tell me.'

He took a deep breath. 'She said it was a lion who killed Mummy.' I stared at him and he shrugged. 'I told you she makes things up.'

———

The Metropolitan Police headquarters on Whitehall was an imposing building I knew well, having been required to convey reports on murder victims from time to time in my previous position. Criminals were delivered round the back in Great Scotland Yard, so the main entrance was mostly used by aggrieved citizens and unwilling witnesses, scurrying in and out hoping no one would see them.

We stopped at the base of the steps and I lit a cigarette to calm my nerves. Having given John a false alibi, it was foolish of me to venture anywhere near this place, but what was the alternative? I couldn't abandon the children to survive on their own, and I couldn't hide them for ever. Sooner or later, they would end up here.

'Go inside and tell the desk sergeant who you are,' I instructed Aiden. 'Ask for Detective Hooper, all right? Say it after me: Hooper.'

'Hooper,' he repeated, humouring me.

I could imagine the conversation they would have, Hooper looking down his nose and recording their answers in his notebook like a venerable secretary taking dictation. It was an unpleasant thought.

'It would be best if you don't mention my name,' I said. 'Say that you slept in a doorway and now here you are.'

Neither child moved.

'Go on,' I insisted, making shooing motions with my hands as if encouraging a recalcitrant donkey.

Still, they wouldn't go in. I had no choice but to take Ciara's hand and lead the two of them up to the door. A constable was coming out, and I recognised him from the club on Rose Street.

'Mr ... Stanhope, isn't it?' he said. 'Have you come to see Detective Inspector Hooper?'

He appeared too old to still be a constable, in his late thirties at least, and broad around the belly.

'No ...' I fumbled in my brain for what to say. 'These are the children of the deceased. They've been found.'

'Excellent!' He ruffled Aiden's hair, which didn't appear to please the boy. 'You'd better come with me, Mr Stanhope.'

'I don't have time now. I have to get to work.'

Down in Westminster, Big Ben was tolling for eight o'clock.

He scratched his head underneath his helmet. 'Your choice. We can come to your address later, if you like?'

He knew that wouldn't be the option I would prefer.

'Let's get it over with then,' I said, and followed him inside.

We waited for twenty minutes in the hallway outside Hooper's office. I considered leaving, but that would look suspicious. Best to appear candid for now and escape as soon as I could.

Aiden was restless and fidgety, while Ciara was sitting still, lost in her own thoughts. Her hair was fighting its way out from the ribbon, though I had brushed the tangles out earlier that morning, surprised at how easily the knack returned.

She shouldn't be here, I thought. She should be on her way to school with a kiss goodbye from her mother.

'Ciara,' I said, in my most gentle voice. 'Aiden told me you saw a ...' I felt idiotic, but the words had to be spoken. 'He told me you saw a *lion* in the courtyard at the club. Is that true?'

She nodded.

'A real, actual lion? A big lion?'

She nodded again, her eyes angled downwards.

Of course, it was absurd; a lion could not possibly have killed Dora Hannigan, least of all with a sword. There were no lions roaming around Soho attacking people. If there were, squads of soldiers would be out hunting them with guns, and ordinary people would be barring their doors and windows. Good grief, it would be the only topic the newspapers would cover for weeks!

And yet, she didn't seem to be trying to deceive me. I wondered if the lion was a fantasy she had created, a way of coping with a memory she couldn't face. If so, I would gladly have extracted it from her brain and placed it into my own. Unlike me, she didn't deserve the agony of witnessing a mother's death.

'Did your mummy fight with the lion?' I asked her.

She shook her head. 'She talked to it.'

Those were the first words she had spoken to me since her mother was killed.

'What did she say?'

She pulled a don't-know face. 'I couldn't hear. I was looking out of the window. It was night-time.'

'Are you sure you weren't dreaming?'

The door opened, and Hooper's head appeared. He beckoned us inside.

It was quite the nicest office I'd ever been in, with scenic, if bland, pictures, wood-panelled walls and a view, between other buildings, of the river. I took it as an indication of the high esteem in which he was held. The last detective I'd met had an office in the clammy basement with pipes running along the ceiling, clonking and hammering like the bowels of a great beast.

'Good morning, Mr Stanhope,' said Hooper. 'And these must be …?'

'Aiden and Ciara Hannigan,' I said. 'They're the children of the deceased.'

'I see.' He bent down to speak to them at eye level. 'We've been worried about you two. I'm very glad you're here.'

He indicated an armchair, and they squashed into it. Ciara picked at the stitching and swung her feet from side to side.

'Where did you find them, Mr Stanhope?'

'In the doorway of my lodging.'

I was keeping my voice steady; just a normal person, doing my duty.

'How very convenient.' Hooper adjusted his spectacles. 'You do keep popping up, don't you?'

'They had my address. You already know that.'

I had decided it was best to be honest where I could, hoping that Hooper would accept these easy truths like the bright, fresh apples at the top of the crate, never noticing the shrivelled, wormy fruit beneath.

He gazed down at Aiden with what seemed like genuine sympathy. 'You've been staying at the …' he grimaced at having to say the name '… the Social and Democratic Club on Rose Street. Is that right?'

'Yes.'

'It's very busy there, I'm sure.' He was trying to put the boy at ease. I could have told him it wouldn't work. 'Lots of people coming and going. And all those foreigners too, speaking languages you don't understand. Must've been awful. Do you know why your mother chose to live in a place like that?'

'No.'

'Do you know what she thought about things? Did she ever talk to you about wanting a revolution, for example?'

'No.' The boy's expression hadn't changed. As with me, he was answering with the fewest possible words, pausing before each one like a novice chess player leaving his hand on a piece to check for any potential threat before letting go.

Hooper switched his attention to Ciara. 'Did your mother ever get cross? Not with you, I mean, with people in industry or government. Respectable, decent people. Was she ever angry about them?'

Ciara didn't understand, and scrunched up her nose as if there was a bad smell.

'She's hardly spoken since she lost her mother,' I said. 'I think she may have a mental derangement of some kind.'

He pushed his fingers through his hair. 'That's unfortunate.' He turned back to Aiden. 'Did you see what happened, young man?'

Aiden glanced at me and shook his head.

'What will happen to them now?' I asked.

'They'll go to Mrs Downes on Endell Street. It's what we call the "halfway house", where all the strays are sent before they're put somewhere permanent.'

Aiden clenched his teeth and edged closer to his sister. Until now, I had believed that Ciara was the one most affected, but perhaps he had been equally damaged. Perhaps it was less obvious with him because he had to look after her as well as himself.

'They're not *strays*,' I said coldly. 'They're victims of a tragedy.'

Hooper shrugged as though the distinction was unimportant. 'It's not for long,' he said. 'A family member will come for them soon, most likely.'

'And if not?'

'They'll be sent to an orphanage, where they'll sleep in the warm and get two square meals a day. They're the lucky ones, if you want my opinion.'

Lucky seemed a contemptuous word to use, under the circumstances. Their mother was gone, and their fate would be decided by people for whom they were nothing more than names on a list, to be allocated by rote.

Something inside me twisted and bent into a new shape.

'Do you have children of your own?' I asked him.

He had returned behind his desk and was arranging his pencils in rows. 'Jack, Robert, Emma and little Jimmy. He's almost a year old now, and he has a temper, I can tell you. Takes after his mother.'

'And if you and your wife died, is that the future you'd want for them?'

He stretched back in his chair. 'My brother would take 'em, and I'd take his brats correspondingly, if the situation warranted it. We're a family, and that's what has to be done. I hope these two will be as fortunate. I'm not without pity for their plight, Mr Stanhope, but I can't give back to them what's been lost.'

'No, but you can find out what happened.'

I had spoken too sharply. Hooper narrowed his eyes at me, working his mouth as if one of his teeth had become loose in its mount.

'Do you know anything about a plot, Mr Stanhope?'

'What plot?'

I didn't want to tell him that J. T. Whitford had already mentioned it to me.

'Ah, well, that's the question, isn't it?'

He raised his eyebrows and stayed silent, presumably hoping I would fill the void with incriminating information, but he didn't know me. I was an expert at duplicity; one part of me constantly watching the other, checking every gesture and tone of voice for mistakes.

'Do you know a man called Thackery?' he asked, eventually.

I felt as though my heart might fall out of my chest. Was my lie discovered after all? I had no choice but to brazen it out.

'No.'

'Sir Reginald Thackery. He's an influential chap, which is why they're all hot and bothered upstairs.' He pointed at the ceiling, indicating, I assumed, his superiors. 'This whole thing's getting a lot of attention I'd rather be without, quite frankly. He owns a mill by the docks, making cloth. A big place it is too, I gather. A thousand men working across three shifts. We found plans at that club to commit arson upon that very mill. Burn the whole thing to the ground. Never mind that Sir Reginald spent his own money to buy it and invested further in machinery and so forth.'

'So?'

Hooper sighed as if to imply that explanations were beneath him. 'On the same evening as the …' he squinted at Aiden, who was staring out of the window '… as the *tragic event*, two men were seen at the mill who shouldn't have been, skulking around. They ran away when they were spotted. We're getting descriptions of them as we speak, though we're quite certain who one of 'em is.' He gestured towards the children. 'Something like the *tragic event* happening at the same place as they're plotting a major crime. It doesn't take a genius to make the connection, does it?'

Now I knew why John Thackery had needed an alibi; he had gone to scout the mill as part of a plan to set fire to it. That mill was the thing his father cared most about, and John wanted to take it away from him.

Of course, he might also have murdered Dora Hannigan and orphaned her two children.

'Do you think Miss Hannigan was involved in the plot?' I asked.

'More than likely.' He looked at me closely. 'You show an awful lot of interest for someone who claims not to be part of all this. Were you really with that fellow what's-his-name?'

'Duport. And yes, of course.' I could hear my voice quivering. 'Why would you doubt it, Detective?'

'It's Detective *Inspector*. And you're each other's alibi, which always makes me suspicious.' He steepled his fingers together, watching me. 'If I find out you're lying, Stanhope, I'll be coming to arrest you.'

There was a knock on the door and a friendly-looking constable came in. He patted Aiden on his head, and the boy flinched away.

'Do they have any possessions?' he asked me. 'Clothes, toys, anything like that?'

'No.' I felt foolish for not having thought of it before. 'I suppose their things are still at the club.'

He led them away and I watched them through the open door. They seemed very small, and I couldn't help but feel I was betraying them.

Aiden looked back once, his dark eyes unreadable.

7

I LEFT THE HOSPITAL at dusk that evening, worn out by the extra duties my foreman had given me for arriving an hour late. He was not a stern man by nature but was so concerned that one of us might realise it, he punished us all the more.

The pharmacy was empty, so I sat at the table in the back room, relishing the silence and solitude. This was my favourite place. It was dusty from the permanent haze of talcum and bicarbonate of soda that Alfie mixed with lavender for tooth powder and kaolin for face powder, and I loved to sit there and surmise the day's events from our footprints: Alfie's chunky ex-army boots, Constance's flat slippers, my own long, slim shoes and Colly's eager paws.

Constance burst in, rosy-cheeked as if she'd run all the way from school.

'Is Father here?' she demanded.

'No. I take it you've had a good day?'

She nodded enthusiastically. 'I am inspired!' Her eyes were positively glowing. 'Where's Father's *Materia Medica*?'

I reached the book down from the highest shelf and handed it to her. It was a big, lumpy thing coming apart at the spine, with discoloured pages that were apt to fall out, but she cradled it in her arms as if it was as precious as a baby.

'Don't tell him, Mr Stanhope. Not yet.'

'Don't tell him what?'

She rolled her eyes as if I was incapable of understanding the simplest thing. 'Isn't it obvious? I've decided to become a doctor!'

She staggered into the pharmacy with the book, and I heard the thud of it being dropped on to the counter, the whisper of the pages being turned and finally her contented sigh as she started reading.

It wasn't all that long ago, a few months at most, that she'd persuaded Alfie to allow her to follow him into pharmacy once her schooling was complete. He considered the long years of study and gruelling examinations to be too much for a young lady, but had been forced to accept her aptitude when she made a batch of cinnamon powders in his absence, and immediately sold a packet of it to the bank manager for one and six. The fellow had returned twice since then for a new supply and would let no one mix the stuff but her, saying it relieved his digestive agonies like nothing else he'd tried.

I must confess, I was jealous. At her age, I had already been removed from school by my father, and even before that our classes were mostly dreary hours of poetry and sewing. The closest we'd come to meeting a member of the medical profession was a visit by a flinty Scottish nurse who'd inspected the skin between our fingers for the itch and scraped our scalps with a comb for nits. She saw us in alphabetical order, starting with Nicola Antrobus, so I had to watch the suffering of more than half the alphabet before she got to P for Pritchard. Lord knows how it felt for poor Susan Watkins.

Now, women could become doctors themselves, apparently. If Jane had ever suggested such a thing to our father, he would have removed every science book he owned – which was several as he had a passing interest in anatomy – and forced her to spend her days playing the piano and singing in the choir.

But that didn't mean he was wrong. No one could doubt she had the brains for the profession, but I knew well how much strength was required to crank open a chest or saw through a bone. And if the argument were made that I was a hypocrite, having myself performed those tasks despite my female physique, I would respond that I have, on occasion, been required to climb on to the table with the 'patient', who was invariably already dead and therefore unaware of the intimacy, to gain the necessary leverage. No lady would be willing to do such a thing, no matter how clever she was.

Constance's ambition would surely prove a step too far for Alfie.

I followed her through to the pharmacy, but she was so engrossed she didn't notice me until I cleared my throat.

'I met a little girl a few days ago,' I said. 'She told me she'd seen a lion in London, roaming free.'

'A lion?'

Her expression was much the same as I suspected my own had been when Aiden told me.

'Yes. Assuming it wasn't a real lion, can you think what she might have seen? Is there a ... I don't know, a place where there are model lions, or a puppet show or something?'

She thought for a moment and then shrugged. 'There's the zoo, of course. Other than that, no. Is it important?'

'Perhaps, yes. She was a witness to something very bad. Her mother was killed. She and her brother are orphans.'

Constance nodded, her face blank, though not through any lack of empathy. Quite the opposite. She had once told me she could hardly remember her own mother and felt her loss not as a person whom she missed, but as a gap in the world, an emptiness where someone ought to be.

'The girl I met is very young,' I conceded. 'It's possible she was confused or dreaming.'

'Perhaps you should take her to the zoo to see a real lion.'

'Perhaps.'

Constance turned to face me, leaving her finger on the page, which, I noticed, described the medicinal properties of ox bile.

'I've never been,' she said. 'You could take the little girl and I could come with you.'

'It's probably expensive.'

I was hoping she would take the hint and stop talking about it, but, of course, she was Constance.

'You can't mope all the time, Mr Stanhope. Have you ever been to the zoo?'

'No, but—'

She frowned at me. 'The girl could look at a real lion and you'd know for sure, wouldn't you? You did say it was important.'

I supposed she might be right, but I was determined not to admit it. With Constance, an inch conceded now would become a yard and then a mile, and I might end up taking her to Africa to see wild lions or buying her one of her own to keep in the yard.

'I'll consider the idea.'

'You're not working on Saturday afternoon, are you? We can go then.'

She nodded firmly as if to suggest that she had solved my problem, and if I wouldn't act upon her solution there was nothing more anyone could do for me.

Over the following days and nights, I found my mind engulfed. At night I was unable to sleep, turning and twisting in the bedsheets, and at work I was continually distracted, putting towels and bandages on the wrong shelves and forgetting the most basic of chores. A pile of letters sat in the tray for two days without being posted.

When I wasn't worrying about the police and the lie I'd told them, I was fretting about the orphans. My own mother had been dead for six years. She had died slowly, bedridden, knowing that the end was coming. I had not been there to read 'Ode to a Nightingale' to her and stroke her cheek. It was not my fault. It was not. I had not even known she was dying. The first I'd heard of it was from Jane, long after it had happened, sitting in a tea shop on Warwick Avenue. It didn't seem real. I wondered whether she was lying, and our mother was alive and well, sipping tea and embroidering cushions in the vicarage parlour. But Jane's breath was uneven and her face flushed. She was trying her hardest not to weep.

'I couldn't find you,' she explained. 'I sent a letter to your last address, but you didn't reply.'

'What name did you use?'

'Your name, Lottie. What was I supposed to do?'

She knew perfectly well what my correct name was.

I didn't see my sister or speak to her for two years after that, and even then it was intermittent and laced with resentment. For the past year, we'd been utterly estranged.

It was far longer since I'd spoken to my brother; not since I'd left home.

And my father? He meant nothing to me now.

I was lost from my family.

I was an orphan too.

––––––

On the Friday after I had left the children with the police, the first day of April, I set out through the evening fog for Rose Street. I had no faith that Hooper would search for a relative of theirs to look after them, so I would have to do it myself.

Of course, someone at the club might be the murderer. I had to be careful. If the killer knew Ciara was a witness, he might want her dead as well.

I knocked on the door, but there was no answer. I knocked again and tried the handle. It turned, so I let myself inside.

The corridor was narrower than I remembered and dim, lit by a single lamp, low on its wick, on a shelf by the back door. People were talking in the rooms on either side, and a woman was singing somewhere upstairs, accompanied by a violin. The smell was musty and thick as though the windows were rarely opened or, given the labyrinthine layout of the building, the air in the distant hallways and stairwells had stagnated, unable to circulate. I put my hand on the wall, expecting it to be damp, but it was dry and flaky under my fingertips. The picture frames nailed to it were coming away, and dust from the holes had collected on the dado rail.

I knew I would never be able to find John Thackery's office again even if I wanted to, and I was too nervous to set off exploring, so I continued down the corridor. Near the end, on the left, a door was marked STEWARD.

I was about to knock when I realised someone was watching me. The back-door window looked out on to the courtyard, and I could see three men, two standing on the ramshackle steps that led up to the first-floor gallery, and one sitting on a box on the ground, squinting at me, smoke drifting from his nostrils. He was bald, with narrow eyes and a wide nose as if he'd been punched a few times. He nudged his friend and pointed in my direction.

I shrank back from the lamplight and tapped on the steward's door, before opening it.

To my surprise, a woman was sitting at a desk, wearing a leather thimble on her index finger. She looked up from her ledger as I came in, indicating one of the chairs.

'Are you the … stewardess?' I asked.

'*Steward* will be fine,' she muttered. 'Just a moment.' She continued at her ledger, adding totals with a scratchy pen, apparently doing the calculations in her head.

I waited. The office was neat and workmanlike, stacked with labelled files. There were twenty or more hooks on one wall, mostly empty but some holding rings of heavy, black keys. On another, a map of Britain and Europe had been pasted like a piece of wallpaper.

Eventually, she did a final tot of the numbers, running her finger down the page and moving her lips slightly, before drawing a confirmatory line under the grand total.

'Right!' she said in an accent straight from the East End. 'Now, what can I do for you?'

'I've come regarding Miss Hannigan. Or rather, her children.'

'Have they been found?'

I thought I detected a note of eagerness in her manner, though it might have been no more than honest concern for their welfare.

'They're with the police.' I wanted her to know they were safely out of anyone's reach. 'I'm hoping to find a relative who'd be willing to take them.'

'I see.' She smiled, but it was a formality. There was no warmth in it. 'And you are?'

'Stanhope,' I answered, immediately wondering if I should have given a false name.

'Mrs Raster. But I'm afraid I can't help you. Our residents are very private.'

She smiled again, this time as a dismissal. She wanted to get back to her accounts.

But I wasn't finished. 'Their mother was murdered right here on your property. Makes you think, doesn't it?'

She sat back and met my eye. It was the first time I'd had her full attention.

'Bad things happen everywhere,' she said.

'I met J.T. Whitford, the journalist on the *Daily Chronicle*. Perhaps you've seen him? I'm sure he'd be interested to know how cooperative you've been. He might want to write an article about it.'

Mrs Raster gazed at the columns of numbers on her desk, taking comfort, I thought, from their neatness and precision. 'I'm the steward here, that's all. Anything's amiss about Miss Hannigan, it's on Mr Cowdery, not me. I told the other gentleman the same thing.'

'What other gentleman? You mean from the police?'

She opened and shut her mouth. 'Yes, exactly. From the police.'

I was sure she was lying, and that meant someone else had been asking questions too. I wondered who. And why.

'This Mr Cowdery you mentioned, is he in charge?'

She rubbed her thimble on the desk, making a squeaking sound. 'They don't hold with one man being placed above another. They don't think it's right. But yes, as much as anyone can be said to be in charge of anything around here, it's him. Leastwise, anything political.'

'You don't take part in the politics?'

'Goes straight over my head, most of it.' She chuckled, displaying brown and broken teeth. 'They talk, talk, talk, while I earn a crust fixing the pipes and counting the rent.' She scratched her head and sniffed her fingers. 'Why do you want to know, anyway?'

'Curiosity. How long did Dora Hannigan live here?'

'Three years, maybe? Something like that. She kept herself to herself, her and the kids.'

'And there's no Mr Hannigan?'

'I'm not one to judge.'

'Was she particularly friendly with anyone here? Anyone I could speak to.'

Mrs Raster shifted in her chair. 'What do you mean?'

'What about Mr Thack … I mean, Mr Duport. Was she friendly with him?'

'I s'pose so, but there was nothing going on. No funny business. They were more like, I don't know, like she was his older sister or something. It was her who vouched for him in the first place.'

'What was she like?'

Mrs Raster smiled. 'Clever, as it happens. She's not like most of 'em. Talk, talk, talk, that's all they ever do.' Her smile faded as she remembered that Miss Hannigan was dead. 'Not Dora, though. She got together all the kids, including her own, and started giving 'em lessons. Reading and writing, sums, needlework for the girls and how to speak English for the foreigns.'

'She ran a school?'

Mrs Raster nodded. 'Nothing official, but she kept 'em in line. She wouldn't suffer any cheek and they had to turn up with their slates and everything, each morning without fail, her own lad included.'

The way she said it made me think she was referring to something specific. 'Was Aiden reluctant to attend?'

'He's a proper boy, that one. He don't like being cooped up. He wants to be outside kicking things around with the lads in the street. Or fighting 'em, of course. Many's the time I had to break up a scrap. But it's natural enough, ain't it? How boys are.'

I thought of Aiden's fierce face. I had already seen that he had a temper.

'Was Miss Hannigan involved in the politics of this place? Was she an anarchist?'

84

'If that's what one of them's called, then yes, I s'pose so. But she was a decent person and always had enough chink on hand to pay the rent.' She opened her ledger. 'Here we are; first of March, three months upfront.'

'I see. So, by my maths, you've been overpaid by two months. You can let her room to someone else and get paid twice.'

Mrs Raster pulled her ledger closer towards her. She seemed unbothered by my implication that she was profiting from Dora Hannigan's death. 'Can't refund the dead,' she said, as though that settled the point. 'Anyway, there's no one in her room yet. It's not as simple as just getting a new lodger. Mr Cowdery has to give 'em the nod.'

I really wanted to see that room. I wanted to inhale its smells and touch its furniture and listen to the sounds of its neighbours through the walls. I wanted to understand more about Dora Hannigan.

'Are her possessions still here somewhere? If so, I should collect the children's clothes for them.'

'I don't know about that. It's not *your* things, is it?'

'What harm can it do?' I fumbled in my pocket and produced a shilling. 'For your trouble. Do we have a deal? Don't bother haggling, this is all I have.'

She took the coin and disappeared through another door. I caught a glimpse of a trolley overspilling with laundry. A man I couldn't see spoke to her in a foreign language and she replied in kind.

When she reappeared, she was wearing a coat and carrying an empty cotton sack. 'Might as well clean it out,' she grunted, and led the way to the courtyard.

I was relieved to see that the men who'd been sitting there before had gone, replaced by a young woman herding two stolid infants in front of her. They stared up at me with open mouths.

We passed the place where Dora Hannigan's body had been buried. The shallow hole had been filled in, but someone had laid a bunch of daffodils on the spot. Mrs Raster paused next to it, bowing her head before moving on.

We climbed up two sets of rickety steps to the top gallery, which creaked and groaned under our feet. She stopped by a door with the number 23 hand-painted on to it.

'Here we are,' she said, and turned the key in the lock.

Inside, there were two beds, a rack for drying clothes, a cupboard and a small chest. The police had been typically careless, strewing the family's possessions across the floor: clothes, an old carpet bag, a child's rag doll and a toy horse carved from mahogany in alternate light and dark stripes.

I sorted through everything, feeling ghoulish. What would Dora Hannigan think, if she could see me? A stranger looking at her chemises and small-clothes, her hairbrush and her pins, her unfinished knitting. I felt a surge of pity for her, interrupted in the midst of her life.

'Has someone else been in here since the police?' I asked.

Mrs Raster folded her arms. 'No. Why would they?'

Again, she was lying, and not well; her neck was the colour of beetroot. I was sure that the other man who'd been asking questions had also gained access to this room. He'd probably bribed her to let him in, much as I had, or he had threatened her – although she didn't seem easily intimidated.

By the side of the bed, I found the ounce of bromide of potash I'd sold her and a box of paper soldiers, but nothing to tell me about her relatives or friends; no letters or cards, no photographs or silhouettes. There were no pictures on the walls either, just a willow-pattern plate over the fireplace that I found hard to look at.

Mrs Raster was watching me, sharp-eyed. 'I've got a daughter,' she announced, picking up a scrappy little cap that must have been Ciara's. 'Mabel, her name is. She'll be getting married soon. He works on the gas, so I s'pose he'll be able to look after her, but you never stop worrying, do you?'

'I don't have any children.'

'Really? Not married? Got a girl in mind, though, have you?'

Not any more, I thought, suffering the familiar clench in my stomach. Even now, over a year afterwards, it still came whenever I thought of her.

I divided everything into two piles on one of the beds: things belonging to the children and everything else. When I'd finished, I indicated the everything-else pile.

'I have no use for this,' I said.

She nodded and scooped Dora Hannigan's possessions into her cotton sack. It was only a third full. She pointed at the other pile.

'And that?'

'That belongs to the children. I'll make sure they get it, I promise. That was our deal. You can go now.'

'All right,' she said, peering under the peak of her bonnet at the door. 'You can have five minutes, and you'll be quicker still, if you know what's good for you.'

I gathered up the children's clothing and Aiden's paper soldiers, hesitating over Ciara's rag doll before putting it in the carpet bag also. I was prejudiced against such ghastly effigies, seeing only malice in their permanent gaiety and wide, unblinking eyes. My Aunt Gwen had given me one she'd made herself for my seventh birthday, together with three matching frocks and hats. I thanked her politely, and then took it upstairs and hurled it into the bottom of my wardrobe. When I came back down, half an hour later, still pink in the face, the atmosphere in the drawing room was tense. Aunt Gwen wouldn't look at me. Afterwards, my mother told me they'd been able to hear, with perfect clarity, the sound from above of me stamping my feet. She made me remove all the wax from the candlesticks in the church as punishment.

Most of the courtyard was visible through the window. In the faint light from the city I had no trouble seeing the doors, the water barrels, the shed and the back gate, two storeys below. Presumably, Ciara had stood here as she watched her mother being murdered. I tried to imagine how that must have felt, and could not. She would have been barefoot and in her nightdress, peering on tiptoe over the sill, unable to comprehend what was happening. She would have woken her brother in desperation, but too late.

And then what? Did they hide in this room, terrified, waiting until the coast was clear? Did they hurry past their mother's newly dug grave?

On some impulse, I tidied up, folding the blankets and opening the window to let in some air. There was no brush for the fireplace and no scuttle or poker either. Perhaps they couldn't afford coal.

What had Mrs Raster said? Miss Hannigan had paid upfront, three months in advance.

Had the police found any money on her body? They had found her purse, with my name inside, but I didn't recall any mention of money.

I had searched every inch of the room; every inch except for that fireplace.

I knelt on the hearth and reached up the chimney as far as I could, holding my breath as soot cascaded down, covering my coat and trousers. I groped around each side of the flue, and then something moved: a loose brick. I pulled it out and, in the gap left behind, I could feel something. I withdrew it and leaned out of the window, beating it against the outside wall, sending clouds of dust billowing into the evening.

It was a leather pouch. I set it on the bed. The leather was soft, and it was fastened with a metal buckle with the initials D. H. inscribed on the front. I opened it up and, at first, I thought it was full of notepaper.

Then, I realised what it was: money. Lots of it. Dozens of pound notes packed tightly together. More money than I'd ever seen in my life.

8

I WON'T CLAIM I didn't feel a burst of excitement. It was a lot of money. In fact, it was a dangerously large amount, certainly too much for Dora Hannigan to have come by honestly, or why had she stuffed it into a chimney?

I felt a pang of fear. I considered putting it back and pretending I'd never discovered it, but what good would that do? Either it would be found and spent by the next residents of the room, thanking God for their luck, or it wouldn't, in which case it would be burned to ash the next time the fire was lit.

I didn't have time to think. Mrs Raster would return soon.

I wrapped the leather pouch tightly into a pair of Aiden's trousers and tucked it at the bottom of the carpet bag.

As I was leaving the room, I heard someone on the gallery steps. I looked over the balcony and saw the bald man who'd been squinting at me earlier coming up. He was hatless and coatless, drops of rain glistening on his jacket and his scalp. I stood aside for him, my heart beating on my ribs like a convict on the bars. He stopped in front of me, standing too close, looking me up and down with the air of an undertaker estimating the quantity of wood required. I became keenly aware of the two-storey drop to the courtyard below.

'I remember you,' he growled, examining my face. 'You've got some explaining to do. You were with the *coppers*.'

'No. I mean … yes, but I didn't choose to come. They forced me to.' I wished just once I could sound confident and perhaps a little dangerous, instead of squeaking like a carriage wheel in need of a drop of oil. 'I'm here to find out if Miss Hannigan's children have any relatives.'

He glared into my eyes, his face inches from mine. If this was the man who had killed Dora Hannigan, he would know to dig a deeper grave this time.

'Where *are* the children?'

I gripped the carpet bag tightly. 'They're safe. The police have them.' I realised how that must sound, as if I was constantly hobnobbing with the constabulary. Nevertheless, he nodded. I had the sense he was relieved but was trying not to show it.

'What's your name?'

'Stanhope. And I'm guessing you're Mr Cowdery.'

'That's right. Edwin Cowdery. And you can take a message back to your friends from me.' He pushed up the brim of my bowler hat with his finger. 'Tell them no one here killed Dora. It wasn't us. Tell them that from me, Mr Stanhope.'

I heard a woman's voice calling up from the courtyard. 'What's going on, Edwin?'

We both looked over the rail. The woman was wearing an apron and a lace cap, and was short, with powerful arms and shoulders, seemingly built for, and perhaps by, manual labour.

'You're not needed here,' he called down to her. 'I'm having a word with this gentleman, that's all.'

She put her hands on her hips and met his eyes. She had the implacability of a tree stump. 'I don't think he's *enjoying* the word you're having.'

He grimaced, breathing heavily through his nose. 'He's working with the *coppers*, Erica.'

She raised her eyebrows. I had the sense that they knew each other well, and this exchange was one fragment of a years-long debate.

'Would you rather they never found Dora's killer? Well then.' She beckoned me down. 'Why don't I see you out, Mr …?'

'Stanhope. Thank you.'

I hurried down the steps, hoping not to hear Cowdery following me.

'The girl's sickly,' he shouted down. 'Ciara, her name is. She has fits. Make sure they know.'

I thought back to that night when she had woken me in the pitch darkness, and the pulling and jerking of her hot little hand in mine.

'I will,' I called back, feeling this was an oddly civilised chat after what had just happened. I almost asked him what he knew about her infirmity, but he opened the door to Miss Hannigan's room and was gone.

The woman, Erica, was waiting at the bottom. 'He's not a bad man,' she confided. 'He's upset about Dora dying that way. It's hit him hard.'

'Did he know her well?'

She took my arm. 'Didn't you say you weren't with the police?'

'I'm just curious.'

She led me back down the hallway towards the front door. I kept a firm hold on the carpet bag, feeling as if I was holding a bomb that might go off at any moment.

On the pavement, I turned to thank her. She surveyed me over the top of her pince-nez with shrewd eyes that would brook no nonsense, and I realised she wasn't as old as I'd first thought; no more than thirty.

'I'm Erica Cowdery,' she said.

'Oh. Are you Mr Cowdery's—'

'Sister,' she interrupted me, her mouth twitching at the corners. 'His *younger* sister. It's been very nice to meet you, Mr Stanhope.'

'You too, Miss Cowdery.'

'Probably best not to get too curious, though, for your own well-being.'

She shut the door before I could reply.

In the street, the wind had picked up. Newspaper pages had blown free and were being whisked along, flipping like acrobats. A small boy was chasing them, leaping and laughing, his arms outstretched and his face a picture of delight.

I envied him so terribly I could have wept.

———

Back in my room, I opened up the pouch and pulled out the notes, spreading them across my bed.

I had made a mistake.

Some of them were, indeed, pounds, but others were higher denominations, fives and tens, which I'd never set eyes on before. I marvelled at the intricacy of the patterns on the paper.

Note by note, I added them up: two hundred and four pounds.

It was remarkable. How could *anyone* have this amount of money? I did a quick calculation and couldn't believe the answer, so did it again; the notes I was holding in my hands would pay my rent for the next *ten years*.

I rustled them between my fingers. Such thin stuff to hold that much power. I pressed them to my face, inhaling the metallic tang of the engraver's ink.

It changed everything.

I had brought up a pot of tea on a tray, and poured myself a cup, watching the steam rise. It was just paper, I reminded myself. I had never yearned for the wealthy life my mother had wanted for me, marrying some gentleman with a job in a bank or a toff with a rich daddy, like John bloody Thackery. The thought of it made me laugh, and I spilled my tea over my trousers, quickly pricking both my humour and my brief avarice. It's hard to feel anything other than foolish while hopping around the room flapping a trouser leg.

When I got back to the money, I had started to think more clearly.

This wealth could change Aiden and Ciara's future. It was enough to fund their care in the very finest orphanage and ensure they benefited from the best education. They could eat well every day: chicken and ham and green vegetables, with apple pie to follow, lemonade in the afternoons and peppermints before bedtime. They could eat like I used to when I was a child, sitting at the table while a maid ladled gravy on to veal shanks. I didn't miss much about my childhood, but memories of that dinner table still made my mouth water.

But nothing was so simple. This money must have belonged to someone else at one time, and whoever it was would likely want it back.

The only person I could think of who was rich enough was Sir Reginald Thackery. Had Dora Hannigan stolen from him? If so, John might have been right; his father could have committed murder to get his property returned.

But he hadn't had it returned, had he? It was right here on my bed.

And there was another possibility. I remembered what Jacob had said: if your father's wealthy, you're wealthy too. John Thackery probably had access to this amount of money.

If so, the lie I had told the police would allow a murderer to escape justice.

I collected the notes and returned them to the pouch, which I shoved under my mattress. It had to be kept secret, or all our lives would be endangered.

The following day was Saturday. I worked at the hospital in the morning and, when I left at midday, people on the streets had their coats over their arms. The sun had found its way through the clouds.

It was perfect weather for the zoo.

I went straight to the police headquarters on Whitehall and asked for Constable Pallett. He appeared after five minutes, jacketless with his sleeves rolled up, his hands in his pockets.

'Constable, I want to visit those children I brought here a few days ago. I have their things.' I held up the carpet bag. 'I'd like to take them out for the afternoon, if that's possible. I was thinking of the zoo.'

'That's very thoughtful of you, sir. But they're with Mrs Downes now, and she don't like to let them out, not without proper authority. She's a bit … particular.'

'I see. That's a shame.'

I admit I was disappointed. I'd started to look forward to our little trip, and Constance had danced around the room when I told her we could go. Drawings of elephants and kangaroos had started appearing around the house. She would not take this news well.

Pallett scratched his chin, still no more bearded than my own. 'Let me check, sir.' Three minutes later he reappeared, now in full uniform. 'Why don't I come along with you, sir, and have a word with Mrs Downes? They're just nippers, and it's not right they can't go out if someone's willing to take 'em. Not after all they've been through.'

'I don't want to keep you from your work, Constable.'

'That's all right, sir. By rights I should be making a list of every resident of Rose Street, name, age and occupation. That's the important task you're detaining me from.'

He laughed, and I can honestly say it was the first time I'd ever heard him make a joke. It didn't suit him. But I was glad of his help and wondered whether his sympathy for the children was rooted in his own upbringing. The rumour was he'd been born in a rookery in Acton town, and had six brothers and four half-brothers, some in prison and one dead, hanged by the neck for garrotting a barman who'd refused him a third bottle of malmsey.

The two of us walked swiftly up Whitehall to Trafalgar Square, where I nodded, as usual, to the statue of General Havelock, stuck on his plinth with a bemused expression, his back permanently and wisely turned to George IV, who was sitting astride a horse and wearing what appeared to be a Roman tunic. What the man himself would have made of such unsuitable garb, I couldn't have said, but it made me feel chilly despite the sunshine.

Endell Street was a busy thoroughfare leading from Long Acre up towards Bloomsbury, jammed tight with carts and carriages pulled by glum horses flicking their tails, bearing little resemblance to George IV's mighty iron steed, save in their immobility. Pallett led me to a row of houses, one of them somewhat prouder than the others, with clean paint and all its windows intact.

Mrs Downes turned out to be an austere woman in a dark green frock. She resembled nothing so much as a pine tree, being narrow yet sturdy at the feet, spreading widely in the lower branches and tapering to a crisp, snowy peak at her bonnet.

Pallett explained our purpose, and she pursed her lips.

'It's most unusual,' she said. 'Other children do get envious, you know. Them that benefit from special treatment soon wish they hadn't, in my experience.'

'I'm sure you're right, Mrs Downes,' replied Pallett, unintimidated. 'But perhaps we can make an exception on this occasion?'

She wrinkled her nose. 'Well, I suppose it don't matter much, all things considered. Wait here.'

Something in her tone made my skin itch.

While she was gone, a skinny boy of perhaps eight years appeared in the hallway. He stopped and watched us, mouth agape. A girl arrived too and stood beside him. Apparently, we were their afternoon's entertainment. They looked alike enough to be brother and sister, both barefoot and dressed in near rags. I would have guessed her age at about eleven, but she was so gaunt it was hard to tell. I smiled at them and she smiled back and then, as if remembering herself, cocked a bony hip and raised her eyebrows at me, her fingers plucking at her ragged collar.

All I could do was shake my head. I wanted to tell her not to do that, not *ever* to do that, but I didn't know who she was, where she came from or where she was going. What had Hooper called this place? A halfway house. A moment of peace, perhaps. Or an intake of breath between two screams.

She ushered her brother away when Mrs Downes reappeared with Aiden and Ciara.

Ciara sat on the carpet and did up her shoes. Aiden, his shoes already on, stood in the hallway and glared at me.

'Would you like to come to the zoo?' I asked him.

'Why?'

It wasn't the reaction I'd expected. Didn't all children want to go to the zoo?

'It'll be fun.' I could hear how feeble that sounded. Their mother was dead, and I was wittering about having fun. Still, I'd started and couldn't seem to stop. 'My landlord's daughter will be coming too. She's very excited.'

'Do we have to go?' he asked.

Mrs Downes gave him a little push towards me. 'You'll do as you're told and be grateful. There's plenty here who'd kill for what you're being offered, as you'll doubtless find out in due course.'

Ciara had finished tying her laces and stood up.

'I thought it might help if Ciara saw a real lion,' I said to Aiden, as one might to an adult. He deserved my honesty. 'She might remember what really happened.'

Aiden folded his arms, still not moving. 'She doesn't know anything.'

Mrs Downes had run out of patience and shoved him on to the doorstep. 'These two have been trouble since they arrived.'

Again, something in her tone scratched at me. 'What do you mean?' I asked. 'What trouble?'

She folded her arms and peered down at Ciara. 'This one's not right.'

'Pardon?'

'She's a lunatic. I was dragged from my bed by one of the others, a good girl, quiet and well-mannered, cos this one was yelling the house down and shaking as if the devil had tooken her.'

She edged an inch or two away from Ciara. The girl didn't seem to notice, and was pulling up her socks.

'Yes, I've seen it too,' I said. 'Afterwards she's quite unaware and resumes her normal behaviour. It's rather …' I searched for the right word to ease her worries '… disconcerting. But not a danger to her health, as far as I can tell.'

Mrs Downes grimaced. 'Maybe so, but this ain't an asylum. I took steps.'

'What steps?'

'As it happens, Miss Lizzie Anderson, the noted mesmerist, was in my charge for a short while some years ago. I could tell she had a gift, and it's only got stronger in the meantime. In demand all over London, she is, but she still comes round here if I have a need.' Mrs Downes paused, as if we might take this opportunity to congratulate her. 'Lizzie talked to the girl, and put her into a spell, as she does, and at the end she said the madness was too strong in one so young. It has overwhelmed her, and there's nought to be done.'

I had once seen a mesmerist, when I accompanied Jacob and Lilya to a show in the days before her sight had left her completely. There was a whole slew of acts offering communion with the spirits, the bringing forth of ghosts and so on. I presumed that Jacob was hoping Lilya might be cured, but she thought the whole affair ridiculous and left before the end. The final act was a mesmerist, and Jacob called out loudly to him with a challenge, asking whether it might be possible to cure a woman who thought she was a man. I hid my face, panicked, but need not have worried. The mesmerist, no fool as it turned out, paused dramatically, training all eyes back on himself, and answered that Jacob had certainly affected a remarkable disguise, and that his beard was almost convincing. Jacob sat down again, sour-faced, and would not speak until we were nearly back at his home, where he explained, between snarled complaints about charlatanism, that he had hoped I might finally be made happy if my body and spirit were rectified. I exchanged angry words with him, annoyed by his disrespect of my circumstance, and was only mollified after two glasses of Lilya's sloe gin.

Mrs Downes half closed the door, peering round it. 'I've done all I can, but I have to think of the others. These two will be going to orphanages on Monday.'

Pallett drew himself up. He was standing on a lower step but was still eye to eye with her. 'You're supposed to keep the children until a family member is found or the search for one is abandoned.' He was always polite, almost theatrically so, yet I could tell he was annoyed.

She shook her head briskly. 'She's a lunatic and I don't have the facility, not for two bob a week. The bindings and laudanum and so forth. They'll have to go.'

She shut the door, and I realised I still had hold of the carpet bag containing their clothes. Somehow, I didn't feel inclined to knock again and ask her to send their things onwards with them.

———

Pallett left us at Seven Dials, his long legs carrying him back to his paperwork, while the children and I walked to the pharmacy to collect Constance. I made them hold my hands at Wardour Street, which was hectic, with broughams rattling past and pedestrians packing the pavement. A lady crossing from the other direction beamed at us, and a driver stopped and waved us over. I nodded my thanks and felt most peculiar, as though I was living somebody else's life.

I was still perplexed by Aiden's reaction to my invitation to the zoo. I would have been overjoyed at his age, and yet he was walking along sullenly, his hands in his pockets.

'I think there are giraffes!' I declared, trying to engender some excitement. 'Don't you want to see one? They have very long necks.'

Ciara raised her arm straight. 'Like this?' She crooked her hand to be the giraffe's head, her thumb becoming its lower jaw, opening and shutting.

'Yes, but *much* bigger.'

In truth, I'd never seen a giraffe except in pictures, and wasn't absolutely sure of their size. I had in mind something like a deformed horse.

'What about you, Aiden?' I said. 'What do you most want to see?'

He kept his eyes straight ahead. 'I don't know what there is.'

'I'm sure there are all sorts. What animals do you like?'

He didn't pause for thought. 'Dogs.'

'Well, they won't have dogs, I don't think.' I was starting to feel impatient. 'But what about lions and tigers?'

He took his sister's arm. 'Ciara will be frightened,' he said. '*I* have to look after her now.'

This time, I caught his meaning. He was angry and hurt. I'd promised to make sure they were cared for and, in his opinion, I'd let them down, giving them to the police and leaving them at the halfway house.

As we reached the pharmacy, I turned him to face me, holding him by the shoulders. He looked back at me, his expression shuttered.

'I'm sorry about how things worked out,' I said, speaking slowly, searching for the right words. 'I know you're grieving for your mother. I'll do my best to find a good orphanage for the two of you. Do you understand?'

Underneath my mattress was enough money to pay for their care for years to come. And, probably, to get us all killed as well. But what use was it if it couldn't be spent?

'It doesn't matter,' he said.

'What do you mean?'

He didn't answer and, when I let go of his shoulders, he pushed open the pharmacy door.

Constance was ready to go, eagerly clutching four paper bags. Alfie took me to one side and spoke quietly.

'These children are not your concern, Leo. Are you sure you should be taking an interest in them?'

Aiden was standing in the middle of the room with his arms folded, and Ciara was kneeling in front of the fireplace, wiggling her fingers exactly as she had the first time she'd visited with her mother. It seemed like months ago, but it was only two weeks to the day, almost to the hour, since Dora Hannigan had asked if I would extend her some credit. She'd probably been thinking about her day's chores, and church tomorrow and school the day after; times tables, spellings and sewing. It seemed inconceivable that she'd been excised from the world, and even more so that the world appeared to have healed around the wound, leaving only these two small scars.

'Yes, I'm sure,' I said to Alfie.

'All right.' He handed me two shillings. 'For your expenses.'

'Thank you.'

I should have turned him down, but I couldn't afford to. I could barely afford my rent. I wouldn't touch the children's money for any sake other than theirs.

I left their bag of clothes in my room, and off we went.

When the omnibus arrived at the Regent Street stop, it was crowded and reeked of sweat. We had to stand in close proximity to other passengers, an inconvenience I had good reason to loathe. I kept one arm across my chest, holding on to the pole as we lurched over the cobbles, while Ciara clung on to my jacket and swung helplessly from side to side.

Eventually, we reached the north-west corner of Regent's Park, which was our stop, and Constance launched herself out and strode down the road towards the entrance, turning from time to time to beckon us to hurry as if she were our teacher and we were late for class. Poor Ciara was quite out of breath by the time we got there.

I paid at the booth and we entered what could only be described as another world.

The nearest I had ever come to visiting a zoo was a dismal menagerie on the Strand, nothing more than a corridor lined with cages containing sad-looking animals with bald patches in their fur and flies crawling across their faces. The solitary lion could have been stuffed, for all the animation he exhibited, and the smell of droppings was so overpowering one could only remain inside for two or three minutes before rushing out to the street to inhale.

The London Zoo was quite different.

The main path was flanked on either side by large cages housing the most colourful birds: parrots, finches and birds of paradise in one; ducks and pelicans in another, with their own pond. The next contained falcons and hawks, glaring at us as if they wanted to peck out our eyes.

And the noise! Squawking, whooping, chuckling and growling; there was every kind of sound one might imagine a creature could make, coming from all directions.

'Which way should we go?' asked Aiden, frowning at the choice of pathways ahead of us.

I checked the sign. 'Perhaps the giraffes first?' I ventured.

I was looking forward to seeing them most of all.

'No, let's start with the lions,' said Constance, already setting off. 'We need to know what Ciara really saw, don't we?' She gave us no choice but to follow, not least because she still had the sandwiches.

We heard them long before we reached them, a rumbling, thunderous burst of noise as if the air was being ripped in two. Ciara held on to my sleeve.

'It's all right,' I assured her. 'They can't hurt you.'

I wondered what she would say, if anything, when she saw one. Perhaps when she set eyes on a real lion – the size of the beast, its mane, teeth and claws – she would realise her mistake. Perhaps I would find out the truth.

The lion house, as it was called, was a long building with a curved roof, reminding me of my brother's toy railway station.

Constance was looking around, shielding her eyes from the sun.

'Are you coming in?' I asked, and she nodded.

A man was wandering behind us, on his own. I noticed him because everyone else seemed to have company. He was a little younger than me, perhaps twenty, and I accidentally caught his eye. He quickly looked down, hiding his face beneath the brim of his brown felt hat.

Inside the lion house, the animal stench was strong, though nowhere near as bad as the menagerie on the Strand. The lady in front of me was fanning herself, and her husband blew out his cheeks.

'They don't need to bite,' he said to her, loudly enough for the whole room to hear. 'The stink alone is enough to kill you!'

We joined the throng at the first cage. Aiden, despite his previous ambivalence, pushed his way through to the front and was soon lost from sight, but Ciara hung back, staying close to me.

Constance took her hand. 'Shall we look together?' she said, and the little girl nodded gratefully.

Left on my own, I had the opportunity to observe my fellow zoo-goers. They appeared to think they were at a society occasion. Almost everyone was well turned out, the ladies in colourful frocks and elegant bonnets, the children clean and pink-cheeked, and the gentlemen in smart coats and top hats which they tipped to one another. They took far less notice of the few men who, like me, were wearing bowlers or flat caps and the clothes they went to work in. One fellow, in a chesterfield and shoulder cape, barged his way in front of me as though I didn't exist, poking my side with his cane and bellowing at his friend to follow.

We had been in the lion house for ten minutes before I even saw a lion, but it was worth it. The crowd thinned at one of the cages, and I spotted Ciara, on her own, apparently having overcome her fear. She was holding on to the bars, no more than a few inches from the beast's fur. His backbone protruded like a line of thick rope under his skin, and his mane was not at all as I remembered, a sort of bushy hat, but flowed from his head down his shoulders to his chest like living gold. His tail flicked gently from side to side with a restrained force, a mere hint of his true power and ferocity. It seemed indecent that such a creature could be held captive.

He climbed to his feet and turned to lie the other way, his face a picture of regal disdain. He didn't so much as glance in our direction. We were jabbering monkeys, grinning and hooting in celebration at his terrible downfall.

The fellow I'd seen before, who'd complained about the smell, reached between the bars and prodded at the golden fur. The lion didn't stir. I almost wished he had. I wondered how quickly the fool would withdraw his hand if one of those huge paws had been raised and a single claw extended.

I'd lost sight of Ciara. I looked around, but couldn't see her. She had been right there. Where could she have gone?

Other children were in the building, shouting and laughing, pulling at their mothers' hands. None of them was Ciara. What colour was her dress? Grey, I was sure, from too many washes and not enough bleach. But what about her coat? Was it dark blue?

How could I not know?

I started walking, scouring the building for her round face, feeling my heart begin to hammer. I didn't want to call out and make a scene. She was probably pressed up against one of the cages, quite safe. I would spot her in a moment, most likely with Aiden, listening as he lectured her about the animals. Any moment now.

But there were Aiden and Constance, and she wasn't with them.

'Have you seen Ciara?' I asked, and they both shook their heads. 'Go and find her, would you?' I was trying to keep my voice steady.

I had made a mistake bringing her here. Such a tiny child, she didn't have the means to understand what had happened. She had said a lion had killed her mother and, even though that was ludicrous, she might have become terrified if one looked at her or bared its teeth.

I didn't know what to do. I felt as if I'd been emptied out. Should I tell a member of staff to form a search party? I would feel so foolish when she turned up, having innocently wandered off. But what if she hadn't, and by delaying I was making it harder to find her?

What if we *never* found her?

With a shock that stung the skin on my face, I remembered the young man in a brown felt hat who'd followed us into the lion house. He'd been on his own, which was unusual in this place. Could he have been spying on us, waiting for his chance? Could he have taken her?

I thought of her mother's corpse lying in a dug-out hollow in a dingy courtyard, her clothes soaked with water, her face grey.

'Ciara!' I shouted. 'Ciara! Ciara!'

9

'CIARA!' I SHOUTED MORE loudly this time, hearing my voice in a high, female register. I didn't care. Nothing was more important than seeing her face poking around a corner, where she'd followed a cat or become distracted by a flower or something, *anything*, as long as she was all right.

How did I lose sight of her? How could I have been so stupid?

A man in uniform approached me, a satchel slung over his shoulder. 'You lost someone?'

'Yes, a little girl. Have you seen her?'

'Name?'

'Ciara Hannigan. She's six. This tall, wearing a blue coat. She has black hair.'

'All right, Mr Hannigan, I'll spread the word.'

I gripped his sleeve. 'A man was following us. He had a brown hat. He might have taken her.'

The fellow looked at me quizzically. 'Why would anyone do that?' He patted my shoulder in a manner that was probably meant to be soothing. 'Don't worry, she'll turn up, they always do. Wait here.'

I didn't want to wait. I wanted to run in circles around the lion house until I found her. Nevertheless, I remained, turning in every direction, scanning every movement.

After a few minutes, Aiden and Constance came back. Constance was wringing her hands and her face was white.

'No sign of her,' she said.

At that moment, I saw the man in uniform coming down the path and, God be praised, Ciara was with him. I had never felt so grateful to see anyone in my life.

'She was by the zebra and antelope enclosure, Mr Hannigan.' He sniffed, making his moustache wriggle on his face. 'Maybe you should pay more attention to where your children are in future?'

I crouched down in front of her. The cloudless sky was making the afternoon chilly, and her teeth were chattering. Her cheeks were pink and wet with tears.

'You must stay close to me,' I told her.

She wiped her face with her sleeve. 'Mummy likes zebras. I wanted to see if she was there.'

I didn't know what to say. I buttoned her coat, pulling it close around her neck, and held her hands in mine until they were fully warmed up.

We ate our sandwiches in silence, sitting on a bench by the reptile house. I could barely taste them. Ciara was between Aiden and me, her feet swinging and sometimes catching me, but I was glad of the pain.

Some boys had started up a game on the lawn. At first it was just throwing a ball to and fro, but now they had divided into two teams and were arguing over the rules. Without asking, Aiden hopped off the bench and went to join them. They were cocksure lads with well-to-do accents, and a couple of them gave him a look as he approached, assessing and dismissing him in a single expression. The largest of them had the ball, and Aiden plucked it out of his hands, standing facing him with it under his arm, appearing relaxed but actually, I could tell, alert and prepared for whatever came next. There was a tense silence, during which I considered intervening, but then they carried on with their debate. It seemed that Aiden would be included or, at least, that none of them would risk trying to eject him.

When I had finished my sandwiches, I tossed the crumbs and crusts on to the grass and watched the seagulls swoop down for them, flapping and fighting. Two came so close we could almost have touched them. Ciara shrank back and pulled her feet up on to the bench, wary of their sharp beaks and fierce eyes.

'It's all right, they won't hurt you,' I assured her. I had an urge to put my arm around her, but I was so used to avoiding close physical contact, I'd forgotten how. 'What you said before, Ciara, about seeing a lion from your window. Was it the same as the ones here?'

She nodded, scrunching herself up even smaller, her eyes fixed on the gulls.

I wished I understood. I saw no sign she was being untruthful or shutting off a memory too harrowing to bear. But it couldn't be random chance that had made her think of a lion; she must have seen *something*.

I was trying to think of a different way to ask the question when Constance leaned across me.

'Perhaps, Ciara, you know a person called lion, like *Mister* Lion, or …' she exchanged a look with me, certain she had found the answer '... or Mister *Lyons*, with a "y". Do you know a Mr Lyons?'

'No,' answered Ciara quickly. 'It was like those ones, except standing up.'

'Standing up?' I wracked my brain for a better way to put it but couldn't think of one. 'You mean on its four feet?'

'No.' She shook her head so firmly her bonnet slipped. 'Standing up.' She climbed on to the bench and stood up straight to show us.

'On its *hind legs*?' I pulled my folio and a pencil from my pocket and handed them to her. 'Can you draw it for me?'

She nodded and knelt on the ground, using the bench as a table, biting her bottom lip in concentration.

Meanwhile, the ball game was livening up. A couple more lads had joined in, so there were seven or eight on each side, and they were calling to each other, making sudden dashes for the ball or pointing to the fellow they thought should receive it. Some had taken off their shirts and were glistening with sweat. I watched them with a dull, formless envy, too familiar to have any bite. In all the hours of my childhood I had spent watching boys play games, never once had I been invited to join them.

When Ciara had finished her picture, she held it up. Her lion had four legs and a mane, roughly speaking, and was rearing, rampant, like on a coat of arms.

'Did a man have this picture on his chest?' I asked her.

She shook her head again, her hair swinging from side to side.

In the game, two boys had started wrestling, tangling on the grass. I realised one of them was Aiden. The other emerged victorious, wrenching the ball free and leaping to his feet, but Aiden was quicker, being slighter and unencumbered by the ball. He took a swing at his opponent and the boy twisted away, the blow landing harmlessly on his shoulder. Immediately, both teams surrounded Aiden, chins jutted forwards. I assumed he would apologise, but he didn't. He raised his fists and stared at them, daring them to take him on. I was on the brink of going to separate them, when a man, clearly the groundskeeper, came running past us, yelling and waggling his finger. I have never seen a group move so fast; one second, they were there and the next, they had scattered in all directions.

Aiden came trotting back to our bench, out of breath and red-faced, his jacket and trousers covered in grass stalks and stains.

'Where shall we go next?' he said.

I searched his face for bruises, but he seemed unhurt. 'Are you all right? I thought they were going to beat you to death.'

He wiped his brow with his sleeve. 'Rich boys. They don't have the stomach for it.'

Ciara showed him her picture, and he rolled his eyes.

'Is this your made-up lion?' he asked.

She looked crestfallen and tossed it aside on the bench.

'Well, I think it's delightful,' I said to her. 'May I keep it?'

Aiden picked it up, took my pencil and wrote at the bottom in large, well-formed letters: *Ciaras mayd up liyon.*

His mother may have taught him to write, I thought, but not to spell. I was about to correct him when I was addressed by a familiar voice. I looked up, and was astonished to see Rosie Flowers standing there, warmly wrapped against the chill. Her children were behind her, two of them eating pies and the third, the smallest, with food around his mouth.

'Rosie!' I exclaimed. 'What on earth brings you here?'

I was amazed to discover I was pleased to see her.

I hadn't spoken to her for a year and had come to believe I never would again. She was part of a history I didn't want to think about. And yet, here and now, she wasn't a memory but a person, her face tipped slightly to one side and her green eyes considering me through her spectacles.

She folded her arms and nodded towards Constance. 'Your young friend here asked me, though we agreed to meet at two o'clock and it must be almost three now.'

'I'm sorry, Mrs Flowers,' said Constance, going pink. 'They wouldn't walk *fast* enough.'

I could scarcely believe it.

'*You* arranged this, Constance?'

I felt as if I'd been staring at one of those optical illusions one sees in magazines, and the true picture had only just become apparent.

'Yes.' She stood up and emptied the last of her crumbs on to the grass, inciting the seagulls to a frenzy. 'You must admit you're despondent, Mr Stanhope. All you do is go to work and come home, or play chess and drink beer with Mr Kleiner, who's even more miserable than you are. You need to go out to places and have nice friends, proper friends, who make you *happy*.'

Rosie raised her eyebrows, and neatly caught the half of a pie her eldest had dropped. The boy was about Ciara's age, but taller and considerably plumper, no doubt indulging in too much of his mother's cooking. Hers were the finest pies in all of London, and her little shop enjoyed a brisk trade. I had walked past it a couple of times in the last few months, and there had been queues outside and along the pavement. I hadn't been tempted to go in; I was sure I had nothing to say to Rosie Flowers. She had caused me greater and more grievous harm than any person alive.

But she didn't know that. I was glad she was free of the guilt, but I found it hard to be in her company. It was too painful not to be able to tell her what I couldn't forgive her for.

'Rosie, I'm sorry. Constance shouldn't have interfered. It was a silly thing to have done.'

Constance went even pinker. She had meant well, but what else could I say?

Rosie pursed her lips. 'Then I suppose I'll bid you good day.'

'No, please,' wheedled Constance. 'Stay for a short while. There's so much more to see. We can all go together.'

Rosie adjusted her spectacles and squinted up at the sunshine. 'We haven't visited the monkeys yet,' she said drily. 'I hear they're riotous.'

I was exhausted and ready to leave, but the children were looking so excited I could hardly deny them. Constance walked quickly off down the path, though she couldn't possibly know where the monkeys were housed. Her confidence was such that Aiden followed her and Ciara followed him, so I had no choice but to go as well.

'Who are they?' asked Rosie as we walked after them. I'd forgotten how short she was, barely reaching my chin.

'They're orphans. Their mother was murdered.'

'Oh.' Her expression hardened. 'Poor little mites. Has the bastard been caught?'

'Not yet. I'm just taking them out for the day.'

'Truly? A single … person like yourself?'

'A single *man*, yes.'

She knew about my deformity: my female body. She had been there when … no, I wouldn't remember it. I could not. I had excavated those thoughts and put them into another place, outside of me, and would never seek them again. After it had happened, she had flogged him with a metal chain, breaking open his skull. She had saved me.

Wasn't it curious that I could be profoundly grateful to her and yet never forgive her, both at the same time? Wasn't it curious, too, that we could walk side by side, in a zoo of all places, surrounded by people who knew nothing of what we'd done together?

How wonderful it was to appear no different from anyone else.

'You don't know much about children, though, do you?' she said, looking ahead at Ciara.

'Why do you say that?'

'Because that girl needs the WC quite badly, I would say, and you haven't noticed.'

———

Once all of us had visited the privy, Rosie produced three more apple and cassia pies from her bag, insisting that Constance and the two orphans should have them ahead of her own children. She also spent a few minutes explaining to Constance how the pastry was made, using cold water and lard, though she might as well have been explaining music to a fish.

We found the monkey house, which wasn't hard, given the volume of the screams and hoots of hilarity within it.

Rosie said something to me as we entered, but I couldn't hear her over the cacophony of screeching and cackling from the monkeys on either side.

'I said, how have you been?' she shouted again.

'What did Constance tell you?'

'That she's worried about you.' Rosie glanced up at my face, a hint of concern in her eyes, and then looked away. 'Though you seem well enough to me.'

Aiden was keeping close to Ciara, who was quite transformed, plucking at her brother's sleeve to move to the next cage, laughing and pointing at the animals as they leapt from branch to branch, clutching fruit in their tiny hands. I found myself strangely resentful that I was still shaking with anxiety while she seemed to have forgotten her ordeal altogether.

'Where did you find them?' Rosie asked, as we reached an ape sitting disconsolately in a puddle of its own piss.

'They were living at a club for people with radical politics. Revolutionaries and the like. They listen to speeches and send letters to Parliament, that sort of thing. Their mother was one of them.'

'Why are *you* involved with something like that?'

I couldn't see her expression, but I thought I caught an amused tone, which irritated me. What gave her the right? Come to think of it, I could barely remember a single sentence she'd ever uttered to me that wasn't scornful or damning. Nevertheless, I answered her honestly. I may have omitted some truths in the past, but I couldn't outright lie to Rosie.

'I'm not. I didn't know the place existed until recently.'

She pulled a face. 'Well, I daresay the world could do with a bit of revolution, what with one thing and another, but speeches and letters don't put food on the table, in my experience.'

Her youngest tugged on her skirt. She lifted him on to her hip, and he buried his damp face in her neck. Even while she was talking to me, her eyes were constantly tracing the movements of the other two, who were skipping from one cage to the next, imitating the animals' calls and their odd gaits.

We stopped at a cage containing creatures no bigger than kittens, with earnest faces and wise eyes. Such agility they had! They swung with ease between the branches like circus acrobats, or better, because they were able to use their tails as extra arms and could quite happily hang from them while they chattered and grinned.

A man was walking up and down the aisle with bags of food we could give to the monkeys, if we dared risk those needle-sharp teeth. He showed the children what to do.

'Hold your hand flat, like this,' he said. 'Then they won't bite, see?'

I watched Ciara as she approached, her tiny hand held out, looking back at me in wonder as a monkey picked the grain from her palm with its fingers. Aiden wasn't so brave and hurled his supply towards the animals from several feet away.

'Are they in danger?' Rosie asked, raising her voice to be heard over the racket.

'I don't know. Ciara may have seen the murderer. I'm honestly not sure.'

Neither of us spoke for a while, going from cage to cage, hardly looking at the animals inside. They took even less notice of us.

And then I had an idea. In retrospect, it was not among my best.

'Maybe *you* could take the children,' I said. 'Just for a short while?' I was relieved at the mere thought of it. She was a mother and would know how to look after them. It was the perfect solution. 'No one will know where they are, and it won't be for long, I promise.'

Rosie glanced up at me, her green eyes glinting in the sunshine that was seeping in through the skylights. 'You'd prefer for me to keep them in my home, is that your plan?'

'Yes, exactly.'

'Just for a short while? Barely any effort required?'

It is possible at this point I should have detected a note of sarcasm in her voice. But I was very tired, and not thinking as clearly as usual.

'Yes, thank you. I can't tell you how helpful that would be.'

'This, because I'm a mother and naturally disposed to the task, while you're free to pursue whatever adventures you choose?' She stood in front of me, still holding her youngest child, whose name I couldn't remember. 'Do you think it's that easy? Do you think you can pass on all your problems to the nearest woman to solve?'

'No, of course not!'

'Must be tempting, I suppose, when you've decided not to be one of us any more, to think yourself better. That's the question, isn't it, Leo? Did you really want to be a man, or just want not to be a woman?'

'Damn it, Rosie!'

I spun round on the spot, too angry and frustrated to stay still. She didn't understand how it was for me, how exhausted I was, all the time. It would be so much *easier* to put on a dress. That was what the world wanted, what God had made me, what my body insisted it was, with its breasts and hips and blood. But it wasn't *true*. It wasn't me.

'You don't understand. I'm not fit for this. I lost Ciara today.'

'Oh Leo! We've all done it. And you found her again, didn't you?' She studied my face for several seconds. I couldn't tell what she was thinking.

'I can pay you, if that helps,' I said. 'I have access to some capital.'

She opened and shut her mouth, and put her son down. 'Sam, go and find your brother and sister.' She turned to me, and I could tell she was properly angry. 'Do you think money will change my answer? Mother of God. You had a wealthy upbringing, I daresay. Dinner on the table every night, and a maid to do your washing, is that how it was? Everything can be bought, can't it, Leo? Everything's for sale.'

'Keep your voice down,' I begged.

'I'll do as I please,' she said firmly. 'And it pleases me to go home and leave you to solve your own problems. I've enough of my own, not that you've asked after any of them. Goodbye, Mr Stanhope.'

She gathered up her children and was gone.

I bit my top lip so hard I could feel the indents with my tongue. I couldn't understand why I could speak to Rosie more easily than to anyone else alive, and yet we couldn't remain civil for more than a few minutes at a time.

Constance found me sitting in a corner with my head in my hands. She was bouncing with excitement.

'There's an elephant called Jumbo, and we can ride on his back for twopence. Can we do it, Mr Stanhope? Can we please?' She looked around. 'Where's Mrs Flowers?'

'She went home.'

'Oh.' She waited one heartbeat, perhaps two. '*Please* can we ride on the elephant?'

I nodded wearily and followed her outside.

The elephant was vast, twice my height or more, ambling towards us and waving its trunk pendulously as if conducting a mournful song in its head. On its back was a contraption that allowed three or four people to be carried on either side of its huge bulk as comfortably as if they were sitting on park benches.

A fellow took my money, and the children climbed the ladder and got on board.

For some reason, I had the feeling someone was watching me. I whirled round, and there, not ten yards away, was the man in the brown felt hat. He dipped the brim again and hurried swiftly towards the exit.

WHEN THE FOUR OF us arrived back at the pharmacy, I could smell Alfie's cod soup from halfway down the passageway.

He raised his eyebrows as we came in.

'You still have them,' he said, more an observation than a complaint.

'I'm sorry. It seemed easier than taking them all the way back to Mrs Downes's house in the dark.'

'Is that a fact?'

'It's just for tonight, I promise. They won't get in the way.'

Constance poured all the soup that was left into a bowl, and we sat around it, dipping pieces of bread and sucking fishy juices into our mouths. It was a feast.

That night, the children took my bed again. On some impulse, I sat on the edge of the mattress and pulled the blankets closely around them.

'Goodnight, Mr Stanhope,' mumbled Aiden. Ciara was already asleep.

I lay down on the rug, listening to the singing of two drunken men in the street. When they finally finished their duet – gone home or passed out – I opened the window and curled up in my chair, breathing in the moist air and watching distant flashes light up the clouds. I counted to fifteen before I heard thunder, so low it was scarcely audible, almost a tremor in the floor and walls. There was a movement in the bed and I jumped up, fearful that Ciara was having another fit, but it was Aiden, his shoulders shaking and his breath catching. He sniffed quietly, and I realised he was crying. I wanted to comfort him, but what do you say to a boy whose mother has been killed? I spent a few minutes trying to find the right words, but by the time I had thought of them, he'd gone back to sleep.

Tomorrow morning, I thought, I will have to return them to the halfway house. I detested the idea of it, but what choice did I have? I wasn't their guardian. All I could do was beg Mrs Downes to keep them for another few days, to give me time to find a decent orphanage. I would pay for it in monthly instalments from the pouch of money. They would have the best life orphans could hope for.

I dozed as the rain fell, but was awake again before dawn, when a blackbird started announcing that Colly was in the yard and we should all watch out.

Not long after that, the church bells began, warning us of a different danger, that we might remain asleep or spend a pleasant morning reading Wilkie Collins when we ought to be at Holy Communion, having our immortal souls redeemed.

I left Aiden and Ciara getting dressed in my room to avoid further antagonising Alfie. He and Constance were bustling about, getting ready. His late wife, Helena, had believed attendance at church was important. He had never confided in me what he believed.

I was sitting alone in the back room with a pot of tea and two shortbread biscuits when Constance interrupted me, her face screwed up in an expression of contempt.

'Apparently, Father's invited Mrs Thing to come with us.'

'Mrs Gower,' I corrected her.

'I can never remember her name.'

'She seems to be doing him good, Constance. He's happier these days, don't you think?'

'Not that I've noticed.'

She looked so miserable, I felt the urge to give her a hug, but of course I couldn't. When I was young, my life had been full of hugging and touching, with my mother and Jane and my father's dogs, and Bridget brushing my hair or straightening my clothes. But now, I had to suppress it. What if she was able to feel the narrowness of my arms, the inward curve of my waist or, worst of all, the edge of my cilice beneath my shirt? Those few inches of air between me and everyone else kept me safe.

'Don't you want to be a family again?'

'We are a family, aren't we?' she said.

I realised she was including me. I had lived above the pharmacy for a quarter of her life.

'Of course,' I replied, but how could it be true? How could they be my family when I kept secrets from them?

Constance didn't seem to notice my reserve and fetched another cup, emptying the rest of the pot into it, tea leaves and all, not bothering with a strainer.

'A boy delivered a letter for you,' she said, pointing to the dresser. 'I think it's for you, anyway.'

I briefly wondered if it was another letter from my sister, but the envelope was of higher quality and the addressee was 'Mr Stanholt'.

I ripped it open.

34 Gordon Square, London W.C.

Dear Mr Stanholt,

I understand from the Police Superintendent that you were instrumental in the rescue of two children. We have not met, but I feel that we should, and at the earliest opportunity. It would be greatly to your benefit to do so. Please visit me at the Canning Town Mill on Barking Road, near the railway line. Any time today would be convenient.

Yours faithfully,
Sir Reginald Thackery

I was perplexed. Why did he want to see me? And what did he mean by *greatly to your benefit*?

'Is it from Mrs Flowers?' asked Constance, ever alert to my social goings-on.

'No. Why would it be?'

She sipped her tea and helped herself to one of my shortbread biscuits. 'I thought you might have written to apologise and this was her letter forgiving you.'

I shook my head, exasperated. 'How on earth would a messenger have made it all the way to Mrs Flowers's shop and back here in that time? And anyway, she knows how to spell my name. Why are you grinning like that?'

'So, you admit you have something to apologise for?'

I pulled a face at her, but I wasn't really cross. 'You are infernal, young Miss Smith.'

'I knew there was a reason she left so quickly. If you haven't apologised yet, you must, and soon. I like her, and I know you do too.'

I decided to change the subject. 'I meant to ask you before. What does bromide of potash cure?'

Despite her youth, she knew almost as much about remedies as her father, especially now she was studying his books during every waking minute.

'Bromide?' she said. 'It settles the nerves and relaxes the muscles.'

It was as I had guessed. 'Could it aid a sufferer with convulsions?'

'Yes, it could. Why do you ask?'

'I'm curious, that's all.'

She seemed intrigued, about to ask me more questions, but her curiosity withered as Alfie came in, accompanied by a well-dressed woman with bright red hair and a frown-shaped mouth. He introduced her as Mrs Gower.

'I've heard so much about you, Mr Stanhope,' she said. When she spoke, her face became quite merry and I could see why he liked her. 'Alfred told me you help orphans. What a kind thing to do.'

Behind her, out of Alfie's eyeline, I could see Constance making the motion of stabbing herself with a table knife.

'Just two,' I said. 'And only temporarily. In fact, I was wondering if you might do me a favour. Would you mind taking them with you to church this morning?'

I needed time to think without distractions.

Mrs Gower looked back at Alfie, and I could see some unspoken communication pass between them. 'Are you not able to take them yourself?'

'Leo doesn't go to church,' said Alfie.

'Oh.' She appeared quite taken aback, as though she hadn't considered non-attendance to be a possibility.

'I'm a vicar's son,' I explained. 'I went enough as a child to last a lifetime.'

We heard footsteps on the stairs, and Aiden and Ciara appeared, wearing the clothes I had recovered from their room at the club. When Aiden saw Mrs Gower, he stood slightly in front of Ciara.

'Good morning,' said Mrs Gower.

I had expected a woman to be more naturally equipped for talking to children, but she was no better at it than I was. Did she have children of her own? I wasn't certain.

Alfie squeezed Aiden's shoulder. 'Of course we'll take them.' The boy seemed to be growing on him.

Aiden chewed his lip, and I wondered whether anarchists went to church. Did they believe in God? By way of contrast, Constance appeared delighted, no doubt preferring the company of other children to being on her own with her father and Mrs Gower. She helped Ciara on with her coat, presumably a cast-off of Aiden's as her fingers were barely visible at the ends of the sleeves. The younger girl looked up at Constance with something close to veneration.

'Is she your mummy?' I heard her whisper, eyeing Mrs Gower.

'No,' Constance whispered back, doing up the younger girl's buttons. 'My mummy's …' She paused momentarily and then recovered herself. 'My mummy's in heaven now.'

Ciara blanched and recoiled, covering her eyes with her hands. She remained like that for several seconds, seeming alternately to stiffen and subside, and I worried she was about to have another fit.

When she lowered her hands, her cheeks were pink. 'Mine is too,' she said.

Constance held the little girl's face between her palms. 'Oh, you're freezing. I have some old gloves and a scarf somewhere. Would you like to help me find them?'

Ciara nodded, and the two of them trotted up the stairs together.

I couldn't help but wonder what Constance would be like now if she'd lost both of her parents at Ciara's age, instead of only her mother. Without Alfie, this confident young woman, full of vitality and kindness, would be a warped reflection, leery and tough. I was grateful beyond words that she was as she was. But, for Ciara, I knew either path was still possible. I felt a shiver run through me.

After a couple of minutes, they came down again, Ciara now resembling a ball of wool with arms and legs. The whole party left through the pharmacy door.

In the silence that followed, I sat on the stool and reread Sir Reginald's letter. He seemed not to have changed in the last eleven years; I could almost hear his voice as he dashed it off to a secretary before moving on to the next matter at hand. I considered declining his invitation but was sure he'd simply become more insistent. I recalled that he didn't like to be denied, once hounding a man with one leg out of a pew he had come to think of as his own. And he might have information that could help the children. Dora Hannigan had worked for him years ago and, according to John, he'd abused her in a dreadful way. *The worst thing*, John had said.

Might Sir Reginald have paid for her silence? Might he have killed her to make certain of it? If so, I could be walking into a very dangerous situation.

Another thought occurred to me, one which forced me to cover my face with my hands. He might recognise me. My better sense told me it was foolishness, and he wouldn't know me even if I was wearing a dress, let alone as I was now.

And yet, John had.

What if John had already told him who I was? I had seen a fervour in his eyes that might lead him to do anything.

No, I didn't believe that. It was paranoia. Not only would it be unspeakably cruel, but that knowledge was his leverage over me. And besides, if Sir Reginald knew who I was, he would have indicated as much in the letter, to make sure I did as he instructed.

Very well, I thought. I am not exposed. Not yet.

I would meet him and hear what he had to say.

———

As I was searching for my other shoe, I was interrupted by a loud knock at the front door. My room looked out over the yard and the houses behind, so I had to go into Alfie's bedroom and peek down at the pavement between the curtains. I was half expecting to see the top of a brown felt hat, but instead I was looking down on a woman's bonnet, sky blue and quite expensive. As she glanced upwards, I stepped back into the shadows.

It was my sister, Jane. I didn't think she'd seen me.

I felt a coldness in my stomach. It was unimaginable that she would visit me here. I could never allow her to meet Alfie and Constance. She might tell them anything, everything, and they would never understand. Alfie would view me with disgust, ashamed that I had lived in his house for three years. And Constance! She had trusted me with her loathing of Mrs Gower, her fears for her father, her ambition of becoming a doctor. And I had been deceiving her all this time, allowing her to think I had once been a boy like any other boy, and was now a man like any other man.

I had wanted to tell them. There was one evening, a few months after I had taken up my lodging, when Alfie first offered me a glass of his whisky. Actually, we had enjoyed a number of glasses, four or five big ones each, and were surprised when Constance came in holding a candle. She was only nine years old then.

Alfie ushered her towards the stairs. 'I thought you were in bed already.'

'I've been reading.'

She held up my copy of *Barnaby Rudge*. I had lent it to her after she told me she'd finished almost every book in her school library and would shortly be reduced to the horrors of W. H. G. Kingston.

'Say goodnight to Mr Stanhope,' Alfie told her, and she did, stopping in the doorway.

'Who's Lottie Pritchard, Mr Stanhope?'

'What?'

'Her name's in the front of the book.' She opened up the flyleaf and there it was, in my handwriting. 'Who is she?'

Whether it was the lateness of the hour, the effect of the whisky or the simplicity of her question I didn't know, but I almost told her. It was the biggest risk I could have taken, but these two were already dear to me. A part of me, a large part, wanted to trust them.

I opened my mouth, but nothing came out.

'Aha!' said Alfie, raising his eyebrows. 'A lady from your past, perhaps?'

'In a way,' I admitted.

'You can have your secrets, Leo,' he said, watching his daughter scamper off to bed. 'But we'll find out everything in the end!'

The opportunity never came up in quite the same way again, and time passed. What might have been possible after a few months became unthinkable after three years. It would no longer be a revelation, it would be a confession, and a terrible one at that. Our friendship would be destroyed.

At ten-thirty, I found a cab on Piccadilly, and the driver agreed to take me as far as the East India Dock at All Hallows, but no farther. He said it wasn't worth getting his throat cut for an extra half a crown.

When I disembarked at the dock it smelled foul, the rancid silt reaching into my throat and squeezing my epiglottis. The wharfs were desolate but for seagulls winging down between crates of cargo.

I passed a sign pointing to 'The Creek', which was far less rustic than it sounded, being sludgy and lined with barges, most of them lying crookedly on the stones. A dozen or more mudlarks were crawling among them, sieving the brackish water with their fingers.

I generally considered the area around my home on Little Pulteney Street to be practically a slum, but it was a paradise compared with this. Yes, Soho was busy and dense with people pushed together in tenements, houses, shops and factories, living over and under each other, sharing rooms and breathing in each other's air, but most of us had enough to eat and the children went to school. Here, the pavement was scattered with beggars, some lying still enough to be corpses and others so thin they looked desiccated, as if poverty had sucked all the blood from their bodies. I placed a farthing into a fellow's palm and was startled when his fingers closed over it.

A crowd of children came rushing out from a building I had assumed derelict and surrounded me, forcing me to wade through them and slap their quick little hands away from my pockets. I couldn't help but think of Aiden and Ciara. This might be their future, if I didn't help them.

The mill was ten minutes' walk beyond the railway bridge, a long shed of brick set back from the road, thrumming with noise. I was amazed. How could it be working on a Sunday?

There was a lane leading down under a railway arch, presumably for the carts carrying raw jute from the docks. On all sides, great puddles had merged into bogs and reed beds, as if the marshes resented man's intrusion and were intent on reclaiming their territory. If I strayed from the lane, I would be knee-deep.

The windows on the mill were black with dirt, though I could make out lamps hanging from the ceiling and the movement of the men inside.

The main door led into a room where a young fellow was sitting eating an apple. He stood up as I entered, hastily thrusting the fruit into a drawer.

'Delivery?' he asked, looking me up and down.

'No. I was invited here by Sir Reginald.'

I held out the letter and he scrutinised it thoroughly, as if suspecting a forgery, before returning it to me.

'This way,' he said, and led me inside.

John Thackery had been right: this truly was a hell on earth, dense with noise and thick with the smell of metal and oil, stinging my eyes as they adjusted to the darkness. Huge machines were lined up in long rows, each of them pounding and roaring, attended by men feeding in coarse threads of jute, their fingers almost touching the teeth of the mechanism, while others collected the cloth as it spewed out, heaving it on to trolleys to be wheeled away. Not one of them would meet my gaze.

As I followed the clerk, I experimented with making a sound of my own, starting with a growl in my throat and rising to a shout, to find out whether I could hear myself. Even at full volume, I could not. It was terrifying, but also strangely liberating, to yell with all your might and yet have no one hear you.

We walked the length of the shed, and the din mercifully reduced towards the end. Here, scores of smaller looms were operated by women, threading and winding strands, their hands darting in and out so nimbly among the wheels and spindles it was impossible to tell what they were doing. One slip, and they would surely lose a finger.

At the back of the building, another door led into a short corridor where bright windows looked out on to the marshes and the railway embankment. The sudden glare made me blink. The noise had diminished to a dull hum, though you could still feel its vibration through the floor.

'How are you able to operate on a Sunday?' I asked the clerk. 'There are laws, surely?'

'All the workers are Jews today,' he replied, with a sly expression. 'The law doesn't apply to them.'

I thought of Jacob. He often worked on a Sunday and took his own Sabbath off, though he usually spent it recovering from too much ale the day before.

'So, you close on Saturdays instead, you mean?'

'No.' He gave me a broad wink. 'On other days, we employ non-Jews.'

'I don't understand. Are *you* Jewish? What about Sir Reginald?'

'Ah, well, you see we're Jews on some days and not on others.'

It was a flagrant violation of the law. I didn't for a second believe they employed men of different religions on different days, which meant they were enabling or, more likely, *requiring* men to work seven days a week. It was inhumane. I was amazed that Sir Reginald could get away with it. But I supposed he had enough influence and money to get away with anything.

At the back of the mill was a paved area leading up to another building, a pair of semi-detached cottages of the quaint sort one might see next to a village square. I supposed they predated the mill, and had watched the bigger, shabbier, noisier buildings multiply around them, casting them into shadow.

The left-hand cottage looked unused, the curtains drawn, but the right-hand one was occupied. As we approached, a secretary emerged and held the door open for us.

The parlour had been converted into an office. Sir Reginald was sitting behind a mahogany desk, annotating a document, his pen pecking at the page.

'My name's Stanhope,' I said. 'You sent me a letter, Mr Thackery ... I mean, Sir Reginald.'

His writing paused, and I sensed he was vexed. I had forgotten to use his proper title, which was foolish on my part. Nothing must suggest we had ever met before.

He indicated a chair without looking up. 'Sit.'

I did as instructed, taking in the room. It was neat and efficient with no sign of ostentation; he was a man dedicated to his work. The one personal item I could see was a picture of the old mill at Ponder's End, though the painter had romanticised it with blossoming trees and neat shiplap boards where in reality there had been rubble and corrugated iron.

He finished his annotation with a firm dot and carefully laid down his fountain pen.

'You've come across a pair of orphans, I believe?'

I didn't respond immediately due to his strange phrasing. *A pair of orphans* made them sound like matching candlesticks. 'Yes, Aiden and Ciara Hannigan.'

He didn't acknowledge their names. 'And how are you involved with this business?'

He was little changed; balder perhaps, and his skin paler and slacker, hanging below his eyes like folds of the cloth that had made his fortune. But his blue eyes were the same, astute and unflinching. When he looked at me, I felt that he could see under my clothes and knew exactly who I was.

'I'm not involved.'

I could hear the light pitch of my voice and feel the roughness of my cilice against my skin.

He went back to examining his document as if my foolish denial had bored him.

'Yesterday, you took them from the place of care provided by the police, and you did not return them. Ergo, you still have them. What I would like to know is: why?'

He was remarkably well-informed. I wondered what else he knew about me.

'Ciara has a malady, and the woman who runs the halfway house was unwilling to care for her.'

He leaned forwards so abruptly I almost jumped back in my chair. 'What kind of malady? Is it serious?'

'She has fits at night.'

'And the boy?'

'No. I mean … he's healthy, as far as I can tell.'

Sir Reginald picked up his pen again, rotating it in his hand. He was trying to hide the fact, but I was certain he felt *relieved* to hear Aiden didn't suffer the same way as Ciara.

'Charles Darwin is right,' he said, allowing no room in his demeanour for disagreement. 'It's simple biology. The stronger blood will always defeat the weaker.'

I wasn't sure how to respond. Was he making a medical judgement or a philosophical one?

Anyway, he didn't seem to feel my input was required.

'You are ideally placed to carry out a service for me,' he announced, without preamble. 'In return, I will pay you one guinea, which is more than generous.'

I kept my mouth shut, assuming he would explain what the service was, but instead he continued looking at me as though it wasn't important, and that I should accept any task he might give me in exchange for such a sum. Again, I felt as though he recognised me, though I was equally sure it was my imagination and he examined everyone with the same intensity.

Without warning, he gripped the edge of his desk and was assailed by a terrible fit of coughing, coming upon him so fast he had no time to inhale. He groped for air, his face flushing purple. I leapt up to beat him on the back, fearing he was choking, but he pushed me away, finally drawing in a gasping, rattling breath.

'Are you all right?' I asked him, shocked by the suddenness of the attack. He was covered in sweat, like a boxer after a brutal bout.

'Of course.' His voice was hoarse, and he spat a glob of phlegm into a tankard apparently put there for that purpose. 'It's nothing. I take it we are agreed?'

'May I ask why you're taking an interest in the children?'

'You may not.' He briefly looked at the piece of paper in front of him, picking up his pen to make a correction and then slamming it down again in exasperation, spraying ink across the desk. 'Look, it's perfectly simple. The task I wish you to perform is the following: you will place them in an orphanage of my choosing and you will tell no one. I've made the arrangements and the police have been informed. All you have to do is deliver them safely this afternoon and have nothing more to do with this matter. Is that clear?'

He evidently expected me to take his money and leave, but this might be my last chance to find out more about Dora Hannigan.

'I was hoping you might know of a relative of theirs, or someone who would be willing—'

'My understanding is they have no relatives, hence my instruction.'

I wondered how he could know that. Was he telling the truth?

'I'm concerned about them, Sir Reginald. Their mother was murdered, and the culprit hasn't been found, as far as I know. And you must be aware that the police uncovered evidence of a plot to set fire to this mill. Do you have any idea what connects these things?'

He produced a bottle of laudanum from his drawer and took a sip, shuddering and gritting his teeth. 'That blasted club. It's filled with Chartists, Owenites, Fenians and God knows what else besides. Radicals and anarchists. They want to blow up the world and to hell with the consequences. I was assured by Hooper that you weren't sympathetic to their cause. I hope he wasn't wrong about that?'

'He wasn't.'

'Good. If I had my way, they'd all be hanged. Thank the Lord they're too bloody incompetent to be dangerous.'

I felt a welling up of resentment. Who was he to decide who should be hanged and who shouldn't on the basis of their beliefs?

'If they're too incompetent to be dangerous, Sir Reginald, I presume you think none of them murdered Miss Hannigan?'

He stared at me, his jaw clenching and unclenching. When he finally spoke, it was in a low voice, measured and precise, as if he wanted me to be entirely certain of what he was saying.

'I'm offering you a very generous payment for a simple task that's in the interests of the infants. They will be well cared for. If you refuse, I must remind you that you removed them from the institution to which they were assigned by the police. You are therefore guilty of kidnapping. If you wish to stay out of prison, I suggest you do as I instruct.'

He reached into his pocket and pulled out a small bag, which he emptied on the table: eight half-crowns and one shilling. He took some trouble to arrange them in a stack on his desk, lining up the edges with precision.

'Why not ask your secretary to do it?'

'Because I'm asking you.'

He seemed to want to keep the whole business as quiet as possible, and I wondered why. But I also knew I had little choice. I was down to a king and two pawns, and checkmate was only a question of time.

'Very well,' I said. 'I'll do it. Where do you want me to take them?'

He watched closely as I put the coins into my pocket, clearly feeling it was the transaction that bound me, not my agreement.

'Do you know the orphanage at Newport Street?'

'I think so. Next to the market.'

It was near my home, and I was slightly familiar with it, having once befriended a student who had lodged in one of the rooms opposite. He had moved back to Birmingham on the completion of his studies, though not before selling me his chess set. It was bequeathed to him by his grandfather, he said, and he was sad to see it go, but the alternative was a week of sobriety.

'You will take them there this afternoon and … and this is important – vital, in fact – you will tell no one where they are. No one at all. Not your wife, your friend, your barber, no one. Do you understand?' He didn't put out a hand for me to shake. We were not equals. 'Do what I've asked and nothing more.'

He picked up his pen again, apparently a signal that our conversation was over.

I examined his face, wondering if he truly was responsible for Dora Hannigan's murder, as John had insisted. I could still feel her cold hand in that dank courtyard, when I had tried to find a sign on her skin that she had defended herself. Like his son, Sir Reginald seemed fired by certainty, although he held the exact opposite views. I could easily imagine him sitting at his desk and instructing a man to put a sword through her and bury her. I could imagine him not giving a damn.

11

I DIDN'T REACH HOME until after three o'clock. I'd walked along the railway embankment to find a station, but it was closed, so I'd been forced to walk for another hour to Aldgate and then wait forty minutes for a Metropolitan Railway train.

Constance was in the back room with Aiden and Ciara. She had placed them on chairs facing her.

'I've been telling them about the bones of the body,' she explained, sounding like a teacher when the headmaster enters the room. 'What's this one, Aiden?' She pointed to her forearm.

'The ulna,' he answered in a flat tone. I'd left the back door open and he gazed through it yearningly.

'And this one, Ciara?' asked Constance, pointing to her collarbone.

'The clavicle,' the little girl replied, looking a good deal more proud than Aiden had. She turned to me with what, at first, I thought was a broad grin, except it wasn't. She was showing me her teeth. 'Look, Mr Stanhope.'

She wiggled an upper front one with her finger, and I felt slightly sick. Then she shut her mouth abruptly, with a rueful expression, and spat into her hand. When she opened her palm, the tooth was there, lying in a pool of pink.

'Oh!' she exclaimed, poking her tongue into the new gap.

'You can put it somewhere for the tooth mouse to find,' I told her. 'Maybe he'll leave you something sweet in return.'

I closed my eyes, realising what I had said. There was no time for a tooth mouse to visit and leave her a pastry. I would be taking her to the orphanage at Newport Street this afternoon. She would never come back here again.

I couldn't face telling her, so I had to watch her wander around the house with her tooth on a saucer, searching for the best spot, eventually deciding on the corner by the stairs. She placed it there with ceremonial care.

'The tooth mouse might be busy, you know,' I said. 'There are so many children. Why don't I give you a penny instead?'

She took the coin, but I could see what she was thinking: a penny was very nice, but what about the tooth mouse? What if he came and left something sweet for her to eat, and she didn't know?

'And for you as well,' I said to Aiden, paying off my guilt in pennies.

But what did I have to feel guilty about? I was doing the right thing, wasn't I?

———

The Newport Street orphanage was almost completely hidden behind high walls and wooden gates. From the pavement, all I could see was the top storey and the roof, which sprouted chimneys of all different shapes and heights like schoolboys lined up for a photograph.

This is it, I thought. I will leave them in this place. It's the best outcome for everyone.

I knocked on the main door with a swift bang-bang-bang and could feel Ciara's hand tighten in mine.

I had packed all their things into the carpet bag, except for their money, which I had kept, for now. I promised myself I would come back and visit them from time to time, and when Aiden reached maturity, I would give it to him. The thought of that moment, of the overjoyed expression on his face, almost soothed my unexpected grief at leaving them.

An elderly woman opened the door. 'Ah, yes!' she exclaimed, peering at us through thick spectacles. 'We were told to expect you. How lovely! Come along in.'

She beckoned us inside, smiling broadly.

The hall was cool and austere, dominated by a large picture of military insignia flanked on either side by rows of smaller paintings of infantrymen in different uniforms. I could hear a woman's voice echoing down the stone stairs, and children repeating what she'd said. That sound – the dull, uninflected chorus of times tables and spellings – slipped me back to my own school in Enfield in an instant; the hard floor under my feet and the lye in my nostrils.

On my last day at school, aged eleven, my teacher had piled half a dozen books into my arms, wiping her eyes, and had gone back for another book and then another, making me promise to keep reading, no matter what. My father had returned every one of them the next day, saying we had quite enough books at home, which would have been completely true if my interests had extended only to dogs, ornithology and anatomy. It was, in fact, one third true; I did quite like watching birds.

'Wait here,' said the elderly woman. 'I'll be back in a jiffy.'

She beamed again at the children and shuffled off.

I must say, I was impressed. Sir Reginald had chosen well. While I would have preferred a less martial decorative style, an orphanage must require a fair degree of regulation, and this place seemed perfectly pleasant and sanitary. It was a world away from *Oliver Twist*.

Ciara kept hold of my hand and pressed herself against my hip. Aiden went to examine the pictures.

'What do you think?' I said to him.

'Do they shoot guns here?'

'I don't know.'

He took one of the picture frames and tilted it, so it was hanging crookedly, and stood back to admire his handiwork. I frowned at him, but he didn't straighten it. They were all exactly aligned except for that one, which was now leaning at an angle like a drunken soldier on parade.

The woman came back with a fellow who I took to be her husband from the way she guided him towards us, her hand at his elbow. He was elderly too, but where she was dressed in a homely fashion, he was neat and smart with not a stray strand of cotton or wisp of hair out of place. He introduced himself as Charles Ramsden.

'Is this the boy Sir Reginald informed us about?' He had a sheet of paper in his hand and peered at it. 'Aiden, is it? How old are you, young man?'

'Ten.'

'Ten, *sir*.'

'Ten, *sir*,' repeated Aiden, though his customary scowl didn't soften.

Mr Ramsden gave me a reserved smile. 'Well, I'm sure we can make something of him.'

He half-bowed in a manner both polite and dismissive, and steered Aiden with a firm hand towards the corridor.

'Lift your chin,' he instructed the boy. 'Slouching leads to laxity.'

I have done my best for him, I thought. He will be happy here and properly educated among others of his age. He will grow up and join the army, as my brother had done. It will be a good life.

I felt a shudder run through me; of course, it would not be like my brother, who was a captain last I heard, directing other men into battle and then retiring to the Mess or shooting at jugs for a bet. Aiden would be a ... I didn't even know the word. A troop? There were plenty of former soldiers in London; some, like Alfie, were whole and well, but I had met his friends. One of them was missing a foot and another was so badly burned only half his face was capable of expression. And there were the silences. In the midst of a story, a name would be mentioned – young McNeal or Ted-a-bed – and a wordless breath would follow before the story could continue. I had the feeling that if one of those silences had lasted just a few seconds longer, every man around the table would've been in tears.

But none of that was my responsibility. I could only help these two as they were now, not as the adults they would become.

'Wait,' I called after Mr Ramsden. 'What about Ciara?'

He turned and peered back at her as if she was a neighbour's cat who'd sneaked in. 'We don't take girls.'

His wife held out her hand. 'You don't want to stay with the boys, do you?'

Ciara buried her face deeper into my coat. I sensed the woman was affronted at having her coaxing skills so summarily spurned.

'I don't understand,' I said. 'Where do girls go?'

'The Good Shepherd orphanage. She'll do lovely there, I'm sure.' Mrs Ramsden folded her arms. 'If she ever comes out.'

'Where's The Good Shepherd orphanage?'

It wouldn't be so bad, I thought, if they could visit one another.

'Leytonstone.'

'But that's … it must be ten miles away!'

Mr Ramsden, who had shown little interest in Ciara's welfare up to this point, wagged his finger to correct me. 'It's eight and a half miles precisely.'

'But they'll be separated,' I protested, realising that was the whole point; boys couldn't be hardened for a life as soldiers in the company of girls.

Aiden twisted out of Mr Ramsden's grasp and ran back to his sister. 'She can't go somewhere on her own, being as she is.'

'Your concern does you credit,' Mr Ramsden said, sternly but not unkindly. 'However, it isn't for you to say. She's a beneficiary of the philanthropy of Sir Reginald and it's up to him to decide how it's administered.'

Aiden glared at him, dark-eyed. I doubted he understood all of Mr Ramsden's words, but he gathered the gist well enough: *do as you're told.*

'No, we must stay together.' He threw me a look. 'You *promised*, Mr Stanhope.'

Mr Ramsden pointed to his piece of paper. 'Sir Reginald left specific instructions. We are to take the boy, and the girl goes to The Good Shepherd. That's what he requires.'

Aiden glanced towards the door and I knew what he was thinking.

Mr Ramsden scratched his head as if pondering the problem, and then made a lunge for Aiden. The boy skipped nimbly backwards and Mr Ramsden stumbled and almost fell, dropping his sheet of paper.

I picked it up for him.

'Please, let's stop and think about this,' I said. 'There must be a way to resolve the situation. Are there other places like this one, but that would take both of them? It's wrong for them to be kept apart when they've so recently lost their mother.'

'It's best to educate boys and girls *separately*,' insisted Mrs Ramsden, indicating the pictures on the walls as if they were proof.

Her husband had recovered his balance. He held out his hand for his piece of paper. I was about to give it to him when I noticed the name written at the top: Aiden Jones.

Beneath that, Ramsden had written Aiden's age and nationality, and that the fees would be paid by Sir Reginald.

'I don't understand,' I said. 'His surname isn't Jones.'

'Of course,' said Ramsden, looking flustered. 'It's just administrative.'

I read it again, turning it over to check both sides. 'But Sir Reginald knows his name is Hannigan. Why would he place him here under an alias?'

The realisation blanched across my skin.

I knew why.

'We have to go,' I said, pulling Ciara towards the door. 'Come on, Aiden. Quickly, please.'

Mr Ramsden trailed us across the hall, appearing to be in two minds as to whether to block our way. 'Sir Reginald gave us strict instructions. He paid six months in advance!'

I reached the door and opened it. 'And a substantial bonus as well, I'm sure. Goodbye, Mr Ramsden.'

And with that, we left the building.

We rushed home as swiftly as Ciara's legs would carry her. When we got into the pharmacy, I bolted the door behind us.

Alfie came through from the back room. 'What's going on?'

'I think they may be in danger.'

I looked out of the window as far as I could in both directions.

'What danger?' I could see his mind working. He wouldn't shy from a fight, but he had Constance to consider. 'Leo—'

'I'll make a new arrangement for them as soon as I can, I promise. In the meantime, we must be vigilant.'

I could think of only one reason why Sir Reginald would place Aiden in an orphanage under a false name.

He wanted the boy to be lost.

12

THAT NIGHT, I SAT in my armchair once again, looking out at the familiar landscape of brick and smoke. There was a time I would have stolen a teaspoonful of chloral hydrate from downstairs to ease me into sleep. It was tempting even now; that yearning had never completely worn off. But I feared those terrible visions. Whatever was to come, I would need a clear head.

Sir Reginald wanted Aiden to be lost, and presumably Ciara as well. Perhaps he knew that she'd witnessed the murder, or perhaps he wanted to hide the evidence of his own past indiscretions. Perhaps both.

I looked over at them; two small shapes under the blanket, Aiden's arm dangling over the edge of the mattress. They didn't deserve any of this.

I had only saved them for a brief few hours. Tomorrow, I was certain, the police would come for them. And for me. Kidnapping was a serious offence.

Before dawn, I felt a tugging at my shirt, and almost jumped out of my chair. For a few seconds I thought the police had arrived already. It was so unfair. I had only tried to do what was best.

'Mr Stanhope!'

It was a child's voice and a child's hand. I reached out and touched Ciara's hair.

'What's wrong?'

I sat up, reality coalescing.

'The tooth mouse hasn't come,' she whispered.

'He's very busy. Maybe he'll leave you something tomorrow.' I rubbed my temples, feeling a headache crawling around the side of my skull, coming to rest over my right eye. 'How do you know he hasn't come?'

'I looked.'

'You mustn't go downstairs on your own. It's not safe.'

Her face was very close to mine, so even in the half-dark I could see her earnest expression. 'I was quick as lightning.'

'Go back to sleep.' I closed my eyes but could tell she was still there. 'What's wrong now?'

'I can't sleep. Aiden's taking up all the space.'

I tried to think what I used to do when I couldn't sleep, back when I was a child. We lived on the edge of the countryside and at night there was no light at all, not even to see my hand in front of my eyes. Sometimes, in that blackness, my mind was able to detach from the world and float above it, all my troubles soothed until morning. But at other times, I grew afraid, hearing the owls as ghosts, and the whistles and moans of the vicarage as monsters, and had to crawl into Jane's bed beside her. On the very worst nights, I would rouse her and beg her to make the nightmares go away, and she would put her arms around me and tell me a story, her voice so close in my ear I didn't know if it was her speaking or me, if it was out loud or only in my head.

'Shall I tell you a story, Ciara?'

She climbed on to the armchair beside me, wriggling to make herself some room, not caring how uncomfortable I was.

I realised, with a twinge of contrition, that I didn't know any stories. Poor Jane. I had woken her on those nightmare nights and then fallen asleep again before she'd finished introducing the first squirrel.

I would have to improvise.

'Once upon a time, there was a …' Ciara closed her eyes and curled up in anticipation '… there was a boy. He was born as a … as a robin.'

'The bird?' she asked, yawning.

'Yes, the bird. His name was Robin too, which is probably why it happened.'

'Robin the robin?'

'Yes,' I agreed, not sure now whether the name had been a wise idea. 'Every day he wished to be a human, but the other robins thought him a fool, and wouldn't listen. He tried to play human games and read books, but he couldn't, because he had wings instead of hands. So, one day, he flew away from his family and …'

I petered out as her breathing slowed, her hair straggling across her face, the soles of her feet pressed against my leg.

I dared not move for fear of waking her, so we remained that way until the dawn light seeped through the curtains.

That morning, we waited in my room for the police to come.

I was supposed to go to work at the hospital, but I couldn't bear the thought of Hooper turning up there to arrest me, so I wrote a note telling my foreman that I had a fever and would be staying in bed. I found a messenger-boy in the street and paid him a penny to deliver it.

Over and over, I repeated the calculation in my head; Mr Ramsden would surely have told Sir Reginald that I had not obeyed his instruction, and Sir Reginald would inform the police immediately. They would arrest me, and the children would be taken away, probably today and at best tomorrow.

I was running out of time.

How could I keep them safe?

I thought of placing them in a different orphanage, a good one, using their real names. But Sir Reginald might still find them and, even if not, there would be questions. Where did they come from, and why did I have them? How was I paying for their care?

As the bells rang for nine o'clock and then ten, the hours seemed to be dawdling just to frustrate me. Whenever the doorbell downstairs jangled, I froze, listening for the officious timbre of a policeman's voice. It was maddening. I began to wish they'd arrive soon and get it over with.

We couldn't go anywhere in case they came while I wasn't here. I didn't want Alfie and Constance to have to deal with the explanations: *Yes, Mr Stanhope was at home earlier. No, I'm sure he hasn't run away.*

Aiden and Ciara didn't appear to notice my disquiet. I was amazed at how resilient they were. Despite having almost been separated at the orphanage, they had after-wards tucked into a dinner of cold chicken and potatoes as if little of note had happened, and this morning had spent two hours playing draughts. By noon, Aiden had got bored and was juggling with screwed-up pieces of paper, showing surprising proficiency, while Ciara lay on the floor, amusing herself with my chess men, sending the knights off on adventures to discover hidden castles.

'Can't we go outside, Mr Stanhope?' asked Aiden, for the third time.

'No,' I answered, a fraction more crossly than I'd intended. 'Please be patient. I'm trying to decide what to do.'

Ciara returned to playing draughts. She had asked her brother to play with her, but he had refused, preferring to continue juggling, so she was taking both sides of the game. It was white's turn and she was sitting cross-legged on that side of the board, her lips pursed. She made her move and crawled round to the black side, her eyes scanning the pieces anew.

That could've been me, I thought, twenty years ago. Oliver rarely agreed to play me at chess. He was good at ball games and fighting, but Jane had sucked up all the brains while they were still in the womb together. He had ventured out first, ever the explorer, so he was technically older, but he was never her match. Their battles were fiery, but brief. I was stuck in the middle, the other one, the non-twin, lesser in every way.

But, like Ciara at her game, I was able to see both sides.

Though I could scarcely tolerate the idea, I could only think of one thing to do. I sat down and wrote a letter.

I had to go outside to find a boy to deliver it, so I gave strict instructions to the children to stay in the house and out of sight. Alfie reluctantly agreed to keep an eye on them, muttering something about having done more than his fair share of raising a child already. But as I closed the door I heard him calling up the stairs, asking if they wanted to watch him make a foam mountain out of baking soda and vinegar. Judging from their cheers, I guessed my coin trick would soon seem rather second-rate.

I found the same boy in the street who'd delivered my earlier note to my foreman. He looked about thirteen years old and as scrawny as they all were, but less suspicious than most, with gentle features beneath the dirt.

'What's your name?'

'Tommy Sollars, sir.' He stood up straight, his eyes darting up and down from my face to my shoes as if he was watching a ball being bounced. 'I live in Cleveland Street, sir,' he added, as though his place of residence was significant.

'Do you know where Maida Vale is? Good. Please deliver this. I'll pay you a penny for the delivery and twopence if you bring it back with a reply.'

That was how desperate I was, relying on my sister for help.

A rainstorm had passed, and the pavements were crowded again by the time she arrived.

Alfie stood back and almost bowed as she entered, such was her presence, in a well-fitted jacket, silk dress and a hat that managed to be both spectacular and reserved. Either she was wearing this garb to intimidate me, or her husband, Howard, had risen another rank or two at the bank. I had never met the man, nor was I ever likely to, but I imagined him as a huge, damp frog, sitting at their home in Maida Vale in a greasy puddle.

'Will you look after Aiden and Ciara while I'm out,' I said to Constance. 'And please do as I asked, all right?'

She nodded.

'Thank you.' I turned to Jane before she could say anything. 'Let's go for a walk, shall we?'

I took her to Soho Square, a patch of grass with pleasant houses arranged around the sides. Water was still dripping from the trees overhead like our own, personal raincloud, but she didn't open her umbrella, perhaps unable to face sharing it with me. She was my sister but would not accept me as her brother.

'Father is dying,' she announced, with the merest catch in her throat. 'The doctors are useless and disagree about everything save one thing: he has a few weeks at most.' She pursed her lips, as though trying to keep her next words inside her mouth. I had already guessed what they were. 'He says he would like to see you, Lottie.'

'Leo,' I corrected her sharply. 'I will answer to nothing else.'

'You were christened Lottie.'

'I was christened *Charlotte*, but that's not my name either. And why does it matter to you anyway? You said you didn't want to hear from me any more.'

She gave a stiff little nod. 'It's Father who wishes to see you, not me.'

I felt a bite of disappointment.

'And yet here we are.'

'Yes,' she said. 'Here we are. Ollie's gone back to India and won't be home again for another year, so there's just the two of us. Will you come and see him, or will you allow Father to die while you sulk?'

'I will consider it. But I have conditions.'

She gave me a look. We had spent our childhood bickering and could veer from amusement to anger, and triumph to resentment, even within a couple of sentences. It was impossible for anyone but us to distinguish between a genuine row and a mere tease. But *we* always knew; the tiny inflections of a word, a blink, a glance, a sly flick of a hand. We never had a second's doubt about what the other intended.

'I had assumed you would. Very well, let's hear them.'

I was somewhat taken aback. I hadn't expected her to be so prepared. But now I came to think about it, I had never in my life beaten her at chess, and the few times I had captured her queen, it had turned out to be a ruse, a prelude to her ultimate victory.

I had to tread carefully.

'Where is Father?'

'He retired to Hampstead, and he's at his house there. I'll give you the address. But you must be quick. I don't know how long he'll last.'

'And he asked for me? Are you certain?'

She cast me another look, and I thought: of course she's certain. She's always certain.

'He's quite lucid most of the time,' she said. 'At least now I've stopped those quacks from filling him with opiates like some oriental.'

'Is he in pain?'

I realised I didn't want him to suffer. No matter that I hated him, I would prefer he lived out his days peacefully, as long as he was far away from me.

'Sometimes. Often. But better that than drooling and comatose, don't you think?' She tapped her umbrella irritably on the ground, conscious that she'd accidentally asked my opinion of our father's treatment. 'He's always had such an acute mind. Exacting, yes, and sometimes more candid than we would like, but always with a purpose.'

I sensed this fabrication was more for her benefit than mine. Yes, he did have an acute mind, but he wasn't exacting, he was dogmatic, and he wasn't candid, he was brutal. My father adored his only son, as he would see Oliver, and doted on his only daughter, as I would see Jane. But I was always the other one, the awkward one; unwanted, unfortunate and unwelcome.

'If I do see him,' I told her, 'I will be myself.' I stood back, looking down at my waistcoat and trousers, the bulge in my groin where I had sewn a roll of cloth to make me appear to have what I did not.

I knew what she was about to say: that for her sake and for his, I should put on a dress and a wig and all the rest of the paraphernalia that women wore, and be obliging and gracious, and pretend to be Lottie. It was a small thing to ask, was it not, to make a dying man content?

But I would not. Not for him, not for anyone. I had made my decision and would never reverse it.

You could have knocked me down with a stalk of grass when she replied, 'I expected as much. It can be as you say.'

She was still walking, even-paced, stepping around the puddles and smiling politely at passers-by. She did not appear to have gone mad.

'You understand what I'm saying? I will see Father as I am now.'

She nodded, not meeting my eye. 'That's acceptable, with the proviso that you don't mention it unless he does.'

'But he *will* mention it. He's mentioned everything he dislikes about me since I was born. He's not going to stop now.'

'You haven't seen him in years, Lottie. What is it? Ten? Eleven? He's changed since Mother died.' She went to take my hand, before realising what she was doing and pulling hers away. 'He's an old man. He wants to see his child again before he goes. Will you deny him that?'

We had completed another lap of the square, and she stopped, clearly hoping our conversation was concluded.

'I have one more requirement,' I told her.

'Another one? I've already agreed that you may go as ...' she pointed at me with her umbrella '... as this. Is that not concession enough?'

'It's not a concession at all, Jane. This is who I am. Why should I dress up as someone else?'

She clenched her hands into fists. 'Can you not, for once in your life, understand the damage you're doing? What you've taken from me? I lost Mother, and now Father will be taken also, and Ollie's in India, but you, my only sister, who could come back to me at any moment you choose, persist in this idiotic ... masquerade.'

'I was never your sister.'

She swallowed, fighting back a sob in her throat. 'You were never so unkind either.'

'What kindness do you think I owe you?'

'A Christian kindness, at least.'

Well, I supposed she did have a point there; it was her Christian kindness I was relying upon. That, and her maternal instincts.

'Very well,' I said. 'I will visit Father this week, if I can.' I didn't mention I was expecting to be arrested within a few hours. 'But there's still one thing I need from you in exchange.'

The children were clean and smelling of soap, having been thoroughly immersed in the tin bath in the back room, scrubbed with pumice and dressed in their least-patched clothes. They were waiting in the doorway when we returned to the pharmacy, as I had instructed. I brought them outside on to the pavement where Alfie and Constance wouldn't be able to hear our conversation.

'This is Mrs Hemmings,' I said to them. 'She will be looking after you for a little while until we find a permanent arrangement.'

Jane bent down. 'You must be Ciara. And this fine young man is Aiden, I presume.' She licked her gloved finger and wiped a smudge from his nose.

Ciara looked up at me with big, round eyes. There was no panic in them, no anxiety about being taken by a stranger. I realised she had lost the ability to fear. I could remember how that felt, as if you're staying still and the world is revolving around you, faster and faster. You can't step in any direction without being whisked away, so you stand and watch until it's all just a blur.

'Aiden doesn't say much, but he's not being rude, it's how he is,' I said quietly to Jane. 'And Ciara is sickly. She's prone to fitting at night. She doesn't seem to hurt herself and remembers nothing of it afterwards, but you have to stay with her until she falls asleep.' I handed the packet of bromide to Jane; the same one I had sold to Dora Hannigan. It seemed like a hundred years ago. 'Dissolve exactly half a teaspoon in water per day. Buy some more if it runs out.'

She took it without comment. She had never been concerned by illness and had sat with me day and night while I sweated and scratched with scarlet fever.

Aiden picked up the carpet bag, ready to go. 'Is it my fault?' he asked. 'Is it because of what I did at the orphanage?'

'What?'

His chin was curling, but he was resisting it. 'Is that why we're being sent away, because I didn't go with that gentleman?'

I was aware of a lump in my own throat. I shook myself and pinched the skin between my thumb and forefinger hard, aiming to raise some blood. I mustn't weep. It was unmanly. My sister had brought it upon me with her cloying regard for our father.

'No, of course not. You were being a good brother, doing your best for your sister. Now I'm trying to do my best for you. Mrs Hemmings has children of about your ages, and you'll enjoy their company, I'm sure.'

My nieces and nephews. I didn't know them. Two of them, I had never so much as laid eyes upon.

At least Aiden and Ciara would be cared for, I thought. For a little while. Jane had many flaws, but she was a good mother and a Christian woman with a charitable nature. She would feed them and clothe them and tell her nursery maid to pick the nits from their hair, and she would take them to church and make sure they said their pleases and thank yous. They would be safe, and she would be gratified; she loved to gather around her the vulnerable and needy and instruct them on how to lead better lives.

Nevertheless, as they disappeared along the pavement, I felt as if I'd lost something precious. I couldn't explain it.

Perhaps I was being silly, preoccupied by my impending arrest or the thought that, if I somehow avoided that fate, I would soon be meeting my father for the first time in eleven years. I didn't know which was worse, though I supposed any conversation with my father would at least have the virtue of brevity. He would never accept me as Leo and would throw me out the second he realised who I was.

It was almost a shame. Before I had left home, my father had known Sir Reginald quite well, and he might know the answers to some of my questions.

I actually felt a pang of disappointment that I would never get the chance to ask him.

13

THE FOLLOWING MORNING, HALF an hour after midday, the police finally arrived.

I had sent the lad Tommy with a note to my foreman informing him that my fever was worsening, and I wouldn't be able to come to work. I could ill-afford the loss of income, but what other choice did I have?

After that, I stood in the doorway of the pharmacy for a while, until Alfie told me to remove myself lest his customers thought some damn fool was preventing them from coming in. Since then I'd been sitting on the stool, from which I had a good view of the black police coach drawing up. Hooper climbed out, followed by the same constable I'd seen before, with receding hair and expansive girth. Hooper squinted up at the sunshine and spoke to the driver who, I noted, waited for them. No, for *us*.

'Mr Stanhope,' said Hooper, removing his bowler as he entered. 'We need a word.'

I led them through to the back room.

I had one faint hope.

'They ran away,' I said.

Hooper folded himself into a chair. 'What did you say?'

'The Hannigan children. They ran away. I don't know where they are now.'

It sounded implausible even to me, and I doubted it would be enough to keep me out of prison. After all, I had kidnapped two children. I was guilty.

Hooper exchanged a look with the constable.

This is it, I thought. I am saying goodbye to this life, this name, these clothes. These are my last moments of truly being me.

Hooper shrugged. 'I don't know what you're talking about. Sir Reginald Thackery assured me they've been taken care of. That's what great men do, Mr Stanhope. They have big hearts to go with their big wallets.'

I could hardly comprehend what he was saying. Sir Reginald must not have carried out his threat to have me arrested for kidnapping. But why? Certainly not to save my skin. He must have reasons of his own, though I couldn't fathom what they might be.

What was he hiding?

Unless, of course, Mr Ramsden hadn't admitted that he didn't have custody of Aiden? He had received payment in advance, plus presumably a bonus, to give the boy a new name and ensure he would never be found. He might have decided to keep his silence and the bribe. But that wasn't likely. Not only was it, at best, a short-term gain, but he didn't seem the type. He was far too subservient.

My brain felt like sludge. I wished everyone would leave me alone for a few hours to actually *think*.

'When did you last see John Duport?' asked Hooper.

'We met at ...' I couldn't remember whether I was supposed to lie about meeting John or not, and my thoughts wouldn't run fast enough for anything but the truth. 'We met at a pub, the Marquis of Granby. The Friday before last, I think it was.'

He pulled out his notebook and peered over his spectacles at it. 'Right. That makes you the last person to see him. No one else knows a thing about the man. No family, no previous address, no anything. Why do you suppose that is?'

'I couldn't tell you. We aren't close.'

'That's what everyone's been saying. Apparently, he has no friends at all, aside from you and Miss Hannigan herself.'

'That doesn't make me guilty of anything.'

'Doesn't it?' Hooper raised his eyebrows and stayed silent, presumably hoping I would babble incontinently and incriminate myself. It was the same trick he'd tried last time, but he had no idea who he was dealing with.

The constable, who had been picking dirt from under his fingernails with one of Alfie's knives, piped up: 'You might as well tell us.'

Hooper rolled his eyes and glared at the fellow, but he was already back at his fingernails.

'Think of it this way,' Hooper said, leaning across the table towards me. 'The victim had your name and address on her person, didn't she?'

'I can't explain that.'

I was feeling light-headed and reckless. Having expected to be arrested and imprisoned, this mere interrogation felt almost playful.

Hooper scratched his beard. 'So you keep saying. But, how I see it, without Mr Duport, your alibi's disappeared. Puff of smoke. So, if he shows up, you'll be sure to tell me, won't you? It's in your interests. Do you understand what I'm saying?'

'Yes, of course.'

'Good.'

As he stood up to go, he caught sight of Ciara's tooth on the saucer on the floor. He stooped to pick it up.

'Whose is this?' he asked.

I almost said it was Constance's, but she was twelve and it was some years since she'd last lost a tooth. Thankfully, my brain found one last teaspoonful of coherence. 'My landlord does dentistry as well as pharmacy. It probably came from one of his customers.'

'I see.'

Hooper put it into his pocket, and I wondered whether he viewed it as evidence or was thinking of adding it to the set in his own mouth.

Once they'd gone, I sat in the back room in a daze, listening to the scratch of Alfie's pen on his ledger and the clink and rustle of coins and notes being counted and scooped into bags. Such commonplace sounds, I barely heard them any more.

This was what I had wanted, wasn't it? Routine. Ordinariness. A quiet life where I was responsible for no one, and no one was responsible for me.

I despaired at how easily that resolve had been broken. All it had taken was two children I'd never even met three weeks before.

And now, for their sakes, I was lying to the police and risking arrest.

I needed help. Fortunately, I knew of someone who might be willing, and who always had an insight different from my own. She had stood by me in my darkest moment.

I left the pharmacy and began the walk to the pie shop thinking: I hope you're at home, Rosie. I need you now.

———

As I opened the door, I was, as ever, assailed. There were bigger shops on grander streets, selling more expensive pies with finer-sounding ingredients, but there were no better pies.

The heat carried with it an aroma that was, for me, more than just a smell. Contained within that pastry, meat and fruit was comfort and peace and the memory of a kitchen, long ago, where Bridget was preparing our breakfasts and chitter-chattering to herself, or perhaps to me, it was hard to tell which.

In addition to Rosie and her three children, the premises was shared with an elderly couple, whose names I habitually failed to remember. It was the female half who greeted me today, her face discoloured and shiny like polished leather; the result, I assumed, of a lifetime spent peering into ovens.

'Mr Stanhope!' She brushed her hands down her apron. 'We ain't seen you around here for quite a while.' She indicated the somewhat depleted racks of pies on the counter. 'We don't have much left, I'm afraid. All the kidney's gone, and the lamb too. Couple of chicken and bacon, and these, which not everyone likes but I think are the best of all: beef cheek and parsnip, with a tiny drop of marmalade to sharpen the taste. I don't know how she came up with that, but it's like rising up to heaven, every mouthful. Rising up with the angels singing. All for sixpence.'

I barely had enough in my wallet for the rent, and had already decided not to spend Sir Reginald's guinea as he would certainly want it back, after I had failed to follow his instruction. Nevertheless, a pie might buy some co-operation, as well as appease my growling stomach.

'I'll take one. Is Rosie here?'

I could hear sounds from the back; a chair leg scraping and a child's voice. I had never been beyond the shop. I imagined a room much like Alfie's, with a table for their evening meal, chairs for them to sit on, pictures on the walls and cupboards for their personal things. And upstairs, a bedroom which Rosie and her husband Jack had once shared.

The leather-faced woman handed me the pie in a paper bag and pursed her lips harder, as though suffering from a toothache. 'I'll caution you to be mindful, Mr Stanhope. Last time you was here, it was most disruptive. *Most* disruptive. She came back soaked to the skin and was in bed for three days afterwards with a fever. And her recently widowed and all. I know it had something to do with you, and the trouble you got her into.'

'I assure you—'

She dropped her voice. 'You never thought to visit, did you? To see how she was getting on. Not once. You should have visited, Mr Stanhope, and that's a fact.'

But I couldn't, I thought, not after what Rosie had done. But of course, Rosie didn't know what she'd done and hadn't intended it. What must she think of me now?

The leather-faced woman went into the back and I could hear their conversation, which sounded as if it might have become heated towards the end. Then Rosie herself came through, her hands white with flour.

She glowered at me. 'What do *you* want?'

I could feel the heat of the pie through the paper bag.

'Can we talk please? I need some help.'

'Is that the only reason?'

I nodded, not wanting to admit that I regretted how we'd parted at the zoo. She surveyed me, rubbing her chin.

'Very well, I suppose. Can you manage to be polite this time?'

———

We slowly circumnavigated the municipal conceit of St Paul's Cathedral, its pale stone walls and decorative columns casting shadows over the orderly shopfronts, listless beggars and gatherings of stray dogs around it.

I explained everything that had happened. The one detail I left out was my first lie to the police. I was too ashamed to tell her that.

Afterwards, she spent several seconds deep in thought, the mist of her breath dissipating in the chill air.

'You've had a lucky escape, Leo.'

'I know. Sir Reginald hid the truth about where the children were, even from the police. I have no idea why.'

'Some men like to control things. Most men, actually.' She wrinkled her nose. 'My guess is he didn't want to admit his plan had failed.'

'What plan?'

She breathed deeply, glancing up at me with a strange expression as if wondering how to break bad news.

'The way I see it, if you'd left those kids at the orphanage as you were supposed to do, no one except you and

Sir What's-his-name would've known where they are. Or who they are.'

'Exactly.'

She turned to me, her hands clutched together. 'Don't you see, Leo? That means if someone had gone looking for them at that place … what did you call it? The halfway house? Well, they wouldn't have found them, would they? And who was the last person to see them? Who took them away and never brought them back?'

Such a sharp pivot on which our fates had balanced. Rosie was right. If Aiden hadn't objected to being separated from Ciara, I wouldn't have seen Mr Ramsden's piece of paper. I would have left them at the orphanage as Sir Reginald had instructed. The children would have disappeared, and I would be the person who had taken them from Mrs Downes's halfway house and never returned them.

'I'd get the blame for their disappearance,' I said. 'I could be accused of selling them or even … even murdering them!'

My legs were feeling weak. I leaned against a metal rail, looking south towards the river. From here, I could smell the oil and hear the creaking of the cranes unloading the ships. Such industry they had, such purpose, while I was like a toy boat bobbing in the bath, waiting for a splash to sink me.

'And at the same time,' continued Rosie, 'his son has scarpered, and your alibi's gone with him. What a coincidence. Seems to me they've tried to make you look guilty of the murder of the mother as well. These rich families, they always stick together against the likes of you and me.'

It took me a moment to untangle what she meant. 'You think John and his father are in cahoots?'

'*In cahoots?*' She grinned, despite her awful conjectures. 'If you mean *together*, then yes I do. No matter how much they disagree, a parent will always help their child. And a son born rich doesn't turn his back on such help when he has need of it.' She faced me, squaring her shoulders. 'There's nothing else for it. You have to tell the police that John Duport and John Thackery are one and the same person.'

'Why?'

'How will it look if you don't? You're keeping a secret for a man who's trying to incriminate you. You don't owe him anything.'

But of course, I did owe him something. Or not *him* exactly, but the boy he'd been: my model, my exemplar. If I gave away his secret, how could I ever object if someone gave away mine?

'No. I won't do that. We don't know he's guilty of anything.'

She shook her head, despairing of my foolishness. 'Then what do you suggest we do?'

I felt embarrassed that she'd jumped to the wrong conclusion. 'No, I can't involve you in this. You might be arrested too.'

'I'll take my chances. You've obviously got yourself into a muddle and I'm going to have to help you out of it.'

I thought of her shop and her children, her care of them as unconscious as breathing.

'You can't be a mother and go hunting for murderers, Rosie.'

'I don't see what one has to do with the other.'

'Yes, you do.'

She folded her arms, reminding me of a firework that has failed to go off and that one shouldn't approach. 'No, I don't. I'll tell you what. I'll absolve you of blame right now.' She crossed herself in the Catholic manner and flicked her hands as if tossing away any responsibility I might bear for her well-being. 'Some man killed that poor woman and orphaned her children, and he deserves to pay. It makes me so angry I could spit. Now, will you come to the shop tomorrow, so we can make a start? I'll give you a pie for your dinner, half price.'

'It's not safe, Rosie. It's not what I intended.'

We had almost gone right round St Paul's and were heading back the way we'd come. She quickened her pace.

'It's been my experience, Leo Stanhope, that you rarely have the slightest idea what you intend.'

As I reached the pharmacy, I could see a figure hovering outside it. I almost convinced myself it was a policeman come to take me into custody after all and was dumbfounded when I realised it was John Thackery, with his hat pulled low over his forehead, his coat collar up and a scarf wrapped around his neck, obscuring much of his face. Indeed, I only recognised him by his nervous stance, hopping from foot to foot.

'We need to talk, Leo,' he said, in an urgent tone. 'Not here, though.'

'The police are looking for you.'

I wasn't sure if I was warning him or just enjoying telling him.

'I know. That's what we need to talk about.'

We walked three hundred yards to the churchyard at St Anne's and sat side by side on a bench, much as we had all those years before. I swished my feet, imagining autumn leaves piling up around us. I used to love kicking them, watching them scatter and swirl, but hated having to sweep them up afterwards. I felt a brief surge of jealousy for my younger self, who had no idea what horrors were to come.

'They haven't found whoever killed Dora,' John said, staring at his feet. 'I don't believe they're trying, quite frankly. They care about my father's bloody mill, but not a human being.' His voice cracked, and he wiped his eyes. 'I miss her, you know, all the time. She was clever and funny, and she believed in a better world, in her own way. She held classes, you know, for the children from the club. All of them, no matter where they were from or how brief a time they were staying for. She said that they must receive an education, or they'll end up as labourers, living and dying at the whims of their masters. She saw the future, you see, more than any of us. I can't believe she's gone.'

I was certain his grief was real. I recognised it. Even a year on, I sometimes imagined I might see the one I had lost, that she would come through the door and embrace me, or I would turn and there she would be, blowing kisses from an upstairs window.

'Dora's wake is on Thursday at three o'clock,' John continued, wiping his eyes, leaving shiny smears on the backs of his gloves. 'It's at the club. You should go.'

'I only met her once.'

'You'll hear about what we're doing. Well, what *they're* doing. Edwin Cowdery will be giving a speech and he's worth listening to. I won't be able to attend, I'm afraid. I'm utterly distraught about it, but I've had to leave the club. Permanently.'

'Why?'

'The thing is, I was seen at the mill. Spotted, you know.' He put his hands over his eyes, shutting out the world. 'The police will arrest me if they find me. I have no choice but to vanish.'

'What do you mean, *vanish*?'

He gave me a thin smile. 'Well, not *me* exactly. But John Duport is no more. I'm sorry.'

I couldn't believe what I was hearing.

'But you're my alibi as much as I'm yours!'

'Yes, quite. That's why I'm here; to tell you to stick to the story, no matter what. You really don't have any choice as far as I can see. I mean, you can't change your mind now, can you?'

'I have other considerations now.'

He looked at me sharply. 'What considerations?'

I realised I had said too much. It would be best to keep the children out of this completely.

'It doesn't matter.'

'It certainly *does* matter.' He was sounding more and more like his father. 'If you don't stick to the story, you'll be arrested for conspiracy, at least. And I can expose the truth about you, remember. We both know that underneath that suit and hat, you're just a woman.'

I was damned if I was going to listen to him making threats after he'd abandoned me to the very lie he'd forced me to tell. Perhaps Rosie had been right after all. Why should I keep this man's secret?

'If you do that, I will inform the police about who *you* are too,' I replied, almost spitting out the words. 'John Thackery, whose childhood governess was murdered and who's been lying about his name. The son of the very man whose mill he was plotting to burn.'

'There's no need for that,' he snapped, as if I was the one being unreasonable. 'I just came here to advise you to stick to what we agreed. It'll be best for both of us.'

Of course, he would say that. He wanted me firmly attached to the lie. And then, when it suited him, he could recant his story to the police and I would look even more guilty. I was utterly trapped.

'Have you visited your father yet?' he asked.

'No.'

He sighed deeply, like a teacher whose worst pupil has failed a simple test.

'Why not?'

I didn't want to discuss my family with him. I didn't even want to think about them.

'That's not your business.'

'I don't understand.' He looked at me earnestly. 'I never did, to be honest. Why would you leave that way? You had everything: a good family, a kind father—'

'You don't know anything.'

'I know you didn't deserve him. You think the reverend was strict, and sometimes I'm sure he was angry with you, but you have no idea how fortunate you were. I would have given anything to be part of your family instead of mine. My own father was ...' He briefly took off his hat and ran his fingers through his hair. 'He was truly cruel. He never forgave me.'

A woman came out of the church, humming a hymn under her breath. She nodded to us and I nodded back, waiting for her to pass out of earshot before continuing.

'He never forgave you for what?'

John laughed briefly and looked away. 'For existing, Leo. For existing.'

Neither of us spoke for half a minute, and then a realisation crept over me. 'Is that why you felt entitled to use me as your alibi? Because you were envious, and resented me for leaving my family?'

He closed his eyes and bowed his head as if praying. 'It wasn't *personal*. The greater good, remember? You left a decent family who treated you well, and this was your chance to make up for that.'

'Like a penance?'

He stood and pushed his hat more firmly on to his head. 'You're choosing to be argumentative. You were always intelligent, but your father thought you were far too wilful, and it seems he was right.' He checked his watch, which was attached to his waistcoat on a chain. For the first time, I noticed how much better dressed he was than before, in a morning coat and ascot tie. 'Six o'clock. I have an appointment. Don't forget what I said, will you? Stick to the story and we'll both be fine.'

He strode away, leaving me in the churchyard, wondering what would happen next. I felt as if I was slipping into a hole, and everything I tried to grab hold of was withering in my hand.

I knew for certain I couldn't trust him. He would desert me and think it justified, even virtuous; a punishment for the sins of my past.

I decided I had to follow him.

He crossed over the road, pausing to light a cigar in the shelter of a doorway, and then turned right and left and right again, taking a zigzag route northwards. He seemed to be in no particular hurry, stopping twice to relight his cigar and once to stroke a dog the size of a small pony. As the streets became wealthier, the cadaverous tenements of Soho gave way to townhouses, and the rumble of industry was replaced by birdsong and wind in the trees. After a mile or so, he reached a strip of grass with houses set either side of it like rows of dentures. He kept his head down and became markedly more cautious, peering nervously from side to side and burying his chin in his scarf. In truth, he could hardly have looked more suspicious, though I was just as bad, and had to scuttle behind a tree when he glanced back over his shoulder.

As he reached the corner, I lost sight of him in the shadow of an imposing church with a rose window like a great eye watching me. I rushed forwards into a square consisting of a small park surrounded by houses, four storeys tall and three windows wide. Each had a porch with steps down to the pavement and a balcony from which one might wave to an adoring crowd.

I looked up at the road name: Gordon Square. It sounded familiar, and then it came to me. I pulled Sir Reginald's letter from my pocket and, sure enough, there it was in his letterhead. Sir Reginald's address was 34 Gordon Square.

John was going to his father's home.

Rosie had been right.

But still I couldn't see him.

I found number 34, and the door was closed. Surely, he hadn't been far enough ahead to enter the house without my noticing?

I checked the streets leading out of the square, but there was no sign of him. He must have gone into one of the other houses or perhaps the park.

It was well kept, divided by paths into lawns where, in warmer weather, nannies could push their perambulators in the shade of the trees, and dotted with benches where a gentleman might read a newspaper between engagements. Not today; it was empty, and a drizzle had drifted in, whispering through the branches of the trees and glistening on the iron railings.

I settled down opposite number 34, wedged between a tree and the fence, feeling oddly detached from the world. The rain was pattering on to the grass, but I was dry under the leaves. No one knew I was there. I could remain in this spot, I told myself, for as long as I wanted, and then I could go. I could escape to some other town, far away, and adopt a new name, just like John. I could become a laboratory assistant in Oxford or a shipping clerk in Southampton. I need never think of Dora Hannigan or her children again.

After half an hour or more, I was jolted to alertness by the rattle of a shiny blue carriage drawing up.

The door to number 34 opened and a lady came out. It took me a few seconds to recognise her. When I had last seen Mrs Thackery – or Lady Thackery as she was now – she had been brisk and bossy, thinking nothing of giving instructions to my mother on the proper way to decorate the church. Now, she was leaning on a stick and hobbling as if each step caused her pain.

Behind her was a young man of about fifteen.

I almost gasped.

He was the absolute image of Aiden.

14

THE YOUNG MAN WAS older, longer and broader than Aiden, but his face was the same triangular shape and his hair was the same too, jet-black and curly, his fringe falling around his eyes. This was Aiden in a few years' time, approaching manhood. Even the reserved way he attended his mother, with minimum eye contact, his attention parsed and rationed, was exactly like the boy I knew.

This must be John's little brother, a child I had given no thought to back in Enfield. Then, he had been a small, round object that fidgeted a lot during sermons. I couldn't even remember his name.

Lady Thackery called back into the house: 'Peter needs to go now.' Her voice was far stronger than her body. 'He mustn't be late.'

Sir Reginald came out on to the step and shook his son's hand, and I could tell the young man was pleased that his father was treating him as an adult and a gentleman. Sir Reginald didn't wait to see his son off but returned inside.

Peter took his mother's arm, and they walked down to the pavement together, their shoulders touching. She didn't concern herself with the rain or look up at the clouds, but concentrated on the slippery steps. I could see her hand shaking as she slid it down the metal handrail.

I huddled behind my tree, out of sight, remembering her keen gaze. Once, at the market in Enfield, she had spent five minutes scolding me for laughing when Jane had slipped on an uneven flagstone and fallen on her behind. But it *had* been funny, and I knew Jane would have laughed just as hard if our places were reversed. Afterwards, we linked arms all the way home. Jane may have been cross that I had laughed, but absolutely no one was permitted to rebuke me for it but her.

Peter said something to his mother, and she put a palm to his cheek and said, 'God bless you.' She fished into her bag and handed him what looked like a pound note. He shoved it into his pocket, and I could see him thanking her, and then he watched her shuffle back into the house while the driver opened the carriage door.

Peter climbed inside and off he went.

The likeness between him and Aiden surely confirmed why Sir Reginald was taking such an interest. He had employed Miss Hannigan as a governess when she was quite young, probably only fifteen or sixteen. It was hardly unusual for the master of the house to take advantage of a girl's innocence, and he must have resumed the arrangement when the family moved back to London, with inevitable results.

I was about to start for home when the carriage stopped again, having done no more than turn the corner. Peter jumped out, and I heard him bark an instruction: 'Take my things to the school, will you? Leave them with the porter and I'll pick them up later.' The driver seemed to be raising an objection and the boy shook his head impatiently. 'That's not necessary. I've made another arrangement.'

He strode off down the pavement, his long coat flapping behind him. I admired his impudence.

As it happened, he was going in the same direction as me, so I followed him. This seemed to be my day for surveillance.

He walked swiftly past Russell Square, stepping around a group of people sheltering under a shop awning. At Theobalds Road he crossed over, heading eastwards.

I was faced by a choice. I could persist in battling through the worsening rain after him, or I could go the other way, where a warm towel and lit fire would be waiting. Naturally, I shoved my hands into my pockets and kept him in view.

When he was almost at Holborn he turned left into a narrow alleyway, which was thankfully more sheltered. The buildings were mismatched and sagging but decorated with brass door knockers and colourful curtains in the windows. My guess was that, on drier days, those doors would be open and young women would be leaning out of them, entreating passing gentlemen to pay a visit. I wasn't judging Peter, not a bit, nor the young women either. I had no prejudice against people making a living.

But he didn't stop at any of the houses. He carried on, head down against the weather, turning right at the end. I hurried forwards, and the alleyway opened into a brightly lit yard. Peter had joined a queue of three or four people waiting at an entrance, where a man was taking payment. Above them, a sign was written in large, ornate letters: THE CALCUTTA MUSIC HALL.

When Peter reached the front of the queue, the doorman doffed his hat. 'Master Thackery, it's a pleasure to see you again.'

The lad lowered his face and glanced around the yard. 'Keep it to yourself, all right?'

The doorman nodded and gestured him through. I noticed he hadn't demanded any money.

I was next in line. 'One and three,' he said to me.

'That lad got in without paying.'

He affected not to have heard me and continued to hold out his hand.

There was really no reason to go inside, and yet I found myself keen to know what Peter Thackery was doing in a place like this. And it was still pouring with rain.

I paid the man, mourning the coins as I handed them over. My resources were growing thin indeed, especially as I would be docked today's wage. I dreaded asking Alfie if I could postpone paying my rent, not because he would decline, but because he wouldn't.

Inside, the tiny foyer was dark and smelled of rot. I pushed through a curtain and entered the theatre, if that was the right word. It was hardly bigger than a school classroom and the stage was formed from crates pushed together with planks laid on top. The audience was crammed in on wooden chairs around little tables, talking loudly among themselves, and the air was thick with smoke, swirling and mixing with the steam lifting from our damp skin and clothes. There was no one on the stage, but the lights were up, shining on a footstool in the shape of an elephant and a painted backdrop of a blue sky, sandy ground and a few vaguely Indian-looking buildings.

A fellow at the back was selling glasses of beer. I could ill-afford one, but I would be conspicuous without a drink, so I bought a half-pint and sat down. The atmosphere was so dense I could hardly see Peter, though he was only a few feet away.

I wondered if he was meeting someone else here, perhaps from his school, absconding as he was. But he didn't speak to anyone, just drank his beer and occasionally craned his neck to see past the men and women in front of him. He was quite out of place in this crowd. His coat alone must have cost five times as much as all of our clothes combined.

Everyone clapped as a fellow came on stage wearing an absurd red tailcoat. He swept his arm across the audience: 'Welcome, ladies and gentlemen, to the exotic and mystical city of Calcutta!' He put one foot on the elephant footstool and beckoned for us to come closer, although, of course, we couldn't. 'It's a land where anything can happen!'

The crowd chortled. They knew the routine. But Peter didn't join in; he just sat and watched impassively.

'Where the women are beautiful,' continued the master of ceremonies, 'and filled with eastern delights!' This didn't make much sense to me, but the rest of the crowd accepted it with an 'ooh!'

'When they sing their songs and dance their mystical dances,' he continued, 'they lure men and women alike into their arms. But beware.' He put his finger to his lips and dropped his voice. 'In the dead of night, in the heat of passion, as you writhe among them in …' He spread his arms and roared the next words: 'in ecstasy!' The crowd shrank back in mock horror and the pianist played a dramatic chord. I must say I found the whole thing preposterous. 'You may find yourself a victim of their sorcery, helpless and entranced!' He stared around the room, wide-eyed, and the audience gasped and clapped, exchanging delighted grins. This was what they had come for. 'And I certainly hope you'll be entranced this evening, ladies and gentlemen, because we have a *wonderful* show for you. First on the bill, please welcome Mr ...' he paused for what seemed like an age '... George ...' another, longer pause '... Galvin!'

He left the stage and a young fellow bounced on and started telling jokes. He was rather long-winded, and the audience quickly grew bored and began talking. He left hastily with a red face and was followed by a short, plump man who imitated the whistles and chirrups of birds, and then a woman carrying a bunch of flowers and singing about her lost love. She was moderately entertaining, and the audience sang along with the last verse.

All except for Peter, who glowered at his beer.

Next, a man with a dog came on stage, the latter arrayed as a soldier, complete with a glengarry cap through which his little ears were protruding. The animal could perform all manner of tricks, including saluting with his paw and marching in time with the music while we clapped along. It was quite marvellous, and the pair were applauded off rapturously. After that, an unassuming man in a grey suit entertained us in a remarkable way, holding a comical conversation with someone locked in a trunk by his side. Except when he opened it, there was nobody there! It was empty. He'd been producing both sides of the exchange himself, one normally and one without moving his lips. I was so absorbed that when I looked for Peter, his chair was vacant, and I panicked that I had lost him. But he returned with a beer in his hand, which he drank swiftly, placing the empty glass under his chair with the others.

Next, a jolly lady sang two very ribald songs, the second about a man who sought shelter in a barn and was seduced by the farmer's daughters, one by one, until, sapped and skittish, he attempted to escape, only to encounter the farmer's lusty wife. We joined in with the choruses, swaying from side to side and holding up our glasses.

All except for Peter.

After her, the master of ceremonies came back on. 'And now,' he announced, beaming, 'something more for your … intoxication and delectation! We are very lucky to have an artist with us tonight who is in demand right across London. The little charmer herself, please welcome, Miss … Vesta … Tilley!'

A youthful person sprang on to the stage dressed as a foppish gentleman in a top hat and cravat, except she was quite clearly a woman. I had read about such performers in the newspapers but had never before seen one. She stood at the front, illuminated by a single lamp, and I examined her face, her hips, the length of her shoes, and wondered if I looked anything like that.

She scratched her behind, and the audience rocked with laughter. She removed a handkerchief from her top pocket and calmly dabbed her forehead with it, and we watched, spellbound. There was none of the jovial give and take of the previous acts; she seemed perfectly self-contained and unaffected, as though she were standing under a streetlamp on Piccadilly.

All our eyes were on her and all our tongues were silent.

And then she started to sing.

Her voice was sweet and light, and she made little attempt to deepen it. In fact, despite her masculine clothes, she was curiously pretty. Her first song was an amusing ditty about herself as a young gentleman, drinking in the taverns, losing money at gambling and trying to seduce a serving girl. At this point she wiggled her hips, apparently taking on the personae of both the young man and his belle at the same time. As she reached the final note, the audience cheered, many of them standing, but she barely acknowledged them, instead gazing downwards, calm and still. Only when there was complete quiet, not a chink of a glass nor a murmur of a conversation, would she start again, this time singing about her lost darling, who possessed such beauty and grace she could never love another.

No, I thought, I am nothing like her. She is singular and deft, holding the gaze of an entire audience, who were mostly drunk by this time, using only a gesture or a heartsick pause. Those clothes were part of her pretence, as inauthentic as the beer bottle she was holding.

As she left the stage, we stood as one, clapping wildly.

I hadn't been taking any notice of Peter, so distracted had I been by Miss Tilley, but he leapt to his feet as well, waving and cheering, calling out for another song. He even started booing when the master of ceremonies came back on to the stage.

'Thank you, ladies and gentlemen!' the man bellowed, as if it was him we were applauding.

Peter sighed deeply, still gazing at the side door through which the girl had left.

Now I knew the truth; the poor clod was in love.

I was about to leave when the next act came on, a man wearing a vast pink dress and bonnet, carrying a live lamb in his arms. He didn't have quite the charisma of Miss Tilley, but he made up for it in volume and scale.

He sang a song about how his poor, innocent sheep had been stolen away in the night by a fierce creature with strong thighs, a deep voice and such muscular intent that, no matter how desperately he protested, he hadn't been able to repel it. Apparently, this metaphor was too subtle for many of the audience, and they became restless. The fellow in front of me called out, 'The sheep's right there, you bunter!' and flicked the dregs of his drink at the stage.

A few people laughed. The shepherdess stopped singing and carefully put down the lamb. The wag was still enjoying the joke with his friends and didn't see the shepherdess climb down, picking his way with a daintiness worthy of the best-brought-up lady. The wag was therefore surprised to find, as he turned back, a fist travelling with some force into his face, and he would have landed in my lap if I hadn't jumped out of the way. As it was, he sprawled at my feet in a puddle of beer, some of which had been mine, with blood already spreading from his nose across his cheek.

His friends pulled him back on to his feet but wisely made no attempt to exact retribution from the shepherdess, such was the latter's imposing height and girth, made somehow more impressive by the dignity with which he straightened his bonnet and fixed the lace around his neckline. He proceeded back to the stage, accompanied by a great roar from the rest of the audience, who were thereafter fully attentive to his act.

Peter drained his glass and stood up unsteadily, edging towards the door, ignoring the calls that he and his flashy hat should get out of the way and stop spoiling the view of decent folks who'd paid for their ticket the same as him; though, of course, he hadn't paid, which I still found curious. I was about to follow him out, when I froze.

The shepherdess had started his song again, trilling about the rampant creature he'd been unable to deny. He extended a long, high note, and shrank back in an imitation of demure fear, his hands shielding his face as the creature itself came on to the stage, growling, stamping and pawing the air, glaring at the audience with eyes that might have been terrifying, had they not been sewn on.

The audience cheered and whooped, but I didn't. I sat there with my mouth open.

The creature was a lion.

15

THE LION AND THE shepherdess danced around the stage. The shepherdess protected her modesty while the lion thrust and swaggered, at one point twirling his tail in his paw and whipping her behind with it. Finally, she gave in, lying back on the stage, legs spread, while the audience, now all on their feet, screamed their encouragement.

I'd seen enough and blundered out through the foyer, almost falling into the yard. I gulped in cold air and lifted my face to the rain.

Was it possible that Ciara had seen a man in a lion suit? It seemed absurd, and yet there he was, with gloves for paws and a mane made of wool, his real eyes peeping through the lion's mouth. She had said the creature had been standing on its hind legs. That answer made more sense than an actual lion loose in London.

At the main road, I heard a low groan from under a jerry-shop awning. Someone was curled up in the doorway, and I realised it was Peter Thackery. As far as I could tell, he was fast asleep, hugging his shiny top hat. He wouldn't stay that way. The first person who came past with ill intent would have that hat, and his wallet, jacket, shoes and anything else that could be sold for more than a farthing. He would be left naked or, quite possibly, dragged off somewhere and stuck with a knife.

I couldn't abandon him.

I prodded him with my foot, and he stirred, opening his eyes.

'Oh,' he said, and was sick on the pavement.

'Are you all right?'

He raised himself on to all fours, gagging again, this time without production. When he seemed to be finished, I pulled him upright, and he sagged against the wall, sweating and blinking.

'I think I've had too much to drink,' he slurred. 'I was at the music hall.' He thumbed back towards the alleyway. 'There's a girl there I want to—'

'Yes, I'm sure. But you should get home now, don't you think?'

He shook his head and waggled a finger at me. 'Not home.'

'Well, you can't stay here. You'll be robbed for certain.'

'Are *you* going to rob me?'

He looked quite forlorn and, more than ever, I was reminded of Aiden. It was impossible to believe they weren't brothers. Or half-brothers.

'No. Where do you need to go?'

'School. I should be there now, but …'

He bent down and was sick again. At least it might sober him up, I thought.

'Where is your school?'

He spat on to the pavement. 'Harrow.'

'Oh, good grief.'

Harrow was miles from here, much farther than any cab would take him.

'Train,' he mumbled. 'From the station. That's how I go there. By train.'

I remembered that the Metropolitan Railway had recently been extended to the north-west of London, branching into the suburbs like a shoot of wisteria.

He managed to stay standing while I hailed a cab and virtually pushed him inside. He fell along the seat, his eyes closed. I sighed and climbed in behind him.

'Baker Street Station,' I called up to the driver.

We set off, joggling over the cobbles.

Peter blinked a couple of times and half opened his eyes. 'Peter Thackery,' he said, pronouncing each syllable with studious care. 'Nice to meet you.'

'Leo Stanhope. I noticed you at the music hall.'

'Ah!' He sat straighter. 'You saw her then. Miss Vesta Tilley. Isn't she a marvel?'

'Yes, she is. Have you seen her before?'

'Many times. Many, many times. I want to dance with her. I love dancing, you know.'

'Do you indeed?' He was looking a little pale again, so I pulled down the window on his side. 'If you're going to vomit again, do it there.'

'And then I intend to marry her.'

'Oh, I see. Does she know?'

He swallowed and sat still, allowing the cool breeze to blow on his face. 'I haven't spoken to her yet.'

'You mean you haven't spoken to her about marriage, or you haven't spoken to her at all?'

He took a deep breath and closed the window. 'At all.'

Youthful love, I thought, is like a leap from a great height. You tumble and spin in joyous descent, but the end is always the same.

'You're a young gentleman,' I said, trying to be kind. 'Your father may not be happy with such a match.'

'Do you know him?' He adopted a mockingly pompous voice, reminding me of a character in a musical play I'd once seen half of, who had wanted to 'rule the Queen's Navee'. 'He's Sir Reginald Thackery, the most famous industrialist.'

'I've met him, very briefly. He didn't seem like an indulgent man.'

'I don't care. If necessary, I shall join Miss Tilley on the stage, and we'll travel the land playing to audiences who appreciate our art and our love.' He attempted to put his hat on, which wasn't possible in the confines of the cab. 'Father can go to hell. If he won't let me marry her, he's an ass.' He was unwittingly concurring with John's opinion of their father. 'Worse than an ass. He's the shit of an ass. He's a maggot in the shit of an ass. No, he's the shit of a maggot in the—'

'All right, I understand.' We were almost at the station. 'Do you know which train you need?'

'It's the last stop on the line and I can walk at the other end. It's not far.' He grinned amiably, if rather lopsidedly. 'I just have to get into the school without them noticing. Frightfully strict.'

I found myself liking this young man, and not only because he so closely resembled Aiden. He seemed to take each minute as it came, with a sort of casual disregard. I envied him his recklessness.

We drew to a halt and he stumbled out, blinking. 'You don't think Father … I mean, if I married Miss Tilley … you don't think he'd cut me off, do you?'

I couldn't tell whether he was truly serious about all this. Did he really believe he might marry a music-hall singer, or was he just playing at believing it? I looked into his eyes, searching for something truthful in them. They were watery and red, and impossible to read.

'Does that matter? If you marry her, you can dance with her every night. Do you truly need money, if you have love?'

He stood still for a few seconds, gripping on to the wheel arch, and then handed his pound note to the driver. 'Take this gentleman wherever he wants to go,' he said. 'Anywhere at all. Damn fine chap.'

'Little Pulteney Street, please,' I told the driver, as Peter reached in through the window to shake my hand.

'You're a bloody good Samaritan, if you ask me,' he said.

I worked the following day. My foreman said he was glad I had recovered from my fever, though I still looked unhealthy to him. I didn't find this surprising; I felt exhausted.

When my shift ended, I hurried out into the dusk. I was looking forward to telling Rosie what I'd learned.

By the time I reached her shop, my stomach was starting to rumble in anticipation. She produced a beautiful pie from under the counter, russet and gold with a tiny touch of black where the gravy had bubbled up through the crust. It was still warm to the touch.

'Pigeon and potato,' she said. 'That'll be sixpence.'

'I thought you said it'd be half price?'

'This one's normally a shilling.'

'Every other pie in the place is sixpence.'

She shrugged. 'If you don't want it, give it back.'

I took the pie.

'Are you sure you want to come with me, Rosie?'

She looked down, buttoning her coat, and when she looked up again, she wouldn't meet my eye.

'Don't be silly.'

We left the shop as evening was descending, shrouding the streets in cobweb-white mist. I explained, through mouthfuls, about the man in a lion costume, John's disappearance and Peter's love for a singer, pausing occasionally to tell Rosie that she truly was the best pie-maker in London.

'There must be more than one lion costume in the city,' she said. 'There are dozens of theatres. It could be a coincidence.'

'It could,' I agreed. 'That's why we're going to the music hall. We need to find out for certain.'

When we got to the alley, the music hall hadn't yet opened for business. We waited outside in the patch of light coming from an upstairs window, where two amiable young women with deeply scooped necklines and bare arms were watching us.

After a few minutes, a man arrived in a cloak and top hat. It took me a moment to realise he was the master of ceremonies. He'd been so dramatic, so larger than life, on the stage, it was peculiar to see him here, in this dull alley. He was shorter than me and, close up, his cloak was fraying, and his tailcoat was old and tatty.

He doffed his hat to us and unlocked the door. As it swung closed behind him, Rosie darted forwards and caught it.

'You see?' she said. 'I told you we were better at this together.'

She slipped inside, so I was spared having to admit she was right. The truth was, she thought of things I didn't and was able to see the world in a different way; a bull-headed, infuriating way, to be sure, but it did sometimes yield results.

There was a narrow hallway and stairs leading up, presumably to apartments above. Ahead of us was an open door. A man came through it, so stooped that his back was higher than his neck. He wasn't wearing a shirt or undershirt, and his chest was matted with thick white hair, like a goat.

'Auditions were this afternoon,' he said.

'Oh no, we're not—'

But Rosie interrupted me. 'Of course. We're very sorry. We were delayed. Is there someone in charge we could speak to about a future date?'

'We've got all we need. What's your act?'

We exchanged a glance.

'Singing,' I said.

'Everyone's a bloody singer. Nothing for you here.'

'This is different,' I insisted. 'She dresses as a man. I'm her manager.'

Rosie turned and glared at me, but it did the trick. The old fellow looked us up and down, nodding thoughtfully, his gaze resting longest on Rosie. 'You might do, darling. Ladygents are very popular these days.' He waved a hand in my direction, without removing his eyes from Rosie's chest. 'Ask for Mr Black. You can't miss 'im.'

The corridor was quiet. A couple of doors were open, one revealing a girl lying across an armchair, one foot on the floor and the other propped up on a cushion, exposing the white flesh of her calf. She looked up at us briefly and went back to inspecting her fingernails.

The last door bore the letters 'P. B.' and was closed. I knocked quietly.

Inside, a voice called: 'Come in.'

A large man was sitting at a desk with his back to us, occupying his chair like a loaf of bread overflowing its tin. On his desk was a bottle of Vin Mariani, half full, and he took a swig directly from it.

'Mr Black?'

'Take a seat,' he said.

His desk was covered with costumes and props: a fan, a lamp, some wooden owls and a china doll that made me shudder. Underneath, the lamb was fast asleep. Behind us, a metal pole had been lodged horizontally between the picture rails, and costumes were hanging from it: a vast frock, an apron and a light brown coat with a fur collar.

Rosie tugged on my sleeve and pointed.

She was right; what I had taken for a coat was actually the lion costume.

Mr Black still had his back to us, so I quietly spun the costume on its hanger. The head was a sort of hood, stuffed in the cheeks, pinched along either side of the nose and folded into little circles for ears. The stitching was poor and oft-repaired, and the material was scuffed and threadbare.

Mr Black turned, taking a deep breath that seemed to flow through his whole body. I thought I recognised him but couldn't think from where.

'Nice to meet you,' he said, his hand enveloping my own. 'Please tell me you're not singers.'

Rosie gave me a severe look and a brisk shake of the head, indicating that under no circumstances was I to maintain the pretence that she would perform as a male impersonator.

'I'm Mr Stanhope, and this is Mrs Flowers,' I said. 'We have some questions about a murder. The killer may have worn a lion costume like this one.'

Rosie shifted in her chair and pursed her lips, apparently of the view that I had been too blunt, as usual.

Black looked from me to Rosie and back again. 'Murdered? Are you being serious or is this part of your act?'

'There's no act,' said Rosie. 'We just want to ask you some questions, that's all. We won't take up much of your time.'

Black sighed and glanced at the clock on his mantel-piece. 'Come with me,' he said.

He took us through a further door and into the theatre itself, which was dark but for a single lamp hanging over the stage. Close up, the trailing vines and painted backdrop were ill-made and old, covered with dust. He perched on the edge of the stage and we sat opposite him in chairs as if we were his audience.

'I hate that office,' he muttered. 'Too hot with the fire lit, but it's the only one we have, so the others insist. Their poor little toes get cold.' His features fitted his face, large and fulsome, but he had sad, chestnut eyes, like a dog too old to chase rats. 'Stanhope, did you say? I've heard your name before.'

'When?'

He took a pull on his cigarette, blowing smoke into the wings of the stage, watching it fade in the shadows. 'Let's get to know each other before we divulge all our mysteries, shall we? You were here yesterday.'

'Yes,' I replied, amazed that he could remember one man among so many.

'I have a gift for faces.' He examined a bandage on his right hand, clenching and unclenching his fist. 'You were sitting behind that cock, weren't you? He got what was coming to him.'

That was why I recognised Black. It was him under the make-up, dress and petticoats.

'You're the shepherdess!' I exclaimed.

He bowed his head. 'Peregrine Black, singer and impresario. And a painter too, once in a while.'

He indicated the walls of the theatre, which were hung with large, gilt-framed pictures. The nearest was of a couple gazing into each other's eyes, and the next was of a singer, her arm extended as she reached for a high note. They were a little florid for my taste, but he had a gift, no doubt.

'You're very talented,' said Rosie, with what sounded like genuine admiration. 'Is this your establishment?'

His mouth twitched into a smile. 'No, I'm just the manager. An employee. Who was murdered?'

'A woman named Dora Hannigan.'

'Ah, yes, of course.'

I sat forwards in my chair. 'Have you heard of her?'

'I read the newspapers. It sounded awful.'

'What wasn't publicised was that her young daughter saw it happen. She said the killer was a man in a lion costume.'

'Well, that's even more awful.' He tapped his cigarette on the edge of a bowl. 'No child should see something like that.'

'Who wears that costume on stage? I saw it yesterday evening.'

He considered my question, rubbing his shoulder, which seemed to be causing him pain. 'It varies. Last night it was Finlay, who does the birdcalls as well. We were short and there was no one else. He hates doing it, but those wretched birdcalls.' He rolled his eyes. 'If he wasn't willing to be the lion as well, I wouldn't book him; I'd rather have another intermission. I doubt he's a murderer, though, unless you count boring the audience to death.'

'Do other people wear it sometimes?'

He shrugged. 'Everything depends on the running order. The role's not difficult. All you have to do is look fierce and steal my innocence.'

Rosie didn't blanch. 'And it's never kept anywhere but here? It's never laundered, for example?'

He sighed, shaking his head. 'Never. We probably should, as it stinks. Finlay sweats like a ham. We used to have a lovely one with proper claws and a horsehair mane. Very realistic.'

'What happened to it?' I asked.

'Stolen, more's the pity. You really can't trust performers.'

'When was that?' I felt as if I was within touching distance of the truth.

He pondered, smoke drifting out of his nose. His cigarette was sweet, giving the auditorium a languid, other-worldly air.

'It must've been the twenty-third of last month. I remember because the music hall was closed. The owner had some of his friends over and wanted them entertained at his house. The lighting was terrible and there was nowhere to get ready. It takes time and effort for me to become Miss Amaryllis, but nobody cares. They think it's easy to turn into somebody else.'

'Who is the owner? And who played the lion that evening, when the other costume was stolen?'

He examined my face, sensing my keenness. I could feel his mind turning.

'Sir Reginald Thackery owns our little enterprise,' he said. 'He bought it last year, more's the pity.'

I admit I was surprised. Sir Reginald didn't seem the type to own a place like this; he was far too priggish. But now I thought about it, Peter Thackery had been able to swan in without paying. The doorman had greeted him by name.

'I didn't realise Sir Reginald was interested in the music hall,' I said slowly.

Black laughed. 'Hardly.'

'Then why?'

'To remake the world as he wishes it to be, Mr Stanhope.'

'I don't understand.'

Black massaged his shoulder again, wincing a little. He peeled back his shirt at the collar, revealing pale, puffy flesh and a vivid red stripe. It reminded me of the grazes under my armpits where my cilice rubbed against my skin. I realised what had caused it: the heavy brassiere he wore on stage.

He blew another lungful of smoke into the air. I had seen him lay out a man with one punch, and yet he held his cigarette with the delicacy of a child about to release a butterfly.

'The masses go to church on Sundays and work every other day of the week, so where are they to enjoy a little frivolity, Mr Stanhope? At the music hall, of course. Have a few drinks, a singalong and a laugh at the upper classes and their careless ways.' He exhaled another puff of smoke. It was making me feel drowsy and I wondered what was in it. 'Sir Reginald doesn't like that sort of thing. It doesn't show due respect to people like himself.'

'You mean he bought the music hall to make sure there were no acts that criticised the upper classes? That seems rather extreme, wouldn't you say?'

Black blinked languidly, taking his time. 'Men like him control the churches and the factories, so why not the music halls as well? Keeps everyone in line. You saw my act? That's what he wants more of. Brawny lions and bird-calls, and nothing that'll get the hoi polloi too riled up.'

'What about the young lady dressed as a man?' I asked. 'Miss Tilley. She was mocking the upper classes, surely.'

'That was because Peter Thackery likes her. He's Sir Reggie's other son. Spoony as a turtle dove.'

'Why do you say Sir Reginald's *other* son? Do you know John Thackery?'

A look crossed his face that I couldn't quite identify: gentle and yet mournful at the same time.

'Of course. His father owns the place.'

A suspicion started to form in my mind.

'That's how you knew my name. John told you.'

'Very good, Mr Stanhope.' He inclined his head in a half-bow.

The suspicion moved almost physically from my mind to my stomach, where it hardened like clay in an oven.

'You've been very open with us, Mr Black. Are you not worried we'll pass on your views to Sir Reginald?'

He snuffed out his cigarette and lit another, taking his time.

'Well, firstly, he already knows what I think. I've never been shy with my opinions, and as soon as he can find someone else to run this place I'll be out on my arse. And secondly, I don't think you will, *Mr* Stanhope.'

He placed a slight emphasis on the 'Mr', and my suspicion was confirmed. John Thackery had told him about me.

One more person knew my secret.

One more person might use that secret against me.

16

THERE WAS A KNOCK at the door, and a young woman entered, carrying a baby wrapped up in a blue shawl. She stopped and bobbed her head as one accustomed to servility.

'Sorry,' she said to Black. 'I'll come back later.'

'No, not at all.' He turned to us. 'This is Mr Stanhope and Mrs … Flowers, wasn't it? This is my wife, Miranda.'

She shook our hands. 'You're blessed with such a pretty name, Mrs Flowers. Not that I mind being a Black, of course.'

She was rather sweet, I thought, with a hamsterish face and milky smell. She was much younger than her husband; probably not yet twenty. I wondered what she thought of him appearing on stage every night dressed as a shepherdess.

She handed him a purse. 'For the bar float,' she said. 'Mr Johnson's counted it.'

'Thank you.'

He kissed her on the forehead and touched the cheek of the baby, who jerked awake, blinked twice and flopped on to its mother's shoulder again.

After they had gone, Black lay back on the stage, so all we could see were his legs, dangling down.

'How long have you been doing this, Mr Black?' I asked.

'Twenty years, nearly. I started out as a singer with a top hat and cane but couldn't make a living at it. They always stuck me on first or after the intermission when everyone's still at the bar. One day someone didn't show up, so I took his place as a maiden in love, whose beau has gone off to war. Then I was a lusty lady for a while, with a limp husband, and after that a duchess, seduced by her charming coachman. We had a prop carriage for that one and wheeled it across the stage on ropes. The audience *loved* it. There were two of us in those days, but he died. A little too fond of his opium. So, I was alone again, and became Miss Amaryllis.' He used his shepherdess voice: 'Terrified of the powerful lion and what he might do to my helpless lambs.'

'Do you prefer acting as a woman? On stage, I mean.'

I could feel Rosie watching me out of the corner of her eye. I had strayed from what we came to find out, but I needed to know. What motivated this huge man to perform every night as he did? He appeared almost to despise it.

'I don't act as a woman, Mr Stanhope,' he said. 'If I did that, the audience would walk out straight away. They'd want their money back, and probably complain to the police. Reality is a bit too sharp for them. Reality isn't *funny*.' He sat up and rapped on the wood with his knuckles. 'The joke is that I'm a man who's *pretending* to be a woman, and not doing it very well. That's what makes them giggle.'

He and Miss Tilley were the same, in a way, using the incongruity of their gender and their clothing to raise a laugh. What meant life and death to me was mere charade to them.

'What else can you tell us, Mr Black?' asked Rosie.

He paused, and I caught that look again; as though he'd been carrying a great burden and was almost ready to put it down.

'John and I sometimes meet.' He glanced towards the door his wife had left through. 'In private, you understand. I want to paint him. His portrait.'

'And have you?'

'Not yet. I've done some sketches, that's all. He's a little reluctant.'

'Why?'

He sighed and indicated the paintings hung on the walls. 'Those are just for decoration, to add to the *atmosphere*. I don't bring my real work to this place to be swilled with ale. You see ...' he breathed out smoke through his nose, making us wait for the punchline like the stage performer he was '... I mostly do nudes.'

'You want to paint John Thackery ... *in the nude?*'

I could feel Rosie tense beside me, and I supposed I must have reacted as well. I admit I was a little shocked. I had seen nude paintings and sculptures before, of course, but they always seemed to belong to another world, long ago and far away.

'Oh, Mr Stanhope, Mrs Flowers, there's no need to be so indignant. It's *art*. George Frederick Watts does it, so why shouldn't I?' He stared wistfully at his pictures on the wall and sniffed, apparently finding them deficient. 'John and I were supposed to meet here after yesterday's performance, but he didn't turn up. It's not like him. He seems to have disappeared, like my bloody sheep.' He smiled, his anxiety hidden beneath the feeble joke rather as a mountain is hidden beneath a scattering of snow.

'Is it unusual for him to miss an appointment?' asked Rosie.

'Well, you know he plays at politics at that vile little club on Rose Street? He uses a false name for some reason, as if anyone cares who anyone else used to be.'

He shuddered, and I thought perhaps he'd remembered that Leo Stanhope wasn't the name I was born with. But then I caught something else in his expression and wondered whether his parents had truly christened him Peregrine and whether their surname had been Black. No, I thought, you are a construction of your own making. You were someone else, once upon a time.

'What of it?' I asked.

'I'm worried they found out he's a Thackery and took *revenge*.' Despite his obvious concern, he couldn't resist rolling the 'r'.

'I saw him yesterday afternoon,' I said. 'He seemed perfectly healthy then.'

I didn't mention that I'd followed John, nor that I'd lost him near his father's house.

Black sighed deeply, his concern assuaged a little.

'If you see him again, tell him to visit me as soon as he can,' he said. 'Or at least send me a note. I worry terribly when I don't hear anything.'

'Of course,' I said. 'But you still haven't told us who played the lion that night at Sir Reginald's house or how the costume was stolen.'

'No one played the lion that night. Sir Reginald told us it was too *risqué* for his important chums. Their wives would be *shocked*, apparently. As if they didn't get up to the same things in the bedroom. Not with their husbands, obviously.' He smiled, but it was thin and reflexive, not reaching his eyes. 'When we got back here, the lion costume was nowhere to be seen, so we've had to go back to using that old thing. And we're two guineas out of pocket too.'

———

Rosie and I made our way out of the alley and into the slums around Farringdon, where the local populace was gathering in doorways or sitting on the pavement, many of them drunk already. Most likely they had no choice but to be outside while their beds were occupied by other people, sharing the rent. No more than a mile from this spot, among the blossoming trees of Mayfair, fat aristocrats were staggering from their carriages and into their homes, ready for a nap before supper. Who could blame men without wages for wanting a little revolution?

We had reached Chancery Lane before either of us spoke.

'There's plenty Mr Black's not telling us, I daresay,' Rosie said. 'Could it have been him?'

'Certainly, although it could also be anyone in the company or the Thackery household, not to mention anyone else who might've crept in. That is even assuming the murderer was wearing a lion suit, which is a ridiculous notion. We only have a six-year-old's word for it.'

'You're not inclined to narrow the field just yet then?'

I caught an amused tone in her voice. I supposed I had sounded rather curmudgeonly.

'Dora Hannigan was buried at the club,' I said, in a gentler tone. 'There must be a reason for that. It's not a coincidence. I think we have to go back there.'

'She lived in the club, though, and taught their children to read and write. She was one of their own. If one of them did something to her then … well, I don't know. It would be a true evil, is what I'm saying.'

Rosie had the strongest sense of justice of anyone I knew; if someone had done a bad thing, she wanted them to pay for it, no matter who they were.

'The wake is tomorrow afternoon,' I said. 'Will you meet me at three o'clock at the pharmacy? There's something I have to do first.'

'What is it?' She peered at me from under her hat, her green eyes glinting in the lamplight. 'You look … scared, is it? What's wrong, Leo?'

'No, not scared. I have to visit someone tomorrow and I'm not looking forward to it, that's all.'

I didn't tell her it was my father I would be visiting, to fulfil my half of the deal with Jane.

As Rosie and I parted, I found I didn't know what to say to her. I couldn't find the right words. A simple cheerio would have sufficed, but instead we shuffled about like two fools, nodding and smiling, until our own ridiculousness overwhelmed us and we walked away in opposite directions. Apparently, we were able to search for a killer together, but not manage the simplest of farewells.

I wasn't far from Jacob's home on Shoe Lane. Despite his cantankerous nature, he often had a perspective on things I hadn't previously considered. Plus, I knew I would miss chess tomorrow for Dora Hannigan's wake, and he would be miserable without me there. He had no patience with the other members of the club and was unbearable if he had to play one of them, growing restless when they moved too quickly, or too slowly, or wore a scarf he found distracting.

It was Lilya who opened the door, with her little dog bustling around her feet.

'Hello, Lilya,' I said.

'Leo.'

She put out a hand, which I took. 'Why does he always make you come downstairs?' I asked. 'You might trip and fall. He should come down.'

She laughed and smoothed her greying hair. 'He makes me do nothing. I can't go out no more, but I can still answer my own door.'

Her face was round and gentle, and her eyes were wise, despite being almost blind. She could tell a bright light from darkness, and claimed she could still see her own hands, although I sometimes wondered if her mind was convincing her that she could discern what she could not. But still, she was able to navigate their home by the tips of her fingers, feeling her way like a cat uses its whiskers, and she could cook as well as ever, and play her guitar. It was one of my great pleasures, to watch her tune it, plucking a note and turning the little screw, her failing eyes closed and her mouth twitching as though the vibration of the string was travelling all the way through her.

'We ate our supper,' she said, 'but I made bread if you want some. Good for the bones.'

I was never certain whether she knew what I was under these clothes. Even if Jacob hadn't told her, she must have felt the narrowness of my shoulders and the scantiness of my wrists. Yet she always treated me as the young man I was.

She led me upstairs, still talking. 'We have cold mutton too, or some cheese maybe, if that crosspatch, my husband, hasn't eaten it all. He thieves it like a greedy old mouse and thinks I don't know.'

Jacob stood up as I reached their little parlour. 'Leo!'

He was already in his dressing gown and pyjamas, but his eyes were crisp and keen under his overflowing eyebrows. His daughter, Millicent, was curled up in the other armchair, knitting what looked like a scarf. She was about Aiden's age and strongly favoured her mother, thank God, with large round eyes and a shrewd expression. She gathered up her yarn and needles as I came in.

'Wait, Milli,' instructed Jacob.

She smiled and placed a kiss on his cheek before scampering away.

Lilya brought through two glasses and a bottle of clear liquid. I had drunk the vicious stuff before, but had no idea what it was called, or even if it had a name. It had been brewed by Jacob's late brother and, when I last looked, there were a dozen or so bottles of it left in the cupboard under the stairs. One day soon, the last of it would be gone, and his brother with it.

I wondered what had released this flood of melancholy. Surely it couldn't be the prospect of seeing my father?

'What is it, Leo?' asked Jacob, once we were alone.

I told him about Aiden and Ciara, and the lad, Peter Thackery.

'Aiden and Peter look similar,' I said, sipping from my glass in a manner Jacob disdained. 'More than similar. They're half-brothers, I'm certain of it.'

Jacob shrugged and threw his own drink down his throat, immediately pouring himself another. 'Nothing surprising there. A wealthy man and a young governess. It's a common story.'

'But Aiden's ten years old.' I did the calculation. 'If Sir Reginald is Aiden's father, it must have happened *after* Dora Hannigan left his employ. She wasn't with them when they lived in Enfield.'

Jacob swilled his glass, grinning as he did when he thought I was being naïve. He saw himself as a man of the world.

'It's simple. He sleeps with the governess, but his wife doesn't like it. So, he dismisses the girl and they carry on. She's his mistress. He probably found a couple of nice rooms in London for them to meet in.'

'And then she became pregnant.'

'Exactly. And fat, tired and ill-tempered.' He rolled his eyes. 'No one wants a mistress who's the same as their wife.'

'So, Sir Reginald killed Miss Hannigan to make sure of her silence?'

If that was true, then Aiden and Ciara were the motive for their mother's murder. What a terrible responsibility for them to carry.

Jacob snorted. 'Over some by-blows with a servant ten years ago? More likely she knew something else about him. Something he didn't want anyone to find out.'

'Blackmail, you think?'

'Why not?'

I thought about the two hundred and four pounds I'd found in her room. There was no need to tell Jacob about it. Not from any lack of trust in him – he had no interest in money – but because it was a threat to the children. The fewer people who knew about it, the better.

'Sir Reginald isn't the only suspect. I met some unsavoury people at the club on Rose Street.'

Jacob sat forwards, always attentive to new things he could castigate. 'Tell me more about this *club*?'

'They're radicals and socialists. Believers in the rights of the common man.'

He laughed. 'Have they met the common man?'

'It's more than just talk. They planned to burn down Sir Reginald's mill.'

'Shame they didn't succeed.'

I was amazed at his hypocrisy. 'You despised them a minute ago, and now you're supporting their cause?'

He grinned, his eyes glinting. 'Once, I would have. Oh yes, in the Ruthenian revolution I was quite the rebel!'

'When was that?'

He shrugged away my question. 'You don't want to know. No one cares any more. It was a long time ago in a different country. I was young and stupid, filled with passion. Now I'm old and my leg hurts.' He stretched it out, grimacing with the pain. 'Even so, one less mill in the world wouldn't bother me. And the stupid arses might set fire to themselves as well, so everybody wins.'

'They might have had a reason to murder Miss Hannigan. Her body was found in the courtyard of the club.'

He jabbed a finger at me. 'You must be careful, Leo. Blackmail and arson, these are not your concerns. Why not lead a quiet life and let the police catch the criminals for once?'

'Because ... because I'm curious. Because the police are too busy condemning the radicals to see anything else. Because those children deserve to know why their mother was killed, and who did it.'

I realised I was furious, not with Jacob but with the world. Someone had snuffed out Dora Hannigan's life like a candle and was living their own as if she and her children didn't matter a jot. It was *wrong*. It was *iniquitous*. I couldn't fix it, but I could make sure that whoever it was faced justice.

I realised that I hadn't thought that way for a long time. I'd forgotten how it felt.

I was yawning by the time I got back to the pharmacy, though it wasn't yet nine o'clock. I ducked down the passageway that led to the back of the house. My mind was elsewhere, on Peregrine Black and whether he could be trusted, and I wasn't thinking about what I was doing. I didn't have to. I'd walked this passage daily for three years, and I knew every crack in the brickwork and slippery stone underfoot. I thought little of it when I heard a crunch behind me; probably one of the neighbours heading to their own back yard or the soil men arriving early to perform their filthy chore.

'Mr Stanhope, is it?'

I turned, and a figure was silhouetted in the passage entrance. He was tall and broad, but I couldn't see any of his features. He had a scarf wrapped around his face and a bowler hat pulled low over his forehead.

'I'm looking for two children.' He spoke without intonation; not a question or a threat, just a statement of fact.

'Who are you?'

I was trying to sound brave but was all too aware that no one would be able to see what happened in this gloomy passageway, or hear my shouts, muffled as they would be by the close walls and narrow entrance.

'Where are they, Mr Stanhope?'

'I don't know.'

'You put them in an orphanage. I want to know which one.'

Of course, I hadn't, but I wouldn't give this man my sister's address. I would rather be beaten black and blue.

'I don't know where they are.'

'Yes, you do.'

He took a step towards me, and I backed up, feeling the corner of the wall behind me with my hand, making a frantic calculation; could I make it to the pharmacy before he caught me? Probably not. I would need to negotiate both the ninety-degree turn and the back gate into the yard.

'Tell me what I want to know,' he said, as if he was asking the price of apples in a grocery. 'Then I'll be gone.'

I was about to sprint for the back gate and to hell with the consequences, when I saw something behind him, and heard a voice.

'Mr Stanhope? Is that you? Is everything all right?'

'Go away, Constance,' I called out to her. 'Quickly now.'

The man turned, and even in the dimness I could see what he was thinking: grab her so I would be forced to answer his question.

That could not happen.

As he took a step towards her, I launched myself at him, hugging him around the neck as if I wanted a piggyback.

'Go, Constance! Run!'

She fled, and the man reversed hard into the wall, knocking all the wind out of me. I tried to cling on, but he did it again, slamming the back of my head against the bricks. I fell to the ground and tried to crawl away, but he grabbed my collar, twisting it in his fist, throttling me against the top button of my shirt. His breath was on my neck. Even in that moment, I thought: He isn't panting. He isn't excited or panicked or overcome with rage. He's fully in control. I'd been threatened before by angry men, avaricious and lustful men, but this was something new. This man might murder me this evening and barely remember it tomorrow.

'Which orphanage?' he said again, and put his knee on my spine, starting to press downwards.

'All right, I'll tell you,' I managed to croak.

His grip loosened, and I drove my elbow into his groin.

He grunted and let go of me, falling to his knees. I shoved him away and ran, tearing round the corner towards the back gate, pulling at the latch to open it.

It was bolted from the inside.

I could hear him stumbling towards me in the dark. Any second now, he would be on me like a dog on a rat.

I reached through the hole in the fence, pulled back the bolt and dived into the yard, managing to re-lock the gate behind me just as he got there.

In the upstairs window of the house next door, a lamp was lit, casting a thin glow. I could see my assailant's forehead over the fence, and his hand writhing and stretching through the hole as if independent of his body. His arm was thicker than mine and he couldn't squeeze it as far. His fingers were groping, touching the edges of the bolt but not quite able to grasp it.

He forced his hand farther through the hole, ripping the stitching of his shirtsleeve.

We were locked in a strange race, him and me. He was straining for the gate bolt while I was fumbling with my key, no more than five yards from him, shaking in my haste to get the door open.

I won the race, but not by enough.

I got inside and was turning to lock the door when he burst through it, knocking me on to my back. I twisted and threw myself under the table, but he grabbed my leg and dragged me out, sending a chair spinning.

I kicked out at him and wriggled free, finding my feet and facing him over the table. He swept an arm across it, scattering bottles and jars, and sending clouds of powder billowing into the air.

'Where are they?' he said again. His eyes were blue and cold.

He took a step to the left and I did the same, keeping the table between us, taking me closer to the front door and the safety of the street.

He picked up Alfie's old scales. I could barely lift them, but he raised them with one hand, like a dock-crane, and hurled them towards me. I sprang out of the way as the metal dishes bounced and spun across the floor. He dashed forwards, and I tried to run, but slipped on the broken glass.

He grabbed me by my throat and slammed me backwards on to the table, pulling a knife from his belt. I felt a cold rush of fear; not of death, but of injury. If I was stabbed, my shirt would be removed to tend the wound and my physical form discovered. At least if I was killed outright, I would be spared that humiliation.

'Tell me,' he snarled.

My eyes were stinging but I forced myself to open them. Above me, the ceiling was yellow and cracked from years of smoke from the stove, steam from the tin bath and fumes from Constance's various experiments.

This was my favourite room in the world.

A fitting place to die.

17

THERE WAS A CRASH as the front door was flung open, and a shout. The fingers at my neck loosened and released. Alfie was hurtling past me. The back door banged, and I could hear footsteps running.

'Are you all right, Mr Stanhope?'

It was Constance, looking down at me with a concerned expression.

'I told you to leave,' I gasped.

She gave me a glass of water, which I used to sluice my stinging eyes.

'I went to get Father. He was in the square with Mrs Th— Mrs Gower.'

I sat up, and realised she wasn't alone. Mrs Gower was standing in the doorway, surveying the room as if she couldn't believe what she was seeing: shards of glass glittering on the floor and hearth, Alfie's old scales broken, chairs on their sides and everything covered in powder. Even the stove.

Alfie came back, breathing hard. 'I caught up to him but couldn't keep hold. He's away towards Piccadilly.' He scratched his head, frowning first at me and then at the ruin around us. 'What the hell happened, Leo?'

'He wanted Aiden and Ciara.'

'Why?'

'I don't know.'

But I could guess easily enough. Sir Reginald must have sent him, wanting to know where I'd hidden the children. He didn't want them found and identified.

Mrs Gower cleared her throat. 'A word please, Alfred.'

He followed her through to the shop.

Constance filled the kettle while I fetched the broom and started sweeping. God only knew how long it would take to clean everything.

When Alfie returned he seemed embarrassed, playing with the lapels of his coat and addressing the cupboard.

'Constance, I'd like to speak with Mr Stanhope alone, please.'

She glared at her father. 'He rescued me,' she said. 'He was very brave.'

He nodded. 'I'm sure you're right.'

'You should be thanking him.'

'Do as I say, Constance.'

She gave him a hard look and marched upstairs, making sure her footsteps echoed loudly through the house.

'I'm sorry, Alfie,' I said.

He righted a chair and sat on it. 'I warned you about getting involved with things like this, Leo.'

'I know.'

'I have to think of Constance. It's not fair to put her in danger.'

'Of course. I understand. I'll find somewhere else to live. Give me a few days.'

I began picking up the larger pieces of glass, gritting my teeth to keep from weeping. I had expected Mrs Gower's arrival to lead to my eviction eventually, but not so soon. I had grown comfortable here. I liked the fraying rug and uneven table and patches of damp creeping around the edges of the window frames. I didn't hear the creaking of the floorboards any more, or the scrape of the pans on the stove or the jangle of the pharmacy doorbell, no more than I heard my own breathing. The walls and ceilings were part of me ... no, part of *us*: Alfie and Constance and me. They smelled of us and sounded like us. I even liked Constance's cooking – or at least, I liked teasing her about it. No one else boiled mutton in quite the way she did, thank God.

This was the only real home I'd ever known.

The following morning, I once again sent a note to my foreman, explaining I had suffered a relapse. Despite the soreness in my back and my neck, I could think of at least three reasons why I would have preferred to go to work. Firstly, the nurses would have offered me salves and sympathy, both of which I felt in need of; secondly, I couldn't afford the continued loss of wages; and finally, a day spent hobbling around the ward with towels and sheets was much preferable to what I actually had to do.

The sun was bright on Little Pulteney Street and I took a route through the alleys to avoid it shining in my eyes. I could hear footsteps behind me with a distinctive squeak but thought little of them until I stopped to buy an apple. When I continued on my way, they were still there. I turned abruptly, and a man in a brown felt hat passed me by.

I was certain he was the same fellow who had followed us at the zoo. I hadn't been able to see him clearly then, but now I could. He was younger than I had thought, with a slim face and tidy moustache. He paid me no attention and carried on towards Wardour Street.

'Hampstead,' I said to the cab driver on Piccadilly. 'Church Row.'

My father's house.

When I was eleven years old, my father bought Oliver a kite. He arrived home with a brown paper parcel and the whole family gathered in the parlour to watch my brother open it. When the kite emerged, flame-red with a silk tail and a string wound tight round a wooden reel, we gasped in admiration.

'Can we fly it right now?' Oliver begged, which was the response my father had hoped for.

I started to pull on my shoes, but Mummy stopped me. 'No, Lottie. Let the boys play.'

I looked at Jane and could tell she was disappointed too. Why couldn't *we* learn to fly the kite? I was four years younger than Oliver, but Jane was the same age as him, born the same day. And it wasn't their birthday, so why was Oliver getting a present and not us?

Oliver and our father returned three hours later, flushed and happy. The kite had flown well. Oliver couldn't stop talking about how high it had risen and how hard it had pulled. He demonstrated over dinner, pinching the string between his thumb and forefinger while our father held up the kite like a trophy.

That night I lay awake.

'It doesn't matter,' Jane insisted, her voice emerging from the darkness like the better part of my impulses. 'It's just a toy.'

'Don't you want to have a go?'

'Of course, but it's Oliver's.'

I couldn't resist. The following afternoon while Oliver was at school, I took the kite from its place of honour on his chest of drawers and crept out of the house before anyone could see me. We went down the hill to the park, that kite and me, and we didn't pass a soul on the way. Such was the strength of the wind I had to lean forward with one hand on my hat, and tuck the kite into my coat so it couldn't escape. Finally, I stood on a wide stretch of grass, legs apart, the reel clutched in my hand.

I hurled the kite into the air and it leapt upwards, thrumming and whipping its tail as the breeze caught hold. It was flying! I unravelled the string as it climbed, bucking and swooping. Some instinct told me to pull harder, sending it higher and higher, hovering and shivering above me like a great, red kestrel.

A gust came, and the reel was wrenched out of my hand. I chased the string as it danced ahead of me, hurling myself forward to catch it as it went slack.

Looking up, I realised why it had stopped. The kite was stuck in the branches of a beech tree, thirty feet or more above my head. The lowest branches were too high for me to reach, so I had only one option: I tugged on the string. It wouldn't free itself, so I tugged harder.

There was a sound; some of it was tearing and some of it was snapping. By the time the kite tumbled down, it wasn't a kite any more. The cross-frame was broken, and the red paper of its sail was in shreds. The silk tail fluttered down on its own and expired in a puddle.

I carried the remains back home and showed them to Mummy, who sent me to my room to change and await my father's punishment.

I wasn't too old to get a beating. Worse, he took away my chess set and all my books, and gave them to impecunious parishioners who, he said, were more deserving of them than me.

The next day, he bought a new kite, exactly like the broken one. Oliver loved it, but our father wouldn't join him again. He said I'd spoiled his gift, and he wouldn't be able to enjoy it any more.

Weeks later, Mummy said she knew I was sorry because I looked so sad all the time. But that was because of my chess set and books. I didn't feel at all guilty about the kite. If our father had taken me with them in the first place, and had shown me how to fly it like he did Oliver, it would never have been broken, would it?

———

Hampstead was a pleasant village north of London. When I was living in Camden Town I used to walk there sometimes to take the air on the heath. From that grassy hill you could look down on the entire city, its buildings flooded by a lake of sulphurous smoke, and imagine yourself an eagle.

Church Row was quiet, aside from a thrush giving full voice in one of the gardens. My father's house was on the south side of the street, and might have been described, by an optimistic letting agent, as a three-storey townhouse, omitting that it was among the narrowest I had ever seen; barely room for a door and a window side by side.

I couldn't imagine why Jane wanted me to visit our father now, so late in his life. As John Thackery had said, he must have thought his daughter had run away, fallen and shamed. How he must have hated me for bringing that disgrace upon him, and how much more he would hate me when he found out the truth.

Needing a few minutes to calm myself, I wandered up the road to the church, a rather grand building for the size of the village. I had a vision of myself at age fourteen, kneeling at the altar rail, my palms pressed tightly together as if I was the most ardent congregant, except I had already given up asking God for the only thing I wanted and was mouthing the words to 'Goosey Goosey Gander'.

I had gained a skill through my adolescence; I could divide myself into two parts. The outer part was my physical self, standing in front of my father as he berated me for some small thing, misplacing my hymn book or forgetting to bring him his pot of tea. He would turn the colour of rhubarb, the veins on his forehead bulging, his mouth ejecting words with perfect, pounding articulation. The other part was inside, buried deep, watching all of this happening with detached curiosity. What a funny man he was, to be so angry over such a tiny slight. How unable he was to control himself, shaking with fury like a four-year-old whose biscuit has been taken away. The poor, strange fellow, he will make himself ill.

He regularly exercised his rage on the outer part of me, but he could never touch that inner one. That was forever beyond his reach, hidden among the stories and daydreams I kept in my head.

I sat on the bench by the gate, feeling the moisture soaking into the seat of my trousers. My father was long retired from the clergy, but I imagined him coming here every Sunday to share his wisdom with the local vicar, a Reverend S. B. Burnaby according to the sign.

'You poor bastard,' I said out loud.

The sun dipped and the temperature dropped. I was starting to shiver.

It was time.

As I knocked on his door, I wondered whether Jane might have brought Aiden and Ciara with her, and my heart was lifted at the thought of seeing them.

A housekeeper answered.

'Yes?'

'My name's Stanhope. I've come to see Reverend Pritchard.'

She opened the door wider, and I entered the house. I was dragged instantly back to my childhood. It smelled of my father: dog hair, old manuscripts, cigar smoke, the starch in his shirts and his vestments drying in front of the fire.

I could hear children's voices at the back of the house, shouting and giggling, and a dog yapping. They sounded happy.

Jane was in the parlour with a book in her hand. She put it face down on the table as I came in, though not before I noticed it was our mother's first edition of *Agnes Grey*, which amused and irritated me in equal measure.

'Good,' she said. 'I wasn't sure if you'd come. Remember, you said you wouldn't raise the topic of your ... appearance. You promised.'

'I know. But I won't hide it either.'

She seemed to feel that the pleasantries were over, and the moment had come for me to do my duty. But I still had questions.

'I met someone we used to know back in Enfield,' I said. 'Reginald Thackery. *Sir* Reginald now. Don't worry, he didn't recognise me.'

Jane pulled a face. 'Yes, I remember him. I found him to be a disagreeable man.' She shifted in her seat. 'You were young, and less, well ...' she trailed off, clasping her interlaced fingers more tightly together. 'I was engaged to be married to Howard, but still living at home, and Father kept inviting the man round. I don't know why.'

It was unusual of Jane to imply criticism of our father, at least in adulthood, and I wondered what had prompted the change.

'He was rich.'

'Yes, he was. He had that cotton mill—'

'Jute.'

'Jute, then. What difference does it make?' She started plucking at her cuffs, a sure sign of annoyance. 'He thought his money would buy him anything he wanted.'

I knew what she meant. I had been considered to be a plain, awkward and sullen girl, yet even I suffered. In fact, some men seemed to believe my limitations were to their advantage and I should be *grateful* for their attentions. Jane had it worse. She was well-mannered and pretty, a clergyman's daughter. A man like Sir Reginald might consider her to be a fine young fruit, ripe to be plucked.

'Did he try to ...?'

'No.' She clenched her fists. 'Well, once, in the garden at home. He said some things and made a grab for me. I ran away and avoided him after that.'

She appeared quite sanguine about it, but I had the urge to snatch up that poker, run to Sir Reginald's house and ram it down his throat. He had frightened my sister. How dare he?

'You'd already gone by that point,' she continued. 'Ollie was in the army and Mummy had taken to her bed. Father and I had to keep things going.'

I could hear the resentment in her voice. She thought we had abandoned her. I supposed we had.

'But you left as well,' I said. 'Eventually.'

She glared at me. 'I got married. That's how things are done. You grow up and have a family of your own. I put off the wedding for months waiting for you to come home and be my bridesmaid.'

I was drawing breath to reply when the housekeeper returned.

'I'm sorry to interrupt, Mrs Hemmings,' she said, addressing my sister. 'You asked to know when he's awake. Well, he is.'

Jane closed her eyes, composing herself. 'Come along,' she said to me. 'I'll take you to him. Remember your promise.'

———

My father's bedroom was small, with a single bed under the window, a mahogany wardrobe and matching chest of drawers, which I recognised. There was no fire, but it was still oppressively warm, heated by the storey below and the houses on either side, and infused with the stink of the bedpan.

He was lying on top of the covers, propped up on pillows, wrapped in a dressing gown. I remembered him as tall, with a substantial belly, bushy beard and thick hair that went in all directions. But the man in the bed was thin-boned, hunched and almost bald, wheezing as he breathed. I would hardly have thought him the same person, until he spoke.

'Who's that?' he rasped. 'Give me my water.'

There was a jug and a glass on the table by his bed. Jane filled the glass and placed it in his outstretched hand.

'It's Jane,' she said. 'And Lottie's here too. You asked for her. Isn't that remarkable? After all this time.'

He turned his face towards us, confirming what I had already guessed. He was completely blind.

'Hello, Father,' I said.

'Charlotte.' He waved his hand at me impatiently. 'Say something more. I want to hear you.'

'I'm sorry you're ill.'

I was conscious of my voice. Was I modulating it higher for his benefit, softening its edges? I couldn't tell.

'Well, yes,' he said. 'Not long now, I daresay.' He was speaking in short bursts, as if his lungs lacked the capacity for long sentences. 'Where have you been? We didn't know what had happened to you.'

'I had to leave. I'm sorry.'

Of course, I wasn't sorry, but what else could I say? I'd been so certain this meeting would be brief and bitter that I hadn't prepared for a civilised conversation.

'Where did you go?' he asked.

'Not far from here, actually. Camden Town. I live in Soho now.'

'Soho isn't a good area.'

'I've seen worse.'

He nodded thoughtfully, stroking his straggly beard, which was dark grey and white, like soot scattered on snow.

'Tell me about your life.'

I searched my mind, but there was almost nothing I could say that wouldn't give away the truth; I had a position at the hospital no woman would be offered and a room in a house with a widower, which my father would consider the height of indecency. Even my chess club didn't allow women.

I looked at Jane, and she shook her head.

'I have a pleasant life,' I said.

He opened his eyes again, and they were clear, though unseeing. 'That's not very ... specific. You and I never quite got on, did we?'

'No, we didn't.'

'Your mother. She coddled you. You were her baby.'

I felt a catch in my throat. 'I loved her too.'

He licked his lips, which were cracked and sore. 'I was afraid for you. The world isn't *kind* to unmarried ladies, Charlotte.'

'You taught me about its unkindness.' Behind me, Jane shifted uneasily. 'Did you think it would make me stronger?'

'No,' he said. 'You were already strong. I wanted you to *learn*. You were so angry all the time. So *difficult*. I didn't want you to end up a spinster. A woman needs a husband.'

'You wanted me to be more compliant, so I was marriageable.'

Jane prodded my back, but I ignored her, wondering what she could possibly have expected. She knew me better than any living soul, but I still seemed to be a complete mystery to her. And yet I hadn't changed a jot. I was the same person I had always been, the person she grew up with. Why couldn't she see me?

My father was sipping from his glass, his hand shaking, slopping water over his dressing gown. When he had finished, he held it out, expecting one of us to collect it and put it down for him. Jane leapt forward to do so, and he closed his fingers over hers.

'You can go now, Jane,' he said. 'We'll be all right.'

She gave me a long look and mouthed the words: 'Five minutes.'

My father licked his lips. 'She's good to me. A fine daughter.' I stayed silent, refusing to rise to his taunt. 'And four grandchildren for me. Are you married now? Do you have any children?'

I was tempted to tell him I had six, all by different fathers, but it wasn't worth it. I wouldn't invent progeny for his sake.

'No.'

He blinked, facing in my direction but not seeing me. 'Children are a blessing. A curse too, of course.'

'Some of them, I would imagine.'

'All of them, in their own way.' He lay back on his pillows and closed his eyes, exhausted by this short conversation. I could hear the clock ticking downstairs, and the wheeze in his throat.

I couldn't think of anything I wanted to ask him about his life now, nor anything I could tell him about my own.

If this strange reunion was to have any value, it would lie in his memories.

'Do you remember Reginald Thackery?' I asked.

I wasn't sure if he was still awake, and I might have thought he had died were it not for his chest rising and falling.

'Yes, I remember him well,' he murmured eventually. 'A wealthy fellow. He had a factory at Ponder's End. I went there once.'

'What kind of man was he, back then?'

He reached out, groping for my hand, and I let him take it, feeling at once repulsion at the intimacy and pity for this dry old man, counting down his final breaths. I could feel his withered skin and matchstick-thin finger-bones.

'Why do you want to know?'

'I met him again recently. I'm curious.'

Again, there was a long pause before he spoke, as if he was gathering what little energy he had left. 'He was an unhappy man. He had everything and nothing. Plenty of money, but no faith. He cared only for things he could see and touch.'

He wiped his mouth and I realised he had some food caught in his beard, a cube of carrot such as one might have in soup. It had probably been fed to him on a spoon. I watched it glistening there, thinking how horrified he would be if he knew. He wore his propriety like armour.

'Do you remember his son too?'

He nodded. 'Yes, of course. John was his name. He came to see me here actually, not a month ago. Maybe less.' He plucked at the blankets irritably. 'I lose track of time, lying in this bed. I can't see the calendar. One day goes into the next.'

'I saw John as well. He's much changed.'

'Yes, he's become interested in *politics*. He was like a … one of those toys that jump up. You had one, I remember.'

'A jack-in-the-box?'

He smiled, the first time I'd seen him do so in eleven years – and longer still since he'd done so because of something I said.

'Yes, exactly. He was like one of those, but it just keeps jumping and never winds down.' In the hallway, the clock started striking the hour, and my father held up his hand for silence, counting the chimes. When they had finished, he sighed deeply. 'I asked him if he knew where you were, but he didn't. He thought all this time that I had known. Odd the way the world works, isn't it?'

'He expressed great respect for you,' I said, feeling strange giving him the compliment. Yet it was the simple truth.

'I took him under my wing back in Enfield. Tried to help him. He wasn't a bad lad, as far as I could tell, though his father didn't agree. He hated the boy.'

I remembered John telling me that Sir Reginald had been cruel and had never forgiven him. When I asked for what, he said: *for existing*. An answer steeped in anguish, I thought, though I had no idea what it meant. How can anyone blame another person simply for existing?

'Do you know why?'

'No. I never understood it.'

'You couldn't understand his dislike of his child?'

He moved his thumb across my palm, kneading my coarse skin, his thin lips pressing together as he realised, I assumed, that I worked for a living. He must think me no lady, these days.

'I know what you thought, Charlotte,' he said. 'But I never disliked you. I cared about you deeply; all three of you. I'm sorry you thought otherwise.'

'And Mother?'

'She was … we weren't alike. She was a lot younger than me. But I was fond of her.'

'You weren't with her when she died.'

'Neither were you.'

His face was composed, but he knew how to wound me.

'No one told me. I had left home.' I could hear the shake in my own voice, just as I had a thousand times as a child. 'You were her husband.'

He nodded, barely perceptibly. 'You're right, of course. I should have been there. I couldn't bear to watch her suffer.'

There were tears in his useless eyes.

At least I knew now why he had me to visit him. He hoped to be forgiven his last debts in this world. But it was too late. Brief remorse on his deathbed didn't make up for abandoning his wife when she needed him most.

Jane's footsteps sounded on the landing. My time was up.

'The Lord will come for me soon,' he said, sounding congested and slow. Sleep was returning. 'He has taken my eyes and soon He will stop my lungs. I just wanted to hear my little girl's voice again.'

———

At the bottom of the stairs, I turned right instead of left, heading towards the sound of children playing in the garden. The back room was filled with our old furniture from the vicarage, the dining table cut down to half its previous glory, its legs incongruously large for the space.

A small, black and white dog jumped up at me, its tail wagging. I was reminded of the one we'd had at the vicarage; a friendly, energetic animal prone to digging up the lawn. I used to love throwing sticks for him.

Beyond the back room, a kitchen had been added to the house. The housekeeper was sitting at the table with a man's jacket over her lap and a needle and thread in her hand.

'Do you need something, sir?'

'No, thank you.'

I carried on through the back door, where three children were lying on the grass, pink and panting from running around. None of them was Aiden or Ciara.

I recognised the elder boy. I'd last met him a year or so before.

'Hello,' he said, getting to his feet. 'I'm Walter.' He pointed at the dog, which had followed me out. 'That's Huffam.'

I wondered how Charles Huffam Dickens would have felt about his namesake.

'Where are Aiden and Ciara?'

The boy looked blank. 'Who?'

Jane had come out behind me, and she took my arm, pulling me back towards the house.

'Please don't talk to them,' she hissed. 'They're not your concern.'

'They're my niece and nephews.'

'They're *Lottie's* niece and nephews.'

I accompanied her back into the kitchen, saying nothing. What she was doing was hateful and wrong, using her children to punish me, but I still didn't want them to hear us. If they were ever going to know of me, I wanted it to be in a pleasant way, a joyful surprise, a dear uncle who they didn't know existed, not as a strange man barking the news at them while their mother tried to shush him.

'Can I get you something?' asked the housekeeper. When neither of us replied she concentrated hard on her sewing, presumably hoping it would render her invisible.

'My God, Jane. Are you denying now that we're siblings at all? They *are* my niece and nephews, regardless of what you say.'

Her face was as hard as china. 'You made your choice.'

I'd had enough of this place.

She followed me to the front door, where I turned to face her. 'And where are Aiden and Ciara? You're supposed to be looking after them.'

'I am,' she said, surprised. 'They're at home. You can't have expected … I mean, they're with the *servants*. You don't think I would have children like that among my own, do you?'

'What do you mean, "children like that"? Do you have any idea what they've suffered?'

'Yes, of course. It's why I took them in, and why I clothed and fed them and gave them a place to sleep.'

She was sounding so reasonable, it made me even more livid.

'What *place*?'

'In the scullery. It's perfectly suitable for—'

'Stop.' I wouldn't listen to her any more. 'Giving them to your servants wasn't what we agreed.'

'We *agreed* it would be temporary until you found their relatives. Have you done so?'

'Not yet.'

'Well then. Do you suppose an orphanage would be any more agreeable?'

I couldn't see her expression in the dimness of the hall, so I didn't know if she considered herself justified to have manipulated the terms of our deal or not.

'I'll collect them from you tomorrow morning,' I snapped. 'Have them ready.'

'I won't be at home. I'll be tending to Father, doing my duty as his daughter.'

'Then I'll meet you here. Bring them with you.'

With a sudden burst of anger, I pushed past her and started up the stairs.

'What are you doing?' She was almost pleading. 'You mustn't tell Father about why you left. You promised.'

'You broke your half of that agreement, so I can do as I please.'

She grabbed my arm, but I pulled away and ran up to the landing.

'Lottie! Please don't—'

I threw open my father's door and shook him by the shoulder. He stirred, his hand groping at his chest for the spectacles that would once have hung there.

'Jane?' he croaked.

'No, not Jane.'

'Charlotte? Is that you? Is that my little girl?'

I should have done it. I should have told him the truth.

I'm not your little girl. I'm not Charlotte or Lottie. I'm Leo Stanhope and I always will be. Nothing of you survives in me. Nothing.

236

But I didn't. He was so frail, his skin like paper pulled thinly over a frame, his hands fluttering towards me.

I stood there looking at him, my lungs heaving in my bound chest.

'Charlotte?' he said again.

'Goodbye, Father,' I replied. 'I hope you find peace.'

18

I STRODE SWIFTLY AND furiously back through the village, ignoring a swan guarding the pond, flapping his wings and extending his neck towards me.

From time to time in my adult life I had dreamed of confronting my father with what I truly was, but now I found my hatred of him, for so long my North Star, felt less certain. He was at the end of his life, regretting the things he'd done. I might have been able to tell the truth to *my father*, the monster of my childhood, but I could never tell that blind and enfeebled old man lying on his deathbed, dying of a cancer he didn't understand, praying for the Lord to be merciful.

I couldn't imagine why He would be; God had never shown any kindness to me. Even the gift of my intellect, for which I was occasionally grateful, served primarily to allow me a true and thorough knowledge of the hopelessness of my situation.

I took the train at Hampstead Heath and was surprised when it terminated at Camden Town, still at least two miles from my home. I was in no mood to wait for an omnibus, so I opted to walk, my ire unextinguished by the gentle rain. My mind quickly turned towards Aiden and Ciara. Tomorrow, I would collect them from my sister, and would have to find somewhere for them to go; an orphanage, I supposed, where Sir Reginald Thackery would never find them.

I had tried everything, but they still kept coming back to me. Stranger still, I found myself pleased at the thought of it, as though I hadn't realised I was thirsty until offered a drink.

Was the idea so foolish? When a child is born to a father, he hasn't lived with the certainty of it growing inside him or felt its kick. He hasn't squeezed it from his womb. The first he sees of it is a wet, red creature swaddled in blankets, mewling and squawking. How long does it take him to love that infant? Minutes? Hours? Days?

Why should my attachment to these children – living, breathing, talking children – take any more time than that?

I shook my head.

Thinking that way was utter foolishness.

———

I was late meeting Rosie at the pharmacy and had to run through the rain, every muscle complaining. She was waiting outside under an umbrella, which she immediately lowered and shook, scattering droplets of water over my trousers.

'I hope you had a nice lunch,' she said, pursing her lips.

'I went to see my father. He's very ill.'

'Oh, I see.' She attempted to adjust her expression to one of sympathy, with limited success. 'Well, that is a shame.'

'Thank you.'

She sniffed, and a little shudder went through her. 'I mean, properly, Leo. I'm sorry. It must be very difficult for you.'

I didn't know how to respond. I wanted to tell her that his dying didn't matter, but it would sound unkind, even to my ears. That damned *pity* again. I was starting to resent it. Hatred is so uncomplicated by comparison.

Through the window, I could see Constance smirking at us.

'Let's go,' I said to Rosie. 'The club isn't very far. And my father did tell me one useful thing. He said that Sir Reginald held a strong dislike for John, his son.'

At the club on Rose Street, a girl was on the door, ten or eleven years old and skinny as a stoat. Her hand was stuck out for payment.

'We're here for Dora Hannigan's wake,' I told her, fumbling in my pocket for a penny.

Rosie shooed her away. 'Little wretch!' she said. 'She's making a fine living, isn't she, charging folks what's rightfully free.'

But I had a suspicion she admired the girl's initiative.

Inside, it was dark and smelled as stale as before. We followed the babble of voices until we found ourselves in the large room I had passed through with Thackery. It reminded me of the village hall in Enfield, with a lectern at the front and rows of seats facing it. Fifty or more people were standing around, clutching glasses of porter and talking earnestly in groups.

'Quite a place, this,' Rosie whispered. 'Never seen anything like it.'

We collected drinks from the table. They seemed to be free, which was just as well, as I was already short for the week's rent.

We stood together near the back, feeling oddly conspicuous. The one person I recognised was Erica Cowdery, who'd escorted me out of the building the last time I was there. She was busily placing pieces of paper on each chair.

When she saw me, she smiled and came over to us, standing so close I could smell her violet nosegay.

'Hello again, Mr Stanhope,' she said. 'I see curiosity got the better of you after all.'

'I'm here to pay my respects.'

'Well, I'm glad.' She squeezed my forearm. 'My brother has something to say to you.' She cast around the room. 'Where is he?'

I introduced her to Rosie, and Miss Cowdery let go of my arm, fidgeting with the collar of her dress and adjusting her mourning hat, a substantial structure resembling the kind of fortress from which one might defend our shores from invading Vikings.

A smartly dressed man approached us, holding a rather stylish black bowler, and I realised he was Edwin Cowdery, Miss Cowdery's brother. He exchanged a look with her and then addressed me.

'Mr Stanhope. I wanted to give you my regards,' he said. 'I was harsh with you last time we met. There'd been a lot going on, and none of it good.'

'I quite understand. This is Mrs Flowers.'

He bowed slightly in Rosie's direction without meeting her eye. 'Pleasure.'

He seemed to have nothing further to say, but wasn't sure how to leave.

'Such a tragedy,' I said, trying to fill the silence.

'Yes.'

'Do you know anything about why she was killed?'

He pulled his face into a smile that nevertheless tugged down at the corners of his mouth. 'You ask a lot of questions.'

I got a glimpse of that temper again. His civility was thin indeed.

Rosie took his arm, which appeared to make him both pleased and anxious at the same time. 'Why don't we go and get a glass of something, you and me.'

She steered him away, towards the drinks table, deep in conversation. I waited with Miss Cowdery, who tried to put her hands into her apron pocket, except she had no apron and ended up folding her arms and standing awkwardly.

In one corner, a fellow was plucking at a violin. Apparently, there was to be music.

'Are you investigating the murder?' she asked eventually. 'How interesting.'

'Did you know Miss Hannigan well?'

'Edwin and Dora ...' She glanced up at me, considering her answer. 'I don't live here, so I didn't see a lot of her. But we were friendly enough, and she used to help us out at the Home.'

'The what?'

She handed me one of the sheets of paper she was holding, which was printed in plain type with no illustration.

———

A special Easter appeal on behalf of the Home for Penitent Females at 57 White Lion Street

From north to south, east to west, their voices reached us:
'We have fallen on hard times and need aid for ourselves.'

In response to their pitiful cries, the Home for Penitent Females opened its doors to any girl or woman who was prepared to work hard and be respectable.
Will you, one and all, share this responsibility with us?
Will you give us something this Easter-time, so we can keep our doors open?

'We're raising money,' she explained. 'I'm the matron. Dora used to visit from time to time, teaching the girls to read and write. Sums too, if they were inclined that way.' She took a couple of deep breaths and closed her eyes. 'Very sad for her children, losing a mother like that. Do you know where they are now?'

It sounded like a casual question, but her face betrayed her: too calm, too reserved. She was desperate to know the answer.

'They'll go to an orphanage.'

She stared at me. 'Surely Dora has family who'll take them in? Do they have no one at all?'

'Not that I or the police have found.'

She put down the papers she was holding and wiped her hands on her skirt, though she seemed unaware she was doing it. I wondered if the mannerism was her way of preparing herself for action.

'Please excuse me, Mr Stanhope.'

She hurried away, and I lost sight of her in the crowd.

Rosie and Mr Cowdery returned. He was holding a shovel.

Rosie looked serious. 'Mr Cowdery here was telling me how it was him who found Miss Hannigan.'

'My dog,' he said, wiping his eyes. 'Best nose in London.'

'What time was it?'

'Shortly after midday, I reckon. Took him out to do his business and he started barking and digging. Frantic, he was. Never dreamed we'd find Dora like that.'

His mouth pulled into a grin-like expression, his only way to avoid weeping.

'And this?' I asked, pointing at the shovel.

'What he used to bury her, whoever he was.'

'How do you know?'

Rosie's attentions seemed to have lanced his suspicion of me.

'It's kept in the shed normally,' he said. 'But it was left under the steps.'

I picked at the spade with my fingernail, and the hard-dried dirt came away, brown dust falling to the floor.

'Why didn't the police confiscate it?'

'I didn't tell 'em. I don't give anything to the coppers as a rule and, besides, it's the only one we have.'

'Does the shed have a lock?' asked Rosie.

'No, we share and share alike here.' He sounded proud, testifying to his creed. 'No man should control another man's means of earning a living.'

'Did you see anything else out of the ordinary? Any footprints?'

'No.' He glanced up at the clock. 'I have to go. Duty calls.'

I gave the shovel back to him and he strode away with it under his arm.

'Not much help there,' whispered Rosie. 'Aside from finding out the killer didn't use his bare hands to dig the hole.'

'It does suggest a lack of preparation, though, wouldn't you say? The killer didn't bring a shovel with him. It was badly planned.' My mind was clicking through the facts, and I confess I felt a brief twinge of pleasure at putting them together. 'What do you make of Mr Cowdery?'

'He's shy of women, I'd say, that one. But he was sweet on Dora Hannigan. Very sweet.'

'Enough to be jealous?'

She sipped her porter and looked away from me, remembering, I supposed, her late husband. She had good reason to be wary of men.

'Perhaps. My guess is things can make him angry, and quicker than they should. He's like a spill of oil that could catch light at any time.'

I was glad I'd brought her. She was good at talking to people. They opened up to her. I just seemed to make them cross.

The room was filling up and guests were starting to seat themselves. We headed for the back row, but by the time we got there, all the chairs had been taken and we had to join the dozen or so others who were standing. They were mostly men; in fact, the whole room was mostly men. From where we were, it was a field of flat caps and bowlers, with a few ladies' taffeta hats dotted among them like glints of anthracite in a coal cellar.

The room fell silent, and I didn't know what to expect; perhaps a minister of some kind, to bless us and pray for the soul of the dead. I certainly didn't expect Edwin Cowdery to get up and stand behind the lectern.

'My old man was an engineer,' he announced, his eyes scanning the room until everyone was quiet. 'And I followed in his footsteps, apprenticed at twelve year old to the Hatcham Iron Works making jackscrews and pistons.

That was twenty-two year ago.' He paused, standing quite still, and you could have heard a feather fall. I was bizarrely reminded of Miss Vesta Tilley at the music hall, holding an audience similarly attentive, though she and Mr Cowdery had little else in common. 'As most of you know, and a few were there to see, it wasn't a good life. Not good at all. The owner, Mr England, he was a hard gentleman, and his men worked all hours, breaking their *backs*, breaking their *hearts*, so he could get rich.

'If a worker lost a hand in the machinery, and was unlucky enough to live, he would be without a wage, without a home, without a cot to lay his head. Even though it wasn't his fault, he'd be gone, and most likely starve to death. It wasn't fair, my friends, it wasn't fair at all.' He grimaced as though the memory of it was a physical pain, and then settled himself, holding his palms together as if in prayer. 'But me, I was an apprentice engineer, on track to become an engineer in my own right, directing men to work to my demands. In due course, I would've become a *senior* engineer with two-score men to toil and die in the factory while I eat cake …' he slapped his belly '… and purchase silk waistcoats in larger and larger sizes. I couldn't do it, my friends. I couldn't abide the injustice. So, what did I do instead, do you suppose?'

There was a murmur from the assembly, but I couldn't catch the words. They all seemed to be saying different things.

Cowdery put his hand to his ear. 'I can't hear you?' he called out, in a theatrical manner. 'Did we buckle under that yoke? Did we let Mr England treat the workers like animals, worse than animals, like carrion? Did we? No, we did not.' His voice dropped almost to a whisper. 'I got the men together, and we fought back. We took our labour away. We found out how many locomotives he could make with an empty factory. And how many was it, do you think? How many?'

'None!' the audience called back to him, delighted to know the answer this time.

'Exactly. None. He wasn't getting so rich now, was he? Had to up the men's wages and agree to contracts, and if a man lost a hand, or lost his hearing from the noise, he had to find him other work, sorting bolts or sweeping up, which wasn't much, but it was better than starving.

'Of course, he gave me the sack, but I didn't care. I didn't want to work for him or anyone like him. Because I'd learned my lesson, hadn't I? You don't buckle. You don't give in. You demand justice from the owners, and you keep demanding it until they treat you with respect, because it's ordinary men who dig the earth, toil in factories, haul on sails and chip away in the mines. So, it's them that deserve protection and decent wages. Not the likes of Mr England, my friends. Not him.'

Cowdery removed his bowler and wiped his forehead with his sleeve. He gazed to his left where the shovel was propped against the wall, remaining silent for so long that the audience began fidgeting in their seats. I could see puzzled glances being exchanged.

'Dora was quite a lady, wasn't she?' he said eventually, almost as if he was talking to himself. 'She never thought of herself as special, but she was. Her death won't go un-noticed, not while I have breath. I'll make sure everyone knows about it.'

He nodded towards someone seated at the front, and I realised it was J. T. Whitford, the journalist from the *Daily Chronicle*. I whispered as much to Rosie, and she craned her neck to see.

'I get the *Daily Chronicle* from time to time,' she whispered. When I looked surprised, she added: 'It's good kindling.'

Cowdery hadn't finished. 'We'll get our revenge, won't we?' He glared around the room, challenging us. 'They won't get away with it. When they're least expecting to, they'll pay for what they've done!'

I noticed his sister, Erica, standing to one side. Cowdery caught her eye and she gave him a stiff shake of her head. When he spoke again, it was more placidly, as if he hadn't threatened death and destruction a moment before.

'Dora was born in Donegal,' he said. 'She used to bend my ear for hours about the sea and the cliffs and the green fields stretching on for miles. Every time she sneezed she told me: "You know, Edwin, snot's not black in Donegal."' He chuckled to himself, shaking his head at the memory.

'Her old man was a cabinetmaker. Beautiful things, she said: chairs inlaid with gold and ivory and tables with marble tops. He used to make toys too, model trains and horses and the like. He did well at his work, educating his children and taking on more men, treating them fairly. He wanted to expand and took out a loan, but times got hard and he couldn't pay it back. The bank put the family out of their house and on to the street, and Dora only eleven. At fourteen she came here. But she was always proud of her upbringing, so we're going to follow the Irish style. Our friend Mr Klaus here will be providing the music.' The fellow who'd been tuning a violin had been joined by two others, one holding a penny whistle and the other what looked like an oversized concertina. 'Irish music played by Germans. Whatever next, eh?'

Most of the audience stood at this point and started carrying the chairs to the side of the room, stacking them against the walls.

'We're not going to dance, are we?' I whispered to Rosie. 'At a funeral? To a *violin*?'

I hadn't danced since I was a child. We had spent hours pirouetting around the parlour while Mummy accompanied us on the piano and instructed us to lift our chins and point our toes. Oliver hated it, so I usually had to take the part of the man, bowing to Jane before we began and asking if she would do me the honour of this waltz. Sometimes I minded, sometimes I didn't.

Rosie took my hand. 'It's a *fiddle*, Leo, not a violin. And this isn't a funeral, it's a wake. An *Irish* wake.'

The penny whistle started with a trilling, energetic tune, accompanied by the stamping feet of the other musicians, and then the violin joined in, climbing swiftly up and down the notes, cycling through tiny variations, gathering vigour and verve while the giant concertina kept the rhythm. And what a rhythm! You couldn't help but dance.

Rosie showed me what to do, putting one of my hands in hers and the other on her waist. I could feel the music in my feet, in my chest, in my fingertips. I began slowly, wary of the soreness of my limbs and back, and kept kicking her ankles and treading on her toes. She stopped me and taught me how to do a sort of sideways canter and, before long, the stiffness had left me completely, and we were spinning around the room with the half a dozen or so other couples. It was chaos, but it didn't matter. We kept bumping into each other and whirling away, laughing and apologising, first to one couple and then the next, dipping and stepping while the little band played and our feet pounded. For the next song, Rosie took both of my hands and we moved together, and apart, and from side to side, and the music gathered pace and we were off again, gyrating around the room until I was giddy and breathless.

As that tune ended, we applauded the band and each other, but we had no time to recover; the next one began, and we bounded away again, round and around, until the whole room was a whirr and I was nothing but my feet and the music and the warmth of Rosie's hand in mine.

Never before had I danced that way. I forgot about my sister, my father and the death of Dora Hannigan. I forgot about everything. For those few minutes, I was happy.

It ended abruptly.

I was facing in the direction of the main door as it burst open. I stopped dancing, but most people hadn't seen, and continued until the band fell silent.

A dozen or more policemen charged in, batons held high. I recognised Constable Pallett among them. He doffed his helmet politely to Rosie as he joined his colleagues in shoving us towards the edges of the room.

Last through the door was Detective Hooper, resembling as ever a heron with a distaste for the pond he was standing in. He pointed directly at Cowdery.

'You're under arrest,' he said. 'Trespassing and conspiring to commit arson. You and Duport were seen creeping around Sir Reginald's mill. And we found your plan to burn it. Your time's up.'

He seemed excited by his authority, enjoying that we were silent and scared. He had us where he wanted us.

Two of the constables grabbed Cowdery, and one of them punched him hard in the face and stomach. He doubled over and fell to his knees. The constable kicked him in the back and he collapsed forward, curling up and covering his mouth.

The crowd surged, starting to shout, and one fellow grabbed at the constable, pulling him away from Cowdery. The policeman swung round and punched him full in the face, and he must have been wearing something over his knuckles, a metal band inside his glove, because the man's face was gashed and bloody as he dropped.

I put myself in front of Rosie, prepared to fight if one of them came near her, though they all looked twice my weight at least.

They hauled Cowdery to his feet and he spat on the floor; a bright, red splash.

'Take him away,' instructed Hooper.

The constables dragged him out between them, taking no great care of his limbs and head on the door jamb.

Hooper noticed me and strode over to where we were standing. His face was flushed pink.

'Mr Stanhope, how interesting to see *you* here. Did your friend John Duport invite you?'

'I haven't seen him.'

'Seems like no one has.'

He turned away from me and addressed the rest of the room, his voice booming as if he were a victorious general.

'You mark my words.' He swept his finger across their faces. 'These are your last days in this bloody place. Go home and don't come back. Count yourself lucky it isn't you in manacles. Edwin Cowdery likes to think he's leading a revolution, but he'll be in the clink tonight with the pimps and the mollies. Won't be so revolutionary after that, will he?'

His accent was shifting; he was sounding more and more like an East End boy with a sharp mind who'd grown up to be a copper and enjoyed hobnobbing with the wealthy and powerful. Under pressure, he was still that boy. His fists were twitching.

A constable approached him and handed him something. Hooper studied it and turned it over in his hand. He squinted towards me, taking in Rosie as well, apparently caught in two minds. Then he made his decision.

'My men have searched Duport's room,' he said. 'They found something of interest. Perhaps you can explain it.'

He handed me a photograph. Rosie peered at it too and I heard her intake of breath.

There were three people in the foreground. In the centre was my father, when he was still tall and straight-backed, his hair grey, but thick and strong. He was wearing the familiar expression that had always frightened me, as if everything I did and everything I was had been found wanting. On one side of him was John Thackery as a young man, shoulders proudly back, looking at the camera. And on the other side, half-turned as if distracted by something out of sight, was me.

I was wearing a pale dress with a frilly neckline and a hat with a bow. What you couldn't tell, unless you knew, was that the dress was covered in little holes where I had picked resentfully at the stitching with my nails.

I could clearly remember that morning. It was late summer in 1869, a couple of months before I left home. One of the ladies at the church had a cousin who was visiting from Hampshire, a Mrs St John, although it was oddly pronounced: *Sinjun*. She had a camera resembling a bellows with a binocular stuck on the front, and she asked people to pose in front of the thing. I had never seen photography done before and watched her with fascination. She noticed my interest and brought me behind the machine to show me how all the parts worked: the glass plate and the little knob that moved the bellows in and out. John Thackery suggested a picture with my father and me. In those days, I rarely looked at myself in a mirror, and even catching my reflection in a shop window made me pinch the skin between my thumb and forefinger. I should simply have said no, and probably Mrs Sinjun would have let me be, but I was craven, and so it was done.

I hadn't seen that photograph in years, but I knew who it belonged to: it was from my father's collection.

'This is obviously John Duport when he was young,' I managed to say, keeping my voice steady.

Hooper raised his eyebrows. 'Yes, but who are the other two, eh? The vicar and the girl?'

'How would I know? It's a very old photograph. What does this have to do with me, Detective?'

'It's Detective *Inspector*, as I believe I've mentioned before. You're mixed up in this somehow, Mr Stanhope, I'm sure of it. Turn it over.'

On the back of the photograph, in handwriting I didn't recognise, was written: *This is Leo Stanhope.*

19

AFTER THE POLICE HAD gone, for five seconds there was silence.

Then everyone started talking at once.

A man climbed on to a chair and appealed for quiet, but no one was listening. A small group had gathered around the stricken fellow on the floor, arguing about how best to treat him, while others were making for the exit. Some preferred standing and yelling.

The one person neither moving nor speaking was Mr Whitford, who was scribbling in his notepad. He looked up and around the room, and I had the impression he was writing down the names of the people there.

'We should leave,' Rosie hissed at me, tugging at my arm. 'No good will come of staying.'

I was too shocked about the photograph to move or respond.

Whitford came over, making as if to doff his hat to Rosie before realising he was holding it in his hand.

'Mrs Stanhope, I presume?'

She reddened. 'Mrs Flowers, actually.'

'Ah, I see. I'm Whitford, and you'll be able to read about all this excitement in the *Daily Chronicle* tomorrow.' He held up his notebook. 'The battle of Rose Street; how a criminal was apprehended.'

'You're sure he's guilty then?' she asked.

'Of trespassing and planning to set fire to Sir Reginald Thackery's blasted mill, with apologies for my language? Yes, he's certainly guilty of that. It's been coming for the last three years, ever since they took this place, stirring up trouble with their speeches and posters and all. It was only a question of time before they went a stage further.'

'What about Miss Hannigan's murder?'

He shrugged. 'Good question. My son, Harry, who works with me on the newspaper, he found out that she and Cowdery had an understanding, so to speak. They both lived in this lushery, so it wasn't hard for them to carry on.'

Rosie gave him one of her looks. 'Does that make him a suspect?'

'Maybe she gave him cause to be jealous.'

Rosie smiled with a sweetness like lemonade, so sharp it makes you wince. 'Will you be printing innuendo, Mr Whitford?'

His ears went pink. 'No, of course not. We'll probably never know who did for her. The police don't care about some dead woman who no one's ever heard of, they care about getting this place shut down. You saw the gang Hooper brought with him. That costs money and takes planning. They don't do that unless someone's paying the bills.'

He was about to leave, but at that moment Erica Cowdery appeared at his side, her face white and her jaw clenched.

'You're the journalist, aren't you?' she said, making it sound like an accusation.

'I'm sorry about your brother. A terrible thing. Unexpected, I'm sure.'

'I wouldn't say so,' she replied. 'They just needed an excuse. You should write about it in that newspaper of yours. The police interrupted a *wake*, of all things, waving their little truncheons. Mr Gladstone's so perturbed by fear of a revolution, like the French have had, that he'll go to any lengths to crush it before it starts, even at the expense of justice and decency. That's the real story, Mr Whitford, and I'm sure you're the man to write it.'

He appeared quite flattered and immediately started writing scratchily in his notebook. 'And yet Mr Cowdery continued to antagonise them. Brave man.'

She narrowed her eyes a little, seeming unsure whether he was mocking her brother.

'Stupid, if you want my opinion. He put the whole movement at risk. I spend my spare time, what little I have of it, making flags, brewing tea, delivering pamphlets, speaking in freezing town halls and collecting farthings in buckets.' She gave the men still left in the room a cold look. 'Real work that needs to be done. Not getting arrested in a ... whatever that was. They go on and on about the rights of man and forget that half of us aren't men. Anyway, I suppose I shall have to go and find a lawyer for Edwin.' She gathered herself and gave me a weary nod. 'Goodbye, Mr Stanhope. I hope we meet again soon, in happier circumstances.'

Outside, Rosie and I navigated between the ragged blankets and empty beer bottles of the passageway sleepers, who hadn't yet returned from their day's begging.

I was still shaking from seeing the photograph. I'd forgotten how I had looked back then; not just the frills and bows, but how I stood, how I smiled, how I held my hands, never sure what to do with them. God, I was good at appearing to be what I was not. Everyone was misled by my physical form. They never guessed I was a boy.

'Rosie, that photograph isn't … it's not *me*. I mean, it's how I *was*, but not by choice. Do you understand?'

'You think I don't know that?'

I felt foolish. Of course she knew. She had seen me at my weakest.

'John told me he had proof of who I was, and it must be that photograph. It was my father's.'

And yet my father was in no state to give him anything. Jane must have handed over the photograph. I didn't want to believe it, but there was no other explanation. My sister held me in so much contempt, she had betrayed me.

'Do you think John Thackery might be the killer?' asked Rosie as we reached Greek Street. 'You said he knew Miss Hannigan well. I still don't know why you won't tell the police that he and Duport are the same man.'

I thought back to John's tearful face in the churchyard at St Anne's.

'He cared about Dora Hannigan. I can't imagine him hurting her. She was the one who introduced him to the club. I got the feeling he idolised her a little bit.'

Rosie didn't immediately reply. I could tell she was turning things over in her mind. 'Some men care about a person so much, they come to think they own them,' she said, eventually. 'If he found out she was Sir Reginald's mistress, he might feel she'd let him down. Forsaken him. That might be a motive to kill her, never mind that it was no business of his and he'd be leaving two children alone in the world.'

'Perhaps. He's a zealot by nature, and that might lead him to a drastic act, though the same could be said about Edwin Cowdery, and perhaps Erica too.'

'She doesn't have much time for her brother, does she? Though she likes you well enough. What about Mr Peregrine Black?' She spoke his name with a theatrical flourish. 'Singer, painter and *impresario*.'

'Not the name he was born with, I imagine.'

'No more than yours, *Leo Stanhope*.'

'Or yours, *Mrs Flowers*.'

She laughed, and kicked a shallow puddle of water at me, and then squeaked when I made to do the same back at her.

'Enough!' she protested. 'Who else might it be?'

'Sir Reginald is certainly capable. I'm sure he's the children's father. Maybe he wanted to silence her, if she was blackmailing him.'

'But over what?' said Rosie. 'It would have to be something that would damage him, wouldn't it? Something that would cost him dearly. And what about the other son?'

'Peter? He's a free spirit, but very young, only fifteen or so. I'm not sure he even knew Dora Hannigan.'

'You like him, though, don't you? When you like someone, it's hard to believe them capable of killing another person.'

I pulled my hat lower over my forehead and didn't reply. She herself had killed, twice, once knowingly and once not. And yet I liked *her*.

For a while we walked on in silence, until we reached the corner of Old Compton Street, where I would go right, and she left.

'Rosie, I want to ask you a question.'

She looked up at me, her head tipped quizzically to one side. 'What is it?'

'With your children, how do you manage without Jack?'

She snorted. 'Are you serious? Without Jack? God, you men. You think nothing can happen without your masculine authority.'

'It's not that. I was wondering how it is, to be both parents at once.'

If it were possible, she looked even more scornful. 'It's all I've ever done! Jack was as much use as mouldy yeast, and a sight less attractive. You're asking the wrong person. Alfie Smith could tell you, I imagine.'

Alfie had looked after Constance on his own for half of her life, despite being a man. Indeed, he seemed weakest in the more obviously paternal area; she was largely impervious to his efforts at discipline.

Rosie looked me straight in the eyes and, even under such a cloudy sky, hers were a bright apple-green. 'You're not thinking of taking care of those children yourself, are you?'

'I haven't made up my mind.'

I was surprised to hear the words emerge from my mouth. It was as if a hitherto unknown part of me had spoken.

'Leo ...' She paused, rethinking what she had been going to say. 'Are you sure about this? They're a big responsibility,

you know, kids. It's like bits of your soul detaching themselves and walking around on their own. You'll not get a
minute ever again without being consumed by fear. And
they're not cheap. There's clothes and food and God knows
what else, and they break things all the time. And the boys
smell. The girls too, but not so bad. And they never shut up,
and when they do you worry they're sick.'

'Thank you for your understanding.'

'Schoolbooks too, don't forget those.' She was ticking off
the list on her fingers. 'And pencils. It's like a river of money
streaming out of your purse. And the cooking is endless.
It never stops. And you'll need another room, under the
circumstances. Would you truly leave Alfie's place?'

I didn't tell her that he'd already given me notice to
leave.

'Do you think I can't manage?'

'Of course you can!' she insisted, with a little too much
conviction. 'You're very … resourceful, I'm sure. It's just
that … don't do this because you're sad. Or lonely.'

'I'm not lonely. Why does everyone keep saying I am?'

'Aye, well, that is a question, isn't it? Your young friend
Constance said you never do anything or go anywhere.
"Moping" was the word she used.'

'Well, she's wrong,' I said firmly. 'I go to work; I play
chess with Jacob; I do lots of things. I went with Alfie to
see his old army friends.'

'That's good,' she said, though I could tell she was
unconvinced. 'Because children don't salve your wounds,
Leo, they rip the stitches out of them.'

I clenched my fingers together so tightly I thought my
joints would crack.

'Why should I be any less capable than anyone else? Is it because of ...' I lowered my voice, but by this time I was properly angry. 'Of what I am?'

She folded her arms. 'If what you are is a man, then most likely, yes. Look around you. How many men do you see caring for their own children, let alone someone else's?'

My rage burned quickly through my better judgement. 'If that's the case, Rosie,' I said, through gritted teeth, 'why are you helping me with this? Who's looking after *your* children while you're here with me?'

She gasped as if she'd been struck, and for a moment I thought she would fly at me. Instead, she took a step away and composed herself, speaking with fierce precision.

'So that's it, is it? I'm to be here when you need me, like last year when it was your Maria and my Jack, but otherwise I should hurry back to my stove and my children with nary a complaint. And when they're all grown up, what should I do then? Bake one final pie and fall down dead, because that's all I'm good for?'

'Rosie, I ...'

'You do what you want. You'll be doing it on your own from now on.'

20

THE FOLLOWING MORNING, I set off early for my father's house.

Rosie's objections had made up my mind.

Indeed, I had stayed awake half the night imagining myself teaching Ciara to read and listening to Aiden recite his times tables. I would settle them into their own bed every evening and wake them every morning. We would be a family. We would be *my* family. The more I thought about it, the righter it felt.

My one quandary was what they should call me. 'Father' sounded too close to my own upbringing, and it wasn't true. 'Leo' would suffice. I knew where this indecision was coming from: a fear that my choice to care for them didn't have a manly cause — to guide these two children and see them grow into fine young adults — but a maternal one — a desire to *nurture* them.

I found myself thinking about my father, resolving to be the opposite of him in every way. Yet, even in doing that, I was more like him than I wanted to admit. He had once told us that his own father, my grandfather, who had died when I was four years old, was a mild fellow, quick to trust and easily bidden. He confided this in a tone laced with scorn, as though we would see the obvious frailty of such a character. Perhaps each generation was destined to counter the last, zigging and zagging from tenderness to brutality and back to tenderness, each believing themselves to be distinct and yet, in truth, being the product of their upbringing as much as if they'd followed in their parents' footsteps. It was a depressing thought, and yet, it seemed to me, we betray our intentions at every turn. My father had continued to keep my grandfather's cane in the porch long after his death, insisting that a parishioner might one day have need of it. No one ever did.

I reached his house as the church bell was pounding out eleven o'clock.

All the shutters were closed. The door was opened by his housekeeper, who was accompanied by the smell of boiling meat and sherry.

Jane stood up when I came into the parlour. Her mouth was resolute, resisting any downward turn, but I could see the doubt and dread in her eyes. For that second, we were as we had once been, linked by some invisible thread more permanent, in its own way, than love: we were siblings. We had grown up in the same bedroom, read the same books, played the same games and shared the ribbons we tied our hair with. I used to be unable to sleep without hearing her breathing in the next bed. She could keep no secrets from me.

'He had a bad night,' she said, 'but he'll hang on for a while yet.' She nodded firmly, agreeing with her own statement, willing it to be true. 'He's as stubborn as a donkey.'

'You're a good daughter,' I said, and meant it. She had sacrificed her own well-being for our father, just as she had for Howard and her children.

She appeared to be on the verge of snapping a response, no doubt that I too could be a daughter to him, if I chose to be, but she thought better of it.

'Those children are in the garden,' she said. 'Do you want to see him again first?'

'No.'

'He's changed his will. He's included you now.'

'What?'

We were surrounded by his books and other oddments: binoculars, spectacles, a notebook, a copy of *The Times* from weeks ago, but I wanted nothing of his. I couldn't imagine anything worse than spending money he'd given me or sitting on a chair that had once belonged to him.

She pulled a handwritten note from her bag. 'He doesn't have much. The house is owned by the church, but there's some capital. Your share will amount to forty pounds or thereabouts. Not bad for someone who hasn't seen him in years.' I could tell she was making an effort to keep her voice steady. 'It's for Charlotte Pritchard, of course, so you'll have to sign the paperwork as such. I'm sure, for forty pounds, you'll find your way to doing that.'

I closed my eyes in exasperation. When we were children, she had often punched me, slapped me, kicked me and once elbowed me in the solar plexus. It was the way of siblings and didn't bother me much at the time, but when I reached the age of thirteen and was her equal in strength and reach, I attempted to hit her back. She responded with a sneer, saying that fighting was infantile and foolish, and I should be capable of settling differences through reasoned argument – at which she happened still to be better than me.

I couldn't win. But at that moment, I was tempted to get a modicum of revenge for all those bruises.

I would do no such thing, of course. I was a gentleman.

'I won't sign with that name because it isn't mine. Did you really think I covet his money? You and Oliver can have it all.'

She considered the question, and it struck me that she might, in fact, be lying; his will might not include me at all. This could be her way of testing my resolve to remain a man.

She gave a brief and disinterested shrug. 'I suppose you do have an income of your own, of a sort.'

I blanched at that. I had neglected to tell my foreman I would not be attending that day. I might be given the sack, and my chances of achieving another position would be slight indeed, without a reference. I had no savings and would be reliant on the charity of my friends for food and lodging within a week.

Of course, my mind strayed to the two hundred and four pounds tucked under my mattress, but I'd vowed that I would only spend it on the children's behalf, never on mine. I would join the beggars on the bridge by the mill first.

I was feeling tired and strangely displaced, here with Jane, as if I might go upstairs to the room we had once shared at the vicarage and go to sleep in my old bed.

'Jane, a photograph has come to light. It's of John Thackery and Father and me ... as I was in Enfield. You gave it to John, didn't you?'

'He came here to pay his respects and asked for a keepsake, and Father wanted him to have it. Where's the harm?'

'Don't you understand? I'm not that person any more.'

She shrugged. 'You are who God made you. You can cut your hair if you like, and wear a man's clothes, but you're Lottie Pritchard and you always will be. Unless you get married, of course.' She smiled at this small irony, but I could see how angry she was, how much she was trying to hurt me.

And then I was sure.

'You told John about me.'

She looked away. 'I had no other choice. Father asked him if he knew where you were, and he became suspicious. Typical of the Thackerys, always thinking they've worked out something no one else knows. I truly thought he was going to accuse us of murdering you, so in the end I told him the truth on condition he kept it to himself.'

I didn't have the words to express how I was feeling.

'He blackmailed me,' I managed, eventually. 'Did you know that? He wanted me to tell the police I was with him when I wasn't.'

She dismissed my protest with a wave. 'I'm sure the whole thing was nonsense. He probably wanted to play at politics without his father finding out. They're all terrified of the man, even Philippa.'

I was too incensed to think clearly. 'Who on earth is Philippa?'

She looked up at the ceiling, astonished at my stupidity. 'Philippa Thackery, his *wife*. Lady Thackery as she is now, I suppose. She wanted to stay in Enfield. She never wanted to go back to London and buy that cotton mill.'

'Jute,' I insisted obstinately, but she wasn't listening.

'It was the right decision for the business, though. Easier to get the cotton on and off the ships if you're near the docks.' I detected a note of envy in her voice. My sister was a woman of extraordinary intelligence who spent most of her time administering servants and attending social functions with her husband. 'Anyway, I'm sure you're mistaken. John Thackery meant no harm. It's not the kind of man he is.'

'But I am?'

'You're not any kind of man.' She took a deep breath and rang the bell. The housekeeper appeared. 'Bring the Hannigan children in, please.'

They were well enough dressed and each was carrying a drawstring sack. Ciara appeared brighter than the last time I'd seen her, and she took my hand and smiled at me. Aiden was serious and hard to fathom, but also rosy-cheeked. Whatever my sister's failings – which were many and not always obvious – she would not see anyone under her roof suffer.

'Hello, Mr Stanhope,' Aiden said, as if we were two gentlemen met for dinner.

Jane presented each of them with a new pair of gloves, for which they thanked her very nicely.

I left the house without saying another word to her.

As we walked down the hill towards the station, I took Ciara's sack and handed her a packet wrapped in waxed paper.

'From the tooth mouse,' I said.

It was a pastry from the shop on Regent's Street, and she set upon it with relish, looking up at me with amazement at the first mouthful as though she had never imagined a thing so delicious.

Aiden seemed a touch peeved until I produced a pastry for him also.

'What happens now?' he asked.

'You're going to stay with me,' I replied, feeling a pride the match of any new father's. 'For ever. We're a family now.'

As we reached Little Pulteney Street, I was mentally listing all the things I still had to do. The top item was to find lodgings. I had contemplated taking a cab to King's Cross Station and going far away, York or Edinburgh, with new names and new clothes. I could almost hear the words in my mouth and feel the itch of it in the soles of my feet: *Come along, now. Hurry up!*

We would never be found.

But how was that any different from what Sir Reginald had wanted to do? Either way, they would be lost, and their mother's murder would go unsolved.

No, we would stay in London and find somewhere decent; nothing extravagant in case I truly had lost my position at the hospital, just a good-sized room for the two of them and a box room for me, with space for a bed and a shelf of books

After that, I would put the children's money into a bank, talk to a lawyer about legal adoption and find a school for them.

And one other thing.

'I want to buy a kite for us to fly in Hyde Park,' I announced. 'The three of us can take it in turns.'

Aiden grinned. It happened so rarely and yet it changed his face completely, transforming it from solemn and long to merry and round.

'A kite? May we really? I've never flown a kite.'

Ted Boyd, who ran the grocery next door, was sitting by his upstairs window. He tapped on the glass and gave me a wave, and I returned the gesture, somewhat perplexed. He'd never been so friendly before.

He opened the window and called down to me: 'You're a credit to the area, Mr Stanhope. A proper credit.'

'Thank you, Mr Boyd,' I called back, puzzled, having no clue what he was talking about.

A police carriage was waiting in the street. Hooper climbed out, unfolding himself like a spider. Another policeman followed him, the same man I'd seen at their headquarters and the club. He was carrying a truncheon, letting it swing freely on the end of a leather strap.

As ever, I felt the urge to run. But I could not. I had responsibilities.

'Mr Stanhope,' Hooper called. 'We've been waiting for you. We'd like a word about this.' He waved a rolled-up newspaper in my direction, but then paused, frowning at the sight of Aiden and Ciara. 'Why have you got *them*? We was told they was in an orphanage.'

I pulled them closer. 'I've decided to adopt them myself. They'll be safe with me.'

'Are you mad?' he sneered.

The constable took a step forwards, and Ciara huddled into my coat and looked up at me with wide eyes. I put my hand on her shoulder and felt her relax, comforted by my presence, and I was immediately overwhelmed. To have someone believe in you that much, rely on you that much, was like nothing I'd ever experienced.

And yet, I couldn't think of a way out of this.

Aiden put down his sack and tugged urgently on my sleeve. Our eyes met, and I could see what he was thinking. I gave him the briefest of nods.

He slipped behind me and took his sister's hand, and they ran.

'Wait!' shouted Hooper, but he was too late.

Aiden pulled his sister over the road and beneath the rails of a parked cart, dodging so fast between two old fellows they didn't even notice.

They would have made it. They were so close. But Aiden didn't know the area well and pulled Ciara into the alley by the butcher. He must have been hoping to lose his pursuers in the maze of streets in the northern part of Soho, but that alley was a dead end.

They were trapped.

The constable lumbered towards the entrance with the truncheon in his fist, followed by Hooper, who was breathing hard, his arms outstretched.

People had stopped to watch. One man caught my eye, and I recognised him. He was wearing a brown felt hat.

As the constable reached the entrance to the alleyway, a carriage drew up, partly blocking my view. Its door was flung open.

'Get out of the way!' Hooper bawled.

Aiden and Ciara hurtled back out of the alley and would have run straight into Hooper's arms, but at that moment a loud bang came from inside the carriage, and Hooper flung himself backwards. I had never heard a gunshot before and it was a shockingly hard, short sound.

'No!' I shouted, but both children were unhurt, still on their feet.

Hooper leapt up and sprinted back towards me, keeping low, his face wild with terror. He wasn't the only one. Another man started to run and then everyone was running, past me and around me. One fellow tripped and fell on to the pavement and continued on all fours.

Aiden had stopped, frozen in place. He was listening to someone in the carriage, and I could just see a gloved hand holding the pistol. He gave a tense nod and seemed about to get inside, but Ciara was hanging back. Aiden said something and then tugged her towards the open door. A hand extended from the carriage and pulled her in. He climbed in behind her, and the door slammed shut.

The driver shook the reins and the carriage drove away at speed.

The man in the brown felt hat raced after it, his coat billowing behind him, but it was too quick, turning the corner at Lexington Street and disappearing from view.

We were left staring dumbly at an empty road.

Hooper had been cowering in a doorway, and now he stood up straight, his face purple with rage.

'Who the hell was that?' he yelled.

'I don't know,' I said. 'I really don't.'

He said something I couldn't hear to the burly constable, who strode towards me. He punched me once on the side of my neck and I fell to my hands and knees. He bent down and punched me again, twice, and then his boot came down on my head, bouncing my skull off the stone.

21

I WOKE UP IN the back room of the pharmacy, lying on the table.

Constance was looking down at me, her face a picture of concentration. She hadn't realised I was awake and was holding my forehead with one hand and a curved needle in the other, a loop of thread hanging down close to my left eye.

'What are you doing?' I asked, trying my damnedest to pronounce the words, but my mouth didn't seem to be working properly.

'Stitches,' she said, and I could see the needle spearing towards my eyebrow. 'Hold still. I was hoping to finish while you were still concussed.'

'Where are Aiden and Ciara?'

Another voice answered, a man I didn't recognise. 'I'm sorry. I chased after that carriage, but I was too late.'

I felt a hollowness open up in my stomach. They had been taken from me. How could I have let this happen? I should have found a way to keep them safe. I should have laid down my life.

'I don't want stitches.'

I could still feel the smallness of Ciara's foot pushed up against me while she slept, and could see Aiden's stern eyes under his fringe.

'You're lucky,' said the male voice. 'She's done them very neatly.'

'It was Mr Stanhope who showed me how,' said Constance, with a note of pride. 'When Colly hurt her paw.' I tried to sit up, but she pushed me down again. 'One more to go. I have some chloral hydrate, if you'd like. It'll help with the pain.'

'No, thank you.'

Tempting as it was, I couldn't sink into that black water. Not now.

'As you wish,' she said. 'But this will hurt.'

She winced as she pushed the needle through my skin.

The agony opened up like a flower. I welcomed it. I deserved it. When I unclenched my fists, there were red welts in my palms where I'd dug in my fingernails.

Constance tied two knots in the thread.

'Thank you,' I croaked. 'I have to leave now.'

I tried again to sit up, but the room wavered and slid around me. A pair of hands lowered me back down and cushioned my head.

'Slowly, old man, you need to rest. You've had a nasty bash. That copper might've killed you if the crowd hadn't stopped him.'

'Who are you?'

'Harry Whitford.'

On his lap, he was holding a brown felt hat.

'Did you say Whitford? Like the journalist?'

He nodded. 'Yes, you've met my father, J. T., I believe? You can call me Harry. It saves confusion. May I call you Leo?'

'You've been following me, Harry.'

'You're an interesting man.' He gave me a little bow, a gesture of respect. 'You've shown an ability to uncover the truth, even when the police are stumped. My father said to keep an eye on you.'

My head was throbbing as though something inside it was growing and would soon burst out. I gingerly prodded the back of my skull and found my hair was greasy with blood.

'I'm not interesting.'

'Our readers disagree.' He handed me a flask. 'It's rough as hell but it does the trick.'

Very slowly, I sat up and took a swig. The liquid tasted metallic in my mouth, burning down my throat. For a second, I thought he'd poisoned me, but then a warmth spread through my chest.

Constance frowned. 'Salicin would be better. What you really need is rest, Mr Stanhope, like Mr Whitford says.'

She started dabbing my face and hair. Gradually, the white cloth turned pink.

'Where's Alfie?'

'He's out.'

Her expression of disgust told me he was with Mrs Gower. It was probably just as well. I had promised him I would find a new place to live and instead was having a head wound stitched by his daughter. He wouldn't be pleased.

'I have to go,' I said. 'I need to find Aiden and Ciara.'

Harry put his hand out for the flask, tipping it up and swilling the liquid around in his mouth before swallowing.

'How? Are you going to knock on every door in London? Look at the state of you.'

He was right, of course. They had been kidnapped for a reason, and that reason must be connected to the murder of their mother. I needed to *think*. But my mind wouldn't come into focus. I felt as though I was looking at the world through gauze.

'A couple of questions, if you don't mind, Leo.' He had his notebook and pen at the ready. 'How old are you, and where are you from?'

'He's from Enfield, aren't you, Mr Stanhope?' said Constance, smiling winningly at the young man. 'He's the son of a vicar.'

'Wait, stop.' My tightly wound world was starting to unravel. 'No questions. I don't want to appear in your newspaper.'

'Ah, well, it might be a bit late for that.' I caught a note of something in his voice. He handed me a copy of the *Daily Chronicle*. 'My guess is this was what the police wanted to talk to you about.'

I opened it up and he pointed to the front-page story, but I could barely make out the words. Constance took it out of my hands and started reading aloud.

'"Police Seek Help Solving Murder at Anarchists' Club". That's the headline, Mr Stanhope. "The murder of Miss Dora Hannigan, found buried in a shallow grave at the Rose Street Club, a haven for anarchists and" … is that "foreigners"? Yes, foreigners … "in Soho, remains unsolved. The police appear to have made little progress beyond app-re-hend-ing Mr Edwin Cowdery, a known felon, for different crimes, those of tres-pass-ing at a mill in the East End and plotting to set fire to it." That sounds awful.'

'Please continue,' said Harry. 'You haven't got to the good bit yet.'

'Yes, of course. "Following its own enquiries, the *Daily Chronicle* understands the police have sought the help of am-a-teur detective Mr Leo Stanhope." Gosh, isn't that a thing, you're an amateur detective! "Mr Stanhope was in-stru-men-tal in solving two previous murders that readers may recall: those of Mr James Bentinck and Miss Maria Mills. In those cases, the per-pe-trators" ... does that mean criminals?'

'Yes.'

'"The perpetrators were convicted and sentenced to be hanged. Mr Stanhope is now investigating the murder of Miss Hannigan and has been seen at the Rose Street Club and elsewhere. The citizens of our city can sleep soundly know-ing the murderer will soon be brought to justice now that Mr Stanhope is on the case!" Well, that's wonderful, isn't it?'

I took the newspaper from her and forced my eyes to focus, reading with a growing sense of dread. There was more, much more, casting me in a heroic light, implying I was poised at every moment to solve crimes the police were too lazy or incompetent to address. I felt sick. This exposure was dangerous; my whole life consisted of secrecy.

'Did you write this?' I stammered.

Harry Whitford nodded. 'My first front page. I don't suppose the police were very keen on it, though.' He grinned proudly, unbothered by my discomfort. 'I know there's more to the story if you're willing to tell me. A woman was murdered and now her children have been kidnapped. Not to mention John Duport has disappeared without a trace. You must tell me everything.'

I climbed off the table, feeling unstable, but just about capable of walking.

Constance glared at me. 'You shouldn't go anywhere except to bed, Mr Stanhope. But if you absolutely must, I'll go with you.'

'Certainly not. Why aren't you at school, anyway?'

Alfie would be vexed that I had allowed her to stitch my wound, but that would feel like a mild breeze compared with the tempest of his anger if I took her with me to search for two kidnapped children.

Constance folded her arms. 'It's lunchtime.'

Harry sucked on his pen. 'Where are you going?'

'Never you mind. But if I can't find Aiden and Ciara, you can write another story for your newspaper, front page, offering a reward. I'll give twenty pounds for their return, or any information about their whereabouts. No, make it fifty. Will that be enough, do you think?'

He made a few more squiggles in his notebook. 'More than. A couple of months ago, we offered a ten-shilling reward for the recovery of a lady's pure-bred dog. We got lots of replies.'

'Good.'

'Not really. Every beggar in London turned up with some mangy hound. Couldn't move for 'em. The place still smells of shit and I'm pretty sure I've got fleas.' He scratched his head. 'And we never did find the lady's bloody dog.'

As I limped down to Piccadilly to get a cab, every part of me felt sore. Blood kept dripping into my eye. All the time

I was thinking: they cannot be dead. They simply cannot. I clung to the belief that if whoever had taken them had wanted to kill them, they would have been shot as soon as they came out of that alley.

A dull ache formed in my stomach that grew, almost crippling me. I had to stop and crouch down, fearful I was rupturing something in my insides.

'Stop being so bloody feeble,' I mumbled out loud.

Nothing mattered except getting Aiden and Ciara back with me, where they belonged. And I knew I couldn't do it on my own.

At Rosie's shop, there was a queue of customers: mothers with small children and working men from the printing presses. Rosie didn't greet me, and instead showed uncharacteristic patience while a lady dithered between chicken with peas and duck with spinach.

I heard a child's voice and whirled round, certain it was Ciara, but it turned out to be a small boy, the son of a customer. I had to lean on the counter for support.

'Rosie,' I muttered, earning an irritated glance from the ditherer.

'Wait your turn please, Mr Stanhope.' Rosie punished me with a formal smile, without really looking at me, and returned to her customer. 'What about a nice lamb and dill, special for Easter?'

'Someone's kidnapped Aiden and Ciara,' I said.

She looked me straight in the eyes, her previous reserve evaporating. 'Are they all right? Who has them?'

'I don't know. They were taken in a carriage by someone with a gun. I need your help, Rosie.'

'A gun? Mother of God.' She undid her apron and hung it on a hook. 'Why didn't you say so before, instead of waiting there like an idiot?'

She disappeared into the back of the shop and returned a few seconds later wearing a coat and hat and holding a flannel, which she tossed in my direction.

'You're bleeding. What happened to you?'

I wiped the blood from my eye and cheek. 'A policeman.'

She seemed to accept that answer as part of the natural order of things.

'We'll start with Sir Reginald Thackery,' I said. 'He might have them.'

In truth, he was the only person I could think of. It had to be him.

Rosie let me get a cab for once. Indeed, she went out to the junction at Farringdon Street and hailed one herself, which proved how appalling my injury must have looked.

For most of the journey we sat in silence, looking out of opposite windows, but as we were passing the Holborn Union Workhouse, I cleared my throat.

'I'm sorry, Rosie. I shouldn't have said what I said to you before. It wasn't fair.'

She didn't immediately reply, her usual approach when I voiced an opinion she considered obvious, which was at least half the time. But gradually, she grew restless, tutting to herself and pursing her lips. Eventually, she turned to me.

'You weren't altogether wrong, is the thing.' She clasped her hands in her lap. 'By rights I *should* be staying at home. I left my children with Albert and Alice, and the shop too. They must be wondering what on earth I'm doing.'

'I'm sure they understand.'

She pulled a face. 'I'm sure they don't. But I meant what I said before. I don't want the total of what I am to be Jack Flowers's sad, lonely widow.'

I felt a tremendous urge to take her hand in mine, to comfort her and me both, but I couldn't. That wasn't how we were.

'*Are* you sad and lonely?' I asked.

She stared at me, her eyes filled with tears. 'How can I be? I love my children more than life itself and I'm with people all the time. It's just ... last year when we were hunting for who killed your Maria and my Jack, we were doing something ... I don't know ... something more *important* than cooking pies.' She gave a little shrug. 'Something beyond the shop my father left me, and the children my husband gave me.'

'I'm glad you did.'

She looked out of the window again, speaking without facing me. 'You say that, but ... where did you go, Leo? All we went through, and you disappeared like it was nothing. Like it didn't matter at all. Did you not once think to come and see how I was doing?'

I couldn't tell her why I had not: that I could never forgive her. Except now, I found myself divided. In my mind, there seemed to be two Rosies – the one who had done me such harm, and the one sitting beside me now, her breath unsteady and her hands fidgeting in her lap.

'I'm sorry.'

She shook her head, but more tenderly now. It was the same expression she used with her children.

'I don't know which of us is the bigger fool,' she said.

Me neither, I thought, as we drew up outside Sir Reginald's house in Gordon Square.

Once before, we had entered a rich man's home. He took us prisoner and … no, I wouldn't think about it. That was in another room, far away across London, and there it would stay.

I had to go inside. This was my single hope.

If Sir Reginald doesn't have Aiden and Ciara, I thought, I have no idea who does.

22

THE DOOR WAS OPENED by a footman. He was very tall and broad, wearing a uniform of military precision, his jacket the exact blue of a jay's feather. You could have put a ruler to the crease in his trousers, and any deviation from the straight would be the fault of the ruler.

'Good afternoon,' he said, not bothering to hide his disdain. 'Are you with the music-hall people? Downstairs and through the basement.'

He went to shut the door, but I put my hand against it. 'No, I'm Mr Stanhope and this is Mrs Flowers. We need to speak to Sir Reginald urgently.'

'I see.'

Something was nagging at me, chewing on my nerve endings and scratching at the palms of my hands. It was him. I recognised his voice and those calculating eyes. This was the man who'd attacked me at the pharmacy. I knew it. And what's more, he knew that I knew it.

'Are the children here?' I demanded. 'Do you have them?'

'Whatever do you mean?'

He surveyed me from his great height, almost sneering, challenging me to take it further.

I didn't know what to do. Even if I'd been able to beat the answer out of him, which I certainly couldn't, it would hardly be possible *here*.

My only option was to beg.

'Please. Was it you in the carriage? I only want to know if they're safe, that's all. Just tell me that much.'

He blinked and rubbed his face with his hands, before glancing over his shoulder into the house. He seemed to be struggling for the right words.

'I don't know anything about that,' he said, in a low voice.

Of course, he might have been lying, but something in his reaction suggested he wasn't. His initial smirk had been deliberate and arrogant, but when I'd told him the children had been kidnapped, he'd been genuinely surprised. He didn't have them.

'Then it's absolutely urgent that we speak to Sir Reginald. It cannot wait.'

'All right, I suppose you'd better come in.'

'Rosie.' I stared at her intently, hoping she would take my suggestion as an instruction. 'You should stay here.'

She blinked twice, fully understanding me and not giving a damn. 'No, I'd rather not.'

Inside, the walls of the hallway were covered with dozens of small pictures of birds, butterflies and lizards, mostly hand drawn, but without any sense of the beauty or vitality of the creatures they depicted. They were anatomical, a product of science rather than art, and the birds, at least, were in something approaching taxonomical order, with eagles and buzzards nearest to me, thrushes and finches chasing each other up the stairs and woodpeckers perching over the door lintels. The whole effect was unsettling, like being trapped in the Hunterian Museum.

The footman indicated a room at the end of the hall. 'You can wait in there with the others. I'll call you if Sir Reginald becomes free.'

'Very well, but I beg you to be quick.'

Through the open door I could see people moving about. A man was calling out instructions in an authoritative tone: 'Higher! Higher! A bit more. Now hold it there. Right there. No, no, no! You're *drooping*, man.'

I recognised the voice, and then saw the fellow himself, Peregrine Black, his attention fixed on something within the room.

'The *actors* are preparing for their performance,' scoffed the footman. 'They'll be entertaining members of the Board of Trade after dinner, so I'm told.'

The room turned out to be a substantial parlour with an elaborate gasolier hanging from the ceiling. There were Union Jack flags either side of the mantelpiece, and at one end a platform had been erected, perhaps eighteen inches above the level of the floor and three yards by two. Hanging over it was a banner bearing the legend: 'The Calcutta Music Hall Touring Company'.

A slack-shouldered stagehand was trying to prop up the single piece of scenery – a fake tree – so the branches would drape attractively. Even at this he was failing, and the poor fellow was receiving the most frightful scolding from Black.

'It must stand up on its own, you utter disaster! When did you last see a tree that couldn't support itself?'

Black spun on the spot, overcome by the man's incompetence. He was about to resume his hectoring when he saw us.

'Mrs Flowers!' he bellowed. 'And … my word, is that you, Mr Stanhope? What on earth happened to your face?'

He approached us, stepping adroitly, for so large a fellow, between a man in a judge's wig and a Chinese woman carrying a baby, which turned out, when she fumbled and dropped it on its head, to be a doll.

'Why are you here?' He appeared anxious, probably recalling his previous criticism of his employer.

'Two children have been kidnapped. We have some questions for Sir Reginald.'

'Is that how …?' He rotated a finger around his face to indicate my injuries.

'Yes. They were taken while in my care.'

It was the first time I'd said it out loud. I pinched myself under my armpit, where my cilice rubbed against my skin.

'Have you seen anything while you've been here?' asked Rosie. 'Or heard any children's voices? It's very important.'

'I haven't seen anyone,' he said. 'But we only arrived an hour ago. My word, you do have an exciting time, don't you? Did you find out who killed Dora Hannigan?'

'You remember her name,' said Rosie, and I could see what she was thinking: that it was odd for someone who wasn't involved to retain that detail.

He waved a hand. 'As I said before, it was in the newspapers.'

'No,' I said firmly. It didn't matter that he was a big man and capable of violence. Nothing would get in my way now. 'John Thackery told you about her, didn't he? She was his governess when he was young.'

Black sighed and closed his eyes, speaking with them still shut. 'Yes, that's true. I didn't know if you'd made that connection.'

'He told me himself. She was the mother of the children that were taken. A boy and a girl.'

He put his hand to his mouth. 'Oh, that's terrible. She's dead, her children kidnapped, and I haven't heard from John in days. Have you seen him again?'

'No. I'm sorry.'

Black gazed out at the garden, seemingly lost in thought. The grass was barren and brown, cast into shadow by a high, featureless wall at the far end.

'He speaks of her often,' he said. 'She was the only one who was kind to him, when he was young.'

'Yes, I heard his father didn't like him.'

'Sir Reginald used to shut him in a cupboard, did you know that? For hours. Isn't that hateful? Who would do that to a child? Miss Hannigan used to get bread and honey for him and slide it under the door. She used to read to him too, he told me.'

I thought of Aiden and Ciara, and shuddered. They might be in just such a place, but with no kindly governess to show them pity. I pushed the thought away; if I dwelled on it, I would go mad.

'That's terrible.'

Black nodded, still staring out at the garden, his eyes following the paved path that led to a wrought-iron bench and an arch with plants growing up and over it. 'He told me that when he was eighteen his father sent him to the Military Academy at Woolwich. He hated it and ran away.' Black pointed at the featureless wall. 'There's a stable behind there, and Sir Reginald locked him in it for three weeks. He punished his own son until he did as he was told and went back to Woolwich. Can you imagine the humiliation?'

'When did you last see him?' asked Rosie.

'Almost two weeks ago, I think. We agreed to meet on Tuesday night, after the performance, but he never turned up.'

'This was for you to paint his portrait, was it?'

He smiled thinly at her. 'Of course.'

Why hadn't John Thackery kept that tryst? I thought back to the day I'd followed him. He had vanished in the square near his father's house. Where could he have gone?

I didn't have time to consider the question further. Sir Reginald came into the room and Black immediately made himself busy near the stage. Sir Reginald watched him go with an expression of revulsion and turned to me, briefly eyeing the sutures above my eyebrow.

'Stanhope,' he said. 'I presume you've come to apologise. Do you have my guinea?'

'No, Sir Reginald. I need to know, do you have Aiden and Ciara Hannigan? They've been kidnapped.'

'What are you babbling about?' He glared at Rosie. 'And who are you?'

'This is Mrs Flowers,' I said. 'She's fully appraised of the situation. She's helping me find them.'

She pursed her lips. 'We're finding them together.'

Sir Reginald barely acknowledged her. 'Are you a cretin, Stanhope? How could you be so stupid? Come with me.'

He led us into a small room covered on all four walls with books, row upon row of them. There was no natural light, but a gas lamp was flickering above our heads. He turned it up using a brass knob on the wall, and as the glow blossomed I saw that most of the books were about science, with titles like *A Treatise on the Blood, Inflammation and Gunshot Wounds*, *The Anatomy of the Human Body* and *A Guide to Hydropathy*, though some were about industry and government and there was a whole shelf full of journals. On a dainty table in the centre of the room, a monkey's paw was mounted on a plinth, raised as if about to catch a ball.

Sir Reginald seemed sicklier than the last time I'd seen him, twice almost coughing, but somehow suppressing it, his knuckles growing white as he gripped the arms of his chair. It was the only one in the room, so we had no choice but to stand in front of him like naughty schoolchildren.

'Do you know where the children might be, Sir Reginald?'

He looked at me as if I had lost my senses. 'Me? What are you talking about?'

'I was hoping that, since I didn't do as you asked, you had taken the task out of my hands.'

'Don't be ridiculous.' His mouth twisted into a sneer. 'I don't *kidnap* people.'

I was watching him closely, desperate for some sign he was lying. 'Your man, the footman, might he have done it? Perhaps believing it was what you wanted?'

'My *footman*? I barely trust him to carry my chamber pot.'

'But you are their father, aren't you, Sir Reginald?' I ignored his glower. Necessity was making me reckless. 'That's why you're so interested in their welfare. Your son Peter resembles Aiden quite closely.'

'Don't be impudent, Stanhope.' This was a simple instruction, issued without heat. I was so far beneath him I didn't warrant his anger.

'We're only trying to understand all the possibilities,' offered Rosie, in a conciliatory tone.

He stood up and pulled a book from the shelf: *On the Origin of Species*.

'Charles Darwin,' he said. 'Have you read it?'

He was only addressing me. He seemed to assume Rosie hadn't.

'A little.'

There had been a copy in the vicarage, and I'd read the first few chapters. I had never wondered about that before; a clergyman owning such a book. If I hadn't known better, I would have thought my father open-minded.

'Then you know what it says, what it *means*. That we progress and progress, and by that progression the strongest of us survive at the expense of the weak.'

'Well, I wouldn't say that's exactly—'

'It's as clear as day.' He licked his finger and turned a couple of pages. 'It's as much about economics as it is biology. Those of us who build something, create something, deserve to rise, and those who dilly-dally and whine about the good of the working man, whatever that means, deserve poverty.' He shook his head, exasperated. 'They're planning a strike, you know, the men at the mill. They're protesting against God knows what, risking their livelihoods out of pure envy. People like that don't have the backbone to do anything for themselves.'

'Like your son John, you mean?' I asked.

He stopped, his hand shaking. 'How do you know him?'

I thought quickly. I didn't want to admit we'd been friendly, years before. It would encourage questions I didn't want to answer.

'Miss Hannigan had been his governess. The police spoke to him.'

Sir Reginald sat down again and opened a drawer in the little table, pulling out his spit cup and a bottle of laudanum.

'Yes,' he said, eventually. 'Like John. Weak blood, you see.'

Rosie looked confused. 'But he's your son,' she said. 'Your blood's the same.'

And then it came to me. John didn't look anything like Aiden and Peter. And John had said his father hated him *for existing*.

'Unless he's not your *natural* son. Is that it? Is John *adopted*?'

Sir Reginald picked at his thumbnail and pulled at the skin with his teeth. All his nails were the same, bitten down, puffy and lacerated around the edges.

'He's the proof, if any were needed. I tried everything for him, but it was impossible. He left the army having never fought a battle or been promoted. Can you imagine that? He doesn't come from my stock. His is a weaker strain.' He tapped his finger on the pages of the book and started to read out loud: '"Each new variety, and ultimately each new species, is produced and maintained by having some advantage over those with which it comes into competition; and the consequent extinction of less-favoured forms almost inevitably follows." Do you see? I have competed, and I have won.'

'And yet you have a sickness, Sir Reginald. It's obvious.'

'I'm not talking about physical strength, I'm talking about *mentality*.' He clenched his fist. 'Intellect, diligence and determination. The power to lead. My line is strong, which is why it deserves to continue, while others die out.'

'Die out? You truly think that?'

'It's science!' He slammed his fist down on the table, making the monkey's paw jump, and then stiffened, his face blossoming red and his chest heaving. He took a sip of laudanum and closed his eyes before continuing. 'Adopting John was the worst mistake I ever made. I regretted it the instant I'd done it. He was a feeble boy and grew into an embittered man. No *substance*.' He banged the table again. 'He had the gall to threaten me. That's why I instructed you to get those two children out of the way.'

'You think *John* might have taken them?'

I hadn't considered the possibility, and yet … at least it would mean they were safe. John had cared about their mother, and I couldn't imagine him hurting them. Unless, of course, he'd killed Dora too, in which case everything I had thought about him was wrong. It occurred to me that I might have been overly influenced by my memories of him as a boy.

Sir Reginald nodded. 'He's got them somewhere, I'm certain, ready to reveal at the worst possible moment for me. He has no consideration for anyone but himself.'

That was true enough. John had chosen to blackmail me without a second thought.

'Was that why you wanted them hidden under a false surname?'

'Correct. But you proved incapable of doing the simplest thing.'

'Do you know where John is now?' asked Rosie.

'I have no idea. And you must stop interfering. No good will come of it.'

'Why?'

'Because things are in motion. Things you don't understand.'

'What things?'

He stood up again, a signal that our meeting was over. 'Follow my instructions this time, will you? It's imperative that you do nothing. Lives depend on it.'

23

WHEN WE WERE ON our own in the hallway, Rosie leaned towards me and whispered: 'I'm going to have a quick poke around. See if there's any sign of them upstairs.'

'Rosie! You can't.'

She cocked her head and blinked three times quickly, all innocence. 'Of course I can. I'm looking for somewhere to wash my face, aren't I?'

'No!' I hissed.

I was almost shaking with exasperation, but before I was able to stop her, she'd rounded the banister and scurried up the stairs.

I couldn't hang about in the hallway, so I went back to the parlour, now even more resembling a makeshift theatre. Some of the performers had already changed into their costumes and were smoking and passing round a bottle, while others were straightening the chairs or arraying lamps at the foot of the stage. The Union Jack flags had been removed from the fireplace so, for the first time, I could see what they had previously obscured: above the mantel was a long sword, set horizontally and supported on brackets at each end. The hilt was simple and black, and the blade cold and clean. It had a purposeful look, like a hunting dog pulling at its leash.

Below, two more brackets were attached to the wall, close together, as if a shorter sword had been hung there.

Except it was missing.

'How do you manage?' asked Black behind me. 'Living in secret as you do.'

'I'm just a normal man,' I replied, a little tartly, not wanting a conversation. Every second spent here was a second not finding Aiden and Ciara.

'A *normal* man?' He seemed disappointed by my mundanity. 'What was your name, before?'

On the few occasions I'd been asked it, that was the question that enraged me the most. What he was really asking was: 'Who are you really?'

'Why does it matter?'

He bowed slightly. 'It doesn't, of course. We're all our own invention, are we not?'

I was too impatient to be polite. 'Is that why you got married?'

'I'm a man of appetites, Mr Stanhope.' He was choosing his words with care. 'I like gin *and* beer. I don't see why I should have to choose between one and the other.'

His face twitched, and I sensed again a vast sadness ... no, it was closer to grief.

'Are you performing this evening, Mr Black?'

He was not yet changed into his finery.

'No, I've been trumped.'

He nodded towards a young woman wearing a delightful cream-coloured frock. I didn't recognise her at first. She looked so different when not in masculine britches.

'Good Lord, is that Vesta Tilley?'

'In the flesh. She has star billing.'

'I thought they didn't like her kind of act. Making fun of the gentry and all that.'

Black looked at me incredulously. 'Oh, they don't mind it for *themselves*, Mr Stanhope. They are *sophisticated* people, able to laugh at their own foibles. It's the stinking masses that mustn't see such things.'

Peter Thackery was hovering near her, clearly desperate to introduce himself. She seemed wary of his intentions and turned away, and his expression soured. When smiling he looked like Ciara, but otherwise he resembled Aiden. It was uncanny.

I wasn't sure if he would remember me – he'd been hopelessly drunk last time I saw him – but he waved with boyish bonhomie.

'We do keep bumping into each other, don't we, Mr …?'

'Stanhope, and yes. I'm looking for two children. Have you seen them? A boy of ten and a girl of six, both dark-haired.'

He wasn't properly listening. His eyes were following Miss Tilley and he was swaying slightly, his arms reaching towards her as if he was about to invite her for a waltz.

'Peter!' I said, a little sharply. 'Have you seen any children here?'

'What? No, why would I have?' He peered at the stitches on my head, even putting out a finger to touch one, until I pulled away. 'My goodness, you have been in the wars, haven't you? Are those boot marks on your—'

'It's not as bad as it looks.'

He leaned towards me and lowered his voice. 'I really must thank you for the good turn you did me. Best not to mention it to anyone else, though, if you wouldn't mind. Father's a bit of a stickler.'

'Of course, I understand.'

Sir Reginald himself came back into the room, firmly guiding Rosie, whose face was living up to her name.

'For goodness' sake, Peter,' he said. 'Stop hanging about here like a love-struck housemaid or I'll send you back to school.'

Peter looked aghast. 'But it's the Easter holidays,' he protested.

Sir Reginald ignored him and surveyed me sternly. 'I did not give you permission to talk to my son nor for this *woman* to wander around my house.'

'I'm sorry, but we need to find—'

He held up his hand for silence and pulled on a brass lever attached to the wall by the fireplace. Somewhere downstairs, I imagined, a bell was ringing. We waited with him like children about to be punished until the footman arrived.

'Mr Stanhope and …' Sir Reginald waved a hand at Rosie '… and this woman are leaving now. Please ensure they do so. And that they do not return.'

———

Outside, I set off as fast as I could.

'Leo!' Rosie called behind me. 'Where are you going? Slow down.'

Reluctantly, I waited for her. She grabbed my arm. 'I checked everywhere I could,' she said. 'There was nothing. A maid caught me poking my head into the main bedroom. There were a lot of medical things in there: instruments and one of those bath chairs for invalids.'

'Lady Thackery is very sickly. More even than her husband.'

'Well, she wasn't there.'

The door to the house opened and Peter Thackery appeared, looking left and right. He closed the door gently, as if he didn't want anyone inside to hear, and came down the steps towards us.

He nodded to Rosie but exclusively addressed me, much as Sir Reginald had done.

'I heard Father talking about those children.'

'Do you know something about them?'

He looked sheepish. 'No. Only that, well, he said he was going to send a note to that policeman, Hooper. He suspects you of kidnapping and murder. He thinks you collaborated with John.' He winked mischievously. 'I say, did you? It would be quite a feat if so.'

'Of course not.'

I didn't have time for this juvenile nonsense and was already moving away from him. The itch to leave this place was coming up through the soles of my shoes.

'Oh.' He seemed disappointed. 'Well anyway, I thought you ought to know, as you were a decent chap to me. One good turn and all that.' He lowered his voice. 'It's just that, well, you might be better off . . .' He didn't finish his sentence but made a galloping motion with his fingers in the air. 'I can provide a bit of funding if you need to get away.'

'That's not necessary.' A thought occurred to me. 'When did you last see your brother?'

'My brother?' He looked perplexed. 'Oh, you mean John? I haven't seen him in ages.'

In my mind, a tiny flame ignited. For the first time since the children had been taken, I was actually *thinking*.

Why had Sir Reginald adopted John, if he felt so strongly about his precious bloodline?

Peter was exactly like Sir Reginald: headstrong and arrogant, though he could be charming when he chose to be. And they shared something in the shapes of their faces and the sharpness of their eyes too. Peter was his father's son, I was sure of it.

But he was nothing like Lady Thackery. Nothing at all.

The tiny flame in my mind grew.

I had assumed Sir Reginald had simply kept Dora Hannigan as his mistress and not cared much about the consequences. But that wasn't true. He had cared about the consequences very much.

And then I was certain. As certain as if I'd witnessed every breath of it.

Peter was Sir Reginald's son. And he was Aiden and Ciara's brother too. Or half-brother. But not in the way I had thought. It was not their father they had in common.

It was their mother.

———

When Peter had gone back inside, I turned to Rosie.

'We need to search Sir Reginald's stable.'

She looked horrified. 'Why? Do you think John might've hidden the children there?'

I thought back to the high wall behind the house and beckoned her to hurry. 'It's possible. This family isn't what it seems.'

'What do you mean?'

I explained as we walked. 'When Sir Reginald and Lady Thackery were first married, no doubt he expected she would soon become pregnant, in the normal way of things. But what if she didn't? What if the years passed, and there was no pregnancy?'

Rosie shrugged. 'It's not so unusual, is it? One of my sisters is childless.' She pondered for a moment. 'Mind you, a man like that, it would make him furious, I imagine.'

'Exactly. I'm sure he sent her to a doctor to be examined – many doctors, probably. But it didn't work, so they adopted John. Lady Thackery doted on him, but not so Sir Reginald. Now, we know why. John was not his flesh and blood.'

'The poor lad,' said Rosie, her face set hard, her sense of injustice provoked. 'It wasn't his fault.'

'No. And as he got older, he started to resent his father. He left the army as soon as he could and became a radical, determined to overthrow Sir Reginald and everyone like him.'

We had reached the corner where I'd last seen John, in the shadow of the church. We turned away from the square, walking as quickly as we could without drawing attention.

'What about Peter?' asked Rosie. 'If they can't have children, where did he come from?'

There was only one plausible explanation. The lad looked so much like an older version of Aiden, they *must* have a parent in common.

299

'I believe Sir Reginald wanted a child of his own blood. But his wife couldn't give him one, so he needed someone else. As it happened, he was employing a governess, Dora Hannigan. She was poor and young, probably no more than fifteen or sixteen years old. The two of them came to an arrangement; he made her pregnant and she gave up the baby for him and Lady Thackery to raise as their own.'

Rosie nodded. 'I've heard of young women having other people's babes. It's a terrible thing. They're not much more than children themselves, but they're used like heifers and then turned out on to the street.'

'She was well paid.'

Rosie looked at me sharply. 'Well, I'm sure that's fine, isn't it? No harm done as long as they gave the girl some money.'

I wondered who else knew Dora had received more than two hundred pounds from Sir Reginald. Probably John, but would anyone else? Her friends at the club might not think so well of her if they learned what she'd done.

'And years later,' I continued, 'she had two children of her own: Aiden and Ciara. They look like Peter because they share the same mother, not the same father.'

We had reached a narrow street, or more properly a mews, that ran behind the houses on Gordon Square, marked at the entrance by a brick arch and stone pillars on either side. The first couple of windows shone with a weak, yellow light, but beyond that it was coal-black.

'The stable must be down there,' said Rosie, as if she was trying to convince herself.

I had no time to confront my own fears; Aiden and Ciara might be imprisoned in one of these stables. I stepped forwards into the gloom.

At first, I couldn't see anything at all, though I was aware of Rosie close to me, her shoes click-clacking on the cobbles. But as my eyes grew accustomed, I could discern the wooden sheds on our left, with signs above their doors: a tanner, a forger and a wheelwright, with a coach wheel hanging from the eaves.

To our right, the stables were lined up like seaside cottages, each one backing on to one of the grand houses on Gordon Square. Most were shut, but the garage doors of one were thrown open, taking up half the width of the mews, awaiting the return of its carriage.

'It'll be near the end,' I whispered to Rosie. 'I counted the houses.'

The mews finished at a sprawling timberyard lit dimly by the lamps of the university behind us. Opposite that was the last stable.

The upstairs windows were dark, their curtains drawn back, and the name 'Thackery' had been inscribed on a wooden plaque on the wall.

I pressed my ear against the door and could hear movements within.

'Are you sure we should be doing this, Leo?' asked Rosie, her voice sounding thin and high.

She was right, of course. If I was caught trespassing on Sir Reginald's property, he would exert the full force of the law. I knew what that meant: discovery, humiliation, the loss of everything and, when I refused to be female, medicines and electricity and that ultimate horror, the red-hot iron, burning me away.

I would kill myself first.

But I couldn't think about that now. I needed to know whether the children were being held in the stable. Nothing else mattered.

'Aiden!' I hissed, as loudly as I dared, but there was no reply.

I pushed and pulled on the door, but it wouldn't budge. I pulled harder and kicked it and then beat my fists against the wood, but I wasn't strong enough to break it.

'Leo!' whispered Rosie. 'Stop! You'll hurt yourself.'

'We have to get inside.'

'I know, but not like that.' She thought for a moment. 'We need something long and thin that we can poke through and lift the latch.'

I was breathing too fast, and it was hurting my chest. I pinched the sore place under my arm where my cilice was scouring my skin into a smooth, leather welt.

'You're right. Do you have a hat pin handy?'

I was almost certain she rolled her eyes. 'No, Leo, I don't. I own one hat pin for church on Sundays. There must be something else here.'

I looked around us.

'Wait.'

The timberyard opposite the stable was disused, a painted sign explaining that the land had been sold to the university. The fence was split and broken, doubtless by thieves looking for wood to sell or burn. I slipped through and searched along the ground until I found what I was looking for: an iron nail, shining in the thin light, almost trodden into the soil.

I held it up, so ecstatic that I didn't think about the faintest of familiar smells, nor the mound of newly dug earth.

Rosie took the nail and poked it between the two garage doors, manoeuvring it until I heard the clunk of the latch inside lifting.

'Jack used to lock me out sometimes,' she said. 'I had to wait until he'd drunk himself into a stupor and then do that.'

I hauled open one of the doors, which was heavy, dragging and rattling over the cobbles, echoing around the mews.

'Keep a lookout,' I said.

Inside, I could hear the nervous movement of the horses' hooves. I edged around the carriage, feeling something at my feet just too late, dislodging it and causing a huge crash. The shafts of the carriage had been propped on a rest, and I'd inadvertently kicked it away. The horses stamped and knocked against the wood of their stalls, breathing heavily. I tried to shush them as best I could, but they wouldn't be touched, jerking their heads up and away from me. I was afraid of being bitten and decided to leave them; if anyone was nearby, they had certainly already heard the commotion.

Beyond the two horses' stalls was a locker, perhaps three feet wide and the height of my chest. I leaned down to look inside, and it was filled with the horses' tack: bridles, reins and winter blankets. The wood felt rough under my fingers, covered with dents and scratches as if something had kicked to get out. But the marks were old, and the bolt was rusted and stiff. No one had been trapped in here for many years. This, I guessed, was where John had been imprisoned after he ran away from the army. I could only imagine his fear, shut in this box with no light nor even room to stand.

Aiden and Ciara could be in a box like this one, crying and hammering to get out. But I had no time to surrender to that terror, not yet; I had to keep searching.

I fumbled back along the wall and found a doorway into a small space. From the breath of cool air on my face, I guessed it was a stairwell leading to the upper floor. I shuffled forwards, my hands groping in front of me as if I was playing blind man's buff, until my fingers touched a banister. I gripped hold of it and tentatively took the first step, heading upwards into complete darkness.

'Aiden!' I called. 'Ciara!'

At the top there was a room with three coffin beds side by side, but only one had any blankets.

There was no sign of the children.

Through the window, I could see Rosie pacing in circles. I opened the sash and was about to call to her when I heard a sound from downstairs; a creaking and then a clatter, like the lid of a crate being dropped.

I stayed completely still, trying not to breathe. There were footsteps and the sound of a match being lit, and then the percussive rumble of the garage door being pulled shut.

'Bloody coachman,' said a man's voice. Despite his words, his tone was sweet and gentle. 'Going off and leaving the bloody door open.' There was a sound of rustling, and then: 'Look what I've got, my darling. You see? You like that? Of course, you do. Here, I've got some for you too. There we are.'

I knew the voice. It was the footman. I listened for an answer, thinking perhaps this was an assignation with one of the maids or even, I had to consider, more than one, but then I realised he was talking to the horses, giving them treats.

He laughed. 'Enough, enough. That's all I have. No more tonight, my darlings, my beauties. Look, see? You've had it all.'

I was hoping he would go back the way he'd come, but the floorboards were warped and, even as I tried my hardest to keep still, they groaned under my weight.

He stopped talking and his footsteps grew louder as he came into the stairwell.

'Is that you, Mr Picken? Are you back?' He paused, listening for an answer, and then called again. 'Bernard?'

To my horror he started up the stairs. I cast around, but there was nowhere to hide, no cupboard or wardrobe or even space under the beds. He would see me as soon as he reached the top. The glow of his candle was growing.

He was far bigger and stronger than me. Even taking him by surprise, I didn't think I could get past him.

I had only one choice.

The window was small, and the sash took up half of it, but I managed to climb on to the sill and wriggle through, so I was sitting on the ledge facing out. My hips were tight against the sides, but I had just enough space to twist round and lower myself down, my feet finding the top of the garage doorframe.

'Mother of God,' I heard Rosie mutter.

'Someone's in there,' I hissed. 'Hide.'

I heard her scamper away as I dropped down, feeling the jolt of the cobbles through my ankles and calves as I landed. I backed against the wall, hidden in the shadows, just as the footman leaned out of the window. He swore and ducked back inside, and then I heard his boots pounding down the stairs, taking two at a time.

I dashed across the mews and through the gap in the timberyard fence, where I crouched down, out of sight.

The front door to the stable opened and I could hear footsteps.

'Who's there?' he shouted, the shine of his lamp swinging from side to side.

I kept completely still, breathing as softly as I could. To my relief, he loped down the mews towards the street.

I didn't want to pass him coming back, so I had no choice but to wait. I was alert to every sound: the horses shifting in their stalls, the squeak of cart wheels on the main road and two men talking in the university playing fields behind me. I almost missed it again, the faintest of smells amidst the woody odour, like a few grains of pepper in a plate of scrambled eggs. But it was there. I hadn't imagined it.

Putrescence. It was unmistakeable. I had suffered it for hours at a time in my previous occupation, assisting a surgeon of the dead. New corpses reeked of leaking bowels and their first, fleshy decay, giving way after a few days to methane from their bloated stomachs and the putrefaction of their blood and bile. I had grown used to it. I would never be able to forget it.

A horrifying thought washed over me. I turned and stared at the place where I had found the nail. The soil had been disturbed, formed into a hump, slightly above the level of the rest of the yard.

I leaned back against the fence, feeling the splinters like pins against my skin.

'No,' I whispered. 'Please, no.'

All I could think about was a grave, with two little bodies inside.

24

I COULDN'T DIG, NOT yet. It would make too much noise. I had to wait in an agony of dread until the footman came back, spitting curses, and slammed the door shut.

My heart was beating so fast I feared it would tear itself apart.

I scrabbled frantically with my hands, scooping the earth and stones to either side, uncaring of my clothes, wiping my face with grubby fingers, barely able to see in the dimness. I knew the grave must be recent because the level of the soil was raised. Older corpses form a dip in the ground as the flesh is eaten away and dirt falls between the bones.

It wasn't long before I touched woven material. I pulled on it, and it was a jacket lapel. Further and further down I went, scraping the dirt from his arms, his shoulders, his neck. When his face emerged from the earth, I stopped, and sat cross-legged beside him.

'Thank God,' I whispered.

How heartless I was. It took several seconds for my elation to be tinged with shame. He was only twenty-seven years old or thereabouts. Not yet half a life.

'Damn it, John.'

I touched something else, cold and metallic, buried next to him. I pulled at it and withdrew a short sword, or perhaps a long dagger, eighteen inches of tapered steel with a leather-covered hilt and ornate guard.

I brushed more earth away, lower down his torso, and found what I'd expected: a gash in his waistcoat, through his shirt and vest, and into his skin. I didn't doubt that it emerged on the other side.

I had been through the routine many times before. I examined his eyelids and fingernails, wiggled his teeth and manipulated his jaw. It was difficult to say exactly how long he'd been dead; a few days, I estimated. Almost certainly before the children were taken.

I heard a sound and nearly jumped out of my shoes, but it was only Rosie.

'Leo! Where are you?'

'Here,' I called quietly. 'In the timberyard. I've found John Thackery. He's dead.'

She came through the gap in the fence, and gasped when she saw what I had dug up. I remembered how, in my earliest days at the hospital, I'd been sick at the sight and stench of a decaying corpse.

'Oh no,' she muttered, looking back in the direction of the mews as if intending to rush away and raise the alarm.

'Rosie, we can't tell anyone. We might draw the attention of the murderer and end up being buried next to him.'

'We can't leave him there to be found, though,' she said. 'It's not right. It's not the Christian thing to do. He has a mother. We have to tell the police.'

'We can't. They'll be even more curious about me than they already are.'

She lowered her head, and I thought she might be praying, or perhaps deciding between her loyalty to me and her Christian duty to the dead.

'So, what's to be done?' she murmured.

I looked at his face, grey and still, and tried to remember the boy I'd known. He had been clever and kind, imagining a fairer world even before the seeds of his dogma had taken root. He would've hated the thought of ending up here, so close to his father's home. I shut my eyes and sent a message of solace to him across the miles and years: *I'm sorry, John. You don't deserve what I'm about to do.*

'We have to leave him and the sword here. Someone will find him tomorrow. The smell will get stronger.'

'Mother of God, Leo.'

'I know.'

I crossed his arms over his chest, smoothed his hair from his forehead and put his hat over his face.

That was how we left him, lying on the ground as if he was worn out from digging a hole and had decided to take a nap under the stars.

Once we were safely among the crowds on Gower Street, I brushed the soil from my hands and clothes.

'That poor, poor man,' said Rosie, shaking her head. 'You were close to joining him too. Where did that footman spring from?'

'There must be a tunnel from the basement of the house. I think I heard him open it. Sir Reginald doesn't want his servants traipsing across his garden to get to the stable. He doesn't even want them looking out on to his garden. Did you notice, there's no door or window on that side of the stable, just a sheer wall.'

Rosie whistled. 'How the rich live.'

For a little while she was silent, but I could tell her thoughts were brewing. Eventually, she said 'yes', quite firmly, as if ending an argument we had never had.

'What?'

'We should go to the police anyway,' she said.

'I thought we agreed—'

'Not about John. They must've been searching for the children since they were kidnapped. Constable Pallett will tell us if they've discovered anything useful.'

I grunted and pointed at my eyebrow. 'It was a policeman who did this to me. They'll do nothing to help us after that article in the *Daily Chronicle*. My guess is they're not even looking. Why would they? Two missing children in all of London.'

'I still think—'

'No, we should go back to the pharmacy. Aiden is resourceful. If they manage to escape their captor, that's where they'll go.'

I imagined them sitting at the table in the back room, guzzling porridge. But another thought kept intruding, no matter how hard I tried to keep it out: their faces scrunched up with fear, somewhere in the dark.

If they were still alive.

When we arrived at the pharmacy, Constance was frying a turbot, suffusing the whole room with a rich, fishy tang. The table was laid for three: Alfie, Constance and Mrs Gower, who was sitting at the end, mashing parsnips with a fork.

'Mrs Flowers!' exclaimed Constance. 'How lovely! Father, Mrs Gower, this is Mrs Flowers who I told you about. She has her own pie shop.'

Pleasantries were duly exchanged, though Rosie appeared unusually subdued. Perhaps she had noticed Alfie's wink at me, or perhaps she found Mrs Gower's serrated courtesy annoying.

'Did you find those two kids?' Alfie asked, eyeing the stitches on my forehead but choosing not to comment on them.

'Not yet. I was hoping they might have come here.'

'No, they haven't,' replied Constance. She had her back to me as she cooked, but I could hear the concern in her voice. 'My God, I do hope they're all right.'

Mrs Gower looked sternly at her stepdaughter-to-be. 'What language! And you a girl of eleven.'

'Twelve,' Constance corrected her, as if it made any difference.

'I owe you the week's rent,' I said to Alfie. 'I promise I'll pay before I leave. I'm sorry, it's just that—'

He waved me aside. 'I know you're good for it. Tell us if there's anything we can do to find those children, won't you?'

'Thank you.'

He pointed at the table. 'There's a letter for you, by the way. A boy came with it a few minutes ago.'

I ripped open the envelope.

It was brutally short.

Stop asking after the dead lady an looking for the orfans rite now
or therell be trubble there lives are at stake Im watching you

I must have made a sound because Alfie and Constance
both stood up, and Rosie's face went white. I showed her
the note, rereading it over her shoulder. The spelling and
grammar were rotten, but the lettering was good: big,
round and legible.

It reminded me of something.

I felt a sting of blood in my cheeks.

I was sure. Or almost sure. But I couldn't check, not
while Rosie was with me. I had to persuade her to leave.
I hated lying to her, but the alternative was far, far worse.

I took back the note.

'This is perfectly clear, Rosie,' I said. 'We need to stop
looking for them, like it says.'

'Why?'

'I don't want something bad to happen.'

She looked confused. 'After all we've done, you'll let
it go, as easy as that? Don't you think whoever sent this
might be lying?'

'Please, Rosie.' I was firm. I needed her to accept my
argument. 'It's too great a risk. Whoever it is has already
committed two murders. Imagine if we continued investigating and the children were harmed. We wouldn't be able
to live with ourselves.'

'I know but ...' She frowned at the piece of paper in
my hand. 'How will the kidnapper even know what we're
doing? We'll be cautious from now on. Careful. No more ...'

No more breaking into stables, she had been going to say,
but she glanced at Alfie and stopped herself.

'What would you do if they were *your* children?' I asked her. 'Please, you have to trust me. Go back to your shop and we'll talk soon.'

'They can spare me for another day or two.'

She was keeping her voice composed for the sake of the others, but I could tell she was annoyed.

'I'll come to your shop tomorrow or the next day. I promise.'

I ushered her towards the front door and almost pushed her out on to the pavement.

'Leo—'

I shut the door and rushed upstairs to my room. In my top drawer, I found Ciara's picture, with Aiden's handwriting at the bottom: *Ciaras mayd up liyon.*

I compared it with the note I'd received from the kidnapper. The lettering matched.

They had both been written by Aiden.

25

AIDEN HAD WRITTEN THAT note. Aiden, who had consumed bowl after bowl of porridge at the table downstairs, who had juggled screwed-up pieces of paper in this very room, who had run off to fight the sons of the gentry at the zoo, who had thrown his grain at the monkeys because he was too afraid to let them eat from his hand. *Aiden*.

Again, my thoughts turned to chloral hydrate. I had an excuse, with my injury, to go downstairs and drink a teaspoonful, and allow the black water to close over my head. I could sink down and drift away.

But I didn't. I wouldn't. Not before I knew why Aiden had written it.

He could have been acting under duress, I thought. I could picture him with a pen and paper, a knife held to his throat, his hands shaking as he wrote the words. If that was what had happened, I truly *should* stop my investigation.

I had to bite my fingers to keep from howling.

I lay down on my hard floor as the light faded. I didn't want to use my bed, the one they had slept in. Their smell was lingering in the blankets. I could almost believe that if I lit a match, they would be there again, whole and real, breathing softly. I was so close to reaching for the matchbox, my hand twitched for it, *ached* for it. But I knew I was being ridiculous.

I forced myself to *think*.

Why would their captor force Aiden to write the note? Why not write it himself?

Perhaps their captor was *unable* to write. My mind drifted towards the footman; he didn't strike me as an especially literate man.

But another possibility pinched at me more ferociously, burrowing into the skin on my arms and legs, into my face, until I stung all over.

Perhaps Aiden wrote the note because he *chose* to.

Perhaps he was trying to stop me from making enquiries because he didn't *want* his mother's killer found.

I couldn't bear to consider it, and yet I couldn't erase the scenario from my mind: confusion in the dark of the courtyard, a sudden sound, a gasp of fright and a turn, a glint of metal and a gush of blood, followed by an awful stillness.

Could Aiden have killed his own mother?

I could guess what came afterwards: the boy realising what he'd done and falling upon her, weeping, and someone hearing and coming, maybe more than one person, and burying her right there in the mud and guiding him away, telling him never, ever to tell a soul. Because he was ten years old and shouldn't be held responsible.

But if that was the case, who had been in the carriage with the gun?

I no longer wanted to know the truth. I didn't care about it. All I wanted to do was find the children and keep them safe.

I didn't sleep. At dawn, I got dressed and was about to leave my room when Alfie called up to tell me Mrs Flowers was here again. As I stumbled down the stairs, I tried to work out what I would say to her.

She was sitting at the table in the back room, her face a picture of determination. She pushed something towards me, which turned out to be a pie wrapped in paper.

'Mutton,' she said. 'No charge, but it's Wednesday's, so it's on your head if you're ill. Now, tell me what's happening. Why did you suddenly decide to stop looking for Aiden and Ciara last night?'

I breathed slowly and folded my arms. All I had to do was stick to my story. 'I'm following the instructions in the note from the kidnapper. I don't want any harm to come to them.'

She shook her head. 'No, there's something else. What aren't you telling me?'

'Nothing.'

She looked away, out of the window at the yard and the back fence. 'I went to see Constable Pallett after I left here last night.'

'What? Why?'

'You wouldn't listen to me, and I thought the police should know about that note. You may think it's an excuse to stop looking for them, but I think it might be important.'

I walked around in small circles, unable to stay still. 'What did Pallett say?'

'Not much. You know how he is. But he did tell me one thing.'

She waited for me to ask.

'All right, what was it?'

'He said that Edwin Cowdery was released from jail yesterday morning.'

'Released? Why? He hasn't been tried yet, and they know he's guilty of plotting arson.'

I couldn't understand it. He was exactly the sort of man the police adored locking up: a socialist, an anarchist and a threat to civil society. Why would they let him out? He had no influence to exert or money to slip into the right pocket.

'I know.' She smoothed out her skirts. 'It's a mystery. It did get me thinking, though.' She paused for a few seconds, still angry with me, making me wait. 'I mean, if Sir Reginald's not the children's father, then who is?'

It was a good question, and I had missed it.

'Not John Thackery,' I said, thinking aloud through the alternatives. 'Do you suppose it might be Edwin Cowdery?'

'That was my conclusion too. He was sweet on her, if I'm any judge, which I am, and Mr Whitford said they had an "understanding", which is a word for … well, one thing leads to another, and another thing leads to children, as often as not.'

Aiden did seem to share Edwin Cowdery's temper.

That hideous thought clawed its way back into my mind, but I forced it down.

'If Mr Cowdery *is* their father, he might've taken them,' Rosie said slowly. 'But he might not view it as kidnapping, do you see? He might view it as *reclaiming* them. And he could've killed their poor mother too.'

My mind was snagging on details. A single thrust of a sword didn't feel like a crime of passion. 'Is Mr Cowdery able to read and write?'

She shrugged. 'I don't know. If he has them, then he must be able to. He wrote that note, didn't he?'

I nodded, but my conclusion was the opposite. If Edwin was holding them, then he must be *illiterate*. Otherwise, why hadn't he written the note himself?

I felt my palms itching. If Aiden had been coerced by Edwin, then he wasn't guilty of anything, and he and Ciara were in great danger; perhaps in the hands of a murderer.

But how could I be sure?

'Wait here,' I told Rosie.

Upstairs, I put on my coat and hat, and studied Ciara's picture of a lion: the mane like a ball of fluff, the claws long and fierce, the tail a single stroke of the pencil, disappearing off the paper. It was all I had of her, but it was also evidence. I folded it carefully and put it in my pocket.

When I came back down, Rosie was standing by the open door.

'Finally!' she announced. 'You've come to your senses.'

'The question is, where's Edwin Cowdery?'

'Constable Pallett said they have a watch on that club, and he's not there, but ...' She pulled a piece of paper from her bag and held it up: the appeal for money Erica Cowdery had been distributing at the wake. 'We could always ask his sister, couldn't we?'

———

From the outside, the Home for Penitent Females was a pleasant-looking house with steps up to a single blue door. Even from the pavement we could hear a babble of voices and the rhythmic clanking of machinery.

Rosie read the sign. 'Penitent?'

'It's another word for desperate.'

'Then why don't they say desperate?'

The door was opened by a young woman in a mob cap wearing a patch over one eye and squinting at us through the other.

'We're here to see Miss Cowdery.'

Inside, the sounds of whirring cogs and squeaking pedals were accompanied by lively voices and, to my surprise, laughter. I poked my head round one door and could barely see as far as the opposite wall, such was the thickness of the steam. Young women were sitting on stools in front of a trough of water in which they were laundering sheets, while others hauled them out and hung them on racks, although I couldn't imagine how anything would ever get dry in the damp atmosphere.

One of the women met my eye and hastily ducked away. She was so thin and hunched I found it hard to believe she was still alive. She disappeared into the haze, the light of her cigarette marking her movements.

'Mr Stanhope!' Erica Cowdery came down the stairs like a mallard coming in to land among a flock of pigeons, scattering them in all directions. 'What a pleasure to see you here. And Mrs Flowers too, of course.' She took my hand and looked earnestly into my eyes. 'What happened to you?'

'An accident. We've come to ask you some questions about your brother. Does he know how to write?'

Miss Cowdery didn't immediately answer, her attention drawn to the laundry room. 'One minute. Ellen Rattle!' She pointed accusingly at the skinny woman. 'If you smoke, you'll put holes in the sheets, won't you?'

The woman sulkily dropped her cigarette on the floor and trod on it, pulling a face as soon as Miss Cowdery's back was turned.

Miss Cowdery brushed her hands down her apron, regaining her composure. 'They're good girls, but they've had hard lives, mistreated by their masters and mistresses. Mostly masters, needless to say. They work here to earn a few pennies and keep a roof over their heads. Would you like to make a contribution to the cause? Sixpence, perhaps?'

I found a twopence and gave it to her. She shoved it into her apron pocket, making no attempt to hide her disappointment.

'Can Edwin write?' I asked again. 'More than his name, I mean.'

She gave me a long look. 'My brother and I aren't idiots, Mr Stanhope. We went to school. We spend half our lives writing letters to raise funds or protest against government. How do you think this place has stayed open as long as it has?' She cast her eyes around the hallway, at the patterned paper peeling off the walls, and the door to the laundry room, so badly warped it couldn't possibly be made to close. 'Though we'll likely have to move soon, I'm told. Colonel Penton wants his land back. Lord knows, he's got a lot and these girls have only a little, but he'll take even that away.'

I didn't have time for sympathy.

'Is your brother the father of Dora Hannigan's children?'

She seemed taken aback by my bluntness, opening and shutting her mouth like a fish before replying. 'Well, yes, that's my understanding, though he didn't want me to know, nor anyone for that matter. I heard them talking once. She was very independent-minded and thought him too impulsive for marriage. He tried not to show it, but I think he still had hopes in that direction. A reconciliation, you might call it. They agreed on so many things, you see. It was her idea to start the strike at the factory, so he told me, because the best time to burn the place down is when it's empty. No working men to get hurt, and no one around to douse the fire.'

'And do you know where he is now?' asked Rosie.

'I don't.' Miss Cowdery's face clouded, and she straightened her lace cap. 'He was let out of prison yesterday, as perhaps you're aware. I wanted him to come here with me, but he wouldn't. Same as ever.' She smiled, but it was rigid, the expression of one who has finally run out of patience and doesn't care who knows it. 'He prefers what he calls a direct approach, and what I call foolhardy and missing the real point. How does it help anyone to burn down a place where men work and earn a living to feed their families?'

'Do you know *why* they let him out of jail?' asked Rosie.

Miss Cowdery brightened a little. 'It's all because of that Mr Duport at the club. Strange as it may sound, it turns out he was rightly named Thackery and was Sir Reginald's own adopted son! Can you believe it?'

I glanced at Rosie, but she was looking down, utter shock written across her face.

'Well,' continued Miss Cowdery, oblivious, 'our solicitor made the argument that Sir Reginald had likely engineered the whole thing from the start. He said Duport, or

Thackery I should say, had been *inserted* into the club by his father to spy on us and report our goings-on.'

'That can't be true,' I said. 'Sir Reginald hated his son.'

'That's what Detective Inspector Hooper said as well,' replied Miss Cowdery, enjoying her story. 'But it opened up the possibility that Duport had *encouraged* Edwin to plan the arson with the specific intention of entrapping him. An element of doubt was cast on their case. Hooper wasn't best pleased, I can tell you. He said it shows how far we've slipped, giving credence to an anarchist over a man of honour and decency. Those were his exact words.'

She produced a fan from her bag and began swishing it to and fro. The hallway was already sweltering, and the movement of the air made it worse.

'Forgive me, Miss Cowdery,' I said gently, 'but you don't seem happy that your brother has been freed.'

I looked at Rosie, who was much better at navigating this sort of thing than me. But she didn't seem to be listening.

'It's not that,' Miss Cowdery replied, a little too hastily. 'In his own way, Edwin loved Dora. We Cowderys are passionate people. Romantics at heart. When he came out of jail yesterday, he was most upset. He had trusted Mr Duport, you see, and to find out he was a Thackery all along … well, it was the last straw.'

'What are you saying?' I asked.

She dipped into her bag for a handkerchief and began dabbing her eyes.

'If I'm honest, I never thought they would actually burn down that mill. I thought it was a bit of fun for them, like a game, thinking about how they *might* go about such a thing. But now, I'm not so sure. I think he might actually do it.'

'We have to find Edwin Cowdery,' said Rosie, as soon as we were outside on the pavement. She set off at a rapid pace and I had to scurry to keep up.

'Rosie, what's wrong?'

'We have to pray he hasn't harmed them.'

'Rosie!'

She turned and glared at me, and I realised her eyes were brimming with tears. 'You don't understand, Leo. It's my fault.'

'What is?'

'After we argued about ... God, I can't even remember what. It doesn't matter now. I thought you were being reckless, allowing John Thackery to blackmail you. I thought it would be best if the police knew that Thackery was Duport, and Duport was Thackery.'

The truth washed over me like the first big wave when you wade into the sea. 'You told the police about John.'

She nodded. 'Yes, but I didn't think ... I didn't realise it would mean they'd release Mr Cowdery.' She stood up straight, squaring her shoulders. 'It's my fault. I told them about Thackery and, because of that, Mr Cowdery was released and was able to kidnap Aiden and Ciara.'

She walked swiftly away from me, and I think I would have let her carry on, would have let her suffer, if she had been right.

But she wasn't right.

'Rosie!' I called after her. 'Edwin Cowdery didn't take them.'

She didn't slow down, but called back over her shoulder. 'He's their father and a criminal, and he's been set free because of me.'

'He didn't write that note, Rosie.'

She stopped and looked up at the sky as if calling on God to give her patience. 'How can you possibly know that?'

I had to tell her. I couldn't abide the thought that she would blame herself.

'Because Aiden wrote it.'

I showed her Ciara's drawing and the kidnapper's note. Her hand was shaking as she held them. Nevertheless, she examined the lettering with care, peering over the top of her spectacles.

'They do look similar,' she said, in a small voice.

'They're identical. Look at the "a" here and here. The same bad spelling and grammar too.'

She wiped her eyes and sniffed. 'Why didn't you tell me about this yesterday, instead of pretending you were giving up?'

I took off my bowler and cautiously rubbed my forehead, avoiding the stitches. There was a cool wind blowing down the street, yet still I felt hot.

'I thought perhaps that Aiden …'

'Oh Leo.' She pursed her lips. 'We're as absurd as each other, don't you think? We shouldn't keep any more secrets. Now I know that Aiden wrote it, the whole thing makes sense. You were brought up as a gentleman, weren't you?' She paused, blanching, realising what she'd said. 'I mean, as a … I mean, *educated*.'

There was no one near enough to hear us, but I still wished she'd be more discreet.

'What of it?'

'You were taught to read and write, but most of us weren't. I never went to school, not one day. My old man said it wasn't worth sending a girl and I was more useful in the shop. Most people write the same way they speak.'

She pointed at the note, and I read it again.

Stop asking after the dead lady an looking for the orfans rite now or therell be trubble there lives are at stake

'See here,' she said. 'He's spelled "looking" right. But "trubble" is wrong, isn't it?'

She wasn't absolutely certain.

'Yes.' I felt a glimmer of anticipation. Perhaps the note was telling us more than it intended. 'And look: the first six words are all correct, but most of the rest aren't. His spelling isn't so much bad as *variable*. He can spell "dead", "looking" and "lives" perfectly well, but not "right" or "orphans".'

She nodded, poring over the piece of paper, her finger running along the words. I couldn't see her face, but I could tell she was trying very hard not to weep. 'And the way it's written is odd too,' she said. '"Stop asking after" is a strange form of words for a lad his age, don't you think? He'd say "stop asking about".' She looked up at me. 'I think someone else was telling him what to write.'

'Yes!' I spun round on the spot, feeling, for the first time, as if we were getting close to the truth. 'It *was* written under duress. Someone else spelled out some of the words

325

for him. Someone who isn't illiterate but wasn't able to write it for themselves.'

I stared at her, realising what we had to do next. Realising the danger.

'Rosie, I know who has them.'

26

THE CAB MADE EXCELLENT pace, diving down side roads and pulling around slow-moving carts, and we reached Gordon Square in less than ten minutes. The curtains of Sir Reginald's house were closed, and there was a wreath on the door.

'Wait here,' I told the driver. 'We may need you again. There's another half a crown if you do.'

I was feeling torn in half: delighted that Aiden almost certainly wasn't guilty of murder, but terrified for him and Ciara.

Rosie pointed at the shapes moving behind the curtains.

'There are people inside,' she said.

It was true, but it meant nothing; in rich people's houses, the servants were always at home.

The footman opened the door, as crisply dressed as before in his pale blue jacket and black, perfectly creased trousers. Instinctively, I felt the bruises on my face.

'Blimey,' he said. 'You again?'

'Is Lady Thackery at home?' I asked. 'It's urgent that we speak to her.'

'We're not open to visitors today,' he said. 'There's been a death in the family. And I was given instructions not to let you in.' He tried to close the door, but I put my foot in the way. 'Are you sure you want to do that?' he asked, almost casually. 'I'd've thought you'd learned your lesson.'

I took a deep breath and prepared myself, glancing back at Rosie for confidence. She nodded almost imperceptibly, and I edged myself in front of her, hearing her irritated 'tut'.

The footman raised his eyebrows, and I'm sure it would have ended badly for me, but at that moment another cab drew up. We watched as the door was flung open and Peregrine Black clambered out, tossing a coin at the cabbie and leaping up the steps.

'What do *you* want?' sneered the footman.

Black shoved past Rosie and me without so much as an acknowledgement. 'Where is that soiled arse? Never mind, I'll find him for myself.'

The footman tried to block his path.

It was so swift, I barely saw it, like the piston on a railway engine; Black's fist shot forwards into the footman's stomach and he went down with a groan, falling to his knees and clutching at the doorframe for support. Black kicked him and stepped over his prone body, taking care to tread on his wrist, seeming pleased by the crack and the footman's squeal of pain.

Black stormed down the hallway, sweeping pictures of birds and butterflies off the walls as he went, leaving a trail of broken wood and glass.

'Sir Reginald!' he yelled. 'Are you at home? It's time for a reckoning!'

I followed him into the parlour, where two pale-faced maids were gaping at us from behind a sofa. The room was no longer set out as a theatre, and now contained armchairs, lamps and a table laid for afternoon tea. Above the mantelpiece, two swords were displayed, one long, one short, both clean and shiny as if they'd been newly polished.

The murder weapon had been replaced.

Black turned angrily towards me and I took a step backwards. I didn't believe he would attack me, but I couldn't be certain. He was panting like a bull.

'That fart of a man killed John! His own son!' He pointed at the garden, sounding close to tears. 'His body was discovered right behind the house.'

'Who told you that?'

I had a fleeting fear he might know that I had been the first person to find John's corpse. I dreaded to think how he might react.

'Policemen!' he exclaimed, as if it was obvious. 'They get drunk and start gossiping worse than ...' He waved his hands around, trying to conjure up the right comparison. 'Worse than *actors*!'

He grabbed the longer sword from above the fireplace and marched back down the hallway, ignoring Rosie, who had reversed against the wall. He threw open every door and peered inside until he reached the little library where Rosie and I had met with Sir Reginald. The handle wouldn't turn. Someone on the other side was holding on to it.

Black rapped on the wood with the hilt of the sword. 'Come out, you coward!'

There was no reply. He rocked back and heaved his considerable weight against the door, and it burst open.

'Murderer!' roared Black, pointing the sword.

Sir Reginald was on his knees on the floor, his face so ruddy it was almost purple.

'Mr Black,' said Rosie. She put her hand gently on the big man's shoulder. 'You can't do this. Think of your wife and child. What will happen to them if you're hanged?'

Black inhaled deeply and repositioned the sword in his hand as if he was about to drive it home, but then breathed out slowly and lowered the point to the floor.

Sir Reginald fell forward on to all fours and retched so excessively I thought his lungs and guts would come up as well. He spat a couple of times and wiped a stream of viscous liquid from his chin.

'I didn't kill John,' he rasped. 'Why would I?'

'You despised him,' I replied. 'He's not of your blood.'

He pulled himself into his chair, groping on the table for his laudanum and dislodging the monkey's paw. He took a swig from the bottle and closed his eyes.

'John was weak,' he said eventually. 'He was my shame, but I never wanted him *dead*.'

'What about Miss Hannigan?' I demanded. 'I know what she did for you. Did she ask for more money, was that it? Was she blackmailing you?'

His hands were shaking. 'No, not money. She would hardly spend what I'd given her before. She wanted to meet Peter and talk to him. It was a ridiculous notion. He's my blood. Dora was just a … *container* for nine months, that's all. But I would never have hurt her. For all her foolish beliefs, I was quite fond of her.'

'What about Lady Thackery? She was upset, wasn't she? Jealous. Where is she now?'

He shook his head. 'I won't tell you. But it's not what you're thinking. It'll be better for everyone if you stop this nonsense right now.'

Black rested the point of the sword against the old man's sternum. It would have taken the slightest of pressures to pierce his skin. 'Answer the question.'

I heard a voice behind me. 'Stop that! Move away immediately!' It was Peter Thackery, sounding remarkably commanding for a lad of fifteen. 'Mr Stanhope, what's happening here?'

'We need to know where Lady Thackery is.'

'Why?'

'She kidnapped the two children I'm searching for.'

He stared at me as if I was mad. 'You think my mother is guilty of kidnapping? My *mother*?'

Black pressed a little on the sword, forcing Sir Reginald backwards in his chair.

I felt a hand on my arm, one of the maids. She couldn't have been older than sixteen, and was still holding a feather duster.

'Mister,' she said, so quietly I could barely hear her. 'I know where Her Ladyship is.'

'No,' said Sir Reginald, his voice constricted and hoarse. 'Don't tell them anything.'

I could see the tussle going on in her mind, whether to disobey her employer or save his life. Common sense won the day. 'Bernie told me ...' She stopped, her eyes flicking from side to side. 'He's the coachman, or he was. Mr Picken, I should call him.'

'Please get on with it.' I was trying to be gentle but couldn't keep the impatience out of my voice.

She nodded and swallowed. 'He told me Her Ladyship made him drive the carriage and snatch two urchins off the street. She had a gun and she shot it at someone, though he was sure she missed. He didn't know what to think. I told him not to worry and it wasn't his fault, but he was scared. He left his position and went back to his brother's without so much as a goodbye. No references neither.'

I almost begged her. 'Where are the children now?'

She looked up at me, straight in the eyes. 'He took 'em to the mill, so he said. That's where they'll be.'

'Thank you.' I turned to Black. 'Peregrine, please don't hurt Sir Reginald. I don't think he did this, and we may need to talk to him again. But stay with him and don't let him send anyone after us.'

He seemed disappointed. 'If I must.'

Rosie pulled on my sleeve. 'Come on, Leo. We may not have much time.'

The footman was sitting at the bottom of the stairs taking short, sharp breaths. His jacket was at his feet, smeared with blood, and he had rolled up one of his shirtsleeves, exposing his wrist, which was hanging at a strange angle. He didn't look up as we passed.

We were out of the door and hurrying down the steps to the pavement when Peter shouted after us. 'Wait for me, Mr Stanhope. I want to make sure you don't hurt my mother.'

'No.'

The cab was waiting. Rosie climbed in and I was about to follow when I heard another shout from the doorway. Peter was standing on the steps. He held up a set of keys and jangled them.

'There's a strike on,' he called. 'The mill will be empty. How will you get in without these?'

He put the keys into his jacket pocket and folded his arms.

I didn't have time to argue any further. 'Very well, come on then. But you must be quick.'

He raised his eyebrows. 'Why?'

It was Rosie who answered. 'Because there's a man with a grudge who wants to set light to the place.'

27

WHEN THE CABBIE HEARD where we wanted to go, he demanded double the half-crown he'd been promised, and Rosie agreed to pay him on condition he broke every rule of traffic in his efforts to get there quickly. To his credit, he did, whipping his horse brutally as we weaved along the road, at one point tipping so far over as we hurtled round a corner I thought we might capsize.

Peter seemed exalted by the whole experience. His eyes were shining. Several times, he put his head out of the window and whooped at people as they dodged out of the way.

'Master Thackery,' said Rosie, in a rare moment he was seated. 'Are you not concerned by what we're doing?'

He grinned. 'This is all a waste of time, I'm sure of it. Mother has never done anything dangerous in her whole life. She can't even walk without a stick.'

The paving ran out at the docks and our cab had to slow down on the muddy tracks. The bridge was the same as the last time I'd been there, lined with beggars unsexed by their emaciation, slouched against the wall or sitting on the ground, hands out for farthings.

We disembarked and hurried down the lane towards the mill. In the shadow of the railway embankment and surrounded by marshes, the buildings resembled ships marooned on a windless lake.

A crowd of a dozen or so men and women were huddled around a brazier of red-hot coals. The mill itself was grim and silent.

Two of the men stood up.

'There's a strike,' one of them said.

'Let us by,' I told him, in no mood to be delayed. 'Our business isn't with you.'

He shrugged and watched us pass, the only noise coming from the squelching of our shoes in the mud.

Peter unlocked the main door and threw it open. I led the way through the anteroom. In the eerie silence, I could hear pigeons trapped in the building, flapping against the skylights.

Our eyes slowly adjusted. The long lines of machines were dormant, half-chewed jute spilling from their mouths. Where in this place might Aiden and Ciara be? They could be locked up in a storeroom or gagged and bound in a cupboard, and I might never be able to find them.

'Aiden!' I shouted. 'Ciara!'

All I wanted was to hear their voices; a cry, a sneeze, a cough – anything would do. I strained in the forbidding silence, but there was nothing.

We searched as thoroughly as we could, walking up and down the lines, looking from side to side, peering under tables and trolleys, opening crates and chests, always thinking: *this* is the place. They will be *here*. Rosie stayed close to me, two lines along, matching my pace, but Peter roamed across the building. At one point I caught sight of him climbing up an immense rack of shelves the height of a cottage, sitting at the top and surveying his father's empire.

Twice, out of the corner of my eye, I was sure I saw movement. The second time, I dashed quickly round the corner to where I thought it was. The dust on the floor was covered with boot prints and skittering trails of rats' paws, and I couldn't tell which were recent and which were old.

'Edwin?' I called out, but there was no reply.

My one comfort was the mechanics of the search: lifting lids, turning handles, occasionally calling out their names. I will do this for ever, if necessary, I thought. I will search inch by inch and hour by hour until I find them.

I did something I'd only done three or four times since I was a child. I prayed under my breath: No matter what you think of me, oh Lord, please let Aiden and Ciara live. Please. I will do anything. I will pretend to be Lottie again, if that's what you want.

The stillness was oppressive. I noticed that Rosie was searching more gingerly than me and in smaller spaces: stock boxes, cupboards and rubbish sacks. I had the feeling she wasn't looking for two grateful children, but for two tiny bodies, curled up.

When we reached the end of the building, she took my hand.

'Leo—'

At that moment, we heard footsteps, growing louder. Through the murk I could see two figures coming towards us, one the unmistakeable frame of Constable Pallett, and the other Hooper, increasing his speed as he saw us.

'What're you doing here?' he demanded.

Peter had seen them too, and loped over to where we were standing, adopting a superior expression exactly like Sir Reginald's. 'They're with me,' he said. 'This is my father's mill. Why are *you* here might be a better question.'

Hooper flagged in the face of such youthful brio. 'We're looking for Edwin Cowdery. Have you seen him?'

'No, Detective,' I said. 'But he might be hiding here somewhere.'

If he *was* here, it would be best that they found him before he carried out his plan.

'It's Detective *Inspector*,' Hooper corrected me, though without much conviction. 'It's my theory Cowdery will have another go at burning down this mill, and we intend to catch 'im at it.' He licked his lips. 'Not to mention, he's a suspect in the murder of John Thackery, who called himself John Duport, with apologies for my bluntness, Master Thackery, him being your brother and all—'

'He wasn't my brother,' interrupted Peter. 'He was adopted.'

'Yes, so I understand,' agreed Hooper. 'Which might explain his duplicity. Be that as it may, he was killed with a sword right through him, same as the girl, only a day after we let Cowdery out of jail. Stands to reason Cowdery's the guilty party.'

I thought Hooper was wrong. I had examined John's body, and he had been dead for a few days. But I couldn't disclose that.

'It's not important.' I spoke so firmly he took a step backwards. 'Dora Hannigan's children are here somewhere, taken against their will by Lady Thackery. They're in danger, do you understand? Now, help us find them.'

337

'You think *Lady Thackery* stole 'em?' Hooper chuckled, shaking his head. 'You're clueless, Stanhope, whatever the newspapers claim.'

I was about to respond, and probably get myself into considerable trouble, when I realised there was one place we hadn't searched. He was right, I *was* clueless.

'There's a pair of cottages,' I said. 'At the back.'

Without waiting for the others, I ran out through the rear door and into the pale glow from the railway embankment. The cottages were on the other side of the paving, which was half-submerged. The wind had kicked up, sending brisk squalls across the pools of water and flogging my coat around my legs.

In the left-hand cottage, the lamps were lit.

Constable Pallett had followed me, with Rosie and Peter a few steps behind. I peered through the window into the front room. It was empty. We stole as quietly as we could around to the back. I had a momentary fear that a carriage would be there, and we would have to deal with the driver, but the patch of mud was bare, glistening in the reflected light.

Pallett tried the handle of the back door, and it opened. Rosie put her hand on his arm.

'Be careful,' she whispered. 'Her Ladyship has a gun.'

Inside, the room was warm and smoky, making my cold fingers ache. On the table, a pile of clothes was still wet from the mangle, as though someone hadn't yet got around to hanging them up. I recognised Aiden's sweater and Ciara's dress.

A child's voice cried out from somewhere upstairs. I'd spent so long yearning to hear it that, when I did, I wasn't sure it was real. But Rosie's head jerked up too, and then I heard it again. Without a doubt, it was Ciara. She sounded close to tears.

'Wait, Mr Stanhope,' instructed Pallett.

I ignored him and headed for the stairs, with Rosie close behind me. It was an effort of will not to run, but I had to stay quiet; with any luck, I could rescue the children before Lady Thackery even knew we were there.

The fourth stair creaked under my weight.

There was a noise and the door to the parlour crashed open. I turned, and Lady Thackery was standing there holding a pistol with both hands, shaking so hard it could have been aimed at any one of us. She was wearing full mourning weeds and her face was contorted as she tried to find the strength in her fingers to pull the trigger. She pointed the gun towards me and I heard a shout and a bang so loud in the confined space of the stairwell it sounded almost muffled, as if I'd been clapped on both ears at once.

Rosie cried out and fell.

Lady Thackery gasped as she saw her son. Pallett lurched forwards and barged into her, throwing her backwards into the parlour.

I knelt next to Rosie, who was lying at the bottom of the stairs, her breathing coming shallow and fast.

Across her upper arm, a red patch was growing.

28

'ROSIE!'

I pulled up her sleeve but couldn't find the wound amidst all the blood. I wiped her skin with my jacket and found where it was pulsing out. At the top of her upper arm, a two-inch trench had been gouged out by the bullet.

'It missed the bone,' I said to her. 'But you're bleeding.'

I turned away, so no one could see, and undid one of my shirt buttons, slipping my hand inside. I could feel where my cilice was tied, squashing my breasts against my chest. I managed to push a finger into the knot and open it, extracting it from under my shirt. This was the first time my breasts had been unbound in company for a long time, but I couldn't worry about it; Rosie was far more important.

I tied it tightly around her arm.

Pallett looked down at my handiwork and then at me, frowning.

'I keep a bandage with me,' I explained. 'Just in case. Now, put your hand against it. More pressure. That's right.'

Rosie winced and shook her head. 'Leo, that's—'

'It doesn't matter.' I did up my jacket and coat, right to the collar. 'You need it more.'

'I'm all right, it's not that bad.' She blinked and licked her lips. 'I'm a bit shocked is all. Go and get the children. I'll feel better for seeing them.'

I took the steps two at a time.

'Aiden! Ciara! It's Leo!'

I heard Aiden's voice in the front bedroom. 'We're here!'

The key was in the lock. I turned it and there they were.

I scooped them up, feeling Aiden's arms tight around my back and Ciara's hair against my cheek, and her chin on my shoulder, and her whole little self. They were here, with me, and safe.

'We were scared,' whispered Ciara. 'The lady wouldn't let us out.'

'Did she hurt you?'

'No.'

I kissed her forehead, grateful beyond words for its warmth and softness.

'I looked after her,' said Aiden.

I ruffled his hair. 'I knew you would. You're a good boy. A good brother.' And then, because I thought he would want to hear it: 'Your mother would be proud of you.'

His face clouded, and I realised I'd said the wrong thing. I had no idea what his mother would be proud of. I'd only met her once.

I picked up Ciara and the three of us went down the stairs together.

In the parlour, Hooper had arrived and was standing in the doorway with his mouth hanging open as if he couldn't believe what he was seeing. Lady Thackery was sitting in an armchair, a black veil covering her face. Peter was beside her on the arm of the chair.

Rosie was lying on the sofa, pale but steadfast, her hand pressed against her upper arm where a red, wet stain had spread through the bandage. Aiden and Ciara eyed the blood warily but allowed her to touch their cheeks.

Pallett was standing by the fireplace holding the gun. In the cramped room he looked like a toy soldier in a doll's house that had been built to a smaller scale.

'Why did you kidnap these children, Your Ladyship?' he asked, pointing at Ciara and Aiden, who had moved close behind me. I could feel Ciara's hand clutching the material of my coat. 'And why did you shoot at us?'

Hooper snorted. 'Don't be ridiculous, Constable. There must be another explanation. Cowdery took 'em, most likely, and was the one who did the shooting. Her Ladyship has nothing to do with any of it.'

'He's not being ridiculous,' Rosie replied calmly. 'It was her, all right.'

Hooper looked pleadingly at Lady Thackery. She took no notice of him.

'My reasons are my own,' she said, and pressed her lips together to prevent any more stray words from escaping.

'Leave her alone,' protested Peter. 'Can't you see she's sick and doesn't know what she's doing?'

'No one does something like that for no reason,' said Pallett.

'Peter, you should leave,' I said. 'There may be things you don't want to hear.' I nodded towards Aiden and Ciara.

'Take them as well, would you? See if you can find some food for them.'

'No,' said Lady Thackery, gripping Peter's hand, her knuckles turning white. 'He should stay with me.'

Peter stood up. 'It's all right, Mother, I won't be far away.'

He left with Aiden and Ciara. She watched them go with a strange expression on her face and then turned her imperious gaze on me.

'I read about you in the newspaper. You interfere where you're not needed.'

I refused to be intimidated by someone who'd just come so close to murdering Rosie.

'Tell us everything,' I said. 'Start with why you killed Dora Hannigan. Your husband paid her to provide him with a son when you could not. Did that make you jealous?'

'A little, perhaps, at the time.' Her breathing was becoming uneven and she seemed to be shrinking, as though she might fall into the gaps between the cushions. 'But afterwards, I was so grateful to have Peter, I forgot all that. I had my boys, and they were all I wanted. It didn't matter that I hadn't given birth to them.'

'Until Dora came back,' I said.

'Yes. Out of the blue, a few weeks ago. She wanted to meet Peter and tell him the truth. She said he deserved to know where he came from. A lot of nonsense about the ruling classes and so on. She wouldn't take no for an answer.'

'She was a woman of strong principles.'

She angled her head in acknowledgement. 'That she was.'

'And what about John, your son? Why did you kill him?'

She bent forwards and opened her mouth very wide. At first, I thought she was going to vomit, but she didn't.

She let out a wail and slammed her hands down on the arms of the chair repeatedly, her feet dancing on the floor and her neck flushing red. As her cry reached the limit of her lungs, she filled them with as much air as she could and wailed again. Her outburst lasted twenty seconds, maybe less, but it felt like an eternity. Watching another person being wracked by such agony was almost impossible.

'Good heavens,' whispered Hooper.

Eventually, she rocked back in her chair, her palms turned upwards as though accepting whatever punishment might come. I had the impression she welcomed it.

'Oh God,' she said, her tone softening, 'from whom all holy desires, all good counsels and all just works do proceed, give unto thy servants that peace which the world cannot give.'

'Lady Thackery, did you kill your son, John?' I asked her again, more insistently this time.

She closed her eyes. 'Yes,' she said, her voice as thin as cobwebs. 'Yes, I murdered John too.'

She was trying to keep her hands still, but they were shaking, sending shivers through her whole body. I tried to imagine the scene, her confronting John at the stable, a sword in her hand, thrusting it into his chest and burying him in the timberyard.

But I could not.

How would she even lift a sword?

'No,' I said. 'I don't believe you killed either of them. You don't have the strength for it. Nor the desire.'

She spoke with absolute conviction. 'You don't know what I'm capable of.'

'But you did capture Aiden and Ciara,' I said. 'And you locked them upstairs.' I clenched my fists, realising the truth, or some of it. Once again, I had seen the whole thing backwards. 'And yet you made sure they were well fed, didn't you? And their clothes washed. In fact, I don't believe you were kidnapping them at all. I believe you were *rescuing* them.'

She looked down at her fingers. A vein on her neck was throbbing.

'Of course,' she said. 'From you.'

I felt my face blaze red.

'From me?'

'You were a danger to them.'

She must have recognised me after all, I thought. Or Sir Reginald had. Or perhaps John had told her. She knew who I was, and she knew *what* I was: an ungodly chimera of woman and man that couldn't be allowed to take charge of children. Aiden and Ciara had been imprisoned and Rosie had been shot, all because of me.

I was to blame.

'Yes!' exclaimed Hooper, smacking his lips. 'Lady Thackery is quite right, Stanhope. You took 'em first.'

Rosie slipped her hand into mine and squeezed it. 'It's not true,' she whispered.

I met Lady Thackery's eyes through her veil. In all this time, she hadn't once looked at me strangely or made some sly allusion to my female body. And if she had recognised me, why didn't she tell Hooper and save herself? And why exactly was she confessing to two murders she couldn't possibly have committed?

The truth unfolded like a map.

'You fool,' I hissed. 'Do you understand what you've done?'

It wasn't me she was rescuing the children from, it was someone else. Someone who *would* hurt them, and who had killed both Dora and John. Someone she was willing to sacrifice herself for.

'Where's Peter?' I asked, a rock-hard lump forming in my stomach.

I ran out to the kitchen, but it was empty.

I sprinted into the rear yard, slipping and sliding in the mud. Dusk had fallen, and I couldn't see more than a few yards ahead. The paving stretched towards the mill, smoke drifting across it like a shroud.

'Aiden! Ciara!'

My voice was deadened by the gloom.

The children had gone.

I had delivered them into the hands of a killer.

I tugged open the door to the mill and ran inside. The whole place was filled with smoke, stinging my eyes and reaching into my throat.

'Aiden! Ciara!'

I blundered towards the outlines of the looms in front of me. There was a sound ahead, a whooshing and crackling, and an orange glow bloomed on one wall. Bundles of jute had been piled up and were smouldering and spitting, flames already licking around their edges. A black silhouette was holding a board and waving it up and down, fanning the fire.

'What are you doing?' I shouted. 'Put that out!'

Edwin Cowdery turned. His face was red, and his eyes were streaming in the heat.

'Mr Stanhope! You should leave right away. This place is going up.'

'Aiden and Ciara are in here somewhere!'

'What? Where?'

'I don't know. Help me find them. Quickly!'

The wood-slat wall had already caught. Flames were crawling upwards through the black smoke.

I ran back down the building, looking left and right, and almost collided with Peter, who was tugging Aiden and Ciara by their wrists. He backed away behind a trolley and pulled something out of his jacket. I saw a glint of metal.

'Peter, I know you killed John and Dora. Don't make it any worse.'

He let go of Aiden and put his arm around Ciara, crouching down and holding a kitchen knife to her throat. She wriggled, trying to get free, but he gripped her harder.

'Leave us alone, Mr Stanhope! Just let it happen, why don't you? My mother has confessed to everything. Let her take the blame. It's what she wants.'

If you harm Ciara, I thought, *I will kill you.*

Aiden had the same look I'd seen when he had joined the ball game at the zoo: alert and poised for action. His eyes were fixed on his half-brother. He had heard Peter's voice, his accent, and I knew what he was thinking: rich boys don't have the stomach for a fight. But Peter had already killed two people.

'Stay calm, Aiden,' I said. 'Let me talk to Peter man to man.'

The air was growing hotter. A lamp hanging on one of the looms burst, sending a spray of oil across the floor.

Peter's face was damp, and his hair was plastered down on his forehead. He wiped his eyes with his sleeve. 'I hate all this,' he said, his voice breaking. 'Truly I do.'

'I give you my word. If you let them go, I'll forget everything. I'll never tell a soul what you've done.'

I could see him trying to decide what to do, licking his lips and rocking slightly. Very slowly, he moved the knife away from Ciara's neck, though he still had hold of her.

She seemed to stiffen and then fall limp over his arm. He dropped her to the ground and shrank away, and for a moment my heart leapt, but she didn't run to me. Her little body started jerking and shaking, her heels thumping on the floor.

Aiden crawled forwards and pulled her head into his lap as she shuddered and shook.

Peter jumped to his feet. 'What's happening?'

There was a movement behind him. I hoped desperately that it was Pallett, but when I saw a face in the flickering light, I realised it was Edwin Cowdery. It was vital that he didn't do anything stupid. All that mattered was getting the children to safety.

I shook my head at him, but he didn't see me. He inched out from his hiding place, his eyes fixed on Peter.

'No, Edwin!'

He launched himself headlong, tackling Peter around his neck. The two of them sprawled on the floor, each trying to get a grip on the other. Against the light of the fire, I couldn't tell which was which.

I raced forwards and grabbed the children, pulling Ciara out of the way. She was still in the midst of her fit, and I pushed my fingers between her teeth to stop her biting her own tongue.

One of the figures rose up, adjusting his balance, a knife in his hand. The man on his back was squeezing the other's neck, and for a few hideous seconds neither was able to move, but then the one on top plunged downward, sending the knife into the chest of the other.

The victor stood, and I could see it was Peter, with a hideous expression on his face, one of boundless satisfaction. He was still holding the knife.

Out of the corner of my eye I caught sight of another figure in the smoke. As it came closer, I realised it was Pallett. I wanted to call out to him, but I was choking. I covered my mouth with my sleeve and shoved the children in his direction.

'Go!' I croaked.

Aiden picked up his sister like a sack and tottered towards Pallett. Through the smoke I watched the young constable gather them up and peer towards me, his hand across his brow, and then turn and carry them out of the mill.

When I looked back, Peter was gone.

I scuttled forwards to where Edwin was lying. His eyes were open, flicking from side to side. He'd been stabbed in the gut. I pressed my hand against the wound, but his blood leaked around my fingers, soaking into my sleeve and pooling on the floor.

He clutched my arm. 'Did I save them?' he asked, his voice hoarse.

'Yes.'

He closed his eyes and his grip relaxed as the pumping of his blood slowed and stopped.

I had no time to pull his body from the mill. If I didn't leave now, I would be trapped. The fire was ravenous. It was like a physical thing, a creature with many fingers, crawling across the walls of the building, exhaling smoke and ash. The carts of raw jute would soon be feeding its appetite. It would consume everything.

'I'm sorry,' I whispered to Edwin.

I could feel the draught being sucked in through the open door by the heat. I staggered towards the oblong of pale light and drank in a lungful of cold, wonderful air.

On the embankment, the lamps were lit, reflected in a flickering line across the marshes.

I heard a footstep behind me and ducked just in time to avoid the swing of the knife.

29

PETER GRUNTED AT THE effort and swung again, spitting and hacking in the smoke.

I stumbled forwards, away from the mill, trying to keep my footing on the marshy ground. My eyes were hot and weepy, and my chest was burning from the inside.

I looked back, and he was following, his hands and face slick with Edwin's blood.

'I saw you,' he called after me, sounding strangely pleased with himself. 'That evening when we went to the music hall. I saw you skulking around near the house and then trailing after me. It wasn't hard to find out who you were and where you lived. You told me yourself.'

I turned to face him, walking backwards, shouting over the roar of the fire. 'You sent the footman after me, looking for Aiden and Ciara.'

He nodded. 'I thought you'd surrender them before the first punch landed. But you're *such* a good Samaritan, aren't you?' Still he came forward, and still I backed away. 'My father was once a great man, Mr Stanhope. Do you know how that feels?'

'Honestly, no.'

The water was growing deeper, and I had to pick up my feet or wade through it.

'But he's become sentimental. It's that stuff he drinks. It dulls the pain, but it dulls the mind as well.' He coughed and tried to spit, trailing phlegm across his chin. 'That Irish whore came to see him. In our house, with my mother in the very next room. The next room! The bloody cheek of it! I assumed he would throw her out with a beating, but he didn't.'

'This was while the music hall was happening at your father's house, wasn't it? You stole the lion costume. You wanted to get close to Miss Vesta Tilley.'

He bit his lip, embarrassed. 'I wanted to be in the performance. Was that too much to ask? I wanted to show her I could do it. But Father refused. He said I was being ridiculous. I went to persuade him, and *she* was there. That Hannigan woman, his whore.'

How foolish I was not to have seen it before. It was obvious. Who but a fifteen-year-old boy would think it was a sensible idea to kill someone while wearing a lion costume?

'Why did that matter to you?'

'She's a bogtrotter, and her offspring likewise. You've seen him, that boy. You must know he's my father's bastard.' He laughed, his arms outstretched to the sky, but when he looked back at me his face was contorted in disgust. 'Some people are born to lead and others to follow. That's what Darwin discovered. The strongest lines survive, but only if they're kept pure. We mustn't be *contaminated* by the weak.'

I missed my step and fell backwards into the shallow water. He waded towards me, halting a few feet away as I regained my footing.

'And John? What about him?'

He spun the knife in his hand and grinned, a little of his previous buoyancy returning. How I wished he was still that boy, skipping school, stealing out in the evenings because he'd fallen in love with a music-hall singer.

'I knew what he was, him and that actor fellow. I caught them in the *act*, as it were.' He laughed at his own feeble joke. 'I invited John to meet me at the stable, away from prying eyes. It seemed an appropriate place, as he did hate it so, but still he came, like a fish to a hook. He was such a bore! Kept whining about the Irish harlot and how sad he was she was dead. It was pathetic. I wondered if he suspected me, but then I thought, why take the chance? He's a fake Thackery anyway, using our name as if he's one of us when he was probably born to a trollop in Finsbury.' Behind him, part of the building's roof collapsed with a whoosh, blowing out more black smoke and ash. He glanced at it quickly and then back at me, waiting for the noise to fade before continuing. 'He'd still have stuck his hand out for the inheritance, when the time came.'

I shook my head. 'John wasn't interested in your father's money. He had principles.'

'Ha! Mr Stanhope, I do believe you're an *idealist*. Everyone's greedy. It's the natural order of things.'

We were nearing the embankment. I could see the fence stretching away on either side. What would I do when I could go no further?

'Lady Thackery knew what you'd done, Peter. She took the children to protect them from you.'

He rotated the knife in my direction. 'It doesn't matter. She's confessed to everything and my father will say the same. I'm going to kill you and leave you to burn, and there'll be no one left to connect those children to my family. I might even let them live.' He paused, wiping his arm across his brow, smearing it with Edwin's blood. 'Or I might not.'

'You're wrong about a lot of things, Peter. Sir Reginald isn't Aiden and Ciara's father.'

He shook himself, his free hand clenching and unclenching. 'What are you talking about? You've seen that boy. We look exactly alike.'

'Yes, you do. But it's your mother you have in common, not your father. Lady Thackery didn't give birth to you. She can't conceive a child, so they found someone to bear one for her: Dora Hannigan. Your pure blood, your precious line, is half from your brother's governess. You murdered your true mother.'

'Nonsense,' he declared, with the confidence he was born to. But I could see a tinge of doubt in his face.

'It's the truth, Peter. Think about it. You're nothing like Lady Thackery, are you? Dora Hannigan was your mother. That's why she didn't put up a fight; she knew who you were. My guess is you told her yourself, boasting before you stabbed her.'

He charged at me and fell, unable to keep his balance in the marsh, grappling for my legs, swinging the knife wildly. I scrambled away, but my foot caught in a hole underneath the water and I flailed backwards, twisting and grovelling in the mud. I struggled to my feet and ran, half wading, half jumping, back towards the mill.

Ahead, the building had partly collapsed. Flames were leaping thirty or more feet into the night sky, cackling joyously, throwing up sparks that rained down on our heads. There was no way through. I would have to take the other route to the road, the lengthier one, right round the cottages and along the far side of the mill.

I turned, and Peter was emerging from the marshes, blocking my path.

He still had the knife in his hand.

'No one else knows what I've done,' he shouted over the din. 'Only you.'

'If we stay here, we'll both die. You know that.'

He twirled the knife and stood up straighter. A blue fire was shimmering across the mud. Even the puddles were alight. How was that possible?

'I'll be back at Harrow in a few days, and when I'm eighteen, Father wants me to go to University College to study law and then enter the business. I'll be an important man and you'll be dead. No one will ever know what happened to you.'

Rosie will know, I thought, but I wasn't going to tell him that. I wouldn't put her in danger as well.

I moved sideways, away from the flames, trying to give myself a route past him, but he mirrored me, narrowing the distance, his arms outstretched as if he was about to tackle an opponent at rugby.

I couldn't dodge past him, and I couldn't beat him in a fight either, not while he was holding that knife. I took a breath, feeling the back of my throat burning.

I had one option.

Keeping my eyes on him, I crouched down and scooped water on to my arms and legs, on to my neck and hair. I took off my coat and pushed it down into the mud, fully submerging it, and wrapped it around my arm.

Peter was watching me closely.

'What are you doing? Stop that.'

I held my sleeve over my mouth and took a step towards the fire.

Even a few inches made a difference. My skin dried instantly and my cheek felt as if it was shrinking on my face, baked by the heat. Every instinct told me to move away, but still I stepped nearer, no more than twenty feet from the blaze. Steam started rising from my coat.

I edged closer. Flames were reaching out to me through the hollow window frames of the mill, and the earth was covered with embers, crunching and hissing under my shoes. The hair on my head was singeing and my skin boiling.

Peter matched me, one hand raised against the blaze as if he would be able to protect himself if the wall fell.

One more step was all I could bear. I took in a single acrid breath so fiery it scorched my insides. I could feel my lungs, the shape of them in my chest, defined by the heat of the air within them.

I had no time left. This was my last chance.

I dashed forwards through the fire, treading in the flames, feeling them grasping for me, clawing at me, biting my feet through the soles of my shoes. I shut my eyes, but still I could see it, glowing red through my eyelids.

A hand tried to grab me, but I beat it away. I heard a scream and trod on something soft, blundering sideways, scrambling over burning wood. Was I alight? I didn't know. I fell and rolled in wetness and then I was on all fours, crawling into the marsh water, with no other thought than getting away, away, away, as fast and as far as I could.

There was a crash behind me, and I swung round. Part of the wall had broken apart and fallen on the spot where I'd been standing a few seconds before. I shuffled backwards on my behind as a roiling mass of burning jute spewed through the gap towards me.

I was lucky. I had reached the paving by the cottages, and it gave me just enough traction to push myself upright and hobble away.

The mill creaked and groaned and finally, with a huge sigh, crumpled in on itself, succumbing utterly to Edwin's fire.

Where there had been a building, now there was an inferno of boiling black smoke and flames. I stood watching it, saying a prayer for Edwin under my breath.

I felt something cold and wet on my face, hissing across the marshland: rain.

It set in fast, going from nothing to a downpour in a few seconds. I stood in it, unable to move, every part of me hurting.

I heard a voice. It sounded like Rosie.

'Leo!'

In the light of the fire, I could see her coming towards me from the far side of the cottages. I tried to answer her, but my voice wouldn't work. My throat was too charred.

I heard another voice, wordless, close behind me. It was Peter, except it wasn't any longer. He was limping, one side of him black and raw where his clothes had burned away. His right leg, arm and side were seared meat, and half his face too. Most of his hair was gone. He had one eye open. I wasn't sure the other was still in its socket.

In his hands, he was clutching the knife.

I staggered backwards and fell, looking up at him. I knew I would soon be dead.

Fleeting thoughts ran through my mind; all the things I had yet to do: see Constance grow up and become a doctor, teach Ciara to read and write, get a dog for Aiden, sit with Alfie for many more glasses of whisky, play endless games of chess with Jacob, have one more argument with Rosie.

I wished for five more minutes, just for that.

Peter seemed to say something, but I couldn't tell what. He raised the knife, but his leg buckled and he collapsed sideways. I heard a crack as his head hit the paving, and he lay still.

Rosie rushed forwards and knelt beside me. 'Mother of God!'

I put my hand to my head and could feel my scalp where the hair had burned away. I managed to climb to my feet and breathe. She put her arm around me, and I leaned against her, before remembering she was injured herself. The blood on her sleeve was shiny and dark in the reflection of the flames.

'I can walk,' I whispered hoarsely.

'Don't be silly.'

'Are Aiden and Ciara all right?'

'Yes. They're with Constable Pallett.'

I looked down at Peter, surprised to see his chest rising and falling. The fire had gathered in ferocity, unhindered by the rain, and would soon take the cottages too.

If we left him, it would kill him for certain.

'Give me a hand,' I croaked. 'Let's get him away from this.'

'Why?'

She was looking me directly in the eyes, rain streaming down her face.

'He'll die otherwise.'

'So? He's murdered two people.'

'Three,' I said, thinking of Edwin.

'Three then.' A note of irritation entered her voice even at that moment. 'Do you truly think they'll convict him, Leo, the son of a gentleman, injured in an attack on his father's property? They'll give him a medal. Trust me, it's better this way.'

She was right, of course, but I couldn't do it. I couldn't leave him to die.

The wind had picked up, sending the flames surging first one way and then the other. We didn't have long.

'If you won't give me a hand, I'll do it on my own.'

I started pulling him, feeling as if my skin would slough off my bones and slop into the mud. I had managed to move him a yard at most when Rosie joined me, and so we dragged him away from the blaze.

I was dimly aware of Pallett arriving, and words being exchanged, and him picking up Peter in his arms and carrying him away.

Finally, I was able to pass out with only one thought in my head: Aiden and Ciara were safe.

30

TWO WEEKS LATER, I was sitting in the yard of the pharmacy, a blanket over my lap. The sun was out and a blackbird was heartily announcing that spring had properly arrived and it was time to get busy.

'Check,' said Jacob.

He had opted to come to me for our weekly chess match, as I wasn't yet well enough to travel. He drew on his cigar, the end of it shining orange. I touched a fingertip to my eyebrow without thinking, but it had gone.

The side of my face felt hard and tight like grease-paper. The doctor who had visited me said he wasn't sure the hair on that side would ever grow back, but ventured that I still had enough to cover the bald patch. He sold me some ointment for the burns and had wanted to perform a more thorough examination, but of course I couldn't allow that.

I looked at the board and was indeed in check. I hadn't been concentrating. I moved my king a square to the left.

A copy of the *Daily Chronicle* was lying folded on the table, next to the board. On the front page was the whole story. I'd written it down as accurately as I could remember. Harry Whitford had come to the pharmacy and sat with me, asking questions, at times disbelieving, demanding the names of witnesses to corroborate my tale. In the end, it had been printed mostly as I'd originally written it and had sold out all across London. Everyone was talking about the shameful Thackery family: the industrialist sickly and not expected to live, his wife arrested for kidnapping, one son a murderer and the other so hating his father he'd conspired against him and died as a consequence.

Hooper got most of the credit. Of Dora Hannigan there was little mention, and of me, thankfully, none at all.

Inside the newspaper, a small report at the bottom of page two told how Mr Peregrine Black, a man of some renown in the music hall, had been given thirty days in the clink for assault. The judge had initially sentenced him to three months, but had been moved, the report said, by the tears of Black's young wife in the gallery. I smiled, as best I could, when I read it. I was sure he would think thirty days a small price to pay, and I vowed to call on him when he got out. Constance was always telling me I needed another friend.

'Look at me, Mr Stanhope!' Ciara was lying on the ground, nose to nose with Colly, Constance's cat.

I was about to tell her to stand up before she made her dress more filthy, but stopped myself. Why shouldn't she roll around in the dirt? Dresses can be washed.

With a wry smile I contemplated how easily we echo our parents; we don't even think, we just regurgitate what we've been told, no matter how corrupt or unfounded, just like Peter Thackery. Despite the evil he had done, I preferred to think of him as a boy who enjoyed dancing and had fallen in love with a music-hall singer, but who had taken his father's views too much to heart.

Inside the house, the clock struck two, and Constance came out into the yard, still in her school dress, followed by Alfie. She handed me a letter with the hospital's crest on the front.

'A boy brought it for you, Mr Stanhope,' she said. 'You know what it says. You've been given the sack again.'

'Constance!' exclaimed Alfie.

I slumped further in my chair. How would I cope without an income or a reference? And how would I find a new place to live?

Jacob drained his whisky, unknowingly provided by Alfie. 'It's for the best,' he growled. 'Carrying other people's bedpans is no task for a man.'

Constance handed me another envelope. 'Fortunately, there's an alternative.'

I ripped it open, and inside was a short note from J. T. Whitford. I read it twice to make sure of what it meant.

'He wants you to write for the *Daily Chronicle*,' Constance announced, beaming. 'He came in earlier and told us all about it. He said the world is changing, and they have a need for a man who knows his strychnine from his coronary embolism, though I told him you were weak as milk on remedies and know precious little about mixing chemicals.'

'Constance!' said Alfie again, but she wouldn't be stopped.

'He insisted you should be given the chance,' she continued. 'He said you could be put to good use sharing your scientific knowledge …' she rolled her eyes at this point '… with the grateful populace for their enrichment and elucidation. Those were his very words.'

'It's just occasional,' I said, rereading the letter. 'It's not a full-time position.'

'But you will do it, won't you, Mr Stanhope?'

I admit I rather liked the idea. 'I suppose I will,' I said. 'I have to pay the rent somehow.'

'Ah, yes,' said Alfie, clearing his throat. 'About that. The thing is, Leo, we think you should stay here and not move out. Especially now …' He nodded towards the children and swallowed. 'I mean, we'd like you to stay.'

'What about Mrs Gower?'

'It's not her decision. Look, one day she and I may get married. I would like to, but not right away.' He glanced at Constance, who kept her face neutral. 'You belong with us, Leo.'

I wanted to say yes. It would be like falling into a soft bed after a long day.

Perhaps, though, it was time for a change; a room with my own front door and my own stove, so I wouldn't have to spend my days deceiving the people I loved.

But I couldn't bear the thought of parting with these two. The time will come, I thought, when I will have to tell them the truth. Just not yet.

'Yes,' I said. 'I would like that.'

Alfie grinned. 'Good, because Constance has been miserable about it for days.'

'You have too!' she exclaimed.

He accepted the point. 'Well, who's going to drink me dry of whisky if you're not here?'

'I should go,' muttered Jacob, guiltily pushing his empty glass next to mine. 'We'll continue our game next week. Especially as I'm winning.' He put out his hand and touched my cheek, but I couldn't feel it through my scarred skin. 'Do as the doctors tell you,' he said.

'Will you be all right getting home? Take a cab, for goodness' sake.'

He tapped his cane on the ground. 'Do you think I'm incapable of finding my way to my own shop? You're worse than Lilya.'

I watched him trudge out, leaning on his cane, one of his braces dangling below the hem of his jacket. I thought of my actual father, still lying sick in Hampstead, as far as I knew. I wondered whether I should visit him again. I hadn't been present when my mother died and I thought she would want me to make up for that. When I'm re-covered, I thought, I will consider it. If he lasts that long. I won't pretend to be Lottie or tell him anything of my life, but I might tolerate a short conversation. Truly, was there anything left in him to be afraid of?

As the clock struck three, I was almost asleep again. The children had gone inside. I heard a sound and looked up to see Erica Cowdery standing over me, silhouetted against the sky.

She was wearing full weeds and a cotton apron. Her brother's funeral had been well attended, Pallett had told me, with all the members of the club turning out to bury the parts of him they'd been able to dig out from under the debris. Pallett seemed grudgingly respectful of their efforts, though he had no sympathy for arson and commented that Edwin Cowdery had got his just deserts.

Miss Cowdery blanched at my appearance, but gathered herself. 'I wasn't sure if you got my letter, Mr Stanhope. I mentioned that I was coming today, but you didn't reply.'

I had read her letter and thrown it away, spending the last two days pretending it had never arrived.

'I'm sorry,' I said. 'I haven't been keeping up with my correspondence.'

She seemed awkward, wringing her hands and briefly hovering over Jacob's old seat as though she might take it, but then not.

'Oh, I see. Well, I'm sure it'll be a relief to you, getting them off your hands, a single man like yourself.'

I tried to reply but couldn't tell her anything without telling her everything, and of course that was impossible.

She interpreted my silence as agreement.

'They'll be well looked after,' she said. 'I'll bring them up as my own. Children need a mother, don't they?'

'You're their aunt,' I corrected her, not truly intending to be objectionable, but I couldn't help myself.

'I know,' she replied, a little haughtily. 'But I'll *become* their mother.' She searched in her bag and produced a folder. 'Would you like to see the paperwork? It's signed by the magistrate.'

'No, it's quite all right.' I didn't need confirmation of what I already knew. 'Best get it over with.'

She followed me as I walked stiffly into the back room. I called the children from upstairs, my throat contracting, sending shooting pains into my chest.

When they came down, Miss Cowdery smiled at them, especially Aiden, no doubt thinking of her late brother.

I had told them that morning what was going to happen.

'This is Miss Cowdery,' I said. 'She's your aunt, so you'll live with her from now on.'

'Do we have to go?' asked Ciara.

I put my hands on her shoulders and looked into her eyes. 'Yes. This is the last time, I promise. Miss Cowdery will look after you very well. She's your family.'

'But I don't want to.'

For their sakes, I thought, I can't waver. I have to be resolute. They should have this new life and they should live it absolutely, through and through.

'I'm sorry,' I said. 'You must.'

'Did we do something wrong?' asked Aiden, his face solemn, not meeting my eye.

'No, of course not. I'll visit you often, and you can visit me. Constance as well.'

One last hug, feeling Ciara's hair against my face and Aiden's head on my shoulder. One last squeeze of their hands.

I gave a box to Aiden. 'This is for both of you.'

Inside was my chess set. It was all I had to give them. I hadn't been well enough to go out and buy a bright red kite.

'I'm very grateful to you, Mr Stanhope,' said Miss Cowdery. 'For finding them and looking after them as you have.' She put a firm hand on my forearm, not noticing my wince. 'Not many men would've done such a thing.'

'This is theirs too.' I handed her the pouch. 'Please open it when you get home.'

I wondered what she would do when she discovered the money inside. I trusted she would use it for their bene-fit, but perhaps instead it would help keep the Home for Penitent Females open for another few months. I didn't know whether I minded that or not.

'You truly must visit us at the Home, Mr Stanhope,' she said, sounding as though she meant it. 'I would like that very much.'

'Yes, of course.'

I smiled, trying to appear less surly than before. I would visit, but not for a while. It would take time for me to gather enough strength to leave them again.

I waved as they left, watching them as they got lost in the crowd on the pavement. They were like any other family, setting out for the market in the sunshine.

I didn't want to speak to Constance or Alfie, so I slowly climbed the stairs to my room and shut the door. Ciara had drawn two new pictures for me, one of Colly and one of a man with a smiling face and his arms outstretched. Aiden had written *Mister Stanhope* underneath it. He must've asked Constance for the spelling.

I held it in my hands and wept, uncaring of the pain from the blisters on my eyelids. I was sure I would never be able to stop.

I already missed the children unbearably, and they had only left a few minutes before. I yearned for them like a drowning man yearns for air, except I felt as if I would be drowning for ever.

There were voices downstairs.

'Leo!' Alfie called up. 'Mrs Flowers is here.'

She was sitting in the back room.

'You're a sight,' she said, not harshly. I was becoming accustomed to the many varieties of acerbity she could muster.

This was the third time I'd seen her since that night at the mill. The first, I'd barely been able to speak, and she'd sat beside my bed knitting a pair of gloves that she presented to me the next time, to keep my hands from the cold, she said, while they were healing. She was considerably better at cooking pies than knitting gloves, as it turned out, and they were much too big and too coarse, making my skin itch.

She had a small box with her, which she opened and offered to me. 'Dried cherries,' she said. 'I thought a pie might be too hard for you to eat. Where are Aiden and Ciara?'

'Miss Cowdery decided she should look after them from now on. She's their aunt, so it's for the best.'

'Oh, Leo. I'm sorry.' She put her hand very lightly on mine and didn't mention it further, which was all I wanted.

I heard the doorbell jangle as another customer came in, and Alfie's solicitous greeting, and, in the yard, Constance's singing as she hung out the washing.

I dozed for a while and, when I awoke, Rosie was still there. We spent the rest of the afternoon that way, side by side in the back room as if it was our own, as if we'd finished our lunch and had nothing better to do but sit together and occasionally boil the kettle for tea.

Acknowledgements

A GREAT MANY HIGHLY-SKILLED people were involved in the making of what you're now holding (if you're reading an ebook, you'll have to use your imagination at this point). I am enormously grateful to all of them.

Carrie Plitt is the best agent ever and I will brook no argument on that. Without her, the Leo Stanhope books would have remained festering in my brain, and I'm eternally grateful that they're not.

Alison Hennessey is Chief of the Ravens, lead therapist for Leo and an absolute genius. She and the whole team at Bloomsbury – including Marigold Atkey, Lilidh Kendrick, Sarah-Jane Forder, Philippa Cotton, Amy Donegan, Maud Davies, the sales teams and many others – are all my heroes. Thank you.

Greg Heinemann has once again designed a knockout cover.

Massive thanks to everyone who helped with the research, including the Wellcome Collection, London Zoo, the V&A, the Ragged School Museum, the Geffrye Museum, Wilton's Music Hall, the Museum of London, the British Library, the National Archives and lots of others! Also, the Beaumont Society, a charity doing important work supporting the transgender community and advising on transgender issues. You can find them at www.beaumontsociety.org.uk.

My wonderful and beloved sons, Seth and Caleb, contributed nothing whatsoever to the writing of this novel, and for that I thank them, because their ideas are usually rubbish.

And finally, Michelle. I'm not nearly a good enough author to sum up what she has contributed to my books or anything else in my life, so I'll just say that it's big – really, really big – and leave it at that.

A Note on the Author

Alex Reeve lives in Buckinghamshire and is a university lecturer. His debut novel, *The House on Half Moon Street*, is the first in the Leo Stanhope Case series and was published in 2018.

@storyjoy

A Note on the Type

The text of this book is set in Bembo, which was first used in 1495 by the Venetian printer Aldus Manutius for Cardinal Bembo's *De Aetna*. The original types were cut for Manutius by Francesco Griffo. Bembo was one of the types used by Claude Garamond (1480–1561) as a model for his Romain de l'Université, and so it was a forerunner of what became the standard European type for the following two centuries. Its modern form follows the original types and was designed for Monotype in 1929.